About the Author

Rachael Johns is an English teacher by trade, a mum 24/7, a chronic arachnophobic and a writer the rest of the time. She rarely sleeps and never irons. A lover of romance and women's fiction, Rachael loves nothing more than sitting in bed with her laptop and electric blanket and imagining her own stories.

Rachael has finalled in a number of competitions, including the Australian Romance Readers Awards. *Jilted* (her first rural romance) won Favourite Australian Contemporary Romance in 2012 and she was voted in the Top Ten of Booktopia's Favourite Australian Author poll in 2013.

Rachael lives in the Perth hills with her hyperactive husband, three mostly gorgeous heroes-in-training, two fat cats, a cantankerous bird and a very badly behaved dog.

Rachael loves to hear from readers and can be contacted via her website www.rachaeljohns.com. She is also on Facebook and Twitter.

Outback
SISTERS

RACHAEL JOHNS

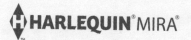

First Published 2016
First Australian Paperback Edition 2016
ISBN 978 176037164 7

OUTBACK SISTERS
© 2016 by Rachael Johns
Australian Copyright 2016
New Zealand Copyright 2016

This is a work of fiction. Names, characters, places, and incidents are either the product of the author's imagination or are used fictitiously, and any resemblance to actual persons, living or dead, business establishments, events, or locales is entirely coincidental.

Published by
Harlequin Mira
An imprint of Harlequin Enterprises (Australia) Pty Ltd.
Level 13, 201 Elizabeth St
SYDNEY NSW 2000
AUSTRALIA

® and TM are trademarks of Harlequin Enterprises Limited or its corporate affiliates. Trademarks indicated with ® are registered in Australia, New Zealand and in other countries.

Cataloguing-in-Publication details are available from the National Library of Australia

www.librariesaustralia.nla.gov.au

Printed and bound in Australia by Griffin Press

MIX
Paper from
responsible sources
FSC
www.fsc.org   FSC® C009448

Dear Lovely Readers

Once upon a time I created a town called Bunyip Bay and a cast of crazy characters who lived there, and decided to write three stories about them. Some of you may have read them—*Outback Dreams, Outback Blaze* and *Outback Ghost*. Although I never intended to write more, the response from you guys was out of this world and so heartwarming to this little writer. When you asked for more Bunyip Bay, I wanted to give you what you requested and really the only characters I could think of, who had become a big part of the stories but hadn't yet starred, were sisters Frankie (who runs the town café) and Simone (a single mum of teenage daughters).

Ideas come to writers from ALL over the place and it was during a conversation on a road trip while touring with my friend and awesome author Fiona Palmer, that the seeds of this story sprouted.

Outback Sisters is a story of family, friendships and following your heart. I hope you have as much fun reading it as I did writing it.

Happy Reading

Rachael Johns
x

In memory of the road trip I took with Fiona Palmer in October 2014. Without our long conversations on the road, I'm not sure Frankie and Simone would ever have gotten their own story.

Chapter One

Francesca Madden, known as Frankie to everyone who mattered, closed the café door behind Stella's bridal party and breathed a sigh of relief. With only four weeks to the big day, excitement was really ramping up—but for some reason she was struggling to get into the mood. She slumped in a chair at the table the group had been sitting at and eyed the half-finished chocolate mud cake. While the meeting had been in progress, Frankie had been so busy helping to serve everyone that she hadn't had time to eat. To say she now felt exhausted—emotionally and physically—would be the understatement of the millennium. She sighed and dragged the plate towards her, hoping, as she dug a fork into the cake, that a little chocolate boost would help renew her energies.

It wasn't that she didn't like weddings. She couldn't be happier for her cousin Adam and his soon-to-be blushing bride, Stella. If any two people deserved happiness it was them, but they weren't the only loved-up couples around here—her thoughts drifted to Faith and Monty, Ruby and Drew, Ryan and Grant; even her niece Harriet had herself a high-school sweetheart, for crying out loud. In fact, it was starting to feel like everyone in the world—or at least in Bunyip Bay—was getting a happy ever after.

Everyone, that is, except her.

Oh, and Simone, but at least her big sister had once experienced the blessing of true love. Although Simone had been widowed for almost ten years, she knew what it felt like to be the centre of someone's world, to be the last thing someone wanted to see when they went to bed and the person they couldn't wait to wake up to in the morning.

Was it wrong that Frankie wanted that too? She had good health and a wonderful business and that was a lot more than some people. Shouldn't the café, her friends and family be enough? She shoved more chocolate cake into her mouth just as one of her waitresses stuck her head out from behind the counter.

'Are you okay if I head off now?' Stacey asked as she scribbled down her hours on the staff clipboard.

Frankie glanced around the café, noted the two elderly diners still nursing cups of tea, decided she could handle them on her own, and hurried to swallow her mouthful. 'Yeah,' she said as she stood and started to collect the plates from the table. 'Thanks for all your help today.'

'No worries. I'll see you Tuesday.' Stacey whipped off her apron, grabbed her bag from under the counter, released her long, wavy, blonde hair from her café cap and all but skipped out the door. It wasn't that she didn't like her job, but rather she had a date with the new vet that she'd been looking forward to all week. Frankie couldn't blame her—Dr Mitchell Clarke was undeniably hot, *and* good with animals. What was there not to love? She lifted a hand to wave. 'Have fun.'

See? Love was everywhere, except she must be in some kind of bubble because no-one had asked her on a date in what felt like forever. All the local guys treated her like a good friend. Maybe she needed to go further afield—jet off on a Contiki tour or something and find romance on foreign shores—because it didn't look like Mr Right was going to come to her. But where would that leave the café?

Telling herself to stop being a sorry-for-herself grump, she finished clearing the table, asked Dolce and Mrs Brady if they wanted refills, silently cheered when they declined and then went to grab a cloth to start the evening wipe down. Frankie was about to begin on the table she'd been sitting at when the door to the café squeaked loudly, signalling another customer. She fixed a smile on her face, despite the fact it was nearly closing time and she was already thinking about curling up on her couch, reading *Picnic at Hanging Rock* with her kittens for company. Halfway to becoming a crazy cat woman, that's what she was.

She opened her mouth to begrudgingly welcome this latecomer but the greeting died on her tongue. Standing in the doorway, his tall, incredibly buff body filling the space, was without a doubt the hottest guy she'd ever laid eyes on. About her age, or maybe a few years older, he wore faded jeans, a navy blue chambray shirt with sleeves pushed up to his elbows and heavy, brown boots— classic farmer attire.

Well, hello there! No farmer around these parts had ever made her stomach flutter the way looking at this guy did. He couldn't be a local because she'd lived in Bunyip Bay all her life and if there was a specimen like this in the region without her knowing … well, that was impossible. His dirty blond hair was cropped close to his head and she had a crazy urge to run right over and sweep her fingers through it. Maybe the sugar had gone to her head.

'Hey there.'

As he spoke, she glanced behind her to check he wasn't talking to a customer she'd missed sneak in, but unless said customer was invisible, he was speaking to her. She turned back and he hit her with a sexy grin that made her feel like she was the centre of his world, which was ridiculous because they'd only just met. Well, technically they hadn't even done that yet but this had to be love at first sight. She felt giddy, like her knees were about to fail her. Visions of puffy white dresses danced in her head.

'Um … Hi …' she stuttered, straightening to a stand as she summoned a smile. *Don't blow this, Frankie. First impressions and everything.* 'What can I get for you?'

In reply, this tall, dashing hunk of a man closed the short distance between them, put his hands on either side of her face, drew her towards him and then lowered his mouth to hers. Her eyes widened as heat flooded from her long-ignored lips right through her body. Places that hadn't felt a man's touch in years lit up and burned. His three-day stubble felt deliciously rough against her chin and she couldn't help but whimper.

Is this a dream? A divinely inappropriate but wonderful dream? If so, she didn't want to ever wake up.

Somewhere—it sounded very, very far away—she vaguely registered the disapproving tutting of the two old women, and the mundane reality of her everyday life threatened to intrude.

Who was this guy? He was the epitome of all she'd ever fantasised about in a man: tall, ruggedly handsome, desperately sexy … but she didn't know him at all. He could be a crazed psycho or an axe murderer for all she knew. A tiny voice told her she should slap him in the face and ask him what he was doing, but that would mean ripping her lips from his, and that would be an atrocity. Whatever this was, she couldn't bear to break the illusion of bliss, so instead, she wrapped her arms around the handsome stranger and pressed her body against his. To hell with local gossips like Dolce and Mrs Brady; hot men and bone-melting kisses like this didn't come along everyday.

He was all firm muscle and yummy hardness and for a few brief seconds, Frankie thought that maybe her luck really had changed. Maybe it was fate that had brought this man of men into her café late on a Friday afternoon. Stranger things had happened at sea, right?

And then he pulled back.

She swallowed a moan of disappointment and pressed a hand against her chest to try to slow her racing heart.

His face was still only centimetres from hers. He had the most beautiful big brown eyes she'd ever seen. 'Hello, Simone,' he whispered. 'It's so great to finally meet you.'

'What?' she cried, stumbling back and bumping awkwardly into the hard corner of a table. Ignoring the pain, she glared at him. 'I'm Frankie!'

'Huh?' He jerked his head back as if she'd slapped him. He couldn't have looked more surprised if she'd admitted to being Frankenstein's monster. And he wasn't quite as handsome with that scowl on his face either.

Of course it had been too good to be true. But hang on, why would a man like him be kissing Simone? As far as Frankie knew—and Simone had always told her everything—her sister didn't have a man in her life. After the recent debacle with Ryan Forrester, Simone had all but sworn off men, deciding that she'd been blessed with love once and that was enough.

'Who are you?' Frankie practically hissed, her heart still racing but now for entirely different, less pleasurable reasons.

'Oh, you must be the sister,' he said, a sheepish smile forming on his face. 'Whoops.'

'*Whoops?*' Frankie tried to ignore how adorable he looked as he ran a hand through his already mussed-up hair.

'I'm sorry.' Whatever-his-name-was held out a hand. 'I'm Logan. Logan Knight?' He spoke as if this name should ring a bell, but she came up blank. When she simply continued glaring at him, he slipped his hand into his jeans pocket and elaborated. 'Simone's friend? We've been online dating for a couple of weeks now. I was driving home from Perth today and thought I'd surprise her. You two could almost pass as twins.'

There was so much alien information in those few lines that Frankie needed a moment. *Online dating? Twins?* She pressed the heel of her hand to her forehead. Maybe she was still dreaming because this conversation was getting weirder by the second.

'Simone *is* your sister?' he asked, sounding a little less certain. 'She *does* work here?'

'Yes and yes.' At least Frankie could answer that without thought.

'Shit.' A crestfallen expression appeared on Logan's face. He cleared his throat. 'I'm really sorry about … you know. I don't usually do things like that, but well, when I saw you, I just kind of—'

'It's okay.' Frankie held up a hand and tried to make a joke. 'You wouldn't believe the number of random hot guys who come in here and kiss me.'

When Logan blushed and looked as if he wasn't sure whether to laugh or not, she gave up the attempt. 'You only just missed her. She's probably at home by now. Maybe you could go see her there.'

'I don't actually know where she lives … or have her number.' He looked a little embarrassed and Frankie couldn't help but find it cute. 'We've only spoken via email. She told me she lives in Bunyip Bay and works here sometimes, so I thought I'd try my luck.'

Frankie nodded. At least it looked like Simone wasn't about to tie the knot without telling her.

'She's never mentioned me?'

'She may have,' Frankie lied. 'I've been a little distracted lately. Let me call her for you.'

Leaving Mr Gorgeous looking a little like a lost puppy, Frankie walked into the kitchen, yanking her mobile phone out of her apron pocket as she went. She generally spoke to Simone four or five times a day, so she was the last person on her recent calls list. She pressed 'call' and drummed the fingernails of her free hand on the kitchen counter as she waited for her sister to pick up.

'I am in teenage daughter hell,' Simone said the moment she answered. 'Harriet wants Jaxon to sleep over tomorrow night. Can you believe it? She's only sixteen for fuck's sake but apparently *I'm* being unreasonable. Can you come over and try to—'

Usually Frankie sympathised with Simone's parenting woes. Although she had no children of her own, everyone knew teenagers were hard work and parenting them alone could be hell. But right now, she had other issues.

'When were you going to tell me you've been online dating?' Frankie interrupted, unable to keep the hurt from her voice. She didn't know why Simone hadn't confided in her.

'Excuse me?' Simone sounded outraged. 'What are you talking about?'

'Your boyfriend just arrived at the café looking for you.' Frankie didn't mention the mistaken identity or the toe-curling kiss that had followed. Her lips still tingled from that kiss. She didn't know if she'd ever recover.

'Boyfriend?'

'You know, Logan? Six foot tall, blond, looks like he's chiselled from a block of marble?'

'Have you been drinking? I have no idea what you are talking about.'

Simone had never been a good liar and from the tone of her voice, Frankie could tell this was the truth. She glanced through the hatch from the kitchen into the café and saw that Logan had found a copy of the latest *Bunyip News* and was sitting on the couch, flicking through it. Man, he was divine. And there was just something extra hot about guys who read: newspapers, books—she wasn't fussy. The beady eyes of Dolce and Mrs Brady, the town's famous gossips, were glued on him and she could only imagine what they were making of this crazy scene. She sighed and gave Simone a condensed, G-rated version of what had just occurred.

'I promise you I've never heard of the man,' Simone exclaimed. 'And I've certainly never signed up to any online dating site. Haven't you heard the horror stories? No-one uses their real photos, everyone lies about their age and their hobbies. If I was that desperate I'd go to one of those speed-dating sessions. At least then you see the person and they can't pretend to be someone they're not.'

All that might be true but it didn't solve the problem of what to do with Logan Knight. 'Well, I don't know where he got your details,' Frankie interrupted, 'but I assure you he's very real, and he seems to know you. What do you want me to tell him?'

Simone swore and Frankie heard a commotion in the background. Her grip tightened on her phone. 'What?'

'Oh no,' Simone gasped. 'You didn't!'

Frankie listened a moment and heard the terror-filled voices of her teenage nieces.

'We didn't mean any harm, Mum,' came Harriet's voice.

'We just want you to be happy,' added sweet little Grace.

'What's going on?' Frankie demanded.

Simone let out an angry puff of air. 'It seems, unbeknownst to me, I *have* been online dating. Sorry, sis, I've got to go. I'm going to grill my daughters, then I'm going to lecture them on the dangers of talking to strangers online, and *then* I'm going to murder them. You'll bail me out of jail, right?'

'No, wait,' Frankie blurted before Simone could disconnect, and then she lowered her voice. 'Logan wants to meet you.'

Simone snorted. 'You'll just have to tell him it's all a big mistake. I'm sure he has a bevy of other online girlfriends to fall back on.'

Frankie shifted from one foot to the other. After the embarrassment of the kiss, she didn't want to go out there and make him feel like even more of an idiot. How would he feel knowing he'd been duped by two teenaged girls?

'I think you should meet him,' she found herself saying.

'What? Geez!' Simone groaned. 'I'm being ambushed from all directions.'

Frankie heard her nieces in the background. 'Go meet Logan, Mum. He's lovely.'

'He seems to be,' Frankie conceded, looking again through the hatch to perve on the man in question. Maybe he had a twin brother? It was hard to imagine there could be two men like him on the planet, but … not totally impossible.

'Is he really that hot?' Simone's question jolted Frankie's thoughts.

She sighed, still staring at him. Logan glanced up, caught her looking and waved. Her heart did some sort of gymnastics in her chest. 'Hot doesn't even begin to cover it.'

'Why do I think I'm going to live to regret this?' Simone asked, and then, 'Tell him I can meet him at the pub in an hour.'

★ ★ ★

Logan put down the newspaper as Frankie emerged from the kitchen. He couldn't believe he'd waltzed in here and kissed her before bothering to introduce himself. He was surprised she hadn't slapped him in the face and he certainly wouldn't have blamed her if she had. What had he been thinking?

He hadn't been, that's what. Instead he'd been overcome with something he'd never felt before. He'd always been impulsive, something Angus felt a constant urge to point out, but what he'd just done was taking things to extremes. If he told his brother about this later, he would omit the kiss. Maybe it was his recent diagnosis wreaking havoc with his emotions or maybe it was simply because Simone's sister was possibly the sexiest woman he'd ever met. She wasn't classically good-looking—not the type that graced movie screens or fashion magazines—but she possessed a natural beauty that shone from somewhere deep within. The little black apron wrapped around her waist, red T-shirt with *Frankie's* scrawled in black across one breast and the skinny faded jeans clinging to her legs highlighted her curvy body. He couldn't help but remember the feel of it pressed against him.

As she walked towards him now, her pale cheeks glowed a pretty red and her hair—a deep rich crimson—hung in a long, practical, but ever so sexy plait over one shoulder. She was like Anne of Green Gables all grown up, and he had a sudden urge to play Gilbert Blythe.

'Simone says she'll meet you at the pub in an hour,' Frankie said, picking up the cloth she'd dumped on a table when he'd walked in. 'Do you know where The Palace is?'

He smiled, hoping to relax her, as she seemed a little jittery. 'Just down the road on the right, yeah?' He felt the need to explain that he was a relative local—so she wouldn't take him for a stalker or anything. 'My family has a farm at Mingenew, so I've been through Bunyip Bay before.'

She nodded and started to wipe the table. 'When you say "family"—you're not married, are you? I don't mean to be rude but you hear all kind of horror stories about online dating and if you hurt Simone, well, don't take this the wrong way, but I'll kill you.'

Logan chuckled at her deadpan tone. It was clear she wasn't joking and he liked that she valued family as much as he did. 'No, I'm not married. Not anymore, anyway.'

'Good.' She turned and he followed her gaze to see two elderly women—the only customers in the café—watching them with great interest. Dropping the cloth again, Frankie crossed to the women and all but shooed them out the door. 'Time to go, ladies. Show's over. Have a nice weekend.'

She shut the door behind them, flipped the sign to closed and let out what sounded like a sigh of relief. 'Local gossips,' she explained, turning back to him. 'You'll be the talk of the town before nightfall.'

Logan grimaced. 'Sorry.'

She shrugged and shot him a smile that hit him right in the solar plexus. 'Everyone needs a little excitement in their lives.'

He got the feeling she wasn't simply referring to the old biddies. 'Can I help you with anything? I'm a pro at washing dishes and it seems that I've got a bit of time to kill.'

'It's fine.' She shook her head, her smile vanishing as quickly as it had arrived. 'I haven't got much to do anyway.' And suddenly she was all business again. 'Well, it was nice meeting you. Hope you enjoy your evening with Simone.'

With that, she went back to her task and it was clear he'd been dismissed.

Damn shame, because he was enjoying her company immensely. They'd barely exchanged a few words but the taste of her lips and her no-nonsense attitude had piqued his interest. He only hoped her sister was half as fascinating.

He stood. 'Well, I might see you round. Have a great weekend.'

'Thanks. You too.' But she barely looked up at him as she spoke.

Feeling odd about leaving a café without so much as a cup of coffee, Logan crossed to the door and let himself out. He stepped onto the main street of Bunyip Bay, wide and near deserted like most country towns at this time on a Friday afternoon. He squinted a few hundred metres up the street to where dusty utes and dirty four-wheel drives were starting to fill the car spaces outside the front of the pub.

Leaving his own ute parked outside the café, he started the short distance towards The Palace. As a journalist, one of his favourite pastimes was people-watching, and small-town pubs were about the best places in the world for such a thing. He'd grab a beer, find a quiet spot in the corner and sit back and watch while he waited for his date.

Chapter Two

Frankie was generally a much better liar than Simone, although she feared Logan might have seen through her fib about almost being finished at the café. The kitchen still needed to be cleaned and she never went home without everything being spick and span, but she'd needed to get him out of her space. After that kiss she could barely breathe with him so close, never mind manage a normal conversation. He'd acted as though it was nothing to simply turn up out of the blue and kiss a stranger like that—like it was something that happened everyday—but she couldn't forget quite so easily.

Careful not to be seen, she watched through the window from behind the café curtain as he sauntered down the street towards the pub. From behind he was just as delicious as he was from the front, if not more so. His jeans were tight across his butt and left little to her imagination. Simone was one lucky gal.

When Logan reached the pub, Frankie finally dragged her eyes away and went back to the task of clearing up. She'd barely made a dent in the mess when her phone beeped, signalling an incoming message.

Help! What the hell am I supposed to wear? You got me into this mess, so come over and help me decide.

Technically it had been Harriet and Grace that had started the ball rolling, but Frankie didn't bother to point this out. It took a great deal of energy to argue with Simone. She glanced around the kitchen—the mess would still be there in the morning and if she got up early, she could deal with it then.

Less than five minutes later she was letting herself into Simone's eternally chaotic house with a cardboard box full of leftover cake. 'Hello?' she called, as she made her way through the trail of shoes and magazines and quirky doorstops that littered the hallway of the 1950s fibro cottage.

'In here!' Simone yelled from her bedroom.

Frankie found her older sister and two nieces crowded around Simone's tiny but cluttered desk, staring intently at her laptop. She rested the cake box precariously on the top of a dresser.

'Have a read of what they've said about me. And would you look at the photo they used? It looks nothing like me. It's over five years old, from before these two turned into monsters and I got wrinkles. No wonder he wants to meet me,' Simone said, springing from her stool and turning to her open wardrobe. 'And then you can help me pick a dress.'

Lord, that could take a while. Frankie glanced over at her sister's collection of outfits. Unlike her, Simone never threw anything out. She still wore things that had been in fashion ten years ago and somehow always managed to look fabulous. And wrinkles? You'd need a magnifying glass to see them, if there were any. Simone had a whimsical, unique style that Frankie had always been a little jealous and a lot in awe of. In contrast, her own wardrobe consisted mostly of skinny jeans, knee-high boots and practical shirts. The very few dresses she owned always made her feel silly when she wore them.

Sixteen-year-old Harriet and thirteen-year-old Grace stepped aside to make room for Frankie. She sat on the wobbly wooden stool and looked at the screen, which showed Simone's profile on RuralMatchmakers.com.au. 'Oh, I read about this site in *The West* only a few weeks ago. Apparently it's had a lot of success helping isolated farmers find love,' she commented before starting to read.

'I'm not sure any farmer—isolated or otherwise—wants to put up with my crap.'

Frankie chose not to respond and started to read. Within a few seconds she was in hysterics.

'*Body type*,' she read aloud, '*feminine and curvaceous, breasts to rival Barbie but the rest of me in much better proportion*. What the hell?'

'Don't!' Simone shrieked. 'I shudder to think what kind of man that profile has attracted, but then I looked at this Logan's profile and read some of his messages and he seems normal enough.'

Normal? Frankie thought of how she'd felt the moment Logan had walked into the café and then moments later when he'd kissed her. Nope, he wasn't normal at all.

'Where's his profile?'

Harriet leaned across the screen and after a few clicks of the mouse, Logan's photo loomed large in front of them. Frankie's heart rate spiked at the sight of his boyish but irresistible grin and she had to close her eyes a moment to settle it. When she opened them again, she barely glanced at the photo, scrolling lower to read all about him.

He was apparently thirty years old, so almost smack bang in the middle of her and Simone. His height had him at over six foot but she could have guessed that from the way he'd had to stoop to kiss her and he hadn't lied about his body type—he was fit, well built and healthy. He didn't smoke, and only drank 'on occasion'. She wondered if that was a lie as most farmers she knew had at least a couple of beers at the end of a hard day. But if a little white lie was the biggest fault she could find, well ... maybe she would sign up to this site after all.

'See, he's a Leo and Mum's Libran.' Harriet pointed at the screen. 'That makes them perfect for each other.'

Frankie raised her eyebrows. Simone was into all that new-age stuff and it seemed to have rubbed off on her daughters, but Frankie thought it all a load of manure.

'It says he's a journalist?' she said, reading further.

'Yep.' Grace nodded, twisting her long golden hair around her index finger. Both of Simone's daughters had luckily missed the family ginger gene and were blessed with golden hair like their father. 'He's a rural journalist. We checked out some of his articles and—'

'He's very prolific,' interrupted Harriet. 'But he also still works on his family's crop and sheep station in Mingenew when they need him.'

Frankie wondered who 'they' were.

'It's not far,' Grace added. 'We only responded to people within a couple of hours' drive. Harriet said long-distance relationships never work.'

'Because Harriet knows so much about relationships,' Simone said sarcastically as she discarded yet another outfit on the bed.

Harriet glared at her mother. 'Well, I'm the only one in this room currently in a relationship.'

'Touché.' Frankie wasn't sure whether to laugh or cry.

'What about this?' Simone held up a cute white dress scattered with black stars. It was ruched from bodice to hip and finished just above the knee. It also had a very low neckline, which would show off her enviable cleavage. Not quite Barbie, but still ...

Frankie swallowed. 'I think it's perfect.'

With a nervous smile, Simone stripped down to her underwear—a black, lacy bra with matching G-string. She always wore sexy lingerie, despite moaning about nobody ever getting to see it. Frankie couldn't help but wonder if Logan would be the exception to that rule and her chest tightened at the thought. Having experienced the magic of his lips, Frankie couldn't help her jealousy, despite knowing how ridiculous it was to feel this way about a man she'd just met.

Stepping into the dress, Simone yanked it up over her boobs, slipped her arms into the tiny sleeves and then spun around. 'Can someone do me up?'

Harriet stepped forward and tugged up the zip. 'You look hot, Mum,' she said, a rare tone of approval in her voice.

'You do,' Frankie had to agree. She didn't know anyone else who could get away with a white dress and black underthings, but on Simone the tiny glimpse of dark lace was incredibly seductive. Sometimes she wondered why some guy hadn't snapped her sister up already, but deep down, Frankie knew it was because no-one had come along who measured up to Jason.

Ignoring their compliments, Simone asked, 'What shoes should I wear?'

The next few minutes were taken up searching through Simone's massive shoe collection. They finally came to a decision, choosing a pair of strappy silver heels.

When Simone rushed off to the bathroom to 'do something about my hair and make-up', Harriet plonked herself down on the bed to grill Frankie.

'So Aunty Eff, is he really as good-looking as in his photo?'

'Oh … yes, like you wouldn't be—' Frankie caught herself gushing about Logan and remembered her place. 'But it doesn't matter what he looks like, pretending to be your mum was very irresponsible—you don't know what kind of people are lurking out there on the internet.'

'We've done cyber safety at school,' Harriet said with a wave of her hand. 'And we weren't stupid.'

Not in the mood to argue with her niece, Frankie decided she'd fulfilled her responsibilities by mentioning the issue. Then, telling herself she was looking out for Simone, she went back to scrutinising Logan's profile. In addition to playing footy, reading, rock-climbing and canoeing—all that physical activity accounted for his lovely body—he also listed baking as a hobby. Interesting; an all-rounder indeed. And apparently he *did* have a brother— she'd have to get Simone to enquire after him.

'Can you stay with the girls while I'm out?' Simone asked on her return to the bedroom. 'I doubt I'll be long and anyway, you can be on call if I need you to check any information about this guy.'

Frankie nodded—it wasn't like she had any better options— and it was always fun hanging out with her nieces. Reading on the couch had seemed an appealing Friday night option less than an hour ago, but now she felt that her favourite pastime wouldn't cut the mustard.

Simone plucked her handbag from where it hung on the end of the bed. Then she took a deep breath and looked at each of them. 'Are you sure I look okay?'

'Gorgeous, Mum.' This from Grace.

'Stop fishing for compliments and get the hell to this date,' Harriet ordered.

'Watch your tongue, young lady.' Simone pointed a finger at her. 'And be good for Frank.'

'You look amazing, Simmo. Have fun.' Frankie summoned a smile as she tried to swallow the lump that had formed in her throat. 'Can't wait to hear all about it.'

Frankie, Harriet and Grace followed Simone to the door and stood on the porch like nervous parents as she climbed into her beaten-up old Pajero.

'Oh bugger, I haven't organised dinner yet,' Simone called, leaning out of the driver's-side window.

'Don't worry about us, just go,' Harriet hollered.

Frankie nodded. 'Yes, go. I'll whip something up for them.'

A man like Logan Knight should not be kept waiting.

With a final wave, Simone reversed her car out of the driveway and started in the direction of the main street. Frankie shook her head, not wanting to think about whether Logan would kiss her sister hello in the manner he'd kissed her earlier.

'Did I see a cake box?' Grace asked, her eyes gleaming with excitement.

Frankie reached out and ruffled her youngest niece's hair. 'Sure did, my sweet. I'll go get it.' Normally she'd have gone to the effort of making her nieces something healthy for dinner, but for some reason she couldn't summon the energy, so they sat down on the couch together and ate cake right from the box. At least, she and Grace did. Harriet moaned about getting fat and grabbed an apple from the kitchen instead.

'You ought to be careful,' she said to Grace when she joined them again. 'Boys don't like fat chicks and if you keep eating junk food the way you do, you'll be the size of a house.'

'Harriet,' Frankie warned. Neither of the girls were fat and this was a ridiculous conversation.

'There's this thing called exercise,' Grace snapped back. 'Of course you wouldn't know about that because the only thing you ever exercise is your tongue.'

Harriet's mouth dropped open and her eyes narrowed at her sister. It wasn't like Grace to stand up for herself and Frankie couldn't help but silently commend her; still, she didn't want to end up umpiring her nieces' bickering all night, so she distracted them.

'What made you two decide to sign your mum up for Rural Matchmakers?'

'Adam and Stella's wedding,' Grace said, dumping her fork into the cake box.

'She'll look like a sad case if she goes alone,' Harriet added, picking up her iPhone and staring at the screen. It was a miracle she'd lasted this long without checking Facebook or Snapchat.

'What about me? You don't have a problem with *me* going to the wedding solo?'

'Oh, Aunty Eff,' Grace said, leaning in to hug her. 'You're so hot and young, you'll pick up some gorgeous guy on the dance floor.'

Hah! The optimism of youth. 'Your mum's not that much older than me,' Frankie said, feeling as if she should stick up for her sister.

'Ah … seven years.' Harriet looked up from social media and the expression on her face said she thought that time period a lifetime—and Frankie supposed it was almost half of Harriet's.

Frankie couldn't help but laugh. If she couldn't be at the pub with Logan, she could think of no place she'd rather be than hanging out with her nieces.

* * *

Of all the ridiculous things her sister and daughters had made her do, going on a blind date with a stranger off the internet was up there at the top, thought Simone as she pushed open the door of The Palace. And she was about to do it in full view of half the town; in lieu of any other nightlife in Bunyip Bay, this was where everyone between the ages of eighteen and eighty congregated on Friday nights. What kind of fool did that make her?

An optimistic one, that's what, because the moment she'd seen Logan Knight's photo on her computer screen, her lady bits had hijacked her brain, reminding her of her non-existent sex life. If Logan looked half as good in person as he did in his profile pic-ture, she was going to give this her best shot. She owed it to her-self and to her daughters, who, she had to admit, had their hearts in the right place when they'd signed her up for online dating. He'd have to be a nice person as well, of course—she wasn't about to jump into bed with a nasty pastie.

As she stepped inside the pub, the familiar smell of beer, cheap perfumes and greasy food wafted over her. The greasy-food aroma had always perplexed her because the food here was uniformly good. Liam, the publican, took pride in his establishment and he was fussy about what came out of the kitchen. Classic rock burst from the surround-sound stereo because that was Liam's favourite music. He'd had a jukebox for about five minutes a few years ago, but when drunk folk started selecting the Spice Girls and One Direction, he'd sold it cheap on Gumtree. There was usually a pool game to join if you so desired and rarely did things get rowdy. These days, especially with English hottie Drew Noble as police sergeant, people thought twice before putting a foot out of line.

'Hi Simmo, can I get you a drink?'

She smiled at Drew, who'd appeared beside her. *Speak of the devil.*

'Would you like to join Rubes and me for dinner?' he added, gesturing to a table in the dining area. He'd been in Australia less than a year but had already become accustomed to the Aussie practice of nicknaming everyone.

She followed his gaze to her dark-haired, gorgeous friend, Ruby Jones, who also happened to be Drew's lucky fiancée. Ruby lifted her hand and waved. Simone wiggled her fingers back and then said to Drew, 'No, thanks. I'm actually meeting someone.' She looked nervously around but couldn't see anyone who resembled Logan.

Credit to Drew, he didn't act shocked. 'In that case, have a good night.'

'Thanks, Drew.' Simone smiled as he walked back to Ruby. She took a few more steps, trying not to make it too obvious that she was meeting a stranger. What if he didn't show? Or, *gulp*, what if he'd somehow already seen her, realised she was years older than her profile picture, and fled out the back? He probably thought her some kind of cougar, preying on younger men on the internet.

'Simone?' A gravelly voice drawled her name at the same time as she felt a light tap on her shoulder. She spun around and came face to face with a tall, blond man who looked like he'd stepped right off the pages of an RM Williams catalogue. A shiver of awareness slithered through her. He wasn't wearing a hat but she could imagine him sitting astride a horse and herding sheep. Hell, she could imagine herself sitting astride him and …

'Yes. Hi.' She blinked—trying to rid that image from her mind before she said something stupid—and held out her hand. 'You must be Logan?'

He nodded, shook her hand lightly and then leaned in to kiss her cheek. 'Sorry about turning up unexpectedly this afternoon, but I was passing through and … well, I couldn't resist. I've really enjoyed getting to know you these past few weeks.'

Warmth rippled across her skin where his lips had been and she resisted the urge to press her fingers to the spot. It might not have been a raunchy lip-lock but it had been so long since a man had kissed her and it was … nice. His attention made her feel like her own woman, rather than just a mum. 'Me too,' she said. 'Shall we get a drink or find a table first?'

'How about a drink, then we can take it to a table? There seems to be plenty to choose from.' He smiled warmly and then touched his hand to her elbow, indicating for her to go ahead of him. She felt a number of curious eyes on them as they walked to the bar. They'd be the number one topic of conversation among certain folks over the next few days, but for once, Simone wouldn't mind the gossip. She had no qualms about rumours involving her and this guy doing the rounds. It would make a nice change from chatter about Harriet and her teenage delinquent boyfriend.

Simone smiled and waved politely at acquaintances before they finally arrived at the bar.

'Evening.' Liam dipped his head and assessed Logan. 'What can I get for you?' he asked eventually.

'My shout,' Logan said, turning to her as he pulled a wallet out of his pocket. 'What are you having?'

'Just a glass of chardonnay, please?' She made a mental note to drink it slowly, not wanting to get tipsy in front of her new, very handsome, prospect.

Logan turned to Liam. 'A chardonnay and a Coke please.'

'You don't drink?' Perhaps she should have opted for a soft drink.

'I enjoy a beer as much as the next bloke,' he confessed, 'but I've got to drive home and I find it's easier not to have anything.'

'Fair enough.' She smiled and an awkward silence descended as they waited for Liam to fetch their drinks. It would be good to ask a question to kickstart the conversation but the problem was she hadn't had enough time to read through all their correspondence. What if she asked him something they'd already discussed? Her hands grew clammy. What had she been thinking? This was a very bad idea.

'How are Harriet and Grace?' Logan asked, as Liam handed them their drinks and they started towards a table.

For a moment his question surprised her, but then she remembered he probably knew a lot more about her than she knew about him and of course her daughters would have ensured they mentioned themselves. They wouldn't want any potential stepdaddies who didn't like kids.

'Terrors,' she said, relaxing a little. The girls were an easy topic of conversation. 'My sister's at home with them now as I'm not sure I can trust Harriet. Last year she told me she was at a friend's when she was actually out joyriding in a stolen car with her boy-friend.' Hah, she bet Harriet hadn't told him about *that*.

Logan chuckled. 'She sounds like quite a character.'

Simone snorted. 'That's one word for it. Shall we sit over there?' She pointed to a table in the far corner of the dining area, where they'd have a little privacy from curious eyes.

'Looks good.' He got there first and held out a seat for her and she smiled her thanks, while silently noting her approval. Too many men these days had forgotten the art of chivalry.

As he sat, Simone sipped her wine and surreptitiously took a closer look at him. He had a perfect layer of stubble on his tanned face and his eyes were a lovely dark-chocolate brown. It made her think of Frankie's famous mud cake.

'So what happened with Harriet and the stolen car?' Logan asked, leaning back in his seat. 'Did she get in trouble with the cops? Is she still with the boyfriend?'

His string of questions reminded her he was a journalist. She bet he found it really easy to get female interviewees to spill gos-sip, although as a rural reporter he probably wrote up much more serious things. 'Yes, she's still with Jaxon. He's not a bad kid really, just bored. We really need to get a youth club or something hap-pening in town as there's not much for the teenagers to do after dark or on the weekends. Luckily the car they took was a family member's, so they got off with a warning. The boys had already been in a bit of trouble, so they had to do community service, but I think they've learned their lesson.'

He grinned. 'I got into a bit of strife myself when I was in my teens.'

She quirked an eyebrow. 'Now that is something I'd love to hear about.'

'Shall we order dinner first?' He picked up the laminated menu. 'Anything you recommend?'

'Well,' Simone said, 'everything's pretty good actually. I usually get the pasta of the day and I always finish with apple pie. No-one makes it like Liam, not even Frankie—but don't tell her I said that.'

With a smile and a nod towards the kitchen, Logan asked, 'Is Liam the chef?'

'No, he's the publican—the guy who served our drinks—but he's also an awesome pastry chef. His two cooks do all the meals but he won't let anyone else make the apple pie.'

'I'll have to leave room for pie then.' He turned back to the menu. His brow furrowed in deep concentration as he read and it had to be the cutest thing Simone had seen since Frankie's kittens. A few moments later he decided. 'I'm having the snapper. Shall I order you the pasta?'

Simone dived on her handbag, which was resting by her feet.

'I'm paying,' Logan said firmly. 'I turned up out of the blue and asked you out, so allow me.'

She raised one eyebrow, thinking it could be quite fun bantering with him. 'Technically I asked you, because I said I could meet you at the pub.'

'It's going to be like that, is it?' But his wide smile said he wasn't annoyed. 'How about you buy the pie we're going to share later?' And before she could reply, he swaggered off to the bar to place their order.

Simone usually didn't share her dessert with anyone, but she reckoned she might make an exception tonight. Her eyes followed Logan as he approached the bar, watching as he chatted to the couple of people drinking there while he waited. He seemed so confident talking to strangers—she liked that about him—and she noticed a couple of the young single women gawking at him. An unfamiliar surge of possessiveness and pride rushed through her.

'Who is *he*? And where have you been hiding him?' Ruby had taken up residence in Logan's chair. She was leaning forward, her waist-length straight hair falling over her shoulders, curiosity dancing in her eyes.

'It's a long story,' she confessed.

'But a good one?' Ruby asked.

'I'm hoping so. He's a journalist-slash-farmer from Mingenew and we've just started seeing each other.' A little white lie was easier than the long, convoluted truth.

'Ooh.' Ruby smiled her approval. 'Where did you meet him?'

'Um … Kinda on the internet. What do you think of him?' she asked before Ruby could interrogate her any further.

Ruby smirked. 'Well, I haven't spoken to him but he looks pretty damn fine from behind. Not that he has anything on Drew, of course.'

'Of course.' Simone laughed and then a fresh wave of nerves hit her. 'Oh, Ruby, I haven't been on a proper date in forever. What if I make a total fool of myself?'

'What about Ryan?'

Simone grimaced. 'As I said, "proper date". Ryan Forrester never thought of me as more than a friend and you know it.'

Ruby shrugged. 'Just relax and let your gorgeous personality shine through. By the way, you look hot in that dress. I'm half in love with you myself.'

'Thanks.'

'But he's coming back, so I'll leave you to it. Have fun and call me later. I want to know *all* the details.' Ruby gave Simone a quick pat of encouragement on her shoulder and walked away.

Logan returned a few moments later. 'I think the publican might have a bit of a crush on you,' he said as he sat down.

'Who? Liam?' She screwed up her face. He wasn't that bad looking, but he'd never shown any interest before. 'People in these parts can be very protective of their own.'

He nodded. 'He grilled me about my background and my intentions before he'd take our order.'

'That's hilarious. What did you tell him?'

'I told him my intentions were honourable but none of his business.'

She couldn't help but laugh. 'And here I was hoping your intentions were entirely dishonourable.'

He winked in reply and the smile she'd had on her face since she'd turned around and seen him for the first time grew a little more. It appeared flirting was like riding a bicycle after all, yet once again she racked her brain for something she could ask him. Conversation needed to be two-sided and so far he'd made most of the effort. Why had she spent so much time worrying about her outfit when she should have been memorising his profile and reading their emails? She couldn't even remember his star sign, never mind anything about this family.

She took another sip of wine. Maybe she could ask him for a quick refresher, tell him she had a shocking memory or something. But that might remind him of their unfavourable age difference. Maybe she could say she'd been drunk during their online interactions, but that would make her sound like an alcoholic. Argh!

'I've just got to pop to the ladies',' she said, practically leaping from her chair and rushing towards the pub's conveniences. He looked slightly confused at her sudden departure. Great, now he probably thought she had a bladder problem. She'd barely bolted the cubicle door before she had her phone out and Frankie on speed dial.

'Hey, sis. How's the date going?'

'Can you check Logan's profile for me? I need a topic of conversation but I don't want to ask him something I'm already supposed to know.'

Frankie laughed. 'Are you serious?'

'Yes,' Simone whispered, her heart racing. 'He's really nice and good-looking and funny and I don't want to blow this by making him think I'm a forgetful fruitcake.'

'If he sticks around, he'll find out eventually,' Frankie pointed out.

'Not helpful, sis. *Please?*'

'Okay, why don't you ask him about the articles he's written lately?' Frankie suggested after a brief pause. 'Most guys love talking about themselves, don't they?'

'Good idea. Thanks.'

'No worries. Where *are* you anyway? At the bar?'

'No,' Simone admitted, glancing around the cubicle, eyeing the graffiti scrawled on the dull beige walls. 'In the bathroom.'

If Frankie had sounded amused before, she positively cracked up now.

'It's not funny,' Simone hissed, thankful no-one else was in the restroom.

'Actually, it is a little bit,' Frankie said once she'd recovered. 'But I'm sorry. Have a good night and call me again if you need to.'

Feeling like a nervous teenager, Simone disconnected, silently thanking the Lord above for her sister. Checking her reflection in the mirror, she reapplied her lipstick, took a deep breath and then went back out to her date.

Chapter Three

Logan smiled as Simone approached after her mad dash to the bathroom. Although she was a few years older than her sister, they were physically very alike. Simone had shorter hair—her red locks hung in chaotic waves to just above her shoulders, a little unkempt as if she'd just tumbled out of bed. But aside from that one difference, she and Frankie could almost have passed as twins.

'You okay?' he asked as she lowered herself into her seat and dropped her handbag to the floor again.

'Great.' She smiled brightly. 'So, tell me about some of the articles you've written recently?'

'Ah, you don't want to hear about that.'

'Of course I do.' She waved her hand and almost knocked over her wine glass. 'Whoops,' she said, righting it quickly.

Was she nervous? He found that endearing and decided that talking about himself for a bit might help put her at ease.

'Well, not too long ago I did an article about online dating in the bush,' he confessed. 'That was enlightening. I went into it thinking that the success rates would be low, but I was pleasantly surprised. The paper got lots of feedback from people wanting to share their stories.'

'Is that why you signed up to the site?'

He deliberated, wondering if he should tell the whole truth or just a portion of it. 'Did we never talk about this?'

She shrugged one shoulder and half-smiled.

'All right, I'll be honest. I signed up for Rural Matchmakers simply because I couldn't get a proper look at the site without being a member. Until then I'd never contemplated meeting potential partners on the internet.'

'Me either.' She made a face and then added, 'Until recently I mean. Go on.'

'I like to be thorough in my research, so I uploaded a photo and filled in my details. I didn't really expect to get much response, but the next morning I woke up to literally hundreds of messages. I deleted most of them—it's amazing what you can tell about a person from what they say online—but something about you stood out.' He shrugged. 'I couldn't help myself, I responded and … well, you know the rest. I feel like I know you almost as well as I know some of my oldest friends; probably better than I know my family.'

Her cheeks flushed and she glanced down at her wine glass. Shit, maybe that admission was a little creepy; he didn't want to scare her off.

'Too full-on?'

'No.' She licked her lips and smiled at him.

'To be honest, I also started investigating the whole online dating thing because of Angus.'

'Your …' She sounded as if she'd forgotten who he was. Poor girl was obviously nervous.

'My brother,' he clarified. 'As I've said, he's been single a long while now and I think it'd be great for him to get out there again.

I thought if the online dating thing worked for me, then maybe I could convince him to consider it.'

Simone opened her mouth as if to say something, but they were interrupted by the arrival of their meals.

'Hi Simone, Hi …' The young waitress's voice trailed off as she put two plates down on the table and looked to him. 'And who are you?'

'Logan,' he offered with a smile. 'Nice to meet you. This fish looks amazing.'

'Wait till you taste it.' She flicked long brown hair that probably should have been tied in a ponytail over her shoulder and grinned at him. 'Enjoy. And let me know if you guys need anything else.'

'Thanks.'

'Yeah, thanks, Tegan,' Simone added as she picked up her fork. She looked back to him as the waitress retreated. 'So, are most of your articles light-hearted like the rural dating one? When you said you were a rural reporter I was thinking about things like the live-export trade crisis and the closure of Aboriginal communities.'

'I've covered both of those stories extensively. I even flew to Indonesia when the live-export problems were rife. But I like to mix up the serious with the human interest stories.'

'That makes sense. I'll be honest, I rarely listen to the news or read the papers because most of what I see when I do depresses me.' She twisted some strands of fettuccine around her fork and lifted it to her lips.

'I know what you mean. To be fair though,' he continued, 'the outback dating one was more serious than it sounds. So many rural towns are shrinking rapidly and many have way more men than women, which is a real problem—not only for communities as a whole but for men's mental health. Online dating might seem a little desperate to some, but it's the only hope many of these isolated farmers have.'

She nodded seriously. 'I've seen that first-hand. Until recently I was worried about my cousin Adam becoming one of those statistics. And it's not just men. I've been widowed for ten years and it's hard enough to meet people, let alone when you have kids. Add living in a small town to that and it can make things nearly impossible. And then there's my younger sister, Frankie.'

'She's single too?' The question slipped out before he knew what he was saying. He hoped he didn't sound too eager.

'I guess the right man just hasn't come along yet, but she's so great. A new cop came to town last year and I thought maybe … but he hooked up with a friend of ours.' Simone sighed. 'At least she's in a social job, being in the café, and could in theory meet new people there.'

'Yes, whereas, since his engagement ended, Angus is practically a hermit. We could be living up north on some remote station and he'd probably meet more people than he does currently.'

'Not a social butterfly then?' Simone asked, smiling as she took another sip of wine.

Logan shook his head. The only new women Angus ever met were the roustabouts or wool classers who came to their property with the shearing teams and even if he wanted to make an effort, they'd probably be too young.

'So Frankie and Angus *both* need to be more proactive.'

'Like us you mean?' He couldn't help looking at Simone and thinking how different she seemed in person to online. It wasn't a bad thing … he liked this Simone as well, but she'd been a lot more chatty over the internet. A lot more forthcoming.

'Exactly.' She slipped another forkful of creamy pasta into her mouth, reminding him he too should start on his meal before it went cold.

'This is better than I imagined,' he said after a few mouthfuls.

'Told ya.' Simone smiled victoriously. 'What's the most recent article you've written?'

'I've just submitted a big feature to *The Australian* on wind-farming.'

Her eyes lit up. 'Ooh, now that's a contentious issue around here at the moment. I hear there's a big renewable energy company trying to lease land off local farmers. I'm fascinated. Are you for or against?'

While finishing his mouthful, Logan deliberated what to say. He'd had numerous arguments with Angus over the last few months about this very issue and he didn't want to get into another one on a first date. Having said that, he wasn't the type of guy to hold back his opinion.

'I don't think it's as black and white as some people want to believe,' he began. 'As with most things, there are advantages and disadvantages, but in this case I think the benefits far outweigh the negatives. The turbines can provide an additional income for farmers, which can help in times of drought. There's also community benefits—employment and ongoing maintenance. Not to mention tourism. '

She smiled and nodded.

'Sorry, I'm probably boring you half to death.'

'On the contrary.' She lifted her wine glass to her lips and took a sip before adding, 'I'm enjoying myself immensely. You don't know how starved I am for adult conversation. Most of my time is spent stopping my teenage daughters from killing each other.'

Logan chuckled, recalling all too well the numerous fights he and Angus had gotten into as teenagers—neither of them backing down until blood was spilled, bones were broken or one of their parents physically dragged them apart. Like most siblings, they had a love-hate relationship. Angus was both his best friend and his worst enemy.

'So what do *you* think about wind farms then?' he asked, trying to forget about Angus and enjoy Simone's company. Just because his brother was intent on living the life of a recluse, didn't mean Logan should feel guilty about getting out and enjoying himself.

'I actually think the turbines themselves are rather beautiful,' Simone confessed, 'but to be honest I don't know enough about them to make an informed decision. I have heard they can be damaging to local wildlife or even hazardous to humans. Do you think there's any truth in that?'

'I've interviewed people on both sides of the fence and I visited a few of the more established Australian wind farms and, in most cases, from what I saw, the livestock weren't affected at all. In fact, cows seem to love wind turbines.'

She raised her eyebrows but her smile said she found this amusing. 'You're a cow whisperer as well now, are you?'

'No.' He laughed. 'But I have got photographic evidence of cows and their love affair with wind turbines.'

'Show me,' she demanded, leaning forward and giving him a glimpse of her cleavage.

'With pleasure.' He swallowed and then whipped out his phone, scrolling back to some of the photos he'd taken while researching the story. They leaned towards each other as he showed her his favourite shot of a black and white heifer rubbing herself affectionately against the great pole of a wind turbine.

'Aw, she's adorable,' Simone said, her voice full of warmth. 'Still, no offence to cattle, but how would they know if the turbines were affecting their health? They're not exactly the smartest creatures on the planet, are they?'

'If I was a cow, I'd take offence to that.' With a grin, Logan put his mobile back in his pocket. 'Plenty of scientific studies have been conducted around wind as a renewable energy and there's not yet been any evidence found to link the turbines with adverse health effects on humans or animals.'

'It certainly sounds like you've done your research. Maybe you should become a politician, you can be very persuasive.' She smiled at him as she twisted some more pasta onto her fork.

He laughed. 'If I can't persuade my own brother to consider wind-farming on our property, I doubt I'd ever be able to convince strangers of the benefits.'

'You want to lease *your* land for wind-farming?'

He simply nodded. In addition to all the reasons he'd listed to Simone, his recent diagnosis meant he had other personal reasons for pursuing an alternative source of income for the family farm, but he wasn't about to share that with her yet.

'And why is your brother so opposed to it?'

Logan shook his head. 'Fuck knows why Angus does or thinks anything.' Then he cringed and hit her with a sheepish smile. 'Sorry. Language.'

She laughed. 'It's okay. I've been told I swear worse than a shearer.'

'But I bet no-one cares when someone as gorgeous as you curses.'

She blushed. 'My mum cares. She reminds me constantly that I'm not too old for her to wash my mouth out with soap.'

He grimaced at the thought, almost able to taste the soap himself. 'She never actually did it though, did she?'

'Hell yeah, she did. First time I was about seven. All I said was "bloody" and she marched me into the bathroom and practically shoved the whole bar of Lux into my gob. You'd think I'd have learned my lesson but I can't help it. I like the way curse words sound on my tongue. Didn't yours ever do the same? Or were you a good boy with a clean mouth back then?'

He couldn't reply; he was too busy laughing at the image of a feisty little redheaded girl with a whole cake of soap in her mouth.

'It's not funny,' she protested, although her tone said she disagreed. 'In fact I think it constitutes child abuse.'

'I'm sorry, you're right,' he conceded, shoving the last piece of his fish into his mouth to stop from cracking up again.

'Thank you.' She nodded her approval. 'So do your parents still live on the farm as well then?'

He almost choked on his snapper. 'My parents are both dead,' he reminded her when he'd swallowed. They'd had the family discussion quite early on in their emails. Simone had shared hilarious tales about her sister, her two daughters, her runaway father and her mother, who'd finally found love in a second marriage and now lived in Perth. And, in turn, he'd spilled his whole sorry life story as well.

'Right. I'm sorry.' She blinked, her cheeks turning crimson. 'I knew that. I feel terrible for bringing it up. It's just—'

'It's all right. Easy mistake.' He forced a smile, trying to relax her again. 'We've covered a lot of ground in a short time. Can I get you another glass of wine?'

'Yes, thanks. That'd be great.'

'I'll be right back.' Silently cursing himself for making her feel bad about her faux pas, Logan pushed back his seat and headed off to the bar. The fifteenth anniversary of his mum's death had passed a couple of months ago and his dad had been dead well over a decade, but whenever someone asked him about his parents, he still felt a sharp spear of grief to his heart. He guessed it might always be that way.

He ordered another chardonnay and then, vowing to get the conversation back on track, he returned to the table and smiled at Simone as he handed her the glass.

'So … why'd *you* join online dating?' he asked.

★ ★ ★

Frankie had finally succumbed to sleep on Simone's couch, but woke just after eleven o'clock to the sound of the front door opening. Her nieces had deserted her but the television still flickered in the corner. Lifting the remote, she muted the already low sound as her sister walked into the room. One look at Simone's face told Frankie the night had been a success.

'Hi, little sis,' Simone said, throwing her handbag onto the floor and squeezing in next to Frankie on the couch. 'Good night?'

'Not as good as yours by the sound of things.' Frankie sat up, yawned and psyched herself up to hear about Simone's night. How the tables had turned. Simone had married her high-school sweetheart young and already had Harriet by the time Frankie started flirting with the opposite sex. So many times, Frankie had called her big sister in the early hours of the morning and shared the highs and lows of her relationship rollercoaster, desperate for Simone's sage advice. Not that it had helped in the end.

'Were the girls good?' Simone asked, also stifling a yawn.

Frankie nodded. 'We ate and then Harriet went off to her room and Grace and I watched a few episodes of *Outlander*. I must have fallen asleep and I guess she went to bed. I'll go check on them.'

Simone grabbed hold of her arm as Frankie attempted to stand, pulling her back onto the couch. 'They'll be fine. They're not babies. I'll check in a moment. Sit with me a while. I'm too psyched to sleep just yet.'

'Okay.' Frankie didn't really want to hear her sister rave about Logan. Any other guy and she'd be over the moon that Simone was getting herself out there again. Ten years was a long time to be alone and just because Frankie was in an extended dating drought, didn't mean she didn't want her sister to find happiness. Guilt tightened her chest.

'Aren't you going to ask me how it was? What he was like?' Simone was practically bouncing in the seat.

'How was it?' Frankie feigned enthusiasm. 'What was he like?' Of course, she already knew the answer to the latter question. In the few moments she'd spent with him, she'd seen enough to know that Logan Knight was like no other guy. They mightn't have shared the world's longest conversation but, be it female intuition or whatever, she knew he was much more than a hot body and a handsome face. 'Did he wonder why you spent so long in the toilet?'

Simone tried to scowl but couldn't bring herself to do so. 'Oh, I honestly don't know where to start. I've had the best night in forever.' She leaned back against her cushions and positively beamed. 'We shared a piece of apple pie.'

'What?' That made Frankie sit up straight. 'But you won't even share dessert with me.'

Simone laughed. 'I know. This was worth the sacrifice.'

Frankie felt a little sick. 'Did he, like … *feed* it to you?'

'No, nothing like that. We had two spoons, but they did clink occasionally and it just felt … intimate. He's such a spunk, which of course you know.' Simone nudged Frankie like this was hilarious.

She nodded half-heartedly. The thought of Logan and Simone sharing dessert reminded Frankie of the kiss. Had Logan mentioned it? She couldn't bring herself to ask for fear of heat rising in her cheeks, giving her ridiculous feelings away.

'But there's such depth to him too,' Simone added. 'We had a fascinating conversation about his work. He's a really intelligent guy.'

'I guess the question is—' Frankie felt like it needed to be asked '—if he's so perfect, why does he need a dating site?'

Simone was quiet a moment, then, 'I take your point, but he travels a lot for work and while that means he meets his fair share of women, long-distance relationships aren't a walk in the park. You and I both know how hard it is to meet people.'

'The right people anyway,' Frankie agreed, thinking of her last attempt at serious. What a train wreck that had been. *Stop being such a wet blanket.* 'I'm sorry, I'm not trying to rain on your parade, I'm just tired. It's been a long week.'

'That's okay. I'm actually exhausted too. It was hard to keep up my side of the conversation without slipping up and sounding like I didn't know something I should.' Simone groaned. 'At one point I asked him if his parents still lived on the farm and he reminded me they are dead.'

'Oh God. The poor bloke. You didn't?'

'It's not my fault. I didn't know! I honestly wished the floor would open and swallow me. I felt terrible and of course I couldn't ask for details because, well ...'

Frankie nodded. 'Yes, I see your dilemma. So, are you going to see him again then?'

'Is the Pope Catholic? I'm not going to let a man like him slip through my fingers. I know it seems sudden but everything happens for a reason and I don't want to be alone forever. Besides, I owe it to the girls to give it my best shot. He's away next week covering some event in Broome but then he'll be back on the farm for a few days. We've arranged to have lunch at the café.'

'*My* café?' Frankie's stomach flipped at the memory of exactly what had happened in her café that afternoon.

Simone frowned. 'Of course—it's the best around, isn't it? So I've got just over a week to do my research. I'm studying Logan Knight and I plan on topping the class. An A-plus for me, little sister. You want to help?'

'What? How?'

'You can be my study partner, read through our emails as well, in case I've missed anything vital.'

Frankie felt as if she'd already read enough. 'Did he say much about his brother at all? Maybe we can double date.' She forced a laugh at the thought.

'Oh yes, his name's Angus—but don't go getting your hopes up. He sounds like a bit of a grump. I'll have to engineer a meeting and check him out before I consider setting him up with my best sister.'

Although Frankie appreciated Simone's sentiment, the phrase 'beggars can't be choosers' immediately came to mind. Besides, if Angus shared the same DNA as Logan, he couldn't be *that* bad. Could he? 'Thanks,' she said, although she felt anything but thankful.

'But hey, if he's not a possibility, maybe you could sign up to online dating as well? It worked for me, right?'

The mere thought made Frankie's skull pound. Simone seemed to have forgotten that it wasn't even her who had done the work—three hours ago she'd been threatening to murder her daughters for it. Deciding it was time to make a move, she stretched her legs out in front of her. 'I'd better be going. I'm glad you had a good night.'

'You can't go yet,' Simone objected. 'Why don't you stay the night? We can grab a bottle of wine, take it into my bedroom and start our study routine. First thing is finding out when and how Logan's parents died. I'm interested in his relationship history too. Did you know he was married?' Simone didn't give Frankie the chance to reply before continuing, 'Of course you didn't. You spent even less time with him than me. He must have been quite young when they tied the knot. I wonder what happened?'

Frankie stood. Although she was curious to learn more about Logan, she decided that for self-preservation, it was better to keep her distance, so she yawned again. 'I'm sorry, I'm stuffed, maybe another night. I've got an early start at the café and the cats will be climbing the walls as I haven't been home since this morning.'

Simone shrugged, dismissing this excuse. 'They've got each other for company.'

'Unfortunately they haven't yet worked out how to open the cat food,' Frankie said, her tone firm. She leaned down and kissed her sister on the cheek. 'See you tomorrow?' Rarely a day went by where they weren't in each other's pockets.

'You betcha,' Simone replied, sounding even more chirpy than usual—and that was saying something. Simone was probably the most positive and optimistic person Frankie knew. Although she'd been through a very dark patch following the death of her husband, she'd eventually made a decision to embrace life and live on for her girls.

Leaving Simone on the couch, Frankie saw herself out, climbed into her hatchback and drove the short distance to her house on the other side of town. As predicted, Fred and George were waiting, peering through the front curtains. She'd barely stepped into the hallway before they were winding themselves around her legs and mewling. She wasn't naive enough to think they'd missed her. Cats only cared about one thing: their stomachs. But Frankie was happy to focus on her pets and on warming up her damn freezing house, anything to distract her from her other thoughts.

On the way to the laundry, she flicked on the reverse-cycle heating, the cats darting in and out around her feet as she made her way down the hallway. She poured some cat biscuits into their bowls and then, because she was feeling generous, opened them a tin of tuna for a treat.

Her heart felt heavy as she brushed her teeth and her eyes were already moist when she began to wash her face. How pathetic. It was stupid to feel like she'd lost something when she'd only met Logan that afternoon. It wasn't like Simone had hooked up with Frankie's ex, or someone she'd been harbouring a secret crush on for years.

'You need to get a grip,' she told her reflection in the mirror.

The last thing she wanted was to strain her cherished relationship with her sister because of some guy she didn't really even know.

Chapter Four

Logan couldn't bring himself to do anything more than kiss Simone on the cheek when he'd bid her goodnight. It had been a good night—the most fun he'd had in ages—and they'd talked easily right up until he'd walked her out to her beaten-up old four-wheel drive, but somehow it felt wrong to kiss both sisters on the same day.

As he walked back to the café where he'd left his ute, the cool August air blew against his face and the street lights of Bunyip Bay shone down upon him and he wondered again whether Frankie had told Simone about his little gaffe that afternoon. He hadn't dared ask—maybe she'd been too embarrassed to mention it. If they ever got serious, it'd probably be one of those stories that reared its head every Christmas, something he'd never be able to live down. He chuckled at the thought—longing for the normality of such a family gathering again.

He climbed into his ute, turned the heating up full bore and then slowly reversed out of his car space. The dulcet tones of the narrator of the audio book he was listening to washed over him as he headed down the main street towards the Brand Highway, but as he picked up speed, he found it harder and harder to concentrate on the story. Squinting, he cursed under his breath as the streetlights of town faded behind him and he struggled to see very far ahead. He couldn't believe how soon his symptoms had worsened, especially when it came to night driving.

Shadows flickered on the road but he couldn't make out if they truly were just shadows or something that could be a hazard like a kangaroo bounding across the road. Or worse, another car coming in the other direction. His fingers gripped the steering wheel so hard he felt his nails digging into his palms. With each passing kilometre, what started as a dull ache in his forehead compounded into a throbbing pain until he could no longer continue.

'Fuck!' Logan slammed the heel of his hand into the steering wheel. The horn blasted but there wasn't a soul around to hear besides him. At this rate, he wouldn't make it home until tomorrow morning. Angry and frustrated, his eyes prickling, he pulled over to the gravel on the edge of the road and killed the engine.

This was not the way he'd hoped to end the day, but he resigned himself to a night in his vehicle with only the warmth of his swag for comfort. It was far too cold to lie in the open air on the ute's tray, so he dragged said swag out and tried to get comfy lying across the passenger's and driver's seats, the hard glass of the window his pillow.

I should have had a beer and taken a room in Bunyip Bay.

Somehow, in the early hours of the morning, despite the gear stick jamming into his side, he managed a few hours' sleep and woke to the sounds of pesky cockatoos flying in flocks overhead and a feeling of ice in his bones. Rubbing his palms up and down his arms, he yawned and glanced out the window, only just able to make out the sun peeking over the horizon through the frosty glass. Still, the low-lying clouds and the mist that painted the landscape took his breath away. There were a few sheep slumbering in a nearby paddock but aside from them, he felt as if he were the only person in the world. Although his muscles ached from his awkward sleeping position, a smile crept onto his face and the darkness that had loomed over him last night didn't seem quite so suffocating.

He packed up his swag, almost froze to death relieving himself behind a tree and then climbed into his ute to continue the drive to Mingenew. Back to the property that had been his parents' pride and joy and was now, he sometimes thought, the only thing that kept his brother going.

It didn't feel long before he slowed the ute at the entrance to the farm. As it always did, his heart stilled a moment at the names on the gate welcoming visitors to KNIGHT'S HILL, TREVOR & CELESTE KNIGHT'S PLACE. Reminders of his parents were everywhere but nowhere more than here on the sign. Neither he nor Angus nor Olivia had ever raised the possibility of taking it down and replacing it. Somewhere in the last few years they'd stopped talking about their folks—something Logan didn't think healthy but he'd never quite been able to rectify it. He sometimes shared the odd anecdote with Olivia, wanting to keep their parents' memories alive for her, but Angus seemed to prefer to keep all his pain and heartbreak locked up inside.

Sometimes Logan thought about provoking him, pushing him to the edge so that he'd snap, get angry and let it all flow out, but the closest he'd ever got was trying to get him to talk about the future direction of the farm. Their discussion about the potential of wind turbines was the latest point of contention.

With a sigh and a determination not to have a depressing weekend, he continued up the track to the main house. As with all farms, there were wheat storage facilities, near-empty dams, the shearing sheds, workers' quarters and various pieces of old machinery put out to pasture on either side of the track, but they'd always been there and Logan barely noticed them. The only time he ever thought about what the farm looked like was when he was travelling for work and thinking of home, but in the last few months, he'd starting started seeing things differently. Taking more notice of his surroundings before it was too late.

Angus's two red kelpies were the only sign of life in the yard, racing towards Logan's ute as he pulled up under an old gum tree.

'Hey boys,' he greeted them, chuckling at the way they always barked like he was a stranger. They fancied themselves more as guard dogs than farm dogs, but they were pretty good at both jobs. At the sound of his voice, they quieted and escorted him up onto the verandah, before falling into two heaps on either side of the front door. He yanked off his boots and headed inside.

Although it was at least ten degrees warmer than outside, the house still felt chilly and Logan hurried down the corridor, one destination in mind—the bathroom and a hot shower.

'Look what the cat dragged in.'

He startled at the sound of Angus's voice as he trekked through to the kitchen and found his brother filling the kettle. 'Good morning.'

'Maybe for some.'

Logan didn't even roll his eyes; he'd be suspicious if Angus *wasn't* in his usual grump. 'What's on the agenda today?'

Angus sighed as he grabbed a mug from the overhead cupboards. 'I noticed a tree down over a fence yesterday. Need to fix that.'

'Must have been that storm we had the other night.'

Angus grunted. 'Pity all that wind didn't bring much rain. Also need to check water levels and start servicing the header. Harvesting will be upon us before we know it. Nice of you to turn up, though. I could use a hand.'

Logan nodded, trying not to feel annoyed. Harvest was still a couple of months away but it was as if every opportunity Angus got, he tried to make Logan feel guilty about leaving him with all this work. But the fact of the matter was, the farm could not support both of them full time and, even before their dad's death, the plan had always been for Angus to take over. 'I've gotta have a shower and eat something, but then I'm all yours. Use and abuse me.'

Whereas most people might laugh at that, Angus merely raised one of his permanently knitted brows. 'You up to it after your shenanigans last night? I'm guessing this girl you've met online turned out to be just as hot in person?'

'Simone was lovely, but nothing happened, if that's what you're insinuating. I'm serious about getting serious and I'm not about to ruin something that could be great by rushing into things. If you must know, I had a few beers over dinner so I stayed at the pub,' Logan finished, unable to meet Angus's gaze.

'Fair enough.' The kettle began to whistle and Logan continued on to the bathroom, leaving Angus to make his coffee.

He stripped quickly and stepped into the steaming shower. At first the heat almost burned his freezing skin, but as he stood there, the hot water slowly warmed him from the outside in. He thought about his date with Simone and smiled; if only he could work out a way to get Angus out there and meeting people as well. It wasn't healthy to be alone so much and now that Olivia was away at uni in Perth, she wouldn't be coming back as often as she had when she was at boarding school.

And their baby sister seemed to be the only person who ever made Angus smile. This weighed heavily on Logan's mind but he'd never mentioned it to her, not wanting her to put her life on hold out of guilt. Instead he'd vowed to return to the farm and check in on Angus as much as he could and to be a practical support as long as possible. Working on the farm today would be good—it'd help him keep his mind off his own woes and hopefully they'd get the chance to have a rational talk about the wind-farming thing. The energy company that was sniffing around the area had a meeting at the end of next month for farmers interested in leasing their land and he wanted Angus to be there. His mission over the next few weeks was to convince him how an opportunity like this could be good for all of them.

With that thought, Logan turned off the shower and stepped out to start the day. Immediately the aroma of bacon and eggs drifted under the door and his stomach groaned.

For all Angus could be a grumpy bastard, deep down he was a great bloke and that was why Logan spent so much damn time worrying about him. It broke his heart to see his big brother's life just going to waste. He hurried to pull on his old jeans and a work shirt, his mouth salivating in anticipation of breakfast with the works.

'Man, that smells good,' Logan said, grinning at Angus as he re-entered the kitchen.

Angus merely laid two plates on the table and indicated for Logan to sit. He did, happy to see he had cooked for himself as well. Logan suspected that often when he was away, his brother lived on Vegemite toast and Weetbix, and not just for breakfast. When he was home, he took it upon himself to ensure the cupboards were well stocked and dinner was something nutritious. He loved cooking and it wasn't always easy to do in motel rooms, so coming home and spending time in the kitchen wasn't a hardship.

They ate and then dumped their dishes in the sink to return to later. Angus filled a couple of flasks with hot coffee and Logan almost made a quip about how domesticated he was, but swallowed it at the last minute, not wanting to piss him off and start the day strained.

Once they were in the ute, bumping across the paddocks, Angus surprised him by initiating conversation. 'What's she like then?'

Logan was surprised to find that the first person who came into his head was Frankie, but he pushed the image aside and smiled. He didn't know Frankie like he'd gotten to know Simone these last few weeks and it wasn't like Simone wasn't also a knock-out. 'She's great. Really warm and bubbly. Lots of fun. An artist. You'd like her.'

Angus snorted. 'Doesn't she have kids?'

It wasn't like Angus to want to talk about women or anything personal, so Logan ignored the irritation that flared within him at Angus's sceptical tone and went with it. 'Yes, two teenage girls. Harriet and Grace.'

'Not worried they might cramp your style?'

'No. Plenty of people manage to have relationships with children in the equation. In fact, I'm really looking forward to meeting them.'

'They'll probably hate you,' Angus said, slowing the ute as they approached the fallen tree.

Logan ran a hand through his hair, losing patience. He glared at Angus. 'Do you always have to be so damn negative about everything?'

'I'm not negative.' Angus shrugged as he stopped the ute. 'I'm simply a realist. Face it, Logan. Your track record with relationships isn't great, and those women didn't have the added baggage of a ready-made family to complicate things. Teenage girls aren't the easiest of people to get along with.'

Logan took a deep breath as he opened the passenger door. There was so much he wanted to say about all that. So he'd been a bit of a player following the break-up of his marriage, but he wasn't the one who'd broken his vows. Had Angus forgotten that? His only mistake was falling for a woman who didn't love him as much as he'd loved her. When a husband cheated on a wife, everyone fell over themselves with sympathy for the woman, but when the roles were reversed, people made excuses. So many people he'd considered friends had assumed Logan must have been a bad husband for Loretta to leave him, and it cut deep that his brother seemed to subscribe to this theory as well.

Still, he was ready to move on from the past. He wanted more out of life than one-night stands. He wanted emotional connection—friendship and companionship as well as sex—something Angus had clearly switched himself off from.

'You're not the only one who has experience raising teenage girls,' he reminded his brother as they both climbed out and slammed their doors. 'I might not have been at home with Olivia as much as you were but I visited her at boarding school and I've been there for her just as much in other ways.'

'Yes, I'm sorry. You're right.' Without another word, Angus opened the ute's tailgate to let the dogs out and then leaned in to grab gloves. He tossed a pair to Logan and then turned to walk towards the fallen tree. With a heavy heart, Logan followed.

He wanted more than anything to fix his brother's pain but he just didn't know how.

Chapter Five

The house phone rang just as Angus Knight sat down to his early lunch—baked beans on toast and a glass of orange juice to wash it all down. He'd been up since the crack of dawn servicing the header and all he'd had was coffee. He looked at the handset and considered ignoring it. Phone calls to the house were few and far between; Logan and Olivia mostly sent messages or called his mobile. Predicting it would be a telemarketer, he took a swig of his juice and then picked up his knife and fork.

Finally the ringing stopped and he grinned in satisfaction as he shoved the first forkful into his mouth. He was a man of simple pleasures but he'd barely swallowed when the damn phone started up again. Glaring at the offender hanging on the kitchen wall, he pushed back his seat and marched across to it, then snatched up the receiver.

'Hello,' he barked.

'Angus?' came a woman's voice.

'Yes. Who's this?'

'It's … Loretta.'

He frowned. What the hell was Logan's cheating ex-wife doing calling?

'Brad just radioed in to say he's seen some sheep on the road. He thinks they're yours.'

Loretta didn't have to say which road—there was only one that both properties used and he had a flock down there because the dam in that paddock was the most full.

'Angus? Are you there?'

'Yes, sorry. Um …' He raked a hand through his hair. 'Thanks for letting me know. I'll head there now.'

'No worries. Brad's trying to get them back in but he thinks you might need to fix the fence. Looks like that's how they got out. See ya.' Loretta disconnected, as eager to be done with the conversation as Angus was.

He couldn't blame Logan for preferring a life of travel to hanging around on the farm—not when the woman who broke his heart was happily shacked up on the property next door—but he missed his little brother when he was away at work. It got lonely, running a farm by himself. A fact he'd never admit to Logan— that would only give him more ammunition in his quest to get Angus to date again, find a hobby, go on a holiday. He admired his brother—liked how he always tried to see the good in people, was always optimistic about the future—but that didn't mean he could pretend to be like that when he wasn't. Nope, Angus was quite happy with the status quo, which was why he didn't want wind-farm developers coming onto his property and changing everything.

He gave one final wistful glance at his unfinished lunch and then stormed down the corridor to the front door. A minute later he was in his ute, dogs on board, charging down the gravel track towards his errant sheep.

As Loretta had indicated, he found his neighbour, Brad, trying to usher the sheep back to where they were supposed to be. Angus cursed at the sight—both thankful and disappointed Logan wasn't here. Thankful because the last thing his brother needed when he was getting on with his life was to have to deal with his ex and her second husband. Disappointed because if Logan were here, they could have dealt with this mess together and he wouldn't have to accept Brad's help.

He parked his ute on the edge of the road and climbed out, nodding at the other man. 'Afternoon, Brad.'

'Angus.' Brad dipped his hat.

'Thanks for calling this in,' Angus said, gesturing to the sheep on the road. He whistled for his dogs as he unlatched the tailgate on the ute. They jumped off and got straight to work.

'No worries, mate.' Brad grinned and Angus flinched, biting down on the impulse to tell this man that they may be neighbours, he may have done him a favour, but they would never be mates. Not after what he'd done to Logan.

Instead, he turned away and helped his dogs do their stuff. Brad insisted on being neighbourly and helping as well; with the four of them working hard, it didn't take long to get the sheep back on his land.

'Need any help with the fence?' Brad asked.

'Nah, I'll be fine.'

'Right. Goodo.' Brad shoved his hands in his pockets but still didn't make a move to go. 'You know, if you ever want to come round for a drink or even a barbecue or something, you're always welcome. Must get pretty lonely with Olivia living in Perth permanently and Logan always off somewhere.'

Often Angus didn't mind the solitude—he and Liv talked on the phone every couple of days—but quiet nights gave him too much time to think. Not that he was going to tell Brad any of this.

Instead Angus found himself saying, 'Actually, Logan has been around quite a bit lately. He's got himself a new woman and she doesn't live far.'

Brad raised his eyebrows. 'Is that right? I'm ... Well, that's great.' He looked as if a load had been lifted and Angus clenched his hands into fists at his sides.

He hadn't told Brad so he could feel less guilty about being a prick. Angus had no time for people who cheated on their partners and he certainly had no time for men who hooked up with other people's wives. If he was going to start socialising—and that was a very big if—the last people he'd be doing so with was Brad and Loretta.

He grabbed his fencing gear from the ute and stalked over to the problem. How the hell it had gotten this bad without him or Logan noticing he had no idea, but he wished Brad would just buzz off and leave him to fix it. He set to work in silence.

'Well, then,' Brad said, finally getting the message and turning back towards his ute, 'glad to be of assistance. Guess I'll see you round.'

Or not. Angus forced himself to lift a hand and wave. He let out a sigh of relief when the other man climbed into his ute and disappeared in a cloud of red dirt.

By the time Angus had fixed the fence and made it back home, his paltry lunch was as cold and unappealing as a plate of wet card-board. He picked it up, scraped the contents into the bin and then dumped the plate in the sink.

On his way out of the kitchen and back down the corridor, he glanced into the office and saw the computer sitting on the clean desk. You could always tell when Logan had been home because he liked things tidy and in their place. Angus liked things clean but he found a bit of clutter comforting. He chuckled at the knowledge that by the time Logan returned in a few days, there'd no doubt be papers spread all over the desk again.

About to continue past, something stopped Angus in his tracks. He'd been a bit hard on Logan this last weekend. His brother had been so full of excitement after his date and all Angus had given him was negativity. He hated himself for raining on Logan's parade but couldn't seem to stop it. With this thought, he went into the office, sat down at the desk, fired up the computer and then typed 'Rural Matchmakers' into the search engine. He'd never been anywhere near one of these sites before but couldn't help being curious about the woman who had Logan so excited. His brother had used the office computer over the weekend and was still signed in, so Angus didn't have to make an account for himself in order to look through the available profiles. He wouldn't snoop at the messages between Logan and Simone, but there was no harm checking her out. Wasn't that what older brothers were supposed to do?

The site was easy to navigate and with a few clicks, Angus found her. As her headshot appeared on the screen, he sucked in a breath, startled by her unique, natural beauty. He couldn't remember having such a visceral reaction to a woman in a long time—maybe he really did need to get out more. A larger-than-life smile had pride of place on Simone's pale face. It was as if she were smiling right at him. Despite being fair, her skin was flawless, not a freckle, wrinkle or blemish in sight, and her lips were full and red; looking at them made his mouth dry. She looked younger than he'd imagined. Then there was her hair—all soft and wavy, so feminine, hanging just past her shoulders, and a rich ruby-red that went perfectly with her sparkly green eyes.

No wonder Logan was smitten.

Angus shifted in the swivel chair, uncomfortable with the unfamiliar sensations Logan's girl had stirred within him. Could he sign up for something like this?

He dismissed the idea almost immediately. The mere thought of having to dress up, go on dates, make polite small talk while he worked out if there was potential for more with someone made his head hurt. And then there was the image rising in his head—a horrible image he would never forget.

No, he couldn't possibly risk anything like that again.

Chapter Six

'Bye, Mum, love you. See you this afternoon.'

Simone's heart swelled as Grace stretched up and kissed her on the cheek. 'Have a good day, honey,' she said, waving off both her girls as they headed down the street to the school bus. Not that Harriet responded. Simone sighed. At least she still had one child who didn't hate her guts and wasn't embarrassed to be seen with her. She'd once read somewhere that having a child was like letting your heart forever walk outside your body and, man, was that the truth. Everyday she prayed that her girls would have a good day; that they—Harriet in particular—wouldn't get into any scrapes.

It was Grace's second year travelling to the high school in Geraldton and thankfully, she seemed to have taken to the extra travel and the greater workload without much drama. Bless her heart. Harriet, on the other hand, lived for the drama. Everything felt like a battle with her at the moment—from the second she reluctantly crawled out of bed in the morning to their final, usually turbulent, words at night.

On Friday night, when the girls had confessed to their online-dating scheme, Simone had felt a mix of emotions. Her first instinct was anger, and then concern for what might have happened—you never knew who they might have met online—and then she'd almost felt closer to Harriet, as if her daughter had finally been thinking about someone besides herself. But by Saturday morning she'd been living with a stranger again. The only time Harriet wanted to speak to her now was to argue about the limits Simone had enforced on her relationship. Quite frankly, she thought she'd been lenient letting Harriet continue seeing Jaxon after the fiasco with the stolen car—not to mention the fire business—but Harriet didn't see it that way. As far as she was concerned, her mother was hell bent on ruining her life.

Her confession of that morning still rang loud and clear in Simone's head. 'I only signed you up for online dating because I hoped if you got a life you'd butt out of mine. But you'll probably stuff things up with Logan like you did with Ryan.'

Usually quick at retorts, Simone hadn't been able to come up with one this time, so had simply ignored her daughter's caustic words. Neither of them had spoken to each other since. Not that that was out of the ordinary—Harriet often left for school in a mood but usually by the end of the day she'd forgotten it or moved onto some other drama. By God, it was draining.

Were she and Frankie such nightmares to their mum during adolescence? Simone didn't think so and wondered why-oh-why she was being punished like this. Hadn't she already been through enough crap? Closing the door behind her, her gaze caught on the photo of her and Jason on their wedding day that still sat in pride of place on the hallway table. When they'd first found out she was pregnant, she'd never imagined she'd have to do this tough parenting gig without him. Not a day went by when she didn't think of him, nor a day where her heart didn't feel empty with missing him.

She sighed, kissed her index finger and then touched the tip of it against his face. The irony of the situation was that Harriet's Jaxon reminded Simone so much of Jason: they were both larrikins with big hearts who sometimes acted before thinking things through. Even their names were similar.

'Not that you'd be able to see the likeness, would you my love,' Simone said, smiling bittersweetly down at her husband. 'Jaxon would never have got within ten feet of Harriet with you around.' Jason had adored Harriet from the moment she was born and they'd shared a special connection right up until he'd died.

Simone went into the kitchen and began the arduous task of cleaning up after breakfast. For two girls, they sure could make a mess. Harriet was 'cleansing'—or so she said—and that meant she blended about a million vegetables each day for breakfast. Meanwhile Grace ate half a box of cereal.

She was tossing all the leftover vegetable scraps into a plastic tub for the neighbours' chooks when her phone beeped with a message. The bus would barely have left Bunyip Bay yet, so it couldn't be the school with bad news.

Wiping her hands on her jeans, she started rifling through the clutter on the bench and on the dining table and finally found her phone under a tea towel. Her stomach did an unfamiliar flip when she saw the name *Logan Knight* on her screen. God, even his name was sexy.

They'd exchanged numbers at the end of their date and had been texting friendly and flirty messages over the weekend. It was a bizarre feeling to have so much interaction with someone besides her mum, Frankie, Harriet or Grace. But lovely all the same. Well aware she had a goofy grin on her face, Simone swiped her finger across the screen and found herself looking at the most beautiful sunrise. In the message were the words: *Cable Beach first thing this morning. Hope you have a lovely day. Chat later. x*

Her whole body warmed as if the sun in the photo was shining down on her. It was such a simple message but exactly what she needed this morning. Well, that or a bottle of wine, and eight o'clock was too early to hit the grog. She tried to ignore the prick of guilt that somehow she was cheating on Jason. He wouldn't want her to be alone forever and Logan accepted that she and the girls were a package deal. Although he hadn't met them yet, they'd interacted with him more than she had, so she was confident they'd get along in person. Knowing Harriet, she'd probably prefer Logan to Simone.

Shoving that thought aside, Simone took a quick snap of the carnage that was her kitchen, pressed send and then typed back: *Jealous. Your morning looks so much more fun than mine. x*

The first time she'd replied to him it had felt a bit odd adding the 'x' to her message—Logan had had longer to get used to their communications than she had—but then she remembered that until now her teenage daughters had been handling her side of the relationship and Harriet and Grace even put smiley faces and hugs and kisses on shopping lists and school essays.

LOL, came his reply.

Her mood vastly improved by their interaction, the last thing she felt like doing was the housework she'd promised herself she'd do today before heading into the studio to begin her paid work. Feeling the need for fresh air and an injection of coffee, she abandoned the kitchen, yanked on her boots, grabbed her bag and left the house. She had a Meals on Wheels committee meeting this afternoon and needed to get to work on her latest commission—a wall hanging of an owl for a local—but nothing would be achieved without caffeine and she wanted to see Frankie. Although they had meant to catch up over the weekend, Simone had been busy ferrying Grace to netball in Geraldton on Saturday and Frankie had been unusually quiet.

Striding down the footpath towards the main street of Bunyip Bay, Simone let her mind wander to her cousin Adam's upcoming

nuptials. Weddings were always lovely but the prospect of poten-
tially having a man to attend with made her even more excited.
Did she have the guts to ask Logan? Was it too soon? Without a
doubt he'd fill a suit, or whatever he chose to wear, just as well as
he filled a pair of jeans. Her mouth went dry at the thought and her
nerves tangled with excitement in her stomach. She hadn't slept
with a man since Jason; he was the only man she'd ever slept with.

Maybe she was getting ahead of herself. After the disaster with
Ryan Forrester—how was she supposed to know he was gay?—
she'd thought herself destined to be a widow for life. Yet although
it was early days, this thing with Logan felt different. She'd all but
given up the idea of dating again but the universe had brought
Logan to her anyway.

'Hey Simmo.'

She turned to the sound of her name as she headed past the
primary school to see Stella Reynolds, Adam's fiancée, coming
out the gate. 'Hi Stella, how are you?'

'Good.' Stella beamed. 'Heidi's really settling into the school
here and everyone is being so supportive and helpful. I couldn't
ask for a better transition for her.'

'That's great,' Simone said. 'You must be so relieved.'

Heidi, at seven years of age, was perhaps the most adorable
thing on the planet, Simone's own daughters aside, of course.
Heidi had Down syndrome and she embraced life—and everyone in it—with such a big heart and a huge smile that your heart
melted every single time you saw her.

'What are you up to now?' Stella asked.

'I was thinking of heading to the café for a cuppa. Want to
come?'

Stella's brow furrowed. 'I thought Frankie closed on Mondays.'

'She does, but I'm family and you will be soon, so we have
special privileges, like taste-test Monday, when she does all her

baking.' Simone held out her arm for Stella to link hers through. 'Come on.'

'If you're sure she won't mind the intrusion, I'll come with you and fetch my car later.'

As the two women approached the strip of shops on the main street, Stella said, 'So, what's this I hear about a new guy in your life?'

Simone groaned, pretending to be annoyed. 'God, is nothing sacred in this town?'

Stella laughed. 'Apparently not. You know what the bush telegraph is like. Adam heard it from Drew, who saw you in the pub, I believe. Are you gonna spill the beans or should I just listen to the idle gossip?'

As they walked, Simone gave Stella a condensed version of how she and Logan had met. By the time they came to the post office, Stella was in hysterics. 'I can't believe your girls did that.'

'Oh, believe it.' Simone shook her head in exasperation. 'I wouldn't put anything past Harriet. At first she pretended it was all for the good of my mental health, but then she told me this morning she just wants me to have a life so I'll butt out of hers.'

Stella gasped and covered her mouth with her hand. 'She didn't?'

Simone shrugged. 'Teenagers. What can you do? And the thing is, if things do work out with Logan, she'll probably take all the credit and try to use it as bargaining power to get her own way.'

With a sympathetic smile, Stella patted Simone's arm. 'I'm just going to check the post.'

As Stella went over to look inside her and Adam's post office box, a shadow came up behind Simone. Something told Simone it would be one of the local gossips.

Sure enough, when she turned around, she came face to face with Mrs Brady, her purple-rinsed hair almost sparkling in the winter sunlight. 'Hello,' she said, preparing herself for some sort of drama.

'I hear you've got a new man in your life too,' Mrs Brady said, her tone disapproving.

It was all Simone could do not to roll her eyes. 'I've just started seeing someone, yes.'

'I hear he's a strapping lad. Quite nice to look at. Vera was having dinner in the pub Friday night and she said he had a handsome face that would be even better if he didn't hide behind an untidy layer of stubble.' She tutted.

'Did she?' Simone smiled tightly. In her opinion, Logan's stubble was just about perfect.

'Hmm.' Mrs Brady frowned. 'He sounds suspiciously like the fella I saw Frankie kissing in the café on Friday afternoon. It was *quite* a display. I was only thankful there were no children present.'

'What? Frankie was kissing someone?' Simone couldn't hide her shock and then cursed herself, because everyone waiting outside for the post office to open had probably also heard it. 'Are you sure?'

Stella returned with a bundle of envelopes and looked from Simone to Mrs Brady in confusion.

'I saw it with my own eyes. I thought *you* would have known,' said Mrs Brady, obviously enjoying herself.

'I'm sorry, Mrs Brady,' Stella said, taking Simone by the arm. 'We're in a bit of a hurry. Chat later.' And with that, Stella tugged Simone along the path. 'What was *that* about?'

'Eff knows.' Simone frowned and glanced behind her as Mrs Brady started up the steps to the post office. Frankie kissing someone? Maybe the old biddy's eyes had been playing tricks on her. Or maybe she was simply confused?

If her sister was seeing anyone, Simone would have been the first to know about it, wouldn't she?

★ ★ ★

Frankie looked up from the kitchen as a knock sounded on the café door. 'Tourists,' she muttered to herself as she continued icing a carrot cake, hoping they'd read the sign on the door and go away. Being open six days a week was enough in a small town—in theory she needed a day's rest but most Mondays she spent baking and preparing for the rest of the week.

When the knock got louder, it dawned on her it must be someone she knew and she stepped sideways to look through the hatch into the dining part of the café. Simone and Stella were out the front, waving through the window like a pair of lunatics. Inwardly rolling her eyes, she forced a smile and lifted her hand to wave.

'There in a minute,' she called, as she finished smoothing the icing and then dumped the spatula back in the bowl. She wiped her hands on her apron and went through to let them in.

'You really should give me a key,' Simone said, sounding far more chirpy than Frankie felt. Her weekend hadn't been bad—the usual working at the café and hanging out with her cats—but she was tired of feeling as if she was living in her own *Groundhog Day*.

'And then I'd never get anything done,' Frankie replied, sounding far more bitter than she'd meant to. Usually, she'd be happy to see her sister and her future cousin-in-law but somehow the conversation always made it around to the wedding. And the truth was, all the talk of love and weddings was starting to get her down. She'd make the cake, she'd attend, she'd be truly happy for Adam and Stella, she'd even don a fancy frock for crying out loud, but right now she felt like everyone's happiness was being paraded under her nose. Maybe she needed a holiday.

'I'd kill for a coffee,' Simone gushed, rushing forward and leaning over to kiss Frankie on the cheek.

'Me too,' Stella said with her usual bright smile—the one that said *I'm blissfully happy and all is right with the world*.

'Murder won't be necessary, but you'll have to turn on the machine and make it yourself.' Frankie headed back to the kitchen, knowing the others would follow. 'Can I get you anything else?'

'No, thanks,' Stella said. 'I ate breakfast at home and although your cakes always tempt me, it's still early and I really must resist if I'm going to fit into my wedding dress.'

There it was—the first mention of the wedding. Frankie's jaw tightened. Before she knew it they'd be talking flowers and bom-bonière and everything else they'd already gone over a zillion times on Friday.

Geez, listen to yourself. Shame washed through her and she was thankful neither Simone nor Stella could read minds. She didn't want to become the bitter spinster who begrudged all her friends and family their happiness. Who knows, maybe she'd catch the bouquet?

'Frankie!' Simone's voice jolted her thoughts. 'Are you okay?'

'Huh? Sure. Why wouldn't I be?'

Stella and Simone both frowned. 'You kind of zoned out a moment there.'

'Oh, no, I'm fine, just had a brilliant idea about your cake, Stella,' Frankie lied, feeling as if her cheekbones would snap from fake smiling.

'Ooh.' Stella's eyes lit up. 'I can't wait to hear it.'

'But first, coffee,' Simone declared.

As her sister got to work making drinks, Frankie picked up the empty icing bowl.

'So, what's this I hear about you kissing some handsome spunk in here on Friday afternoon?' Simone asked as the coffee machine whirred to life.

Frankie's heart slammed into her ribs and she almost dropped the bowl. Thank God she was facing away from Simone as her cheeks filled with heat—embarrassment, guilt and the simple memory of Logan's lips on hers. She honestly had no idea how to reply and the time was ticking; with each passing second her guilt amplified and the silence grew more uncomfortable. She'd never had any secrets from Simone before but when she'd failed to confess Logan's mistake on Friday night, she'd all but decided to lock it in the vault. And it looked like Logan had made the same decision.

'Frankie?' Simone prodded, sounding a tad concerned.

She dumped the bowl in the sink and attempted a disbelieving laugh as she turned to face her sister. 'What? Who told you that?' Of course she knew even before Simone replied that it could only be one of two people.

'Mrs Brady.' Simone raised her eyebrows.

Frankie swallowed as heat flooded to her cheeks. 'It was nothing. Logan mistook me for you and he greeted me with a little kiss, not much more than a peck on the cheek, really.'

'That's not the way Mrs Brady told it,' Simone teased.

Frankie tried not to sound defensive. 'Who are you going to believe? Me or that old busybody?'

'You, of course.' Simone half-laughed. 'But why didn't you say anything?'

Frankie shrugged. 'I think he was a little embarrassed, and there wasn't an appropriate moment—you were about to go on a date with him! And it wasn't like it meant anything.'

Lies, all lies. However much it shouldn't, however much she tried to deny it, the kiss had meant something to her. The memory of his lips on hers had haunted her all weekend.

'When do we get to meet this infamous Logan?' Stella asked, leaning against the work bench. 'Before the wedding, I hope. I imagine I'll be a little preoccupied by then.'

Frankie swallowed; weren't they getting a little ahead of themselves? Simone and Logan had only just met and the wedding was still weeks away. 'Are you going to ask him to come with you?'

'I'm not sure. He travels a bit for work and I'd like to get to know him better myself before I share him around, if you don't mind.'

Stella nodded. 'Totally understandable. When Adam and I first got together, I couldn't get enough of him. I didn't want to share him with anyone, not even Heidi.'

'Here you are. Coffees all round,' Simone said, handing a mug to Frankie and another to Stella. She picked up her own and nodded towards a table. 'You got time for a break, sis?'

Frankie wished she could say no, but she didn't want them to think her rude. 'I can spare five minutes, then I've got to make some muffins.'

The three women sat at the table furthest from the front window, so passers-by wouldn't see them.

'Frankie,' Stella said, nursing her mug between her palms, 'what was your idea about my cake?'

Sheesh. Frankie had to think quick. 'How about we make the top layer a rainbow cake? Only inside—but lots of bright colours—something fun for Heidi.'

Stella's smile stretched right up to her eyes. 'I think that's a wonderful idea. It won't be too much work for you?'

'No.' Frankie shook her head. 'It's not that hard.' Just time-consuming, but the way she felt right now, keeping herself busy would be a good thing.

'Thanks, Frankie.' Stella stretched across the table and squeezed her hand. 'It means so much to me that you are all going to be involved in the wedding in your own special ways. And I know it means a lot to Adam as well.'

At Stella's heartfelt gesture, Frankie felt some of her irritation and frustration ebb away. 'We're just so happy you found each other,' she said honestly. 'We couldn't have asked for anyone better for our cousin.'

'Amen, sister.' Simone raised her mug in a toast.

Frankie couldn't help but laugh. She *was* blessed to have so many wonderful people in her life and if she wanted to find love, then maybe it was time to stop feeling sorry for herself and actually take matters into her own hands. If online dating worked for Simone, why the heck wouldn't it work for her? She'd always felt as if it were a cheat's way to meet guys, but maybe it was time to swallow her pride. There had to be another man out there who could make her insides tingle and her knees quiver the way Logan had.

First thing that evening she was setting up an account at Rural Matchmakers.

Chapter Seven

'Hubba, hubba. Who is that?'

'I don't know but he's too old for you and I saw him first.'

Frankie closed her eyes as she overheard Monique and Cara—her Tuesday trainee—out by the counter. Normally she would laugh at such sentiment—they often played the 'first dibs' game when a good-looking man entered the café—but today she guessed without looking who they were talking about and it made her insides twist. It had been well over a week since he'd waltzed into their lives and in that time the only contact she'd had with him was through Simone, relaying their various emails, phone calls and messages. For two people who'd only met the one time, things seemed to be progressing fairly quickly and Frankie hated that she couldn't be one hundred per cent supportive of her sister.

Yet, whenever she closed her eyes at night, Logan's face appeared in her head and the memory of his kiss was as strong as it had been eleven days ago.

She should have chucked a sickie today, but that was hard to do when you were the boss. And a day off wasn't an option; Simone looked after the café whenever Frankie wasn't there but today she had a prior engagement.

Knowing she couldn't avoid him forever, Frankie forced herself to peer through the hatch. Her heart fluttered at the sight of him. He had his hands in his pockets and was reading some of the vintage signs on the walls, looking even sexier than he had the other day. If that were possible. Seriously, it should be illegal to look that good in faded jeans. She sucked in a breath, fighting the urge to escape out the back door, to make some excuse and leave Monique in charge to supervise the lunchtime craziness. She couldn't avoid him forever. If things kept progressing the way they were with Simone, then Logan might become a permanent fixture in their lives, so she needed to take control of this teen-like crush.

'Settle, girls,' she hissed as she came out of the kitchen. 'That's Simone's new guy.' The reminder was as much to her hormones as it was to her employees, who pouted just the same.

She walked around the counter to Logan. 'Hi there,' she said, not at all sounding like herself. Thankfully, he didn't actually know her and didn't appear to notice.

His smile widened as he turned away from the wall to look at her. 'And so we meet again.'

All Frankie could do was nod.

Logan rubbed his jaw and said, 'I wanted to say sorry again about the mix-up the other day. When I kissed you. I didn't mean—'

'It's all right,' Frankie rushed to assure him, a slither of heat snaking through her at the recollection. Her cheeks warmed. Would she ever be able to bring herself to forget it? *Focus on your sister*, she told herself. 'Simone said she was meeting you for lunch?'

He nodded and glanced down at his watch. Her eyes followed, her gaze snagging on his wrists. Dammit, even they were sexy. 'I'm a little early,' he said apologetically.

Frankie forced a laugh and snapped her eyes back up to meet his. 'Well, you'd best sit down and make yourself comfortable because Simmo is notorious for being late. Can I get you a coffee or something while you wait?'

'Simone told me you make a white hot chocolate that is out of this world.' He shrugged one shoulder. 'I know it's not really the type of thing you drink *before* lunch, but I'm thinking it sounds good all the same.'

Trying not to focus on his sheepish grin, Frankie said, 'One white hot chocolate coming right up.' She turned away quickly, happy to have something to occupy herself, and took greater care than ever before in creating her most popular winter drink. When she was finished, she placed two tiny shortbread biscuits on the edge of the saucer and then looked up.

Logan had deposited himself at a table by the window and was reading a book. She blinked and did a double take. It wasn't that she didn't think blokes read books but she couldn't remember the last time she'd seen one doing so in her café. Usually lone male diners occupied themselves with newspapers or smart phones.

Just act normal. She held her chin high, but her fingers trembled and she clung to the cup and saucer so as not to spill the hot chocolate as she made her way over to the table.

'What are you reading?' she asked as she placed his drink down in front of him.

He looked up, smiled again and turned the cover of the book so she could see.

Her eyes widened and she couldn't hide her shock. '*Picnic at Hanging Rock?*'

He gave her a bemused frown. 'Something wrong with it?'

'No ... it's just ... I—I'm reading it too.'

'No way?' He put the book down and his half-frown transformed into something that made her toes curl in their shoes.

'Yes way.' She nodded. *Play it cool. It's just a wacky coincidence. Doesn't mean anything.*

'I've read it a couple of times. It's an old favourite,' he admitted. She looked from him to the book and noticed a couple of stains on the well-worn cover. The sight warmed her heart, because she loved her books to pieces as well.

'It took me a couple of chapters to get into it but now I'm hooked.'

'Have you seen the movie?'

She shook her head. 'No, it was on TV a few months back and I almost watched it, but I much prefer to read a book before I see a movie. Still, that was what put the seed into my head—it made me realise there are so many Australian treasures I've never picked up. I've read lots of English and American classics, but barely any Aussie literature.'

'I did a couple of units in Australian fiction during my journalism degree, but it wasn't a hardship. I love this stuff.'

They talked for ten whole minutes about the book—about how Joan Lindsay doesn't go over the top with character description, yet each character seems so real; about how the mystery that kickstarts the story has a rippling effect that spreads wide among the characters and beyond.

'I actually thought I was reading a true story,' Frankie confessed.

'Apparently that's a common response,' Logan said in a way that didn't make her feel like an idiot at all. 'So, you're a big reader then?'

'I guess. I've always loved reading; it's my way to wind down at the end of a long day.'

'Me too. What's your favourite genre?'

'I read anything and everything. Except paranormal. I don't do vampires and shape shifters and stuff.'

He laughed and cocked his head to one side. 'You're telling me you didn't even read *Twilight*?'

She closed her eyes and sighed. 'Okay, caught, but in my defence I was in my late teens when it came out. *Everyone* was reading it.'

'It's all right. Your secret's safe with me.' He winked. 'I read it too. Team Edward or Team Jacob?'

She was about to reply when a customer—not a local—called from the counter, 'Is there anyone taking orders around here?'

'Go,' Logan whispered before she could make her excuses. 'I'll be fine with my book.'

As she turned away from him, she couldn't help smiling at their conversation. Why did he have to be so easy to talk to, so interesting, as well as so incredibly hot? *Why* did he have to be going out with Simone?

'What can I get for you?' she asked the tall, aggrieved-looking man as she rounded the counter. At the same time Cara appeared from the kitchen, drying her hands against her apron. 'Sorry,' she mouthed at Frankie.

'It's fine. I'll do this.' Frankie smiled at her; after all, she'd been the one slacking off.

When she turned back to the man, he was glaring at her as if she'd made him wait an hour, not all of two minutes. 'I'll have a Coke and one of those homemade pies,' he said, thrusting his finger at the glass display counter, 'and it better be good.'

'It will be,' Frankie promised. 'Take a seat. I'll bring them both out to you.'

She set to work heating his pie—resisting the urge to spit in it—as other customers started to dribble into the café. By the time she delivered the pie to Mr Cranky, a queue was forming at the counter, and as much as Frankie longed to resume her conversation with Logan, she had to go and assist her staff.

The next fifteen minutes or so were busy, but she couldn't help noticing that Simone hadn't turned up yet. Knowing her sister, she'd gotten caught up in her latest work of art, but Frankie felt sorry for Logan, sitting alone. She wished she could go over and talk books some more with him. Finally, as the lunch rush thinned and she was considering calling her sister, the door of the café opened and in rushed Simone, the ends of her colourful scarf flying behind her. Even with her hair windblown and her face flushed, she managed to look beautiful.

'So sorry I'm late,' Frankie heard Simone gush as she dumped her handbag on the floor.

'It's fine.' Logan stood and then Frankie watched as he leaned over and pecked Simone on the cheek. They didn't kiss like two people who were falling madly in love, but something sharp and prickly still twisted in Frankie's heart at the sight of the two of them together. She stared miserably as Logan pulled out a chair for Simone and she sat. They smiled at each other warmly and began to talk as if they were the only people in the world.

Feeling like a terrible sister, Frankie retreated into the kitchen to scrub dishes and distract herself. She'd leave Cara and Monique to take orders and serve.

* * *

'Busy morning?' Logan asked as Simone settled into the seat opposite him. Their knees briefly brushed against each other and he moved slightly so as not to crowd her.

'You have no idea. I've been working on the bombonières for my cousin's wedding and I lost track of time.' She smiled as she swept a hand through her hair. Her fingers were speckled with some kind of paint and her nails cut short and practical. An artist's hands, he thought—different from Frankie's, which he'd noticed had been immaculately clean.

'Sounds like fun.'

'It is,' she said, 'but I'm sorry to have kept you waiting.'

'It's not a problem. I had my book and I ordered one of Frankie's white hot chocolates to ward my hunger off. You were right, they're pretty damn good.'

Simone glanced towards the counter as if just realising she hadn't said hello to her sister yet, but Frankie was no longer in sight. 'Everything Frankie cooks is amazing. Apparently she takes after our father. Mum and I can boil eggs and make spaghetti but that's about the extent of our culinary skills. I feel sorry for my girls. Lucky for me, Harriet is always watching her weight and Grace is quite happy with eggs and spaghetti.'

Logan chuckled, enjoying the way she spoke as if he knew them. If her daughters were half as captivating as their mother and aunt, they'd be lots of fun.

'What about you?' she asked, unravelling the scarf from around her neck and dropping it into her lap. 'Can you cook?'

'Yes, as a matter of fact, I can. Angus and Olivia tease me about being a culinary snob, but I enjoy good food—cooking *and* eating it. After Mum died, I kinda fell into the role of feeding the family. I even did the birthday cakes.' He kept a straight face and added, 'I was particularly proud of the My Little Pony I did for Olivia's tenth birthday.'

She raised an eyebrow. 'I'm impressed. There must be a big age gap between you boys and her?'

'Yes. Fourteen years between me and her. Think she was an accident.'

Simone smiled knowingly. 'And how old was Olivia when your Mum died?'

'Only three.'

'Oh God.' Simone pressed a hand against her chest. 'That's how old Grace was when Jason died. Harriet was six. There's no good age to lose your parents, but it must have been particularly hard for your sister, growing up without her mum.'

Logan nodded, trying to ignore the lump in his throat that formed whenever he thought about it. Losing Mum was bad enough but thank God Olivia hadn't been old enough to comprehend that their dad had *chosen* to leave them, chosen to end his life. 'Angus did the best he could, though.'

'I'm sure you both did,' Simone said, reaching across and touching his hand.

He smiled his appreciation and turned his hand to take hold of hers. The connection was nice. Angus might think of him as some kind of wild playboy, but the truth was it had been quite some time since Logan had been in a relationship, since he'd had someone to share stuff with and confide in. He missed it.

'Shall we order?' Simone asked, breaking the silence, retrieving her hand and nodding at the counter. 'I'm in the mood for some soup. What about you?'

Logan had already perused the menu. 'I might try a homemade sausage roll and some sweet potato fries. See if Frankie's really as talented as you make out.'

Simone laughed and went to stand. 'My shout since I kept you waiting and I can sweet-talk the owner. Who, yes, I promise you, is that talented. Do you want a drink as well?'

'Just some water, please.'

Simone went to order and Logan checked his email on his phone. He'd be working from home the next few weeks—while also doing his bit on the farm—and one of the editors he worked with had promised to send him a few leads for possible stories. He'd just finished deleting some junk mail when Simone returned.

'All ordered. Now, tell me about your week in Broome. The photos you sent looked fabulous. I've never been but it's definitely on the bucket list.'

'It was great. I've travelled around Australia a lot, but it still baffles me how different various parts of this country are. When the plane hovers over the Kimberleys, the rich contrasting colours below just take your breath away.'

As they waited for their lunch, he told her about the article he'd been researching on the Camel Cup—the main reason for his trip. 'It's only a new thing but it's building appeal quickly and I'm sure it'll soon be one of outback Australia's big events. I thought the Henley-on-Todd regatta in Alice Springs was hilarious, but I hadn't seen anything until I saw camels racing.'

'I can't imagine a camel running,' she admitted, her forehead furrowed as though she were trying to do exactly that.

'It's a sight to behold. I'm still not sure they're really cut out for racing. While I was there, I was constantly waiting for someone to announce that it was actually all a big joke, but the competitors and the onlookers took it fairly seriously.'

A young blonde waitress brought their lunch out and once they'd thanked her, conversation continued easily as they hoovered up their meals. The rumours were right. Frankie's pastry was the flakiest he'd ever tasted and he couldn't quite make out the secret ingredient in the meat that gave the sausage roll its edge, but he vowed to get it out of her one day.

'Enough talking about me,' Logan said. 'Tell me about these bon-bon-what-nots?'

She laughed. 'Bombonière.'

'Yes, those. What exactly are they?'

'Well, they can be anything really—they're gifts brides and grooms give their guests. In this case, I'm hand-painting some little tins with Adam's and Stella's names and the date of the wedding. They're going to fill them with chocolates.'

'Yum.' Logan patted his stomach. 'This is the wedding I'm coming to?'

She blushed a little. 'Yes, if you don't mind. I'll pay your accommodation and everything, but if you ...'

He cut in and grinned. 'I'm looking forward to it. And I'm also looking forward to seeing your studio—and some of your art.'

'Are you inviting yourself back to my place, Logan?' Her smile said she didn't mind his forwardness at all.

'What if I am?' Although this was her sister's café, he didn't want to be one of those customers who overstayed their welcome. Besides, he was curious to see where Simone lived and worked.

She grinned and pushed back her seat. 'I'd say I hope you don't mind a little bit of mess.'

'Not at all.' He also stood.

'I'll just go say goodbye to Frankie.' Rewrapping her scarf around her neck as she walked, Simone disappeared into the kitchen. Logan deliberated about following and thanking Frankie himself—asking about that pastry—but before he'd made a decision, Simone was back, a slight frown on her face.

'Frankie's apparently not feeling great. She's gone home sick. That's weird. She almost never goes home sick.'

'Did you want to go check on her?' he asked, concerned; Frankie had seemed full of life and more than healthy an hour ago. 'She seemed fine when I came in earlier.'

'Nah. Let's let her rest. I'll make her a batch of chicken soup later and take it round tonight.'

'I thought you couldn't cook.'

'I can't.' Simone sighed. 'It'll probably do her more harm than good, but there's nothing I wouldn't do for my little sister.'

'Okay. If you're sure. Let's go then.' Logan held open the café door for Simone. 'Shall I follow you in my ute?'

'Perfect.' She grinned and headed for her four-wheel drive.

A few moments later, Logan turned into the driveway of a 1950s fibro cottage, typical of so many in rural Australia. It had a wide verandah at the front with a door in the middle and windows on either side. Simone's garden was a jungle of plants—some natives, some cottage flowers—and sculptures—some big, some small. He climbed out the ute and followed her up the winding garden path to the verandah, which was full of hanging baskets, overflowing with greenery, more sculptures and an array of mismatched cane furniture.

'This is … eclectic,' he said, as she unlocked the front door.

'If that's your kind way of saying untidy, wait until you come inside.' She laughed as she pushed open the door and the moment he stepped inside, he saw she hadn't been exaggerating.

There was stuff everywhere. Not rubbish, not dirt, just lots and lots of … stuff. Photos in frames lined the hallway floor as if no-one had ever gotten around to hanging them up. He made a mental note to offer to do so for her. Then he caught sight of a small frame on the hallway table—a much younger Simone in a wedding dress and a handsome young bloke, who had to be her husband. They looked blissfully in love and he couldn't help wondering if she was truly ready to move on.

'Do you collect doorstops?' he asked, turning away from the frame and counting at least five doorstops within two metres.

'Maybe.' She cocked her head to one side. 'I guess I just thought they were cute. Come on in, don't stand there in the cold.' She gestured for him to follow her and as they headed down the hallway, he began to see evidence of her teenage daughters. They passed one bedroom, in which a single bed looked as if it might collapse under the mountain of teddy bears and another, the only tidy room in the house it seemed, that had walls covered with boy band posters.

'I'm sorry about the mess.' She looked sheepishly at the pile of paints and little tins covering the table as they entered the kitchen. 'I was working inside because it gets cold in my studio in the winter, but I should have anticipated you coming around. I'm sorry … I'm … nervous. I haven't done this whole dating thing for a long time. I'm severely out of practice.'

Although she didn't spell it out, he knew she wasn't simply referring to not tidying up the house for company and his heart went out to her. It was hard enough getting back in the saddle after a divorce, but it must be a hundred times more daunting after being widowed.

He crossed the room, closing the gap between them, and put his hands on her arms. 'Relax,' he told her, meeting her gaze. 'We don't have to rush anything. I'm enjoying getting to know you. Let's just take things slowly and see where they lead. Okay?'

She rubbed her lips together. 'Are you sure?'

He nodded. Good things were worth waiting for and he wasn't going to rush her into anything.

'I really like you,' she told him, 'and you're very attractive.' She blushed, the pink in her cheeks making her very attractive as well.

'Ditto,' he said, smiling down at her.

She laughed nervously and he wanted more than anything to put her at ease. 'How about you show me your studio? I'd love to see some of your work.'

'Okay.' She took a deep breath as if glad to have had that conversation out of the way. 'Can I get you a drink or anything first?'

He glanced around, wondering if she'd be able to find a mug beneath all the clutter. 'I'm okay for now.' He dropped his hands from her arms and took one of her hands in his. 'Lead the way.'

Hand in hand, they went out the back door and through a jungle of plants along a cobbled path to a shed far down the end of the property. From the outside it looked like nothing more than a place for storing crap, but inside it was amazing.

'Wow.' He looked around as Simone tugged on blinds and let the afternoon sunlight spill into her studio. Like the house, there were tables so covered in stuff you couldn't see their surfaces and there were art supplies everywhere. Balls of yarn, scraps of material, buttons and sequins and ribbons. But it was the finished products scattered around the shed—some perched on easels, others like the photos in her hallway, just waiting for someone to do something with them—that left him speechless.

He took a few moments just to admire her obvious talent. There were beautiful sceneries, people's faces, shells, animals, even a row of teapots—all created with textiles. He'd never been a huge lover of art but it was impossible not to be impressed. 'You sell this stuff?'

'Yeah, some of it.' She leaned against a work bench and smiled at her surroundings. She looked right at home among the organised chaos. 'The little craft shop in the main street sells some of my smaller pieces and there's a couple of galleries in Perth that display my work too.'

He continued to admire her work—some pieces complete, others obviously in progress. Nothing he could think to say seemed good enough. 'You are—these are—I've never quite seen anything so detailed. These are amazing.'

Simone beamed. 'Thanks. This is my happy place. When the girls are making me want to take up smoking or drinking or tear my hair out, I come here and escape to my art. I'm lucky. I love doing it, and people seem to love looking at it. Come and see what I'm working on now.'

He followed her to her workbench and found it surprisingly uncluttered compared with the tables. On it lay a piece of thick calico with the outline of three butterflies in some kind of black silk.

'Cute,' he said. 'My sister loves butterflies.'

'Who doesn't?' Simone laughed. 'I'm making this for Adam and Stella for a wedding present. The butterflies represent them and Stella's little girl, Heidi, who helped bring them together. Each one will be unique and reflect their personalities.'

'She has a daughter?'

'Yes. Heidi has Down Syndrome and her father didn't want her, so Stella became a single mum very young. It's tough enough being a single mum, but being a single mum of a special needs child ... Well, Stella is amazing. And in my opinion, Heidi is something of a miracle worker.'

That piqued Logan's interest. 'How so?'

'Long story short, Adam's little sister, my cousin, went missing when she was seven years old and until last year, we didn't know what had happened to her.'

'Jesus.'

Simone nodded and continued. 'It devastated our family but it hit Adam's mum, Esther, the hardest, of course. She totally withdrew from society and didn't leave the farm. Ever.'

'Wow.' And Logan had thought his family had had their fair share of affliction. Stories like this made him remember that no-one was immune from tragedy, but you did have the choice about how you responded to it. This Esther woman reminded him of Angus.

'I know, right? But because of Heidi, we eventually found out what happened to our cousin.' She paused, took a deep breath and then told him everything. Her story blew his mind.

'And your aunt?' he asked her when she'd finished. 'She's better now?'

'She'll always grieve her lost daughter, but Heidi and Stella have helped fill that gap in her life and given her the courage and will to start living again, so you'll see why I wanted to make them something really special for a wedding present.'

'I do indeed and I bet they'll love it.' He leaned a little closer to peer down at the gift again. 'It's so much more meaningful than towels or another set of pots and pans.'

'Speaking of pots and pans, I should go make that chicken soup.' Simone straightened, already turning to the door. 'You don't mind do you? It's just that once the girls get home from school, the afternoon usually gets away from me.'

'Of course not.' He checked the time on his watch. 'How about I help?'

Simone grinned. 'I was kinda hoping you would.'

They headed out the studio, back up the path and into the house, where Simone began to hunt through her freezer and fridge for supplies. She conjured up a bag of frozen chicken pieces and held them up to Logan. 'These will do, right?'

'Yep.'

'What veggies do we need?'

He shrugged and pushed up his sleeves, ready to work. 'Onions, carrots, celery are a good start. Whatever herbs you have growing. But anything will do, really. That's the great thing about soup.'

Simone's head disappeared into the fridge. 'Luckily Harriet fancies herself as a vegetarian at the moment, so we should have plenty.'

She retrieved some celery, carrot, broccoli and an onion and laid them out on the bench.

'Have you got any pasta?' Logan asked. 'It's a good way to make the soup a little more like a chunky meal.'

'Good idea,' Simone said, diving into the pantry and re-emerging with a packet of macaroni. 'Will this do?'

'Perfect.'

The two of them set to work alongside each other on the bench. The last time Logan had cooked with someone, he'd been married and, although it was only five years ago, that suddenly seemed a very long time. It felt good to be doing something so normal with a woman again. They talked and laughed as they worked, conversation only pausing when he went to the bathroom.

'Mmm,' he said when he returned a few minutes later to find the kitchen filling with the comforting scents of homemade soup. 'Not bad for someone who claims they can't cook.'

Simone grinned. 'I had a little help. Now let me get you a drink while it simmers.'

She made them both a cup of tea and they sat at the table. 'Have you talked any more to Angus about the wind-farming?' she asked.

Logan groaned. He didn't want thoughts of his brother's stubbornness ruining what was proving to be a very pleasant afternoon.

She smiled sympathetically. 'That bad, hey?'

He nodded. 'We had words about it again before I went to Broome—he just refuses to see that it could really work for us. Farming is uncertain—we're at the mercy of Mother Nature and she isn't always kind—so why not make things a little more financially secure for ourselves?'

Simone shrugged one shoulder. 'What does your sister think?'

He was about to say he hadn't brought Olivia into the argument yet, when they both screwed up their noses.

'Oh no!' Simone leaped to her feet, her chair crashing to the tiles in her haste to get to the stove. 'Damn. Shit. Bugger it. I've stuffed it.' She switched off the gas and peered dismally into the pot.

Frowning, Logan stood and went to join her. 'How did that stick so quickly?' Then he saw the empty packet of macaroni beside the stove and his mouth dropped open. A bubble of amusement stirred within him. 'Did you put *all* that pasta in?'

She nodded sheepishly, her eyes wide and the expression on her face telling him she didn't find this quite as amusing as he did. 'Wasn't I supposed to?'

He lost the battle with laughter and eventually Simone saw the funny side too.

'I'm sorry,' she said, giggling. 'You probably want a girlfriend who knows how to cook.'

He shook his head. 'Actually, that's not high on my list of priorities. I can cook perfectly well myself, so there are a few other qualities that are a bit more important to me.'

'What exactly are those qualities?' Simone asked, her tongue darting out to moisten her lower lip.

He opened his mouth to tell her he wanted someone who made him laugh, someone who turned him on and someone he could talk with, but his words were lost in what sounded like a hurricane coming down the hallway. He snapped his head around to see two teenage girls. Although they had blonde hair instead of Simone's rich red, they were both stunning and it was clear they were her daughters.

The older of the two stopped in her tracks. 'Oh. Shit,' she said, storming over to the window and yanking it open. 'Have you been cooking again, Mum?'

'And it's lovely to see you too, Harriet. Did you have a good day at school?' Simone's tone did not match her words.

The girl rolled her eyes and then seemed to register him. 'Logan!' she exclaimed, her sullen expression lifting as she eyed him as if her were a long lost friend. 'So good to finally meet you.'

He lifted a hand in a slight wave. 'Hey. You must be Harriet.'

She nodded. 'Yes.' Then gestured to the shorter girl. 'And this shrimp is Grace.'

'Hello.' Grace briefly met his gaze and offered a little smile before looking back to the floor. She reminded him a bit of Olivia at that age, shy and not quite grown into herself.

'Hi,' he said, feeling uncharacteristically nervous, as if this were some kind of test. 'It's good to meet you both too. I've heard a lot about you.'

'We know.' Harriet smirked as if something hilarious was going on. 'All good, I bet.'

'Of course.' Logan nodded uncertainly. Simone had never said a harsh word about her girls during their online exchanges, although in person she'd alluded to the normal teenage dramas. Five seconds in Harriet's company and he reckoned she could have said a whole lot worse. Maybe Angus had a point about dating women with children, but Logan wasn't the type to let a sixteen-year-old scare him off.

'Are you staying for dinner?' Harriet asked, yanking open the fridge and retrieving a tub of yoghurt. She turned back to him. 'I promise we won't let Mum poison you.'

He quirked an eyebrow. He wanted to stand up for Simone but it probably wasn't his place to reprimand her daughter. Instead, he shook his head. 'Thanks for the offer, but I've got to get back to the farm.' He didn't want to risk another night on the side of the road so he needed to head off before dark. 'Maybe some other time.'

Harriet shrugged. 'Whatever.' And then tore the foil lid off her yoghurt.

'Is your farm big?' Grace asked, glancing up at him again.

'Big enough for me. You interested in farming?'

She shrugged one shoulder. 'My dad's parents have a farm. I like them well enough.'

Grace sounded as if she didn't want to show too much enthusiasm in front of her big sister. An idea popped into Logan's head. 'You three should come for a drive on the weekend.' He looked sideways to Simone. 'What about it? Want to come out for a barbecue lunch on Sunday? I promise not to burn the sausages,' he teased, 'and you can meet Angus. It'll do him good to have some company.'

Simone raised an eyebrow. 'I can hardly wait.'

'Ah … he's not as bad as all that,' Logan said, feeling a little contrite at the way he sometimes painted his brother. 'What do you say?'

'Sounds good. Can we bring anything? Like drinks or something I can buy in a packet.'

Logan laughed. 'Just yourselves.'

Agreeing to finalise the details on the phone, he said good-bye to Harriet and Grace and then followed Simone back down the corridor. They stood on the porch awkwardly for a few long moments. It reminded Logan of his first ever real date, when he'd spent most of the night contemplating whether or not to kiss the girl goodnight. So much so that he'd forgotten to actually talk to her.

He knew he should kiss Simone—how could he not?— but it felt wrong to do so with her daughters just inside, and he'd meant what he'd said about not rushing her into anything.

'Thanks for a lovely afternoon,' he said eventually, then leaned forward and brushed his lips against her cheek.

That would have to do for now.

Chapter Eight

'I thought you liked Logan,' Simone said, her fingers clenched tightly around the steering wheel and her jaw set rigid as she drove towards Mingenew. She was trying not to lose her shit with Harriet—she didn't want them both to be in a mood when they arrived at the farm—but her patience was wearing thin. Simone resisted the urge to tell her daughter to take her feet off the dash. Some wars simply weren't worth fighting and she was already nervous as it was.

'I do.' Harriet, sitting in the passenger seat, sighed loudly as if her life was over. 'But that doesn't mean I want to waste a perfectly good Sunday afternoon playing happy families, when I should be supporting my boyfriend at the game.'

'The game' was the local under-18s footy team—hardly the AFL—but Simone reminded herself that at sixteen, little things mattered a lot.

'I'm sure Jaxon will tell you all about it later. Please, at least try to have a good time.'

In reply, Harriet gave another dramatic sigh, crossed her arms and turned her whole body so she was looking out the window.

Simone rolled her eyes and kept on driving. It was too late to relent now. Maybe she should have allowed Harriet to stay in town—Frankie was there in case of an emergency—but Logan had invited all of them and she didn't want to offend him. Not all men would go to such efforts to get to know their girlfriend's kids. Besides, it could be Harriet's punishment for setting up this whole online dating thing behind her back. She dared not say this to Harriet or she might to throw it back in her face and decide to tell Logan the truth.

Simone shuddered, uncomfortable with the deception but unsure how to handle it. It had been more than two weeks now, so probably best to just let it go. What would he say if he found out? Would he find it amusing if he discovered he'd been sharing intimacies with her daughters back at the beginning or would it change things between them? He might be embarrassed that they knew so much about him. Maybe she should tell him herself before somebody else did.

Argh! Not wanting to think about this conundrum, she glanced in the rear-view mirror. 'You okay, Grace?' Her youngest daughter had been excited about the prospect of getting out of Bunyip Bay for the day but so far she'd barely said a word on their journey.

'All good, Mum,' Grace squeaked from the back seat before burying her nose in her book again. So much like Frankie at that age, no wonder they got along so well. And maybe Simone and Harriet were alike, which was why they kept butting heads.

The girls were quiet for the rest of the drive, leaving Simone alone with her thoughts. The closer they got to Logan's farm, the more her pulse skittered. So far they'd met in her territory and venturing outside of that, going to visit him on his farm, somehow seemed like a big step. He'd get to spend some real time with her kids and she would quite possibly meet the mysterious Angus.

What if he didn't like her? The way Logan spoke, he sounded like someone who was hard to please.

She tried to tell herself it didn't matter what Angus thought—that as long as Logan and the girls got along, they'd be okay—but by the time she slowed the Pajero in front of Knight's Hill, her stomach was aflutter with nerves.

'We're here,' she said as she turned down the gravel track. Logan had said the house was about a kilometre off the road, so she had maybe a minute to prepare herself.

'No shit,' Harriet snapped.

'Don't swear,' Simone said automatically.

'That's rich coming from you.' Simone could feel Harriet's glare on her and she really didn't want to argue right now.

'Shut up, Harriet. Leave Mum alone,' Grace said, dumping her book on the seat beside her.

'Thank you, Grace.' Simone took a deep breath. 'But Harriet's right. I need to watch my language as well. How about we all agree to try a little bit harder to speak like ladies?'

'What. Ever.'

Simone ignored Harriet's insolent tone and continued on down the bumpy farm track. Only a couple of hours from Bunyip Bay, Mingenew was further inland and a little drier, but the property looked much the same as Adam's, the Forresters', her in-laws' and all her other friends' farms. Somehow this familiarity helped ease her anxiety a little.

'Hey, there's Logan,' came Grace's voice from the back seat.

A large house came into view and Simone saw Logan out the front, waving. She waited for another sarcastic remark from Harriet, but was surprised to see a smile find its way onto her older daughter's face. Maybe she wouldn't be a total nightmare after all.

Logan, wearing faded jeans and a simple black hoodie, gestured for her to park under an old gum tree just to the right of the house and jogged over to them. He opened Simone's door for her, startling her when he leaned forward and greeted her with a peck on the cheek.

'It's great to see you again,' he said, his smile feeling like it was reaching out and wrapping itself around her.

'Thanks.' She swallowed, slightly embarrassed by his show of affection in front of the girls. 'You too. We found your farm easily enough.'

Harriet and Grace climbed out and slammed their doors.

'Oh, isn't he just the cutest thing,' Harriet gushed and Simone turned to see her squatting down and rubbing the ears of a young red kelpie. Harriet had always adored animals when she was little and it was nice to see this rare display of excitement. Last year, when a cat on Adam's farm had kittens, Harriet and Grace had begged her for one, but she'd refused. The idea of having another living thing to look after had filled Simone with horror and dread. Sometimes she felt like she was only just managing to keep her daughters alive.

Logan chuckled, put his palm in the small of Simone's back and ushered her around the four-wheel drive. 'That's Rascal and he's a devil. Angus is very original with his names.'

The girls laughed. Simone forgot about whatever it was she'd been thinking about, every cell in her body focused on the tiny touch of Logan's hand.

'He's got another dog—Max—but he's out with Angus right now,' Logan said.

'Oh, Angus isn't here?' Simone asked, feeling a weird sense of disappointment. She'd been strangely looking forward to meeting him after Logan's descriptions.

'He'll be back for lunch. He promised to make an appearance.'

Simone smiled and nodded, feeling completely weird about this situation. It was like her body was here, but her mind was still catching up. 'I brought cake,' she said brightly, suddenly remembering the box in the boot.

Logan raised a sceptical eyebrow at her and she laughed, relaxing a little at his easy way. 'Don't stress. Frankie made it. She said to say hi.'

He wiped his hand theatrically across his brow. 'Phew.'

Without thinking, Simone elbowed him in the ribs and couldn't help but notice how solid he was. She blushed, hoping neither he nor the girls could read her mind, which was currently visualising him bare-chested. It was a very attractive picture indeed.

'Ow.' He doubled over, feigning pain. 'Okay, okay, I asked for that. Where is this cake?'

Simone nodded to the back of the vehicle and Logan opened it up and retrieved the cake. 'Hmm … smells delicious. Now, ladies, shall we?' He gestured to the house.

The four of them, Rascal in tow, weaved through the front garden, slightly overgrown and in dire need of water, like much of the landscape in these parts.

As if reading her thoughts, Logan said, 'Neither Angus nor I are green thumbs and there always seems something that needs doing more.'

'I know what you mean.' Simone thought of her own garden, which basically looked after itself, although she did make an effort with her potted colour and hanging baskets.

'I thought we could eat out here,' Logan suggested as they climbed up onto the verandah and he gestured to a gorgeous wooden outdoor setting. 'The weather's quite nice today and it always feels wrong to eat a barbecue inside.'

'Suits me.' Harriet sat herself down on an old rocking chair at the corner of the verandah, curled up her legs beside her and looked down at her phone. 'What's your wi-fi password?'

'Harriet!' Simone exclaimed.

'It's fine,' Logan said, tossing Simone a warm smile and then rolling off said password. 'Can I get anyone a drink or would you like the grand tour first?'

'The grand tour?' Grace's brow furrowed.

Logan chuckled. 'You're right, it probably won't be very grand, but Mum always showed visitors around the house when they arrived. Come to think of it, I never quite knew why.'

Simone grinned. 'My mum does exactly the same but I must admit I like it when other people do. I'm nosy by nature.'

'In that case, be my guest.' Logan gestured to the front door and as Simone and Grace started towards it, he linked arms with both of them.

Simone glanced at her daughter and saw that Grace was blushing. Who could blame her? Logan had a knack for making a girl feel special.

'My apologies for the mess,' he said. 'I do my best but Angus is a shocking housekeeper.'

They stepped into a long hallway with gorgeous polished floorboards, high ceilings and antique furniture that made the artist in Simone swoon. Everything was so neat and tidy, she wondered what Logan must have thought of her place. 'Wow,' she breathed, reaching out and touching a finger to the beautiful turn-of-the-century hall table. 'This is gorgeous.'

'Thanks.' He smiled. 'Mum loved everything old-fashioned and we haven't really changed anything.'

'I must admit,' Simone confessed, 'when I heard you lived with your brother, I envisaged some kind of bachelor pad with big screen TVs, leather couches and smelly socks.'

'Trust me, Angus has plenty of smelly socks in his room.'

'I think it's beautiful,' Grace said, her eyes wide as she glanced around her.

'Aw, thanks buddy.' Logan ruffled her hair and her beam grew wider. If he did that to Harriet she'd have screamed blue murder for messing up her 'do.

The three of them continued on—Logan showing them where the kitchen and bathroom were and then allowing them a quick squiz into the bedrooms. Logan's was pristine—like some kind of hotel room, bar the shelves overflowing with books. The absent Olivia's was suitably pink and girly, with a few posters of bands that Harriet also liked, reminding Simone that Logan's sister wasn't much older than her daughters.

'And this is my big bro's room,' Logan said, pushing open a door. 'Don't tell him I showed you or he'll skin me alive.'

Warm and cosy were the first words that came into Simone's head as she looked into Angus's space. She inhaled some kind of earthy, musky scent that she kinda liked—and it wasn't half as messy as Logan made out. Lived in, yes; in fact, it reminded her a lot of her own house, minus all the art and teenage girl paraphernalia. There was a pile of old *Farmer's Weekly* by the bed and a stack of CDs on the floor by an old stereo, which made her wonder what kind of music he listened to.

Their snooping was interrupted by the deep clearing of a throat behind them.

Simone spun around and found herself looking into the black, stormy eyes of a man who had to be Logan's brother. Her breath stalled in her throat. Although Angus was dark and bearded, and Logan blond with a little stubble, it was clear they both shared the same favourable DNA. When God had handed out good looks, he'd given these boys a double dose of chiselled—even Angus's scowl was sexy, making her heart turn in her chest. The brothers reminded her a little of Ridge and Thorne from *The Bold and the Beautiful*. Was that show even on anymore? Her mum used to watch it religiously every afternoon.

'Angus, I'd like you to meet Simone and her daughter, Grace. You may have seen Harriet on your way in?' Logan spoke as if they hadn't just been sprung trespassing on his brother's privacy, but Simone's cheeks flared with heat. *Such* a great start to their relationship. What must he think of her?

'If you don't mind.' Angus stretched past the trio and pulled his bedroom door shut with a thud that reverberated right through Simone's body. For a moment she thought he wasn't going to bother even acknowledging them but he nodded curtly. 'Nice to meet you.'

'Yes, you too.' Simone smiled awkwardly and although he didn't smile back, she felt his intent gaze, almost as if he were touching her. She wished they could turn back time and meet under better circumstances.

Grace didn't say a word and Simone reached out and took hold of her hand, giving it a reassuring squeeze.

'Well, let's go fire up the barbecue,' Logan suggested, his tone light. 'Angus, do you want to get our guests some drinks?'

She was almost certain Angus would refuse and retreat to his bedroom, never to be seen again, but she was pleasantly surprised when he said, 'Of course. Would you like a glass of wine, Simone?'

'Oh, yes, please, that would be lovely.'

'White or red?'

'White, please.' She was being so damn polite she barely recognised herself but she so wanted Logan's brother to like her.

'Good. And what about you, Grace?' Simone wasn't sure but thought she saw a glimpse of a smile as Angus spoke to her daughter. 'Lemonade? Juice?'

'Just some water, thanks,' Grace replied, before retrieving her hand and escaping back down the corridor to the verandah. Poor love, she hated any form of confrontation.

Angus went to the kitchen and Logan took Simone's hand and started in the same direction as Grace.

'Well, that went well,' Simone said, mortified.

'Relax,' Logan whispered, his thumb sweeping across her wrist. 'Angus's bark is worse than his bite.'

Simone wasn't so sure and she vowed to try to win him over by the time they left that afternoon. Whatever it took.

★ ★ ★

Angus couldn't remember the last time they'd entertained and he had to admit it wasn't as bad as he'd feared it would be. The food was good, the teenage girls friendly enough and Simone as gorgeous in person as he remembered from her online photo. After a few minutes in her charming company, he'd forgiven her for prying into his bedroom. It wasn't like he'd found her in there alone—although that was a thought in itself; a dangerous one that he quickly pushed from his mind. No, Logan had been the one to intrude and he was such an open book himself he never thought to consider other people's privacy.

As they ate and talked—Logan orchestrating the conversation—Angus caught himself looking at Simone a few too many times. He couldn't help himself. She had such a captivating, fresh face and every time she smiled, something felt like it shifted inside him. Her laughter was the most beautiful sound he'd heard in a long time—so open and honest and rich that he found himself wishing he could think of something funny to say just to hear it again. Uncomfortable with these thoughts, he turned to Harriet, who was sitting beside him, and tried to make conversation.

'Are you at school in Geraldton?'

She simply nodded, indicating he wasn't the only non-talkative one at the table.

'You're lucky you live close enough that you don't have to go to boarding school,' he said. 'My little sister Olivia would have loved to have been able to be at high school closer to home. She's not much older than you actually.'

'I wish I *was* at boarding school,' Harriet retorted. Making no comment about Olivia, she turned to glare at her mother. 'Then maybe Mum would stop trying to rule my life.'

Angus glanced across at Simone, who was thankfully engrossed in conversation with Logan and Grace and hadn't heard her daughter's jibe. 'I'm sure she means well,' he said.

Harriet shrugged. 'Maybe. Did you really hate boarding school?'

'I wouldn't say I hated it,' he confessed, 'but I missed the farm. City life is not for me. I like the open air. I like to be able to see the stars at night with only the sounds of the wind and the sheep.'

'You make it sound romantic,' she said with a sigh.

He couldn't help chuckling; he was possibly the least romantic bloke on the planet.

'Did you get into any trouble at boarding school?'

'I got into a few fights over the girls from St Mary's but I didn't get expelled, unlike some.' Angus glanced at Logan.

Harriet gasped. 'Logan got expelled?'

The other three looked up from their conversation and Logan grimaced.

'What did you get expelled for?' Harriet asked in obvious admiration.

'Who's up for dessert?' Logan said, getting to his feet and starting to gather the empty plates. 'Frankie's famous chocolate cake won't last forever.'

Angus laughed and stood to help clear the table. He couldn't remember the last time he'd enjoyed sitting down to lunch so much.

'Not a story for teenage girls,' Logan hissed as the two men carried the plates into the kitchen.

'Sorry,' Angus lied. Logan was probably right but seeing him blush had been worth it.

'What do you think of her?'

'Who? Harriet?'

Logan glared at him, a rare expression of nervousness flickering across his face. 'No, *Simone.*'

Angus sighed and patted his brother on the shoulder. At first he'd thought Logan was pursuing this relationship to prove a point, but now he'd met Simone and her charming girls, he thought maybe there was a future for them. 'She's great, mate. I can see why you like her so much. Gorgeous *and* nice. Almost too good to be true. No idea what she sees in a loser like you.'

Logan grinned. 'She has a sister, you know?'

He shook his head. 'We've been through this before.' Logan might be able to overlook the fact that the Knight brothers were unlucky in love, but Angus wasn't going to be burned again. 'I'm not interested.'

'Okay, okay. You can't blame me for trying.' Logan sighed as he grabbed the cake box off the table. 'Can you bring out a knife and plates?'

The group devoured the chocolate cake in record time. Angus's hopes of some being left over for smoko tomorrow were dashed when Grace helped herself to the last slice. For someone so small, she sure managed to eat a lot.

'Who's up for a ride on the quad bike?' Logan asked, when they had finished eating.

Grace's eyes sparkled but Harriet shook her head. 'Do you know how dangerous those things are? I heard they accounted for more farm deaths than anything else last year.'

Grace let out an audible sigh, a frown tainting her lips.

'You'd be right,' Logan said, smiling in his easy manner. 'I actually wrote an article about the dangers after a friend's little boy was killed on their property up north, so I won't be taking any stupid risks. I always use a helmet and anyone who rides with me will be wearing one as well.'

'Can I, Mum?' Grace asked, looking to Simone.

Simone reached over and patted her hand. 'Sure, honey. Just do whatever Logan tells you.'

'I will. Promise. Just gotta go to the bathroom first.' She pushed back her seat and leaped up, hurrying off in excitement.

Logan chuckled and turned to Simone. 'We've got two bikes. You could come as well if you like?'

She looked from him to Harriet and then back again. 'Not really my thing, to be honest. Harriet and I will clean up here instead.'

'You don't have to do that,' Logan said. 'Angus and I can take care of that later.'

Angus nodded. 'There's really not much.'

After a few more minutes of ridiculous arguing over who was going to scrub the dirty dishes, Logan and Grace headed off to the shed and Harriet took herself over to the old rocking chair at the corner of the verandah and slumped down into it with a dramatic sigh.

'Um, missy, cleaning up?' Simone reminded her.

Harriet groaned and although he wasn't close enough to be certain, Angus guessed she rolled her eyes as well.

'Honestly, we'll do it later,' he said, then called across to Harriet, 'My sister has a massive DVD collection. You want to watch one?'

She considered this a moment as if contemplating whether agreeing would ruin her tough-girl image, but eventually said, '*Yes*. Anything to take my mind off football.'

Angus frowned and looked to Simone for clarification.

She shook her head. 'Don't ask.'

Only when Harriet was ensconced on the couch in front of *Pitch Perfect* did Angus realise it left him alone with Simone. He couldn't remember the last time he'd been alone with a woman who wasn't his sister. What the heck were they supposed to talk about? She smiled at him awkwardly from where she was standing in the hallway just outside the lounge room.

'You're not at all what I imagined,' he blurted in his efforts to think of something to say.

She quirked one eyebrow. 'What exactly had you imagined?'

He shrugged. 'Someone younger, a little more polished.'

She blinked, widened her eyes and then she half-chuckled.

'Shit. That didn't come out right.' He ran a hand through his hair, thinking that he should have volunteered to take Grace quad-biking and given the lovebirds some one-on-one time. Or as close as they could get, with a surly teenager in the other room.

'You don't say?' Simone sounded amused.

'I'm sorry. I'm not good with words.' *Or women.* 'All I meant was that you seem really nice, normal, whereas Logan's usual type is stuck-up bitch.' He shrugged. 'At least that's how they sound. You're the first he's brought home in quite some time.'

She burst into laughter at that, making him smile also. 'I'll take that as a compliment.'

'Please do,' he said, nodding as his cheeks flamed. 'Can I get you another drink?'

'Better make it a soft drink. I don't want to get done for drink driving on the way home.'

He fetched two Cokes from the fridge and they took them back out onto the verandah. Simone sat down on the top step and there really wasn't any option but to sit down right beside her. Angus tried to ignore the fact that her shapely legs—barely hidden beneath their tight denim jeans—were a mere ruler's length from his thighs. Not that it meant anything bar the fact he hadn't been near a female body in a long while. The old trip-to-Perth-meet-a-girl-in-a-bar-one-night stand didn't have the same appeal as it once did.

Simone took a sip from her can and then sighed. 'It's truly beautiful out here. So peaceful.'

Angus met her attempt at small talk with, 'I like it.' And then more silence followed. Normally he didn't mind peace and quiet but sitting next to Simone, he felt the need to say something to stop thinking. 'How long have you been a single mum?'

She turned her head slowly to look at him. 'Ten years. How much has Logan told you?'

'Nothing really. Just that you're a widow with two gorgeous girls.' Not quite as gorgeous as their mother, but he guessed they'd grow up to be.

She snorted. 'And now you've seen them for yourself, you must think your brother's insane.'

'I've known he's insane for a long time. As for your girls … they seem like normal teenagers to me. Well, Harriet does. Grace is sweet.' He chuckled. Despite Harriet's efforts to be difficult, he couldn't help liking her. 'What happened?' he found himself asking. 'To your husband?'

She rubbed her lips together for a few moments and he was about to apologise for prying when she said, 'He shot himself.'

Angus's heart slammed into his throat as he struggled to find adequate words. He only hoped she hadn't been the one to find him because he knew first-hand what kind of nightmare that was. How the images and questions never went away.

'Not like it sounds,' she rushed on. 'He'd been out shooting a fox on the farm … the gun was in his holster … he climbed a fence … and well … somehow it went off. He was with his dad and the ambulance rushed him to hospital but they lost him on the way to Geraldton.' Her voice cracked a little on that last word.

Geez. Not what he'd been imagining but just as horrific. Without thinking, he put his hand on her knee and squeezed. 'I'm sorry for your loss.'

'Thank you.' She met his gaze and for a moment they just stayed that way—his hand on her knee, her eyes searching his as . if she could see deep into his soul. He had a weird urge to tell her about his own losses, but then she glanced down at her knee and he tore his hand away. What the hell had he been doing?

'The girls must have been little,' he said, wanting to banish the weirdness that had settled between them.

Simone cleared her throat and nodded. 'Yep. Harriet was six and Grace just three. He doted on them.'

'And you would have been young too.'

'Teen mum, child bride, widowed in my early twenties.'

'Fuck. That must have been tough.' He cursed the words the moment they were out. Talk about stating the bloody obvious.

'Some days I didn't think I could get out of bed. If it wasn't for my sister Frankie, Mum and Jason's family, I'm not sure the three of us would have gotten through it. But hey, I'm not the only one that has been through hardships. I'm still alive, I'm healthy, I have two mostly adorable children and I've experienced true love. That's a lot more than some people can say.'

So that's why she and Logan got along—they were both the glass-half-full type of people. He thought of his own losses.

'It sounds like you guys have had a pretty tough life, too,' she added before he could say anything else.

He had no idea how much his brother had told Simone about their family and he didn't like talking about the past anyway, so he turned the conversation back on her.

'Where'd you and your husband meet?'

'First day of pre-primary.' A wistful smile flashed across her face. 'It was your clichéd childhood sweetheart situation. He pulled my pigtails and chased me around the school yard, I ran away from him screaming "boy's germs". First kiss was kiss chasey in the playground, then it was a love-hate thing until high school.

Everyone said we were too young and it'd never last but we were head over heels. When I got pregnant, everyone reckoned we only got married 'cos of the baby, but we truly were blissfully happy. He was my best friend. My soul mate. I never imagined not growing old with him.'

Angus didn't get emotional about much, but he felt a lump forming in his throat. Was that why he and Sarah hadn't survived the crap life had thrown at them? Because they weren't soul mates?

'Have you been on your own ever since?' he asked, not wanting to think about Sarah or any of that.

She cocked her head at him and smiled in a manner that made his insides tighten. He couldn't think of anyone who had a brighter smile. 'Yep. Most men aren't that excited about taking on another man's children.'

'Not only men,' he said. So much for not thinking about Sarah.

'Logan tells me you brought up your sister after your parents died?'

He nodded. When was Logan coming back? He should be the one entertaining his girlfriend.

'I'm guessing that would have made your love life pretty tricky as well?' There was an awkward pause and then she added, 'I'm sorry. None of my damn business. I have a habit of speaking before thinking.'

She sounded mortified and he wanted to put her at ease. 'What love life? I was engaged when Dad … when he died and my fiancée Sarah wasn't too keen on raising my little sister. We parted ways and since then Olivia has been my focus.' That wasn't the whole story, but opening up any further would likely have her reaching for the tissues.

Simone smiled, looking right into his eyes. 'What a stupid woman.'

Warmth spread through him at the compliment behind her words and he damped down the impulse to stand up for his ex. If he'd told her everything, Simone might have been more understanding. As a mother she would understand Sarah's grief.

'Actually, she's quite smart. Got a PhD in environmental science or something now.'

She laughed. 'I'm betting that certificate doesn't keep her warm at night.'

'No, maybe not.' He too found himself chuckling at the image. 'But she had her reasons.'

'So what's Olivia like? Did she give you the kind of grief Harriet is giving me or am I just lucky? I guess it would have been hard playing the role of protective older brother and mum and dad.'

He wanted to tell her that Olivia had caused him all sorts of trouble to make her feel a little bit better about her stormy relationship with Harriet, but the truth was Olivia had been an angel most of the time. The bright spark in his otherwise dull existence. Without her to go on for, he doubted he'd have gotten up in the mornings, never mind found the energy or motivation to work.

'We had the usual ups and downs,' he began, 'but I think it was harder on Olivia not having a woman around than it was on Logan and me looking after her. Blokes don't really get the hype about shopping for Barbies and ballgowns, and she missed out, not having anyone to discuss women's stuff with.'

'I can imagine,' Simone said. 'Lord knows how I'd have managed with a pair of boys. I can't even kick a football.' She paused a moment, then asked, 'Did you and Logan really go shopping for ball dresses?'

Relieved their conversation was headed for lighter territory, Angus nodded. 'Yep—we took our duty as big brothers seriously. Poor Liv wanted to get this short red dress with a low-cut cleavage line or whatever you'd call it, and we both overruled her. She ended up with a very demure navy blue dress, floor length and with a very high neckline, but she looked gorgeous.'

'I'll bet she did,' Simone said. 'Maybe I should take you and Logan with me when we start shopping for Harriet's ball dress. I can only imagine the nightmare that's going to be.'

He laughed. 'Don't stress too much about Harriet. She'll come good in the end, I promise.'

'Maybe.' Simone shrugged and gave him a what-can-you-do? smile. 'The question is, how many grey hairs will I have by then?'

Grey hairs or not, she'd still be beautiful. Angus swallowed that thought and asked her about her art. She was more than happy to talk about her passion and he found all she said fascinating. When they heard the roar of the quad bike approaching, he glanced down at his watch and realised that almost an hour had passed. He couldn't believe how fast the time had flown and tried to swallow his disappointment when Grace came racing towards them, Logan only a few paces behind.

'Have fun, honey?' Simone asked, rising. This made Angus eye-level with her butt and he quickly averted his gaze.

Grace nodded so much Angus was surprised she didn't get whiplash. 'It was awesome. Logan took me all over the farm and even let me have a go myself.'

Simone pulled her daughter into a hug and glanced over the top of her head at Logan. 'Thank you so much.'

He grinned back. 'It was my pleasure. I hope my brother behaved himself.'

Simone met Angus's gaze and the look she gave him—as if they shared a secret—made his pulse quicken. 'He was the perfect host,' she said.

'Well, that's a relief. I'm just going to grab some water. Do you want to go for a walk?'

'That sounds lovely,' Simone said.

Logan went into the house to get his water and returned with a bottle less than a minute later. Grace retreated to the lounge room with Harriet, and Angus watched, something inside him squeezing, as his brother took Simone's hand and led her off down the winding garden path.

He shook his head in an effort to rid the unfamiliar feeling, and then went inside to start on the dishes.

Chapter Nine

'I'm sorry about leaving you with Angus for so long,' Logan said as he led Simone, hand in hand, across the paddocks towards his favourite spot on the farm. It had been their place for adventure when they were kids and now it provided solitude when he needed to be alone with his thoughts. 'Grace was having so much fun and I couldn't bear to disappoint her. We only came back when the diesel was running low.'

Simone laughed. 'Honestly, Angus was the perfect host. He got me another drink, refused to let me clean the kitchen and made interesting conversation.'

'Really?' Logan couldn't hide his surprise. 'Wonders never cease. What did you talk about?'

'Oh, just stuff. Work. The trouble with teenage girls. We talked a bit about your sister.'

'About Liv? What did he say? Did he sound depressed?'

'No.' Simone shook her head. 'He told me about the time you all went shopping for a ballgown. Why? Do you think he's depressed?'

He let out a deep sigh and kicked away a lone gumnut. 'I dunno. I just worry about him being out here alone for days, sometimes weeks, at a time. It's not healthy. Besides the farm, what has he got to live for? I can't help worrying he'll go the same way as Dad.'

Simone frowned. 'Did your dad … did he …?'

'Yes.' Logan closed his eyes briefly. 'He killed himself. Depression got him in the end.'

'Shit.' She squeezed his hand. 'I understand your concern and I'm no expert, but Angus didn't seem depressed to me. He spoke with great passion for the farm, and about you and Olivia. Not everyone's a social butterfly, but from what you've told me about your dad, it sounds like maybe he wasn't coping with his grief.'

'Angus found him, you know. Hanging from a rope in the shearing shed.' Logan could barely get the words out. He'd been away at the time—first year of uni—but he had a good enough imagination and that image had never left him. How much worse must it have been for Angus?

'Oh God. That's something no-one should ever have to see. Did he get counselling?'

Logan snorted. 'Angus didn't have time for stuff like that. He threw himself into farm work and looking after Olivia and Sarah and—' He shut up before he said too much. Of course Angus would expect he'd eventually share their family history with Simone but it still felt wrong talking about the one thing that Angus himself refused to speak about. Yet how could he explain to Simone that it wasn't simply losing their dad or Angus's split with Sarah that made him worry? Angus had lost so much more than a parent and a lover.

'He told me about his fiancée leaving him.'

Logan couldn't believe it. 'He told you about Sarah?'

Simone nodded. 'We were talking about how hard it is to date with kids and he told me she left because she didn't want to raise Olivia. She sounds like a cow.'

Ah, so he hadn't quite told her everything. 'She was young … it was … hard for everyone.'

'You're right, I shouldn't judge. Speaking of being young, I can't thank you enough for spending some time with Grace. She never causes any fuss and I think I'm sometimes guilty of over-looking her.'

'Nah.' He shook his head as they approached a gate and he had to let go of her hand to open it. 'You're a great mum. Grace is great. Even Harriet is great … in a kinda scary way.'

'What on earth did I do to find you?' Simone asked as she walked through the gate.

'You signed up to Rural Matchmakers with a whole lot of other desperados.'

She laughed. 'It's not nice to talk about yourself in such a way.'

He merely smiled as he closed the gate behind them and took her hand again.

'Do you really not mind about the girls?'

He frowned. 'I'm not sure I understand the question.'

'You're still young. Don't you want to have kids of your own?'

He slowed and turned to her. 'I'm honestly not sure. You don't want to have any more?'

She shrugged. 'I hadn't thought about it.'

He reached out a hand and brushed a strand of flyaway hair behind her ear. She blinked her beautiful green eyes. Maybe this was the time to confess about *his* eyes. They were talking the big issues after all. Relationship deal breakers. But the winter sun was shining above them and he didn't want to ruin what was turning out to be a very good day. They were still getting to know each other … they'd barely even kissed. Maybe they wouldn't even make the distance. If he felt things were getting serious, then he'd tell her.

'You know … you're not that old. Plenty of women haven't even started their families at thirty-five.'

She bit her lower lip and nodded.

'Saying that, kids are great,' he said, 'but I'd rather be with someone I love and can have fun with than someone I think will make good babies with me. And you already have two awesome daughters—having kids is a major lucky-dip.'

She raised one eyebrow and smiled at him. 'Grace is sweet. Spend enough time with Harriet and you might change your mind.'

He laughed. 'I like Harriet. She has spark.'

'That's one way to put it.'

He nodded ahead to a cluster of trees on the edge of the usually dry creek bed. The rains hadn't been bad this year, so there was a rare trickle of water in it. 'This,' he exclaimed, leading her over, 'is one of my favourite spots in the whole world.'

She smiled as he led her over to some big rocks in the middle of the trees that he and Angus had pretended were a fort when they were kids. He smiled whenever he thought about the battles they'd had here, the war wounds they'd returned home with. Mum often joked about needing to buy bandages and antiseptic cream in bulk.

'Sit,' he said, pulling her down next to him on one of the rocks. 'You've read the Faraway Tree books, right?'

She chuckled. 'Who hasn't? Dad was an English teacher and he read to Frankie and I since we were babies. Frankie adored Moonface and … what was the name of that blonde fairy?'

'Silky.'

'That's it. Frankie longed to have blonde, frizzy hair like her.'

'I guess we always want what we can't have,' Logan said, 'but I reckon the colour you and Frankie have is just perfect.'

'Are you blind or something? This hair is the bane of my existence.'

For a moment every muscle in his body froze. If only she knew, but he couldn't bring himself to go there yet. It was hard to summon the smile that Simone's joke required, but he did his best. 'We used to pretend this was the Enchanted Forest.'

Unaware of his discomfort, she glanced around. 'Frankie would have loved that. She was never without a book as a kid.' Simone was quiet a moment and then turned to look at him, an earnest expression on his face. 'Hey, do you think we could convince Angus to come to the wedding too? As Frankie's date?'

His own woes forgotten, he smothered a snort. 'Good luck with that. I'd have more luck convincing him to look into this renewable energy project, and you know how I'm going with that.'

She sighed, leaned over and picked up a leaf, which she proceeded to rip into pieces. 'I just don't want Frankie to be by herself. As glad as I am you're coming with me, I feel bad about leaving her to go solo.'

'She hasn't been in a relationship for a while then?'

Simone shook her head. 'A few years ago she was burned by a guy in Perth—it cut her pretty deep.'

'What happened?' he asked, then quickly followed with, 'You don't have to say. Not my business.'

'She was working at a café and got friendly with one of the local businessmen who came in. They started dating and for a while Frankie was so happy. Then the night they were going to take the next step, he booked a room at a city hotel and arranged to meet her there. He never turned up. She found out later it was because he'd been with his wife … in hospital … while she was having his baby.'

Logan clenched his free hand into a fist. 'What a bastard.'

'Yep. Better she found out sooner rather than later, but that experience really fucked her up. She came home to Bunyip Bay, bought the café and threw her heart and soul into that to try to erase the pain. As far as I know—and I would know because she tells me everything—there's been no-one else since.'

Logan couldn't understand why some smart guy hadn't snapped Frankie up. He'd only met her the two times, but those brief interactions were enough to tell him that if she were emotionally available, anyone would be crazy to pass her by. He racked his brain for a mate who might be happy to accompany a pretty girl to a wedding but came up blank; all his good friends were currently coupled up.

'I'll ask Angus,' he said, surprising himself. 'But no promises.'

'Thank you.' Simone squeezed his hand again and beamed at him. He smiled back.

Her face was mere inches from his and they were in the middle of nowhere, with no audience. Perfect opportunity to kiss her. Uncharacteristic nerves tumbled in his gut, but he took a quick breath, leaned forward and pressed his lips against hers.

* * *

'Nope. Nope. Nope.' Frankie sighed, took another sip of her Milo and continued scrolling through the list of potential dates on RuralMatchmakers.com.au. A number of men had sent her virtual flowers and indicated they'd like to connect, but she'd managed to find something unsatisfactory about each and every one: their hair looked creepy or their religious or political views didn't match hers. One said his favourite movie was *Magic Mike* and although he had a handsome face and the rest of his profile seemed promising, she just couldn't get excited about a man who liked watching other men get their gear off.

She was about to give up and go read on the couch when she heard a key turn in her front door. Every muscle in her body tightened. Simone was the only person who had a spare key and it didn't take a genius to guess why she'd decided to drop by. Psyching herself up to be a supportive and excited sister, Frankie rolled back her chair, stood and went out to meet her. Fred and George—who'd been sleeping on either side of her computer— roused, leaped off the desk and followed her out of the study.

She met Simone in the hallway. One look at the expression on her face told Frankie that the excursion to Logan's farm had been a success.

'Want a drink?' she asked. A post-mortem of Simone's day might require something stronger than malted milk.

'Love one.' Simone smiled as she bent down and scooped up the cats, one in each arm, and cuddled them against her. 'Hello, cuties. How you doing today?'

The two felines meowed and struggled to escape.

'It's like that, is it?' Simone laughed as she deposited them back on the floor. Fred and George scuttled off to the kitchen and Frankie followed, her thoughts already on the bottle of white wine in her fridge.

'I'm guessing you had a good day?' she asked as she entered the kitchen and collected the bottle and two glasses.

Simone nodded, then sank down into a chair at the tiny kitchen table. 'It was fabulous. But I'm exhausted now.'

'And the girls?' Frankie asked. 'Did they have a good day too?'

'Grace had a blast. Logan took her out on the quad bike for over an hour. She was in heaven. Of course Harriet whined and carried on about being there because it meant she missed spending the day with loverboy.' Simone rolled her eyes. 'She's on the phone with him now. I ordered Grace to call me if she takes so much as one step out of the house.'

Frankie laughed as she plonked a glass of chardonnay down in front of her sister, then leaned back against the bench and took a much-needed gulp of her own. 'So Logan got along okay with the girls then?'

'Oh yeah, he's great with them. Especially Grace. At one stage, I thought she was going to spend more time with him than I was.'

'But that wasn't the case?'

Simone shook her head. 'We had a lovely lunch, then he took
Grace for a ride, Harriet sulked in front of the TV and I hung out
with Angus.'

'The grumpy brother?'

'He wasn't as bad as all that.' Simone smiled. 'In fact, I think
you'd like him. He's tall and well built like Logan, but he has this
scruffy mop of dark chocolate hair and a beard. He looks very hot
when he's trying not to smile.'

Frankie grimaced. She wasn't a scruffy-beard type of girl. She
much preferred Logan's cropped-hair look. 'And does he do that
a lot? Try not to smile? Sounds like a riot.'

'He was very entertaining actually. But Logan worries about
him—thinks he spends too much time on his lonesome. *We*
thought it might be good if we could get him to come to the
wedding. As your date.'

It took a few seconds for this to register and then Frankie almost
choked on her wine.

'What? No.' She shook her head. 'I don't need a date,' she lied,
thinking of the hours she'd just spent scrolling through profiles
in the hope of someone who might fill that particular bill. She
didn't want to be a charity case—she especially didn't want Logan
to think of her that way. To pity her like he obviously pitied his
brother. 'I'm quite comfortable, quite happy on my own. I don't
need a guy in my life to complete me. I have the café, and my
friends, and my family, and my cats.'

On cue, Fred started winding himself around her legs and she
put down her glass and snatched him up, relishing the comfort of
his warm, furry little body. He started nibbling on her plait.

Simone held up her hands. 'I'm not asking you to marry the
guy. I was just trying to be helpful. You were the one wondering
if Logan had a brother, remember? Forget I mentioned it.'

Frankie sighed. 'I'm sorry. I appreciate the thought and ... you're right, it would be nice to have a man in my life who has two legs instead of four. In fact ... I've just taken a leaf out of your book—or rather your daughters'—and signed up to Rural Matchmakers.'

'You have?' Simone's eyes widened and she grinned.

'Yes. I have. Although I doubt I'll find anyone suitable by the wedding.'

Simone shrugged. 'You never know. A lot can happen in two weeks. I can vouch for that.'

And that brought the conversation back to *him*. Frankie held Fred a little tighter and forced herself to ask, 'Things going to work out with Logan then?'

'It's early days, but I kinda feel like I've landed on my feet,' Simone confessed, twirling her wine glass between her fingers. 'It's hard enough to find a nice guy these days, never mind one who also looks like an underwear model *and* doesn't mind the fact that I have kids.'

And is an incredible kisser, added Frankie silently. She snatched the glass of wine off the bench and took a gulp.

'We kissed today,' Simone confessed and Frankie's chest tightened.

'Oh?' she managed, despite the fact she felt like she was having some kind of heart attack.

Simone nodded, giving nothing away.

Frankie was torn between wanting to know details and preferring to stay in the dark, but as a supportive sister it was her duty to pry and Simone would worry if she didn't. 'And?' she asked.

'And ...' Simone rubbed her lips together, her brow furrowed slightly as if in contemplation. 'It was nice.'

'Nice?' Frankie spluttered. That was not a word she considered adequate where kissing and Logan Knight were concerned. The mere thought of his lips on hers still turned all her internal organs inside out.

'Yes,' Simone said. 'Pleasant … easy … I dunno. There was nothing *wrong* with it, but I couldn't stop thinking about Jason. I kept imagining that he was watching and that thought made me feel a little weird. Which is not a good way to feel when your tongue is down someone else's throat.'

'No.' Frankie swallowed, not wanting to think about how well acquainted Simone's and Logan's tongues might have gotten that afternoon. That thought made her feel a little weird. But she had no right to feel that way. Trying to detach herself from the scenario, she thought about what she would say if the guy Simone had kissed was somebody different. 'I can imagine it must be hard putting yourself out there again,' she said, 'but Jason has been gone a long time. He was a great guy and I know you miss him terribly, but you're not cheating on him. I'm sure he'd want you to move on and find happiness again.'

Simone puffed out a long breath. 'I know you're right. It's just all a bit sudden, but I'd be a fool to let this one slip through my fingers, wouldn't I?'

'Uh huh.' Frankie nodded, her jaw clenched tightly as she forced an encouraging smile.

Simone pushed back her seat and closed the distance between them. Frankie stilled as her sister wrapped her arms around her, cushioning Fred between them. He mewed his discontent and Simone laughed, stepping back for Frankie to release her feline bundle.

'Thank you,' Simone said as Fred scampered away to join his brother under the table. 'You are the best sister ever, you know that? I'd go insane if I couldn't talk this through with you.'

Frankie forced a smile. The thoughts going through her head right now didn't make her a very good sister at all. Her only hope was meeting someone else to take her mind off yet another Mr Unavailable. What was wrong with her that on the rare occasion she felt something for a guy, he was always claimed by someone else?

'When are you seeing each other next?' she asked.

'He's pretty busy helping Angus on the farm this week and also has some writing deadlines, but he mentioned something about meeting in Geraldton one day for lunch.'

Geraldton. Thank God. Frankie didn't think she could handle watching Logan and Simone sit through another romantic lunch right under her nose. 'Great.'

'We've got the hens night next Friday, but if Angus agrees to come to the wedding with you, I was thinking we could go visit them on Saturday or Sunday so you could meet before the big day.'

'Okay.' It sounded horribly like a blind date but Frankie told herself this was a good thing. Simone had said Angus was good-looking and not as grumpy as all that, so maybe her ridiculous hormones could transfer their affections onto him. Even if he was half as hot as Logan, he'd be better looking than most men. Besides, looks weren't everything and she had to admit it would be nice not to be the only person with no-one to dance with at the wedding.

'Excellent.' Simone clapped her hands together in excitement. 'We always said we wanted to double date. This is our chance.'

'Wouldn't it be a bit weird, sisters dating brothers?'

'No,' Simone scoffed. 'Happens all the time. And anyway, I'm not asking you to marry the guy. Just consider it a good opportunity to meet your future brother-in-law.'

Chapter Ten

As Angus lifted the next lamb into the circular crutching cradle, he glanced over at Logan, who had the brand marker ready to clip the animal's ear. Behind him, the pen of lambs cried out for their mums, who waited on the other side of the yard. The mums would baa back, making the sheep yards rather noisy.

Unlike the sheep, Logan had been quiet all morning. In fact, he'd been acting a little strange ever since Simone and her kids had come round for lunch on Sunday. Angus guessed that's what love did to a guy. He remembered falling in love with Sarah and being unable to think about much else, but in hindsight, Sarah wasn't half as stunning or fun to be around as Simone. He'd been thinking quite a lot about her the last couple of days, but that was likely down to the fact that, apart from his sister, he'd barely been near another woman in years—and certainly hadn't enjoyed their company the way he had Simone's.

Sighing at that unhelpful thought, he waited for Logan to finish the clip and swing the lamb around. This one was a male, so when Logan was finished, Angus used the elastrator, making sure he had both balls in the rings before letting them go. Over the years, the brothers had tagged more sheep than Angus could remember and they didn't need to converse while doing so. They worked like a factory line—sheep in the cradle, ear clipped, balls rung off if necessary, vitamin injection and finally the tag pierced onto their ear; start all over again with the next lamb—but usually Logan kept up a steady stream of conversation. He'd prefer Logan to be badgering him about his renewable energy ideas than this odd silence but since they'd last fought about that a week ago, Logan hadn't raised it again.

Sometimes Angus got annoyed with Logan's excessive chatter, but today, his silence made him nervous. It was like their roles had been reversed, and Angus didn't like it one bit. As he crunched an ear tag onto the bleating lamb, he racked his brain for some kind of small talk.

'Remember when Liv wanted to get her ears pierced?' he asked eventually.

Logan made a noncommittal grunt and Angus raised his eyebrows.

'She pestered and pestered me, remember? Sarah said I should just let her have it done—that lots of little girls got their ears pierced when they were younger than her—but I kept thinking of how it felt to crunch an ear tag on a lamb and couldn't bear the thought of the pain Olivia might feel.'

Logan made a half-hearted attempt at a chuckle and his lips lifted slightly at the edges. 'So that's why you made me take her in the end?'

'Damn straight. Did I never tell you this before?'

Logan shook his head as Angus lifted another lamb onto the cradle. This time a female, which made the process marginally quicker. 'You generally don't tell me much at all. Man of few words is what you are.'

'As are you today,' Angus noted as Logan clipped the lamb's ear. 'Any reason for that?'

'Nah. Just exhausted. I've been burning the candle at both ends.' As if to prove his point, he yawned and then swung the lamb back to Angus.

'What are you writing at the moment?'

Logan shrugged and then wiped sweat off his brow. 'This and that.'

'Or have you been up late talking to Simone?' Angus couldn't help being curious. The distance between Bunyip Bay and Mingenew meant it wasn't easy for them to catch up in person, but he'd heard Logan on the phone the last couple of nights and it had been obvious who he'd been talking to.

'That too,' Logan said, finally cracking a smile.

'So you really like this one?'

'What's not to like?'

The answer to that question was nothing, but Angus kept that to himself. 'I'm happy for ya,' he said instead. 'Maybe that online dating palaver isn't as ridiculous as I first thought.'

Logan froze, the clippers in midair. 'You think you might give it a go?'

Angus laughed. 'Let's not get carried away. I'm merely conceding that maybe I was wrong about you not meeting someone that way. I see now I was wrong about you not being serious about settling down.'

Logan smirked. 'Apology accepted.'

Stifling his own chuckle and glad to have Logan a little closer to his usual self, Angus said, 'I never said I was sorry. When are you seeing her again?'

'I'm gonna try to meet her for lunch in Gero sometime this week. When you can spare me?'

Angus gestured to the pen of lambs. 'We're flying through these little guys. I can probably do without you later in the week.'

'Goodo.' Logan tossed him an appreciative smile. 'And while I've got you in a good mood ...'

Here it comes, thought Angus.

'Simone and I were wondering if you'd come to the wedding with Frankie, her sister?'

'What? You've asked her to marry you?' He hadn't been expecting *that*. Thoughts of wind-farming sidelined by Logan's request, Angus continued, 'What's the damn hurry?'

'No.' Logan gave him a look of horror. 'Not *our* wedding. That *would* be fast. Their cousin is getting married in Kalbarri in a couple of weeks. I'm going with Simone and her sister doesn't have a date.'

'Why not? What's wrong with this Frankie?' Angus had visions of her being the ugly sister, because let's face it, no-one would ever outshine Simone.

'Nothing,' Logan said a little too emphatically. 'She's gorgeous. I think she's just too busy to meet anyone—she runs the café in Bunyip Bay.'

'I know it.' Angus had stopped there a couple of times with Olivia and he had to admit the food was good. Better than good.

'Well, there you go. Nothing wrong with her. If anything, it's the men in the area that need their heads read. So you'll come?'

'Sorry. I don't have anything suitable to wear.' Angus turned to grab hold of the next lamb and gave it a scratch with the scabby guard vaccine.

'Not a problem,' came his brother's quick response. 'I'll lend you a suit. I don't think it's an overly fancy wedding anyway. They're going to Kalbarri rather than having it in Bunyip Bay, to keep it intimate.'

Intimate. That sounded like a good idea. Logan's wedding to Loretta had been a mammoth event. Mingenew wasn't a big place, but it had felt like every man and woman in town had attended, along with their dogs and extended family—and look how that had turned out. Man, he hated weddings.

'Won't it be weird going to a wedding of people we've never met?' he asked, trying a different tack.

Logan shook his head. 'Of course not. At most weddings the guests only know the bride's or groom's side well. I've gone to heaps where I've only known my date and I've had fun at every single one of them.'

The tone of Logan's voice and the way he wriggled his eyebrows told Angus exactly the kind of fun he was referring too. But even if Frankie were that way inclined, they'd have to think about the fact that if Logan and Simone kept seeing each other, a one-night stand could be awkward afterwards. They could even end up related. 'You've got an answer for everything, haven't you?'

'Pretty much.' Logan looked unashamedly proud of this fact and for some bizarre reason, Angus found himself wavering.

'Come on,' Logan continued. 'I'm not asking you to give up your hermit existence permanently, just for the weekend. If that thought pains you too much, put yourself in Frankie's shoes. No girl likes to go to a wedding alone.' And then he hit him in his soft-spot. 'Imagine if it was Liv. Wouldn't you want some knight in shining armour to rescue her?'

Angus groaned, rubbed his jaw and raised his eyebrows. 'I'm no knight in shining armour.'

'Maybe not, but it could be fun,' Logan said, sounding like he was running out of arguments.

And then Angus had an idea. 'Tell you what,' he said, 'how about we make a deal? I'll go to the wedding with Simone's sister if you agree to stop trying to convince me to attend the renewable energy meeting. I'm not interested and I know this farm is both of ours, but I don't want any other party coming in and telling us what we can and can't do on our own land.'

Shock flashed across Logan's face. As he deliberated, Angus prepared himself for another argument. If past discussions were anything to go by, no way would his brother back down on this. He knew Logan didn't want to be so tied to the farm anymore and that he saw this as the perfect way to achieve his goal.

'Okay,' Logan finally breathed, defeat etched across his face.

Angus almost lost his grip on the lamb he'd just grabbed. 'Okay?'

'Yep. You've got yourself a deal.' Angus could see it physically pained his brother to agree, but it was a testament to how Logan felt about Simone that he did. 'Looks like we're going to a wedding!'

'I suppose you want me to get a haircut as well.'

'You really should,' Logan conceded. 'And that beard could do with a trim.'

Angus gave Logan the finger, rubbed his beard affectionately and then got back to the sheep.

Chapter Eleven

Simone gave each of her daughters a kiss goodnight and practically threw them at Jason's parents, who'd agreed to look after them while she attended Stella's hens night. She waited until she was out of view of the old farmhouse and then pressed her foot down on the accelerator, red dust flying up behind the Pajero as she drove towards the main road. Joan and Eddie McArthur lived about fifteen kilometres east of Bunyip Bay and thanks to the girls dilly-dallying to pack their overnight bags, Simone was already running late. The phone coverage was crap out this way, so she couldn't call Frankie or the others, but they never expected her to be early anyway.

She passed the time bopping along to The McClymonts and as she entered the outskirts of town, her mobile started ringing on speaker phone.

'Hey Mum,' she said as she accepted the call.

'What are you and my darling girls up to tonight?' Ruth asked by way of a greeting.

'I've just dropped them off at the farm. It's Stella's hens tonight at Ruby's, I'm heading there now.'

'I'll bet that will be a bit of fun. Do Jason's parents know about your new man?'

Simone frowned as she turned off the highway into town. 'How did *you* know about Logan?' Although it was a stupid question; the Madden girls talked. 'Frankie, Harriet or Grace?'

'Harriet—she seemed quite proud of herself for setting you up.'

'She's lucky I didn't kill her. And I haven't told Joan and Eddie yet but I think they'd be happy if I found someone else. They've said on more than one occasion that I should put myself out there again.' She shuddered at that awful expression—but that's the way people spoke, as if she was some product that had been returned and needed to be re-shelved for purchase.

'Will their financial support continue if you and this Logan fella get serious?' Ruth asked, her tone anxious.

When Jason died, Simone had used his life insurance to buy a house in Bunyip Bay. Although owning her own home had meant she'd never been in dire financial trouble, the McArthurs continued to pay her an allowance from the farm, wanting to look after their son's wife and children. 'Mum, I have no idea, but it wouldn't matter either way. You know I've saved that money for the girls. We've never relied on it; we get by okay on what I earn.'

Ruth sighed and Simone hoped she wasn't going to pry into how much she earned from her art. She'd always got the impression Ruth and Graham, and even to an extent her real dad, didn't take her art seriously, but plenty of other people were prepared to pay good money for her creations.

'That's good then. You know I can't help worrying.'

Simone turned into Ruby and Drew's driveway and smiled at the sight of Faith Forrester's ute up ahead. 'I know. It's a mother's prerogative.'

'Anyway, tell me about this Logan fella. I've heard he's tall, blond and quite a looker.'

'Harriet said that?' Simone's cheeks burned at the thought of her mum and her daughter discussing her love life.

'Yes, so what else is he like?'

'He's a journalist and also helps his brother out on their farm,' Simone said as she parked between Faith Forrester's ute and Frankie's hatchback in front of the impressive house that used to be Ruby's parents' place.

'I don't want his resume, I want to know what he's like? Does he make you laugh? Does he make you … *scream*?' Ruth giggled like a teenage girl.

'Mum!' Simone gripped her fingers tightly around the steering wheel.

'What? You're an adult now. You have two teenage daughters. I know you've had sex and we've all been hoping that one day you'd have some again.'

Oh. My. God! Simone swallowed, unable to believe they were having this conversation. She and Logan had kissed again in Geraldton—and whenever his lips touched hers, her heart skipped a beat, but it felt more like nerves than anticipation. Truthfully, she was afraid her body had forgotten how to feel those things, terrified her hormones had grown sick of all those years waiting and up and left. 'It's early days, but I'm bringing him to the wedding next weekend. You'll get to meet him then.' She hoped this news would distract her mother's inappropriate thoughts.

'I can't wait. And I've got an idea!'

By the time Simone disconnected the call and climbed out of the Pajero, she'd somehow agreed to her mother's crazy plan. And maybe it was for the best. Maybe she just needed to jump in, head first, so she didn't have time for the crippling fear that consumed her every time she thought about being with a man again.

As she headed up the garden path towards the house, she heard the sounds of Taylor Swift's latest album inside. Considering that, like the wedding, Stella's hens night was going to be a small affair—only her closest friends and soon-to-be cousins-in-law in attendance—the party sounded in full swing.

Poor Stella was estranged from her own family, but Adam's parents had welcomed her with open arms. It was hard to believe they'd barely even known each other a year. She hadn't replaced the little girl they'd lost all those years ago, but Esther and Dave loved Stella like a daughter and Heidi as if she were their grand-daughter by blood.

Hitching her overnight bag up on her shoulder, Simone lifted her hand to ring the bell but the door was flung open before she could do so.

'What took you so long?' Ruby asked as she reached out and dragged her inside.

'Teenagers cannot be rushed,' Simone replied as she kicked the door shut behind them.

'Harriet and Grace take after their mother,' called Frankie from somewhere further inside the house. 'Simone can't be rushed either.'

Simone stuck out her tongue in the direction of the voice and Ruby laughed. 'I love you two,' she said, threading her arm through Simone's. 'I always wanted a sister.'

'They have their uses,' Simone conceded. 'The girls and I would likely starve to death if it wasn't for Frankie.'

'Wait till you see the feast she's conjured up for tonight.' Ruby led Simone into the lounge room where Stella, Faith and Frankie were draped over the leather couches, glasses in hand.

She waved at her sister and then bent down to envelop Faith in a huge hug. Faith had grown up in Bunyip Bay and although she and her long-time best friend, now fiancé, Daniel Montgomery—better known to his mates as Monty—had come back for a visit just after Christmas, they were once again busy with their new lives on their property down south and everyone missed them.

'Look at you,' Simone exclaimed. 'Pregnancy suits you. Monty must be looking after you.'

Faith grinned. 'I have no complaints. The man is a saint.'

Simone smiled and then glanced at the coffee table in front of them, laid out with a mouth-watering array of homemade dips and nibbles, all beautifully displayed in Frankie's trademark style. Although her stomach rumbled at the sight, it was the glistening bottle of bubbly Simone was interested in. She thrust her index finger towards it. 'I need me a glass of that. Now.'

The perfect host, Ruby slipped her arm free of Simone's and turned to fill the empty glass that sat on the table.

'Sorry we didn't wait,' Stella said apologetically. 'I was a little nervous about leaving Heidi for the night and Frankie thought this might help.' She held up her crystal flute.

'No worries.' Simone sat down on the couch next to Stella and patted her knee.

'There isn't much a few bubbles won't fix.' Frankie lifted her glass and took another sip.

Simone took her glass and downed about half of it in one mouthful. She let out a sigh of contentment as she felt the tension caused by another fight with Harriet ebbing away. 'That stuff is good.'

'Only the best for our bride.' Ruby winked at Stella as she topped up everyone's glasses.

Poor Faith was sipping on a glass of mineral water. 'I would kill for some of that,' she said, flicking her long brown hair over her shoulder and frowning.

'Surely you can have one glass,' Stella said.

Faith shook her head. 'One glass is never enough. Better if I abstain. It's only nine months, right? Less now.' She placed her hands on her growing bump and looked from Stella to Simone and back again. 'And it'll be worth it in the end. Right?'

'Totally.' Stella nodded, her smile wide.

Simone raised an eyebrow and took a slug of her drink, then, 'No comment. If it weren't for my delightful little angels I wouldn't have been late tonight. You'd think they were packing for a month-long cruise, not a weekend away.'

Frankie snorted. 'So what was your excuse for the nineteen years before they came along?'

Simone glared at her, pretending to be annoyed.

'Where are the girls?' Faith asked. 'I'm hoping to catch up with them and the rest of the gang sometime this week.'

'The gang' referred to the netball team Faith used to coach before she and Monty moved to Mount Barker. As key players in Adam and Stella's bridal party, Faith and Monty had returned for the wedding and the fun and frivolity leading up to it.

'They're staying with Jason's folks on the farm for the weekend.'

Frankie chuckled. 'Bet Harriet is pleased about that. She'll miss another footy match because I can't see Mrs McArthur bringing her all the way into town to see her boyfriend.'

'No, the guys have a bye this weekend, thank God, and the boyfriend's gone to Perth with his parents,' Simone explained, taking another much-needed sip.

The other women laughed, recalling what it felt like to be sixteen and in love. Simone and Stella had both ended up pregnant to their first loves. She shuddered at the thought, thinking she really needed to try to talk to Harriet about contraception again—she was not old enough to be a granny yet.

'Anyway, now that you're here,' Ruby said, leaning down and sliding a box out from under the coffee table, 'we can really get started.' She reached into the box and pulled out a bright pink satin sash and held it up so they could all read the word 'bride' scrawled across it in sparkly silver cursive writing.

'Oh, no,' Stella squealed, shaking her head. 'I'm not wearing that. You said this was going to be a civilised night.'

'Sure you are.' Ruby used her stern voice, the one she used when giving horse-riding lessons, and tossed the sash over to Stella. It floated down into her lap and Faith snatched it up and then draped it over her, giggling.

'Gorgeous.'

Stella rolled her eyes but the smile on her face said she didn't mind the attention one bit.

'Just because we're staying in, doesn't mean we can't have a proper hens night,' Ruby said, pulling out a tiara that at first glance looked very regal, but under closer scrutiny seemed to have miniature penises sticking out the top of it.

'Ruby!' Stella exclaimed, her cheeks turning a deep shade of crimson as the tiara was placed on her head.

Frankie and Faith were quick to grab their phones to commemorate the event.

Stella pointed a finger at them. 'Do not put any of this on Facebook!'

Simone's eyes widened as she stifled a laugh. 'What on earth else do you have in that box?'

In reply, Ruby wriggled her eyebrows up and down. 'Don't worry, girls, I didn't forget any of you.' And then she stuck her hand back into the box and pulled out four matching 'bridesmaid' sashes and some weird reddish-beige necklaces.

Simone narrowed her eyes as she tried to work them out, then, '*Oh my!*' She slammed her hand over her mouth.

'More penises!' shrieked Stella, losing her battle with hysterics. 'I didn't know you were such a naughty girl.'

'Me either,' Simone mused, taking another slug of her drink. When she'd first moved back to Bunyip Bay, Ruby Jones had seemed the shy and retiring type, but hooking up with Drew Noble had allowed her true self to be revealed. And when she wanted to be, she could be the life of the party.

Ruby shrugged. 'Come on, ladies, you can't have a hens night without a few fake cocks!'

'What would Drew think about these?' Frankie asked, fingering hers as Ruby handed them all out. It squeaked like a dog's chew toy and they all cracked up again.

'What Drew doesn't know won't hurt him,' Ruby said. 'Besides, I'm sure the boys are getting up to their own fun.'

A worried look crossed Stella's face. 'You don't think they'll do anything stupid to Adam, do you?'

The men were at The Palace, getting up to who knows what kind of mischief. Even though Drew was a cop, she doubted he'd be able to stop Monty and the footy guys having their fun with Adam if that's what they so desired. 'They'll be fine,' Simone lied. 'Liam doesn't allow strippers in his pub.'

'Really?' Ruby and Stella said at the same time.

'Yep.' Faith nodded. 'Years ago he had a bunch of skimpies in for one night and one of them stole all the takings from the till and did a runner. He's borne a grudge against all skimpies, strippers and the like since.'

'They'll probably just have a few quiet beers and a game of pool,' Frankie said, eyeing the box warily. 'You got anything else in there?'

Ruby shook her head. 'I contemplated buying us Pin the Cock on Jock, but thought better of it. I do have some penis-shaped after-dinner mints for later though.'

'Splendid.' For someone dosed up on champagne, Frankie sounded a little grumpy.

Simone frowned, wondering if everything was okay. The last week had gone quickly and they hadn't spoken as much as they usually did. Not that they'd had a fight or anything, but they'd both been busy. Lunch in Geraldton with Logan had taken up most of Simone's Wednesday and the rest of her week had been filled with the usual Meals on Wheels, school canteen duties and time spent finishing the wedding bombonière. The only times she'd seen Frankie were the two shifts she'd done in the café, and even then they'd been like ships passing in the night, with Frankie rushing home to do 'cake preparation' the moment Simone arrived. There appeared to be a lot more to making a wedding cake than any of them had anticipated. Maybe that's why Frankie was in a mood: stress.

'And I do have a couple of pre-dinner games,' Ruby said, tearing Simone's mind away from her sister. She picked up a few clipboards and some pink pens from the floor next to the box and started handing them around.

'What's this about?' Faith asked, glaring down at her clipboard. 'I hope I don't have to think too hard. Pregnancy brain has well and truly hijacked my mind.'

Simone tossed her a sympathetic smile. 'It never ends … pregnancy brain turns into baby brain and then you blink and your cute little cherubs have turned into scary monsters who give you *teenager* brain and that's—'

'Don't scare the pregnant woman,' Frankie interrupted as Faith's eyes widened in fear.

'Ladies.' Ruby tapped the side of her champagne flute with her pen. 'This is a quiz about Adam and Stella. For every question you get wrong you have to take a sip of your drink. You ready?'

'Hang on,' Simone said. 'What do we get if we get the question right?'

Ruby's brow furrowed a moment. 'You get to take a sip of your drink.'

They all laughed again.

'Sounds good to me.' Frankie took a sip of hers for good measure. 'What's the first question?'

Ruby cleared her throat. 'In which season did Adam and Stella meet?'

'Oh, I know this one.' Faith bounced in her seat, her hand shooting up into the air.

'Write it down,' Ruby said, her tone amused.

Simone scribbled 'summer' down onto her pad, but Frankie looked at Stella. 'Did you arrive in late November or early December?'

Stella opened her mouth but Ruby held up her hand. 'Don't say a word. No questions, Frankie, that's cheating. Right ... next question. What did Stella cook the first time she and Adam ate dinner together?'

'I think I'm going to get one hundred per cent,' Stella said and then took another sip of her drink.

There were twenty questions in all—some easy, some tricky— and by the time Ruby had called out the answers, they'd gone through another two bottles of champagne between them.

'I'm feeling quite light-headed,' Stella confessed, a big grin on her face.

'That's the idea,' Ruby said. 'Do you want another game or shall we eat now?'

The unanimous decision was food, so Frankie and Faith went into the kitchen to ready the feast they'd prepared earlier that day. For a small wedding, there was going to be a big bridal party, with Simone, Frankie, Ruby and Faith as bridesmaids; Monty, Drew and two blokes from the local football team as groomsmen; and of course gorgeous little Heidi as flower girl.

Ruby, Stella and Simone took the glasses and what was left of the last bottle of bubbly over to the dining room and took their places at the table.

'Wow, this is beautiful.' Simone admired the table as she sat down. Not a fake penis in sight; instead there were gorgeous pink candles, a lace tablecloth and shiny cutlery—far removed from the mismatched knives and forks she had at her place. Someone had even folded the pale pink napkins into swans. Impressive.

'Yes,' Stella agreed, sounding a little choked up. 'I can't thank you enough for going to all this trouble, girls.'

'Hey, I did nothing,' Simone said, feeling a little guilty about that now. She'd had a crazy week and no-one would have wanted her to help Frankie with the food anyway, but she could have contributed to the table design.

'You're worth it,' Ruby said and Simone had to agree with that.

'I was beginning to think my spunky cousin would be alone for life and then you drove into town like an early Christmas present and swept him off his Blundies.'

Stella laughed. 'Speaking of spunky men … when are you going to update us all about how things are going with Mr Logan Knight?'

'Ooh, yes,' Faith said as she and Frankie entered from the kitchen with trays of steaming food. 'I need all the goss on this new guy of yours. Ruby said he's quite good-looking.'

'Understatement of the century,' Frankie said, dumping a casserole dish of what smelt like curry on the table.

For a moment Simone forgot about Logan as she inhaled the tantalising scents.

Frankie and Faith finished laying the food out on the table and then took their spots. 'Dig in,' Frankie said, taking another sip of her champagne.

'Well, Simmo?' Faith began, when they all had bowls laden with rice, curry and accompaniments. 'Tell me all about your new man. I feel so out of everything now I'm so far away.'

'He's …' Simone was at a loss for words. Many a time she'd put her friends in the hot seat about their new love interests, but she shifted in her own seat at the prospect of talking about hers.

Truth was, she thought she should be more excited than she was about this newfound relationship. For the last few years she'd been hankering to get back in the saddle. Her lady bits were so dry she thought they may have shrivelled up and died but she'd been desperate to see if she could breathe some life back into them. She'd well and truly landed on her feet with Logan, who was undeniably hot, smart, patient and liked her kids, but the thought of taking things to the next level—of even getting naked with him—scared the bejesus out of her.

What if she'd forgotten how to do it? She'd only ever been with one man and she'd been Jason's first as well, whereas the way Angus had spoken, it sounded like Logan was a bit of a Casanova. It still perplexed her why he was bothering with someone like her when he must have a hundred women knocking at his door.

Simone glanced around the table to see the others all leaning forward, their eyes gleaming in anticipation.

'He's what exactly?' Faith asked, before shoving a forkful of curry and rice into her mouth.

'He's absolutely gorgeous,' she said, her cheeks heating with all the attention. 'Inside and out.'

'Have you got a photo?' Faith wanted to know.

'No.' Simone shook her head and then suddenly recalled the selfie Logan had taken of them when they were out to lunch in Geraldton. He'd messaged it to her later that night. 'Actually, yes.' She pulled out her phone and scrolled through her messages to find it. 'Here.'

Her phone was passed around the table and Simone watched in amusement at the expressions on her friends' faces and the noises escaping their mouths as they scrutinised him.

'Not bad at all,' Faith declared when she finally handed the phone back. 'So, what's he like in bed?'

★ ★ ★

The last thing Frankie wanted to hear about was how good Logan was in bed, but she couldn't for the life of her think of an excuse to get up and flee the room. Every muscle in her body tensed as their friends turned their eyes to Simone in anticipation. Frankie didn't think they'd slept together yet, but she wasn't a hundred per cent sure. She was fairly certain that Simone would have told her if they'd taken that step, but then again, she'd kinda been avoiding her sister the last few days for fear of hearing something she didn't want to hear.

'We haven't done the deed yet,' Simone confessed, and Frankie couldn't help but let out the breath she'd been holding. Thankfully none of the others—all focused on Simone—noticed her display of relief.

'It's hard,' Simone said. 'Although we've talked lots on the phone, we've only actually seen each other in person a few times. I could hardly jump into bed with him at my house when the girls were home. Besides, I wasn't ready yet. The next time we saw each other was at his farm with his brother and my daughters hanging around.'

'Ever heard of taking a walk and doing it in a paddock?' Faith suggested with a snort of laughter. 'First time Monty and I had sex was on the ground, under the stars. It was oh, so romantic.'

'I thought you were drunk?' Frankie said, unable to help herself.

'Well, I was …' Faith conceded, 'and the morning after I was mortified, but the sex was fan-fucking-tastic.'

They all laughed, even Frankie—the alcohol having well and truly gone to their heads; although Faith didn't seem to need any liquid assistance to be frank with her anecdotes.

'Didn't you have lunch in Geraldton this week?' Stella asked. 'No opportunity to sneak away to a hotel somewhere?'

'I'm shocked by all of you,' Simone exclaimed. 'What kind of hussy do you think I am?'

'I'm sorry,' Ruby said, not sounding so at all, 'but ever since I've met you, you've been waxing lyrical about needing some action down under and here you are with this extremely sexy man and you haven't made use of him yet?'

'I don't want to rush into things and ruin them.' Simone glanced down at her plate and for a second Frankie felt sorry for her being under the spotlight—then she remembered her sister was the one with Logan Knight on speed dial and all sympathy evaporated.

'Don't wait too long,' Faith warned, nodding towards Simone's phone. 'Otherwise someone else might swoop in and snap him up.'

'I won't,' Simone said, then inhaled deeply. 'In fact, I'm thinking next weekend might be the right time, at the wedding.'

Stella's eyes widened. 'I hope you don't mean during the actual ceremony. I want all eyes to be on me.'

Simone laughed. 'They will be. You'll make a beautiful bride. I meant the night time. I've just spoken to Mum and I think we've worked out the logistics to make it possible.'

'Do tell,' said the others in unison.

Despite herself, Frankie was all ears.

'Well, Mum booked an apartment with two rooms for her, Graham and Frankie,' Simone spoke as if Frankie wasn't even there, 'and I'd booked another one for me and the girls. Mum's going to pretend she wants to spend quality time with her grand-daughters and have them in with her. Frankie can share with me so I won't have to worry about the girls when I bring Logan back to my room.'

While Stella, Ruby and Faith applauded this cunning plan, Frankie struggled to keep down the curry she'd eaten. She was surrounded by women who were no doubt getting it on a daily basis and her older sister, who was planning to break her sexual drought next weekend. She'd never felt more like an old maid in her life. The closest she was going to get to a penis anytime soon was the fake one hanging around her neck.

'And where will Angus be?' she asked, making a mental note to buy herself some high-grade earplugs because hotel walls were often thin and she didn't want to have to listen to Logan and Simone consummating their relationship all freaking night.

'In the room he and Logan have booked. Unless you two hit it off.' Simone shot her a teasing grin.

'Who's Angus?' Stella and Faith both wanted to know.

'Logan's brother. He's coming to the wedding as Frankie's date,' Simone explained.

'Ooh.' Ruby looked to Frankie. 'Is he as hot as his brother?'

Frankie shrugged one shoulder. 'I don't know,' she said, although she doubted anyone could be *quite* as hot as Logan. It was this line of thinking that had made it practically impossible for her to identify any men on Rural Matchmakers she wanted to make contact with. Damn the man. 'But we're meeting on Sunday.'

'A blind date!' Faith exclaimed. 'How exciting.' If Frankie wasn't mistaken, she sounded more sympathetic than excited.

'Did I forget to mention?' Simone said, grimacing. 'Logan had to cancel Sunday lunch. He's had to go to Perth today at the last minute to cover some protest march for a friend who's in hospital with swine flu, and he'll be there all weekend.'

'Oh.' Frankie didn't know what to say about this news. She guessed she was both disappointed and relieved at not having to see Logan again so soon, but now she faced the prospect of attending a wedding with a total stranger.

'Sorry, sis.' Simone reached over and squeezed her hand. Frankie tried not to flinch. 'But I promise you, it'll be okay. Angus is lovely.'

Before Frankie could respond, Faith said, 'Imagine if you fall head over heels for him. It'd be so funny if you two ended up with brothers.'

'Yes!' Stella shrieked, catching the enthusiasm. 'You could have a double wedding!'

'And we could all be bridesmaids!' Ruby gushed. 'I can throw you a hens night if you want.'

Although Simone also seemed to find this hilarious, Frankie couldn't bring herself to even crack a smile. If they were going to continue on like this, it was going to be a long night.

Chapter Twelve

'I can't believe you conned me into this,' Angus said to Logan as they drove through the tiny fishing port of Gregory. Having left the farm that morning, they were well over halfway to Kalbarri. 'I should never have let you talk me into trying on your suit.'

Logan chuckled, his fingers caressing the steering wheel as he drove. 'I can hardly believe it either, but I have a good feeling about this weekend. You never know, you might actually enjoy yourself.'

Angus snorted. 'Hanging out with a bunch of strangers, making small talk with your girlfriend's sister, watching two people I've never met before tie the knot ... what could be better?'

'That's the spirit,' Logan said, stifling a smile and trying not to think about the fact Angus was only here because they'd made a deal to forget about the renewable energy development. Maybe if he told Angus the truth about why he wanted to pursue this option he'd look at things differently, but Logan wasn't ready to have that conversation with anyone yet.

He rubbed his eyes and focused on the road. As long as he was the only one who knew about his diagnosis, it didn't feel real. If the doctors were right, it could be years before it really became an issue and who knows what kind of medical advances they'd have made by then? Maybe he was worrying for nothing. It made his head hurt thinking about it, so he vowed to try to put it out of his mind for the rest of the weekend.

'Remind me again who's getting married,' Angus said, folding his arms and staring at the road ahead. 'Simone's brother?'

Logan shook his head. 'Simone and Frankie's cousin, Adam. I haven't met him yet but he sounds like a top bloke. He has a farm just outside of Bunyip Bay. From what Simone tells me, he's had a pretty rough trot of it.'

'What do you mean?'

'His little sister went missing when he was ten and they only found out what happened to her recently. It's a pretty spinny story actually, how they eventually found out the truth.' He set about relaying the story that Simone had told him and, like he had, Angus found parts of it hard to believe.

'Ghosts aside, that's one sad story,' Angus said. 'I guess we're not the only family that has been through tough times. I'm glad they got some kind of closure in the end.'

'I think the worst thing would be not knowing, always hoping.'

They stewed on this thought a while, driving a few more kilometres until Angus pointed at a white hatchback ahead, which they were rapidly catching up to. 'That car has Bunyip Bay number plates. Wonder if it's also going to the wedding?'

Logan was about to reply when without warning a kangaroo darted out from the side of the road into the direct path of the hatchback. 'Shit!' He planted his foot on the brakes as the other car did the same. While he narrowly missed a collision, the poor kangaroo wasn't so lucky. They watched as it slammed into the hatchback, flipped onto the roof and then miraculously landed on its feet on the other side of the car and bounded off into the scrub, seemingly unharmed.

'Shit!' Angus exclaimed as the car in front pulled over.

The driver got out and Logan's heart jolted in his chest as he recognised her. 'Frankie,' he breathed, a weird feeling coming over him. He never felt quite himself around her—possibly because of their embarrassing and unfortunate first encounter—but he needed to get over that and check that she was all right.

'*That's* Simone's sister?' Angus asked as Logan pulled his car over onto the gravel strip at the side of the road, behind the little white hatchback.

'Yep.' He nodded, unclicked his seatbelt, took a deep breath and then climbed out of his vehicle, Angus following closely behind.

'You all right?' Logan yelled as he jogged over.

Frankie's long red hair was up in a high, practical ponytail and she looked vulnerable, her face pale. She barely acknowledged him and he guessed she must be in shock. He reached out a hand to comfort her but she shrugged him away. While the two men trekked around to the front of Frankie's vehicle, she went to the back and threw open the boot.

'Holy fuck!' they heard her shriek.

'The kangaroo must be okay and the car looks all right as well,' Angus called over the top of the vehicle. 'Barely a scratch.'

'I don't give a freaking hoot about the car. Or the kangaroo for that matter—it should learn some road sense!' she yelled back. 'I care about the cake, or what *was* the cake five minutes ago. Oh, Lord, what am I going to do?'

Frowning as realisation dawned—Logan remembered Simone saying something about Frankie staying up till all hours making the most amazing wedding cake ever—he walked around to the back of the vehicle and saw exactly what had sent Frankie into such a tizz.

Holy fuck, indeed.

Broken sugar flowers, soft pink icing and different types of cake were all mixed up in a chaos of colour in the boot of the car.

There was icing smeared across the back window where the cake had slammed into the glass and then ricocheted into the back seat. Although there was a delicious vanilla scent in the air, what they were looking at was barely recognisable as any kind of dessert, never mind a wedding cake.

'This is a nightmare.' Frankie glared at Logan as if it were his fault.

He nodded glumly. There were no words that could comfort her.

'It's not even dusk yet. What the fuck was a kangaroo doing on the road at this time of day?'

It was obviously a rhetorical question and Logan knew better than to reply. Frankie looked adorable when she was angry and he wanted to tell her it wasn't as bad as it appeared, but as someone who had a bit of experience baking cakes for special occasions, he knew that would be a lie. With the wedding reception just over twenty-four hours away, this was a disaster of epic proportions. He felt Frankie's pain as if it were his own.

'I think I'm going to be sick,' she said, turning away from him as she doubled over and placed her palms on her knees. She didn't vomit, but it sounded like she was hyperventilating. Logan looked to his brother for help but Angus merely shrugged, no use at all. These were not the terms under which he'd imagined them meeting.

Feeling totally helpless, Logan gave Frankie a moment to pull herself together as he turned back to assess the extent of the cake wreckage. A cake topper of the bride and groom and a cute little flower girl poked out of what must have once been the top layer of the cake. As trucks and cars roared past them along the highway, he plucked it from the debris and wiped it free of icing. At least the pièce de résistance wasn't broken. Although this was likely little consolation, because nothing else looked to be salvageable.

With a sigh, he tucked the bride, groom and flower girl into his shirt pocket, then went over to his ute and retrieved a bottle of water and the ancient packet of tissues that lived under the passenger seat.

'Bit of a fruitcake,' Angus whispered to him, nodding over to Frankie as Logan passed. 'She always like this?'

'She's in shock, you idiot,' Logan said, shaking his head as he walked back to Frankie, who was still breathing heavily. Sometimes Angus had no heart at all.

'Hey,' he said, gently touching her arm. 'Would you like some water?'

She slowly turned to look at him and her cheeks were streaked with tears. His heart melted and he fought the urge to close the distance between them and kiss away each tiny droplet.

'I'd prefer a miracle, please,' she whispered, smiling sadly at him. 'A cake miracle to be precise.'

He smiled back, impressed she could raise a bit of humour at a time like this. Instinctively, he reached over and took her hand, squeezing it slightly, wanting her to know she was not alone.

She glanced down at his hand and then back to his eyes. 'Know any cake magicians?' she asked, her voice shaky. 'Your brother isn't a cake magician, is he?'

As if knowing he was being discussed, Angus appeared beside them and as Frankie looked up, Logan dropped her hand in case his brother got the wrong idea.

'Frankie, I'd like you to meet Angus,' Logan said, gesturing between them. 'Angus, meet Frankie.'

Angus nodded his head once. 'Hey, nice to meet you.'

Frankie eyed him hopefully. 'You're not a cake magician, are you?'

He chuckled and shook his head. 'Sorry. Logan's the baker in the family.'

Logan started. 'I hardly think making a few kids' birthday cakes is on the same level as this.'

'What am I going to tell Adam and Stella?' Frankie looked from one man to the next as if either might have the answer, her tone desperate once again.

'The truth?' Angus suggested, lifting one shoulder.

She all but glared at him and he shoved his hands in his pockets and stared down at the red gravel.

'Let's not tell them anything just yet,' Logan said, his mind already ticking over. They needed to think creatively.

'What?!'

'Relax,' he said at her outrage. 'We've got twenty-four hours until we need the cake, right?' She didn't reply, merely lifted one eyebrow at him like he were crazy, so he continued. 'What say we try to make another one?'

Her eyes narrowed. 'Do you know how long that took me to make? I've been up every night this week making those flowers and although it's not your traditional fruit cake, those layers required time. The mud cake needed to cool a whole day before I put on the icing and the top layer had five different colours of cake—it was a bit of fun for Heidi.'

Logan took a deep breath, not sure Frankie was quite ready to hear that maybe the cake they made instead wouldn't quite be up to her usual standard but surely any cake would be better than none. 'Where's Simone?' he asked instead. She'd know how to calm her sister.

'I decided to drive on my own so I didn't have any distractions. I wanted to focus on the cake to avoid anything like this happening. Damn kangaroo.' She puffed out a breath. 'And Simone's always late anyway; waiting for her would have driven me insane.'

Logan cracked a smile. 'I understand. Angus is exactly the same. It was a miracle he was on time today.'

'Hey!' Angus objected. 'I'm right here you know.'

At that moment, Simone's old four-wheel drive appeared over the horizon. She was driving what looked like a hundred miles an hour, but she slowed and swerved over to park behind Logan's car the moment she recognised them. Three doors were flung open and Simone, Harriet and Grace came running over.

'Oh my God,' Simone shrieked, looking between the three of them. 'Did you guys have an accident?'

'Your sister hit a kangaroo,' Angus informed her.

She smiled at him and then dropped to her knees beside Frankie and Logan. 'Fuck. Are you okay?'

'Language, Mum,' Harriet sang. Everyone ignored her.

'You okay, Aunty Eff?' Grace asked softly.

'I'm fine.' Frankie sighed. 'But the cake is cactus.'

Simone, Harriet and Grace turned their heads to the boot of Frankie's car and their eyes widened. Simone swore again and this time neither of her daughters chastised her.

Silence reigned a few long moments. Harriet was the first to break it. 'Man, that would have been delicious!'

'Thanks for stating the obvious. Feel free to help yourself,' Frankie snapped.

Simone wrapped an arm around her sister and pulled her close. 'It's all right,' she whispered. 'We'll make it all right. I'll help you make another one.'

Frankie pulled out of her embrace and glared at her. 'Are you all insane? Kalbarri isn't exactly a metropolis. Where the hell are we going to get everything we need to make a wedding cake? Where the hell are we going to *make* said wedding cake?' Her voice was getting higher and higher with each question. 'And have you forgotten you are a disaster area when it comes to cooking? As if I'd let you anywhere near a wedding cake.'

Hurt flashed across Simone's face, but she didn't dispute Frankie's statement. Her shoulders slumped and she looked as woebegone as Frankie. Logan recalled what had happened when they'd attempted to make chicken soup.

He hated seeing them both so despondent. Weddings were supposed to be happy times. This weekend was supposed to be fun. It had barely even started and it was turning into a catastrophe.

'It still tastes good.' Harriet's voice broke his reverie and he turned to see her and Grace munching on bits of ruined cake. Angus dipped a finger in and nodded enthusiastically. Logan scowled at them, particularly annoyed at Angus. How the hell could they eat cake at a time like this?

'Of course it's good,' Frankie said, looking up. Logan froze, waiting for her to snap again, but instead she burst into laughter. It had to be one of the most beautiful sounds in the world.

He and Simone exchanged worried glances. Her eyes pleaded with him to come up with a plan and he wanted more than anything to do just that.

Chapter Thirteen

'Relax,' Simone instructed Angus as she weaved her arm through his and pushed open the door to the resort's restaurant where her family and friends were gathered for dinner. 'You've already met Harriet and she's the scariest person here.'

He grinned down at her as they stepped inside and she couldn't help thinking again how lovely his smile was when he decided to use it. So far, the weekend wasn't panning out at all how she'd expected or hoped, but she told herself that at least she had Angus to keep her company while Logan tried to help Frankie create another cake. She had to admit her new boyfriend was a superhero—he'd driven a shaking Frankie all the way to Kalbarri with Simone and Angus following in the other vehicles. Then he'd instructed them to look after her while he made some 'inquiries'.

Simone and Angus had plied Frankie with a stiff drink and her breathing had almost returned to normal by the time Logan came back and informed them that he'd come up with a plan. At first Frankie had resisted, but they'd convinced her that Logan's proposition was better than the alternative: telling Stella and Adam they wouldn't have a wedding cake.

'Well, hello there.' Aunty Esther's voice jolted Simone from her thoughts and she turned her head to meet her aunt's scrutinising gaze. 'This must be Logan?' She looked Angus up and down as if he were a model in a men's clothing catalogue. Approval was evident in Esther's smile. Simone suspected her aunt had already had a few drinks, but she was the mother of the groom, so who was going to stop her?

'Actually, no,' she said, grabbing hold of Angus's hand, both as a show of comfort and also so he couldn't turn and run, as it looked like he wanted desperately to do. She'd promised Logan she'd look after him tonight. 'This is Angus. Logan's brother.'

'Oh?' Esther's brow creased. 'Where's Logan then?'

'Um …' Simone racked her brain for a good excuse, cursing herself for not coming up with this stuff before they entered.

'He had a last-minute deadline come up,' Angus informed her, extracting his hand from Simone's and offering it to Aunty Esther. 'But I'm sure you'll meet him tomorrow.'

'Okay then,' Esther said, smiling again as her hand was enveloped by Angus's massive one. She blushed a little and Simone couldn't blame her—both the brothers had that effect. 'What about Frankie then? I haven't seen her yet?'

'She has a migraine,' Simone said, thinking quickly. 'She's gone to bed in the hope it'll be gone by tomorrow.'

'That's terrible.' Aunty Esther frowned again. 'Maybe we should take her some dinner?'

'No! I'll go check on her later,' Simone blurted. 'I think she just needs rest.'

Esther nodded, apparently satisfied with this scenario. 'Well then, time you come and meet the clan, Angus.'

As Esther gestured for them to follow her, Simone and Angus exchanged a look of relief. 'Thanks,' she whispered to him. 'Frankie would be appalled if everyone found out the truth.'

They'd threatened Harriet and Grace with a fate worse than death if they so much as breathed a word to anyone about the cake disaster, but both girls seemed to have forgotten the drama the moment their grandma's car had rolled into the resort car park.

As Simone's mum and stepdad lived in Perth, the girls didn't see their adored grandmother as often as they liked, so they were overjoyed to be rooming in with Ruth and 'Grandad Graham'. Simone hadn't seen either of the girls for a couple of hours but was relieved to find them both now sitting at the long table with the rest of her family and the bridal party; Harriet looked far less sullen than she usually did and Grace slurped happily on a glass of Coke.

Everyone sitting at the table looked up when Simone and Angus arrived.

'Hi all,' Simone said, waving. Ruby, the only one of her friends who had met Logan, looked confused. 'This is Angus,' Simone explained, 'Frankie's date for the wedding. Unfortunately Frankie has a migraine and can't join us tonight and Logan, my ... boyfriend—' the word still felt odd on her tongue, '—has some unexpected work to do.'

Although Simone knew Angus wasn't very comfortable in social scenarios, he was the perfect guest as she went around the table introducing everyone. 'You've met Aunty Esther, this is her husband, Dave, and beside them is Drew and Ruby.' She paused for handshakes and greetings to be exchanged. 'On the other side we have Faith and Monty—our friends who moved south—and the blushing bride, Stella and my ratbag cousin, Adam, who also happens to be the groom.' Angus smiled, looking like he was trying to remember all their names.

'And last but not least,' Simone said, gesturing between Adam and Stella, 'is Heidi. She's chief flower girl tomorrow and daughter of the bride.'

As Angus grinned at Heidi, she launched herself from her seat and rushed around the table to give him one of her famous hugs. Simone couldn't help but admire his lovely arms—strong, tanned and muscular from outdoor labouring—as they enveloped the little girl. She'd always had a thing for arms.

'It's a pleasure to meet you,' Angus said.

Heidi giggled and stepped back slightly to look at him. 'You Aunty Simmo's boyfriend?' she asked, her eyes wide with curiosity.

Everyone laughed and Angus's cheeks flushed red, only just visible through his beard. 'No. We're just friends,' he said.

'I be your friend too?'

Angus ruffled the ringlets atop Heidi's head. 'I'd like that very much.'

Simone and Angus took their seats in the middle of the long table—Angus next to Monty and Simone next to her mother. Heidi immediately crawled onto Angus's lap. Stella tried to lure her back but she fervently refused and Angus didn't appear too flummoxed by it all. They ordered dinner and then various conversations sprouted around the table as they drank wine and beer and waited for their meals. Heidi stayed on Angus's lap, colouring in her Disney Princesses book as he discussed farming and the upcoming harvest season with Adam, Monty and Uncle Dave. He appeared in his element with these born-and-bred farmers and Simone loved hearing his passion as he spoke about his and Logan's property.

When the waitresses brought out the dinner, Stella convinced Heidi to sit back with her, and as they all began to eat, conversation around the table turned to tomorrow's big event.

'I hope the weather holds out,' Ruby said, biting her lip. 'The forecast is for rain in the afternoon.'

'So we'll get a little wet.' Stella shrugged one shoulder and looked at Adam. 'So what. It'll still be perfect.'

A smile stretched across Adam's face and he leaned across Heidi and kissed Stella full on the lips. Everyone cheered and even Heidi beamed. Just looking at these two, you could tell how perfect they were for each other. Both tanned, fit and gorgeous, they looked good together but it was so much more than that. They made each other smile in a way no-one else did, they finished each other's sentences, and when they looked at each other, it was like they shared a secret from the rest of the world.

Simone couldn't help but watch, a wistful sigh escaping her mouth as she silently acknowledged sparks didn't fly like that when she and Logan kissed. His lips were soft and sweet but they didn't cause her heart to skip a beat. Were they flogging a dead horse or did she just need more time? She couldn't help feeling slightly relieved that he'd be otherwise engaged tonight when they were supposed to be taking the next big step in their relationship—especially after she'd told everyone about her plans at the hens night. How Frankie, Stella, Faith and Ruby would laugh if they knew how much she was dithering over this decision.

Maybe she just needed to go for it, throw caution to the wind and leave her head behind when she took him into the bedroom?

'You okay?' Angus leaned towards her and she caught a whiff of some delicious scent wafting off him; something exotic and enticing that she swore had a hint of dark chocolate. Her spine tingled but she made a concerted effort not to inhale deeply and let it consume her.

'Sure,' she lied. 'Are you?' After all, he was the one who didn't know anyone.

He nodded. 'This lot seem like a good bunch, and Heidi said I could help colour in one of her pictures after dinner.'

Simone laughed at the idea of Angus bent over a colouring book. He really was not at all like Logan portrayed him. 'Thanks for agreeing to come to the wedding with Frankie. No-one likes to be alone at these things.'

'I wonder how they're doing?' Angus asked, his voice still low.

'Probably a lot better than if we were there offering assistance,' she replied.

His lips quirked upwards. 'I hear you are almost as bad a chef as me.'

She smiled back. 'I think it's safe to say I'm probably much worse.'

Not long after that, Heidi returned to her new best friend, climbed back up into his lap and resumed her colouring in. As promised, she handed Angus a pencil and instructed him to 'help'.

Simone took a sip of her wine and tried to focus on the conversations going on around her, rather than staring at Angus and Heidi. It was adorable the way he interacted with her, speaking as if she were his equal and asking her opinion on which colour he should use next. And if he'd looked sexy before, he looked even more delicious when his face adopted an expression of deep concentration and he tried not to colour outside the lines. She couldn't help smiling—it was easy to see how he'd have made an awesome surrogate dad for his little sister, but it was sad that he'd never had the opportunity to father his own children. Again she thought of the fiancée who had left him, and wondered why.

Across the table, Ruby and Stella were discussing what time they all needed to be up to get ready tomorrow morning. 'Well, the hair and make-up lady is arriving at seven-thirty,' Stella said.

On the other side, Simone's mum and daughters were trying to work out what movie they would watch tonight and she tried to make the right noises for each suggestion.

'I think I'll get an early night,' Graham said when a recent romantic comedy was decided on.

'You gonna watch too, Mum?' Grace asked.

Ruth jumped in, 'Your mum needs to get an early night as she'll be up at the crack of dawn for hair and make-up.'

Harriet grinned, seemingly pleased with the news her annoying mother wouldn't be joining them. Simone struggled not to feel disheartened by the fact her oldest daughter would rather hang out with anyone but her.

Ruth met her eye and winked over the top of the girls' heads. Not privy to the cake disaster, she still thought Simone and Logan would be sharing a room that night. Instead Simone faced the prospect of going to bed all alone, with not even Frankie next door to talk to. While it would give her another night to rally her courage before taking the next step, it did feel a bit of a let down after all the anticipation. Sighing, she picked up her glass of wine and took a big gulp.

★ ★ ★

Frankie stood in the immaculate kitchen the resort manager had generously offered them and took a deep breath. Now was not the time to start hyperventilating again—she had serious work to do. The afternoon had been a whirlwind: the kangaroo, the cake disaster, meeting Angus and not feeling the instant attraction she was hoping for, then Logan coming up with his plan to save the day.

Which brought them to this moment.

The sexiest guy on the planet, the man she'd been trying to forget since the kiss in her café and who was now going to save her butt, was standing before her, his shirt sleeves rolled up ready to work. She couldn't help glancing down to admire his smooth, tanned, muscular forearms. She squeezed her lips together to stop from whimpering at the sight. *Work, work, work.* She repeated the word in her head, hoping if she thought it enough she'd remember that was the only reason she now faced the prospect of a night alone with Logan Knight. Her insides quivered at the thought and she stood there gawking at him like some mute idiot.

'Shall we get started?' he asked, breaking the awkward silence that had descended the moment they'd ushered Simone and Angus out of the kitchen.

'Yes,' she managed, hoping there wasn't drool on her chin. 'Good idea.'

Logan surveyed the stuff they'd bought that afternoon. They'd cleared out the local IGA of baking supplies and although whatever they created wouldn't be quite the same as the cake she'd dedicated the last two weeks of her life to making, he'd promised her it'd be something spectacular.

'I'm so sorry about this,' she gushed for what had to be about the fifth time in the last hour. Tonight was supposed to be his big night with Simone and she'd hijacked it.

He shrugged one delectable shoulder and hit her with a smile so potent she almost lost her balance. 'Stop apologising. Now, don't be shy about ordering me around. I'm at your service. This is your gig. I'm just the hired help.'

Frankie swallowed as her mind snagged on his declaration. What would he do if she told him she needed him to work in his underwear? She imagined he'd wear snug, black boxers and ... *No!*

She shook her head—self-loathing and guilt squeezing her heart—she shouldn't be imagining *that* at all. He was here with Simone. Her sister, her best friend.

'Okay!' The determined tone was as much for herself as for him. 'First things first—making the cupcakes. I'll start the first batch. Can you turn the oven on and get the patty pans sorted? And then you can start on the stand.'

It had been his idea to make a cupcake tower and when she'd pointed out that they didn't have any kind of stand, he'd promised her a solution for that as well. He'd bought some thick card from the newsagent, several rolls of aluminum foil, ribbon and a sixpack of little glasses. She been dubious but he'd told her to trust him and really, what choice did she have?

'Yes, sir.' He nodded and saluted her, his silliness making her laugh as he dug out the silver patty pans. Maybe this wouldn't be as bad as she'd first imagined—and maybe spending some real time with him would help her see past his incredible looks and the memory of his lips on hers the first time they'd met. She valued her relationship with Simone more than anything in the world and she knew it was wrong to be thinking about her sister's boyfriend in this way.

As Logan got to work, Frankie located the equipment she needed. What a stroke of luck that the person Logan had managed to sweet-talk into lending them her kitchen happened to have a whiz-bang Kenwood mixer and a lot of the other tools they would need. The manager had snuck off to her room when they'd arrived, promising to make herself scarce but telling them to call on her if they couldn't find anything or required assistance. Frankie felt bad about putting the nice woman out, but drastic times called for drastic measures and every time she thought about the sight of the wrecked cake in the back of her car, she remembered how drastic this situation was.

She did not want to be the one to ruin Adam and Stella's wedding day.

'Who taught you to cook?' Logan asked as she began measuring out her ingredients.

'No-one,' she said, embracing his attempt at small talk. 'I think I probably taught myself out of necessity. Apparently Dad was a good cook, but Mum was dismal and when Dad left, I got sick of her boring dinners. She didn't have much imagination in the kitchen, and to give her some due, it's not easy coming up with interesting food for two kids after you've spent the day working—ask Simone. Before I took over, dinner at our place mostly alternated between spaghetti bolognaise with Dolmio's sauce, sausages and instant mashed potatoes, and shepherd's pie, also with instant mash.'

Logan laughed and screwed up his nose. 'What did you cook instead?'

'Oh, everything. I used to experiment with the few ingredients Mum kept in the cupboard and often what I created wasn't half bad. By the time I was ten, I was doing most of the cooking. Mum used to give Simone her bank card and we'd do the food shopping on our own. What about you? How'd you learn?'

'My mum was the opposite of yours,' Logan said, a wistful smile crossing his face. 'She loved cooking and every meal was different and magnificent. I don't remember Dad ever making so much as a piece of toast—and while Angus loved being Dad's right-hand man on the farm, I'd often stay at home with Mum and help make dinner. Much to Dad's disgust, I asked for a recipe book for my tenth birthday, but after Mum died I think he was grateful that he didn't have to worry about putting meals on the table as well as everything else.'

'I can't imagine losing my mum,' Frankie confessed, a chill washing over her at the thought. 'How old were you?'

'I was seventeen. Doing my year twelve exams. She was driving to Perth to take me out to celebrate when a truck hit her head on, on the Brand Highway.'

Frankie couldn't help but gasp at the brutal image. Although she knew Logan's parents were both dead, Simone had never told her the details.

He nodded and his voice cracked a little as he spoke. 'Only consolation is she would have died on impact.'

Frankie's heart went out to him. Although he was speaking about something that happened a long time ago, the expression on his face told her the pain was just as strong as it would have been that day. She wished she could say something, do something to comfort him, but no words seemed right. 'I bet it's not much consolation. I don't know how I'd cope if something like that happened.'

Logan shrugged. 'It wasn't easy. I took a few years off studying and hung about at home, helping Dad and Angus with the farm and my little sister. But life goes on, well, for most of us. Dad couldn't cope. He took his own life a few years later.'

'No!' She couldn't keep the shock from her voice. 'I knew you and Angus raised your sister but I didn't know—'

'He hung himself in the shearing shed,' Logan confessed, glancing down at the benchtop.

'That's awful,' she whispered, her words sounding futile even to her own ears. Silence hung between them a few long moments and then Logan turned his head and met her gaze.

'I'm sorry, I don't know why I'm telling you this. As if today isn't stressful enough.'

Despite the topic of conversation, the way he looked at her took her breath away. Sensations she knew she shouldn't be feeling flooded through her body and at that moment she didn't care about the cake, she only wished Logan would keep looking at her that way, keep opening up his heart.

It wasn't her right to wish this—not when he was here in Kalbarri with her sister—but she couldn't help her feelings, no matter how much she knew they were wrong. And the more time she spent in his company, the worse they got. 'It's fine,' she said, struggling to breathe steadily as she gestured to the mess already forming on the bench. 'We've got hours ahead of us. Gotta keep each other awake somehow.'

His solemn expression transformed into a light one again and he nodded. 'Damn straight. By tomorrow morning we'll have a magnificent cake—or rather, cakes—and I shall know all of your deepest, darkest secrets.'

She shivered at the thought. 'I don't really have any,' she lied, looking away.

'I'll be the judge of that,' Logan said. 'What was the name of your first boyfriend?'

'Adam,' she told him, with a half chuckle.

'Ha! You mean *this* Adam?'

'Yep. At least I wanted him to be my boyfriend, but everyone else told me my cousin couldn't be my boyfriend. It broke my heart.'

She looked up at the expression on his face and smiled as well. 'It's okay, you're allowed to laugh. From a very early age, I've had a habit of falling for Mr Wrong.'

Chapter Fourteen

Angus knew he shouldn't be having this much fun with his brother's girlfriend—not while Logan was slaving away with Frankie fashioning a replacement wedding cake—but he couldn't help himself. Following dinner, Adam's mum Esther had whisked Heidi off to bed and Simone's mum, stepdad and daughters had retreated to their apartment to watch a movie. The bride, groom and their bridal party had chosen to stay on and enjoy a few more drinks. It had been a long time since he'd last sat up with a bunch of adults like this—had a meal and enjoyed the conversation following.

Maybe this was what his life would have been like if his parents hadn't died, if he hadn't ended up as Olivia's guardian, if he and Sarah hadn't suffered their own tragic loss. Things might have been very, very different. He didn't begrudge the sacrifices he'd made for Olivia. To be honest, most of the time he didn't think he missed having a social life, but sitting here with Simone made him wonder if maybe it was time to make some changes.

'Want a top-up?' Simone asked as she pushed back her chair and gestured at his empty bottle.

'Sure, but it's my shout,' he said, standing and reaching into his pocket for his wallet.

She hit him with her potent smile. 'I'm not going to argue with that.'

'Who else wants another one?' Angus asked the rest of their party.

'Actually I think I'll call it a night,' said Faith, who Simone had told him wasn't drinking because she was pregnant.

'Are you okay?' asked her boyfriend, Monty, reaching over to grab her hand, concern in his tone and on his face. Angus remembered feeling anxious and protective when Sarah was expecting, but he pushed that thought aside.

Faith smiled back at Monty. 'I'm fine, just tired. I need my beauty sleep for tomorrow.'

'There's nothing like pregnancy fatigue,' Simone said and Stella nodded her agreement. Angus remembered that too; Sarah had slept and slept and slept.

The others declined another drink and after bidding Faith and Monty goodnight, he headed over to the bar to get their drinks.

'We're just about to close up,' the barman said, as he placed a bottle of beer and another glass of wine on the bar.

'No worries,' Angus said, handing over his money. When he returned to the table he found that Ruby and Drew, and Stella and Adam were also leaving.

Goodnights were exchanged and before he knew it he was all alone with Simone, except for the few staff members wiping and setting tables for the breakfast service.

She glanced around and then looked up at him. 'Do you get the feeling we're not wanted here anymore?'

'Perhaps.'

'Pity. I was enjoying myself and I didn't want to rush this.' She picked up the wine glass he'd just put in front of her and twirled it between her two fingers. 'Do you want to go watch TV or something in my and Frankie's apartment?'

No, his subconscious told him firmly. *Not a good idea.* But he'd had such an enjoyable night and it was still early; he didn't want it to end just yet. Besides, it wasn't like she was offering anything sinister. Just a little bit of TV.

'Okay,' he said, telling himself that he'd sit with her while he finished his beer and then he'd get an early night, maybe stop in on Logan and Frankie and see how the cake making was going.

Without another word, they stood and Angus saw the relieved expressions on the resort staff's faces as he held the door open for Simone.

'Thanks for keeping me company tonight,' she said in a near whisper as they walked quietly down the row of townhouses to her accommodation. Her shoulder was about an inch from his and he'd never felt more aware of another person—at least not for as long as he could remember.

Although it wasn't even eleven o'clock yet, the resort was deserted, everyone already barricaded in their rooms, and Angus felt like a criminal trespassing on someone else's land. Palm trees swished gently in the wind and the beer bottle felt cold in his hand as Simone stopped and fumbled in her pocket for her key.

Ignoring the voice of caution inside his head, he followed her into the apartment as she flicked on the lights. 'Well, here we are,' she said, turning to look at him and then gesturing to the one small couch that occupied the lounge room. 'Make yourself at home.'

'I wonder how Logan and Frankie are doing?' he asked, forcing himself to focus on something other than how amazing Simone looked, standing before him in a flowing hippy-type skirt and a figure-hugging black crochet top. Forcing himself to remember why exactly they were here.

She kicked off her shoes and flopped back onto the couch. 'They'll be fine. If anyone can fix this cake mess, they can. Are you gonna sit?'

In absence of any other chairs, Angus perched on the edge of the couch beside her and took a long drag on his beer. He felt crazily like a young bloke on his first date, which was pathetic, because he wasn't young and this wasn't any kind of date. Simone would probably laugh or feel very uncomfortable if she was aware of some of the thoughts he was trying to suppress.

She leaned forward to retrieve the television remote from the coffee table and her top rode up slightly in the process, giving him a quick glimpse of smooth skin. He sucked in a breath and took another gulp of his beer. Within seconds the television flashed to life and she began to flick through the channels, giving him a moment to think cool thoughts.

'The usual Friday night crap,' she said, settling on one of the Harry Potter movies. 'You seen this before?'

He nodded. 'Liv went through a stage where she was obsessed with the books and the movies. Do your girls like them?'

She leaned back against the couch and pursed her lips a moment. 'I think Grace has read some of them. Frankie gave the whole set to the girls for Christmas one year.'

Angus couldn't help thinking how much Frankie and Logan had in common, including a love of books and culinary talents; far more, it seemed, than Logan and Simone had in common.

'If Harriet's read them,' Simone added, 'I'd be the last person she'd tell.'

Although her tone told him she was trying to make light of this, he saw the hurt in her eyes as she spoke about her older daughter and he desperately wanted to say something to make her smile again. 'Sounds like she's at least read The Teenager's Guide to Making Their Parents Crazy.'

'Hah, yes. I reckon she wrote the book.' Simone nodded as she lifted her glass to her lips. He tried not to focus on the colour or plushness of them as they closed around the rim. What the hell was he doing here?

As Simone drank, so did he, downing the last dregs of his beer. He placed the empty bottle down on the coffee table. 'I suppose I'd better head off,' he said, not making a move to get up.

'Really?' Simone frowned at him. 'Don't leave me all alone with my mother guilt. This weekend was supposed to be fun. Let's have some fun!'

'What do you suggest?' he asked, his chest tightening.

She shrugged one shoulder and her jumper slipped slightly, exposing another glimpse of skin. 'We could play a board game ... if we had any. Do you have any cards on you? I'll whip your butt at poker.'

He made a show of patting his pockets. 'Damn, I think I left them at home.'

She sighed and he racked his brain for a suggestion, wanting to please her more than anything.

'I know,' she said suddenly, grabbing the remote again and flicking through to a music station. 'Let's dance.'

He raised an eyebrow as she leaped to her feet and pushed the coffee table over to the edge of the room. Again, he swallowed as he copped an eyeful of pert butt and smooth naked skin as her top shifted. 'Dance?' She had to be kidding. 'I'm not sure I've had enough to drink.'

'Don't be a spoilsport.' She reached over and grabbed his hand, tugging him to his feet. 'I love dancing. It's good exercise. Consider it practice for tomorrow night.'

'Logan never mentioned anything about dancing,' Angus said, his breath hitching in his throat at the realisation of how close he was to this stunning woman, at the feel of her soft hand in his work-roughened one.

She laughed, rolled her eyes and dropped his hand. 'So you *are* grumpy. Logan said you were, but I refused to believe it. You seemed quite nice to me.'

It was the sweetest compliment anyone had paid him in a long while and as she lifted her arms above her head and started to move her body in time with the music, he found himself trying to do the same. It was a boppy song and he wasn't coordinated at the best of times, and it was hard not to look like a total fool when all he could think about was how damn sexy she was. That long skirt wafted around her feet as she swished her hips from side to side and his mouth went dry. He tried to avert his gaze, but all his eyes wanted to do was zone in on her breasts and the cleavage all too visible in her low-cut top.

Only because she's the first woman you've had much to do with in a while, he told himself. But that wasn't strictly true—there'd been one-night stands in his not too distant past and none of those girls had made him feel like Simone did.

She cocked her head and dropped her hands to one side, looking at him. 'You're not very good at this, are you?'

He scowled, but she flashed her eyes at him, he couldn't help flirting right back. 'You call that dancing?'

Her mouth opened and she perched her hands on her hips. 'Are you insulting my dancing, Angus Knight?'

Fuck, no; he could watch her dance all bloody night. 'It's not bad,' he conceded, 'but not what I'm used to.'

'Oh yeah? And what exactly are you used to?' she asked, grinning.

'They made us learn ballroom dancing at boarding school. You know: the waltz, the tango, stuff like that?'

'Wow, I'm impressed. I always wanted to learn proper dancing.'

'I could teach you,' he offered, cursing the words the moment they were out of his mouth. Just the thought of holding her as close as was required for such an activity made his heart race. Not an appropriate response to your brother's girlfriend.

'Would you?' Her words were barely a whisper and her eyes looked straight into his, making him giddy.

He swallowed. 'We'd need different music.'

Her lower lip dropped in a pout but then right on cue the song on the television changed to a slow ballad, pretty much perfect for their requirements. *Well then …*

Against his better judgement, Angus raised his hands, put one palm against Simone's hip and the other against her shoulder, pulling her close against him. She fit perfectly and she smelt angelic—some kind of floral perfume.

'What now?' she asked, gazing up at him with her soulful green eyes. She had the longest eyelashes and almost invisible smile lines around her eyes. All he could think about was slipping his hand up into her luscious red curls, pulling her head towards him and doing what he'd imagined doing ever since he'd walked into his house and found her snooping in his bedroom.

⋆ ⋆ ⋆

'Mmm … those smell amazing,' Logan said, his stomach growling as Frankie pulled another tray of cupcakes out of the oven, taking their total tally up to a hundred. That was the amount they'd calculated was necessary to make a fabulous cupcake tower, but the hard work—the decorating—was still to come.

Frankie looked at him, her expression like a stern schoolmistress. 'Don't even think about it, mister. No, taste-testing until we're absolutely certain we've got all we need.'

'Come on?' he pleaded. 'What if we accidentally put salt in the mixture instead of sugar? Wouldn't it be better if we found out before it was too—'

'Fine.' Rolling her eyes, she cut him off and plucked one piping hot cupcake out of the tray she'd just placed on the stovetop. 'Knock yourself out. But if it tastes bad, I'm warning you, I'll cry.'

He took the offering, inhaling the delicious aroma of freshly baked chocolate as he peeled off the patty pan. It was so hot his fingers almost burned and he blew gently on the cake before taking a bite. The flavours simply melted on his tongue. Frankie was a baking genius.

'Well?' she asked, her expression anxious as she waited for his verdict.

He made a show of finishing his mouthful, then glanced down at the rest of the cupcake in his hand and frowned. 'They're not good,' he said, deadpan.

'*What?*' Her hand flew to her chest and her eyes widened in horror.

He grinned. 'They're fucking fantastic.' And then he shoved the rest into his mouth, wishing he could devour a few more.

Frankie let out a visible breath and her forehead relaxed as she lifted her hand and socked him hard on the arm. 'You utter shit! I can't believe you did that.'

'Ouch,' he yelped, laughing as he rubbed his arm.

'You deserved that,' she said, her tone lighter now, and he had to concede he did. 'If I didn't need you so much right now, you'd be a dead man.'

'I'm sorry.' He stifled a laugh; the bruise on his arm was worth the expression on her face. It was getting late and his eyes were gritty from fatigue, but he couldn't deny the last few hours together had been fun.

Despite Frankie being a bit of a control freak in the kitchen, they worked well together, and he didn't mind being ordered around by someone as talented as her. As they baked, she'd taught him a few tricks of the trade and, in addition to cooking and reading, they'd found so many other mutual interests that the conversation never waned. Initially she'd been a bit jittery but he'd put that down to stress. They'd talked about everything from the mundane to the intense, from favourite movies to greatest fears and why they'd chosen their careers, and she'd soon relaxed. She'd listened and seemed to understand that although farming was in his blood, he'd hadn't wanted to follow in his father's and grandparents' footprints. It was something his dad and brother had never understood—although their farm couldn't sustain more than one full-time income, he'd always been made to feel guilty for bailing out.

And Frankie had inspired him with her passion and drive to start her own café. After she'd made the statement about always falling for Mr Wrong, he'd pushed her for more details—despite knowing he might be heading into murky waters. She'd confided how she'd fled a broken relationship in Perth, and he'd felt that anger once again towards her ex, even though he'd already heard part of the story from Simone. He hoped one day she'd discover that not all men were cheating scumbags.

After only a few hours of conversation, Logan felt as if he knew Frankie almost as well as, if not better than, he knew Simone.

'Do you want a drink?' he asked, thinking that they both deserved a quick break. Although he'd made it sound like he didn't think creating a wedding cake overnight was an impossible feat, they weren't out of the woods yet. He had grave fears that they could very well miss their deadline. The cake might not be needed until the evening, but Frankie was expected to report for bridesmaid duties bright and early.

'I'd love a coffee,' she said, surveying the mess in front of them. 'And I suppose we should clean this lot up before we get on with the rest of the decorations. Do you think the chocolate will set in time?'

Once again panic crossed her face. 'Of course.' He injected a confidence he didn't feel into his voice as he turned to fill up the kettle. 'But worst-case scenario, the silver cachou and pre-made sugar rosettes will do the trick. I promise.'

'I hope so.'

While he made their drinks, Frankie swiped the empty flour packets and egg cartons into the rubbish bin till it was near bursting.

'Here, I'll take that out,' he said, stooping to collect it. 'You sit down for a few minutes and drink your coffee.'

She sighed and glanced at her watch.

'Two minutes is not going to ruin us,' he said, reading her thoughts. 'You need to recharge.' And so did he.

Relenting, she picked up the steaming mug and perched herself on one of the stools at the breakfast bar while he trekked outside. It was darker than Logan expected and he couldn't find the porch light but he could just make out the rubbish bin in the corner of the yard. He deposited the trash and had almost made it back to the door when he tripped on a pot plant he hadn't seen.

'Shit,' he hissed, as he stumbled to the ground. Instinctively his arms shot out to save him, but his leg hit something hard and sharp on the way down. Annoyed at himself and ignoring the pain that now throbbed just below his knee, he scrambled to his feet, dusted himself off and took a deep breath. He didn't want to have to explain to Frankie what had happened, so he summoned a smile and carefully made his way back inside.

'This is the best. Coffee. Ever,' Frankie announced as he quietly shut the door behind him. She was still perched on the stool, her eyes closed and her fingers wrapped around the mug. His pain all but evaporated as she opened her eyes and hit him with a satisfied smile. If good coffee gave her that expression he could only imagine what good sex would do.

Where did that come from? Cursing the thought the moment it entered his head, he smiled awkwardly and then picked up his own much-needed caffeine. 'I've been meaning to ask you. Did you ever finish *Picnic at Hanging Rock*?' He wanted to distract himself with safe conversation.

She nodded. 'Yep, but I wasn't too sure about the ending. It was weird.'

Mug in hand, he leaned back against the kitchen counter. 'Did you read the chapter that was added after Joan Lindsay's death?'

'I … think I did.'

'That explains it.' He was about to tell her how Lindsay's editor had removed this chapter prior to original publication, and that it was only published posthumously, when Frankie shrieked.

'Oh my God!' Her hand shot to cover her mouth and then she lowered her voice to speak again. 'What have you done to your leg?'

Following her gaze, he looked down to see a dark red patch seeping through his jeans just below his knee. 'I tripped when I went outside.' He shrugged, feigning nonchalance. 'Must have knocked it when I fell.'

'It must have been a pretty hard knock,' she said, placing her mug on the bench and sliding off the stool. 'We should check that out. I wonder if there's a first-aid kit around here.'

Before he could tell her he'd be fine, she started opening and closing cupboards. 'Bingo.' She tucked a small red box under her arm. 'Go sit on one of the dining chairs and I'll take a look.'

Guessing she wouldn't let him ignore this, he did as he was told, sinking into a seat. Luckily these Levis were old and quite loose so he could roll up the cuff and reveal the cut without taking them off. The last thing he needed was to get naked in front of Frankie—they'd barely recovered from his ill-considered kiss.

'Ouch,' she said as she dropped to her knees in front of him and examined his leg. She opened the first-aid kit on the floor beside her and retrieved some tissues. 'I'll be gentle,' she promised as she pressed the tissues against his leg to soak up the blood. 'I hope you don't need stitches.'

'No time for stitches,' he said. 'Here, let me do that.'

As he held the wad of tissue firmly against his leg, she grabbed a tube of antiseptic cream and a large bandage. The bleeding stopped and he scrunched the tissue up in his hand, watching as Frankie squeezed some cream onto her fingers.

The cream was cold and he breathed in sharply as she touched it to his wound, but his reaction was as much about her fingers brushing against his skin than the chill. *Oh Jesus. This isn't good.*

'Is that okay?' She glanced up at him as she rubbed the cream into his leg. As he gazed down at her, he could barely even remember why she was doing it, his eyes drawn to the sweet curve of her lips. The memory of the day they'd met landed once again in his head and his chest tightened at the thought. He still couldn't believe he'd just walked in and done that without first making sure who she was—hell, he couldn't believe he'd done it full stop. But there'd just been something about Frankie that had caused all his common sense and propriety to take a hike.

And that something still lingered between them, no matter how much he liked and respected Simone, no matter how much he tried to ignore it.

'I'm fine,' he managed. 'I'm sure it's not as bad as it looks.' He willed her to get the bandage on quickly so he could tug down his jeans, stand up and put some space between them before he did something stupid. This wasn't right.

'There,' she said, smiling as she pressed gently at the edges of the bandage. Her grin did crazy things to his insides. 'But smoko's over now. It's time to get back to work.'

That was a very good idea. Even if Frankie did feel the same connection he did—and he had no idea if that were the case—they had a cake to make and he couldn't forget that the only reason he was even here was because of her sister.

Logan nodded and yanked down his jeans, wincing as the material scraped against his wound. Right now, a little gash was the least of his worries.

Chapter Fifteen

Simone wasn't sure who kissed who first but Angus's lips were on hers and she could no longer think straight. As the music blared on the TV behind them, all she could register was the feel of his hard body pressed against her and the tantalising slide of his tongue into her mouth. He tasted of beer and the steak he'd had for dinner. Nothing had ever tasted so good. Sensations she hadn't been sure she'd ever feel again flooded her body, spurring her hands to sneak their way into his hair and deepen the kiss even more. The coarse hair of his beard rubbed against her face, driving her wild as she imagined how it would feel on other parts of her body.

His hands slid from her face, not at all gentle or reserved as they skimmed over her shoulders and came to land on her breasts. His thumbs tweaked her nipples through the wool of her crochet jumper and she felt them harden beneath his touch.

'Oh God,' she panted, wanton need flooding her as she pushed herself closer to him and felt what was undeniably an erection pressing into her belly. It had been so long since she'd felt anything of the sort and her thighs pressed together in anticipation. She wanted it. She wanted him. Nothing else mattered right now except the need consuming her body. Her lady bits throbbed with desire and breathing didn't seem nearly as necessary as tasting and touching him.

Indicating he felt exactly the same, Angus pushed her back against the wall behind them and dropped his lips to her neck, scorching her bare skin as he tasted her. She moaned, her head rolling back as her hands palmed the wall for fear that if she didn't hold onto something, she'd collapse.

And then—oh then—he lifted her jumper and the thin cotton T-shirt beneath it right over her head, exposing her breasts in their silky red bra.

'Fuck, you're beautiful,' he all but breathed as he raised his head to admire her. She smiled up at him, every part of her burning for him as she registered the desire in his eyes. She felt more desirable than she had in years and couldn't bring herself to reply, so instead she reached out and ran her hand down his chest.

Rock-hard muscle rippled beneath her touch, spurring her to go lower. Still lost in his gaze, she pressed her hand against the mound in his jeans and he swore again, before dipping his head and capturing her mouth. His tongue duelling with hers, she moved her hand slowly up and down and then boldly planted it inside his waistband. She heard his sharp intake of air and it corresponded with hers as she felt his hot, silky length. Every cell in her body quivered as she closed her hand around him and squeezed hard. It had been so long since she'd held a man in this way and she'd forgotten the power it invoked. The fact she could make him hard and desperate was a heady drug and, like an addict, she wanted more.

Stilling her hand and reluctantly tearing her lips from his, she looked into his eyes. 'I think we should take this into the bedroom.'

Angus nodded and offered her his hand so she could lead him.

He'd barely kicked the door shut behind them before their lips reconnected and their hands were all over each other again. There was little finesse as they stripped off their clothes. They didn't make it to the bed, dragging each other to the floor, which thankfully was covered in a plush, thick carpet. Simone wouldn't have cared if there were hard, icy-cold tiles beneath them.

She reached for Angus, pulling him down so his heavy length was pressed against her as he once again kissed her into oblivion. Their legs entwined, their hands roved over each other, touching intimately yet barely making an indent in their cravings.

He explored her neck, her breasts, her less-than-perfect belly, yet every sound he made was one of admiration. She raked her fingers over his back, cupped his tight buttocks and yanked him against her so that his erection was almost inside her. But as his lips found hers again, he slipped his hand between their sweat-soaked bodies and touched her in a way that made her cry out.

'You like?' he asked, his voice low as he pulled back to look at her.

If not for the sliver of moonlight sneaking in through a gap in the curtains they'd have been in pitch darkness, but her eyes had acclimatised enough that she could see him and what she saw she liked, very much. She nodded and his lips twisted into an assured grin as he resumed his efforts, delving his finger deep inside her.

Pleasure rippled through her as he touched her exactly how, exactly where, she needed. It wasn't long before her breathing quickened and she was quivering beneath his touch. She cried out, digging her nails into his shoulders as he covered his mouth with hers, silencing her scream.

She couldn't remember ever being so vocal during sex—granted it had been a long time—but Angus brought out the wild animal in her. Hungry for more, she clung to him as she wrapped her legs around him. His penis slid right into her and she moaned as her body accommodated him.

He felt enormous. He felt divine.

They began to move together, her butt rubbing against the carpet as another orgasm rose within her. Angus knew all the right buttons to push. All her nerves and anxieties about sleeping with a man again flew out of the window as they came in spectacular unity. Had that ever happened before?

'Jesus,' Angus hissed, his breath hot against her neck. And that pretty much summed up everything going through Simone's mind as well.

As they lay there together, their bodies slick, their hearts racing and the scent of sex emanating off them, she couldn't quite believe what she'd just done. Had she jumped into bed—or rather fallen to the floor—with Angus because she'd overindulged on wine? Part of her wished she could accept this explanation but she'd only had a few glasses and …

Who was she kidding? There'd been something between the two of them from the moment she'd laid eyes on him—a spark that hadn't been there when she'd met Logan, or if she was honest with herself, when she'd thought herself in lust with Ryan. The feelings Angus ignited didn't take any effort whatsoever. And fighting them had been impossible.

'We didn't use a condom,' Angus whispered after a long silence.

'It's okay,' she replied, 'I'm safe.' She'd only just finished her period, which was a good thing, considering she'd given not one thought to contraception until now. She'd gone on the pill briefly last year, when it looked like she and Ryan were getting closer, but she was so damn terrible at remembering to take it that she'd stopped. Since then, she hadn't needed to worry about such things and she'd never considered that when she finally had sex again it would be like this—on the floor with the brother of the man she was supposed to be dating.

She pushed that guilty thought aside, not wanting to ruin the moment. Obviously this was something she would need to address but right now the only thing she wanted to address was the delicious male lying on top of her. Already she felt her desire rising once again. She cupped his face and pressed her lips to his, a non-verbal thanks for making her feel alive, making her feel like a woman again.

* * *

It was turning into the longest night of Frankie's life. Not because of the stressful situation with the cake or the fact she'd been awake hours past her bedtime, but because being alone with Logan set every cell in her body on fire.

One minute they were working hard, chatting amicably and the next minute there was weirdness between them. There'd definitely been weirdness when she'd been tending his cut. It had taken everything she had to stop her hands shaking, every ounce of her self-control to stop from curling her fingers around his calf and running her hand up and down his leg. Good grief! What would he have thought if she'd done so? What would Simone say if she knew how Frankie's mind had been working when it should have been focusing on the cake? Her sister had willingly given up a night of hot sex with her boyfriend so that Frankie didn't have a nervous breakdown, and what did she do to repay her? Kept imagining she was having hot sex with him instead.

It was an honest-to-God miracle she'd achieved anything over the last few hours.

And the worst thing of it all was she couldn't work out whether the weirdness was just her or whether Logan felt it also. Occasionally when she'd looked up from a task, she'd caught him watching her and their gazes had held a fraction too long. She'd swear she felt an actual electrical impulse between them but then Logan would look away again, go back to whatever it was he was doing, and she'd convince herself that any feelings he might have for her were platonic or concoctions of her vivid imagination.

And that made her feel like weeping because after hours in his company, she hadn't discovered he told really bad jokes or was in a secret cult or watched *Magic Mike* in his free time. She hadn't discovered anything remotely unlikeable about him, except the fact he was clumsy in the dark—and even that was kind of adorable. Instead, her inappropriate feelings had multiplied a zillionfold.

Thank God they were finally finished and, despite her distraction, had somehow managed the impossible and created a beautiful cupcake tower that made her throat close over with emotion when she looked at it. If anything, it was better than what she'd spent the last week or so labouring over, and much of that was down to Logan. He'd excelled himself, not only by being her assistant, but by fashioning the most amazing cupcake stand. Looking at their magnificent creation now, she had to squeeze her eyelids together to stop herself from crying.

'Hey.' She felt Logan take a step closer to her and every organ in her body froze as he placed a comforting arm around her shoulder. 'There's no need to cry. We did it. You might even get a few hours' sleep before having to report for bridesmaid duties.'

Just the way he said 'we'—as if they were a team—made her shiver. In response he rubbed his palm up and down her arm, which only made her more emotional. She sniffed, opened her eyes and turned her head to look at him. He was so close she could see the fine hairs of stubble poking out of his chin and the speckles of grey in his dark eyes.

'I'm crying because I'm—' She meant to say 'happy' but the word died on her tongue. Yes, she was relieved about the cake, but her heart ached with the knowledge that Logan was off-limits. It was bitterly cruel that she'd met the man of her dreams and once again, he was unavailable. Talk about Mr Wrong.

'I know …' he whispered, and her aching heart stilled as he lifted a hand and cupped it against her cheek, meeting her gaze with his own intent one.

Before Frankie knew what was happening, their lips met with what felt like an electric shock. A very pleasurable one that turned every bone in her body to jelly. His lips were soft but firm and sweet on her mouth and his hands cupped her face as if she were the most precious thing in the world. She'd imagined this moment a hundred times, yet nothing compared to the reality. She closed her eyes as his tongue swept along the line of her lips. Whimpering inside, she opened for him, wanting to enjoy the taste of him, wanting this moment to never end, but …

This is wrong. Wrong. Wrong. Wrong.

Alarm bells sounded loud and clear inside her head. Her conscience warred with her body—her brain yelling at her to pull back, while her hormones screamed like wild banshees for her to keep going. She despised cheaters, and here she was kissing her sister's boyfriend. She couldn't hate herself more.

Logan must have realised what they were doing at the same moment, for he tore his mouth from hers and huffed out a breath. Then they simply stared at each other, neither of them saying anything for quite some time. The room was silent—all Frankie could hear was the frantic beating of her own heart. Her fingers tingled with the need to touch him, yet this time she summoned all her willpower to resist.

'Sorry,' Logan said finally, rubbing his hand over his jaw. 'That was …'

Lovely. Amazing. Magical. Even better than the first time we kissed? Because this time he wasn't just a pretty face. This time he was a man she truly liked and respected.

'Wrong?' she finished for him. 'I know.' Her voice cracked on the admission as guilt swept over her.

He took a deep breath, his eyes undeniably hot with desire. 'But good.'

'So good,' she whispered back, unable to tear her gaze from his. She wanted him more than she'd ever wanted any man— any*thing*—in her life, and the way he kissed her, the way he looked at her, told her he felt exactly the same way.

He took a step back, putting necessary distance between them. 'If only we'd met earlier, under different circumstances. I'd be lying if I didn't admit I have really strong feelings for you,' he continued. 'I have done since the day we met, but I've tried to ignore them, not wanting to hurt Simone.'

'Me too.' Frankie's eyes burned with tears again as she nodded. Hurting her sister was the last thing she ever wanted to do. What a god-awful mess!

'The last few hours with you have been so much fun, but also infuriating. Being near you drives me crazy, but my feelings aren't simply carnal, they run way deeper than that.'

She understood. She felt exactly the same. In any other situation, his words would have been music to her ears, but she heard the 'but' behind them and knew what was coming.

'But I've been cheated on before,' Logan said, 'and it's awful. I know you don't want to sneak around behind Simone's back any more than I do.'

'Of course not,' she whispered, thanking the Lord that one of them had some restraint, as she wasn't sure she'd have stopped if he hadn't. 'So what do we do now?'

Although she didn't want to hurt Simone, he couldn't be considering staying with her, could he? Not now. There was no way Frankie could cope if she had to keep seeing him and pretend she didn't want to jump his bones. And then there was acting normal around Simone—that was going to be hard enough. They'd never had secrets from each other, but this kiss was one thing she would have to take to the grave.

'I'm going to end it with her,' he said and all she could do was nod again, relief combining with the terrible guilt that was weighing down her heart.

But that relief was short-lived. She wasn't stupid. She knew as well as he did that he couldn't dump her sister and then start going out with her the very next day. 'And ... after that?'

The way he looked at her made her heart skip a beat. 'I want to pursue this with you, Frankie. More than anything. But I don't want to come between you and Simone. What do *you* think we should do?'

She sighed. That was the million-dollar question. What was the protocol in situations like this? Was there a specific time period they should wait before announcing they were seeing each other? Would they find the answer on Google or were they being ridiculous even contemplating getting together?

'I want to be with you too,' she admitted, 'but I'm not sure how to make that happen without hurting the closest person in the world to me.' It broke her heart confessing this, but right now the thing she wanted most in the world seemed impossible.

'I understand.' Logan smiled sadly and reached out. She felt his hand close around hers. He squeezed gently and although his warmth enveloped her, this time it was a show of support, not the start of something else. 'Let's just get through the weekend,' he said. 'I'll talk to Simone and we'll take it from there.'

'Okay.' She extracted her hand from his for fear that if she didn't, she'd never want to let go. Who knew for how long the memories of this kiss would have to be enough. 'Thank you again for helping me with the cake.'

'It was my pleasure,' he said. 'I didn't want to be anywhere else. Now, let's get you to bed. Don't think about the cake again. I'll get Angus to help me carry it over to the function room and I promise you we'll get it there safely.'

Despite her eyes struggling to stay open and her limbs heavy with fatigue, Frankie couldn't help wishing she was taking Logan to bed with her. Something fluttered low in her belly at the thought. How the hell she'd get any sleep after what had just almost happened between them, she didn't know. She only hoped that tomorrow she'd make it through the day on adrenalin.

After one final look of admiration at their creation, Frankie and Logan left the cottage, closing the door quietly behind them.

It was four o'clock in the morning and still pitch dark outside. Logan got out his phone and used his flashlight app to light the way for them out of the manager's courtyard, which was adjacent to the rest of the resort.

Once they were in the main complex, a row of low garden lights that edged the paths between the villas lit the way.

'Do you want me to walk you to your room?' Logan asked.

'No, I'll be fine.' *Safer not to*, Frankie thought. Somewhere in the distance she heard the eager crow of a rooster. 'I'll see you in a few hours.'

'You will.' He looked down at her and for a moment she wondered if he might kiss her again, but instead he sighed, shoved his hands in his pockets, turned and stalked in the direction of the villa he was sharing with Angus.

It wasn't cold but she shivered as she watched him go.

* * *

The sound of the key turning in the apartment door startled Angus and Simone from their bubble of bliss. Reality struck like a hard blow to the side of his head as he looked down at the beautiful woman in his arms. She froze and her eyes widened as if she too had just realised exactly what they'd done. While they'd been in the throes of passion, alternating between dozing and having sex for what felt like hours on end, they'd entirely forgotten the world around them, the people they loved. But now the truth of the situation came crashing in.

He was a bastard of the highest order, sleeping with his brother's girl, and he had to get out of there quick fast.

'Frankie,' she whispered, her tone urgent.

But he was already on the edge of the bed, scrambling around in the dark for his clothes. Simone switched on the bedside lamp and he found his jeans, his jocks and shirt. He shoved them on in record time, fumbling with the buttons, making the mistake of turning around while he did so. Simone was sitting up in bed, her face pale and the sheet tugged up around her neck, but it was thin and the curve of her breasts was visible through the sheet, her nipples still peaked, reminding him of moments earlier, when he'd had them in his mouth.

God, she was hot. Recalling how she'd tasted had his dick hardening again, but that didn't make what they'd done right.

'I'm sorry,' he whispered, needing to say something, but not wanting to risk Frankie hearing that Simone had a guest.

She shook her head. 'It's okay. It takes two to tango.'

He half-smiled. They'd barely gotten through the first waltz before he'd kissed her—or had she kissed him? He couldn't recall, but they certainly hadn't made it to the tango. 'It shouldn't have happened.'

'I know.'

She sounded close to tears and all he wanted to do was climb back into bed, take her into his arms and comfort her, but that was a stupid idea for so many reasons.

Number one: his brother.

Number two: he didn't get close to women anymore. Sex, yes; when he needed to scratch the itch, he knew where to find some-one, no strings attached. But this thing with Simone felt terrify-ingly like more than just sex. Simply being around her had him losing control of all his senses.

'Look,' he said, perching on the edge of the bed as he began to tug on his socks and boots. 'Don't beat yourself up too much. No-one need ever know about this. I don't want to ruin things between you and Logan—'

'Logan!' Simone's eyes widened. 'I can't continue things with Logan after this.'

He lifted a finger to his lips to remind her to keep her voice down. The last thing they needed was Frankie walking in. 'Okay.

Whatever. That's your prerogative.' Guilt swamped him at the thought that he'd ruined his little brother's chance at love. He wasn't sure how he was ever going to look Logan in the eye again. Hell, he was no better than Loretta. 'But nothing more can happen between us, you understand that right?'

'Of course.' A cocktail of anger and hurt flashed in her eyes. 'No more Knight brothers for me.'

Her breasts heaved in annoyance and he sucked in a breath, muscles all over his body tightening at the sight. Simone saw and yanked the sheet higher up around her neck, folding her arms over her chest as she glared at him.

'Sorry.' He looked away, silently cursing as he finished pulling on his boots. Then he stood, shoved his hands in his pockets and lingered awkwardly.

'Waiting for something?'

He nodded towards the door. 'What if Frankie's still out there?'

'Oh. Shit.' She pursed her lips a moment, then, 'Turn around while I get dressed.'

It seemed pointless when he'd already seen every last inch of her naked, but he did as he was told while Simone found something to wear.

'Wait here,' she said after a moment and then he heard the door open and close again.

He let out a long breath, his heart hammering. He'd climb out the window if they didn't have those damn locks that prohibited them opening the whole way.

After what felt like an eternity, Simone returned, looking frustratingly sexy in a pair of stripy pink flannel pyjamas and holding the black top he'd yanked off her. 'Good find,' he whispered, nodding towards the top, offering her a conciliatory smile.

She didn't return it. 'Frankie must have gone straight to bed. She's probably knackered. The coast's clear.'

He nodded as Simone opened the bedroom door and gestured for him to go through it. Although part of him couldn't wait to escape, it felt wrong just … leaving. He paused in the doorway and looked down at her but she refused to meet his gaze. The word 'sorry' lingered again on his tongue, but he couldn't completely regret what had happened between them, so he swallowed it and kept walking.

He'd only taken a few steps when she rushed up behind him.

'What if Logan sees or hears you come in?' she whispered.

Fuck. He hadn't thought of that. This deception game was hard; he didn't know how anyone managed it on a long-term basis. He glanced down at his outfit, wondering if he could get away with saying he couldn't sleep and had gone for an early run. Logan wasn't stupid.

'I'll work something out,' he promised, turning to meet Simone's gaze yet again. 'You try to get some rest.' Lord knew they'd all need their energy to get through tomorrow.

'Okay. Good luck.' Her voice was softer this time and it only made leaving even harder.

'Thanks,' he whispered, resisting the urge to reach out and squeeze her hand. If he touched her again, who knew what kind of trouble they would land in. Without another word, he let himself out into the early morning.

Angus felt like a burglar sneaking into the villa he and Logan had rented. His heart raced and his fingers shook as he turned the key in the door, trying to be as quiet as possible. But his efforts were for nothing.

'Where the hell have you been?' Logan asked from where he was perched on the edge of the tiny couch, drinking a coffee. He looked as tired as Angus felt.

'Couldn't sleep in the strange bed, thought I'd go for a run. You guys finished then?'

Ignoring the question, Logan raised an eyebrow. 'In yesterday's clothes?'

'I didn't pack suitable exercise gear,' he said, thinking quickly, 'so I just threw these on again.'

'You could've brushed your hair before you went out,' Logan said with a slight chuckle.

Angus's hand automatically went up to touch his hair, which he guessed looked ruffled because of what he'd just been up to with Simone. Thank God it was his brother not his sister he had to answer to. Olivia would have taken one look and known he was hiding something. Even when she was little she'd always had an uncanny ability to read her brothers like they were picture books. 'Didn't think I'd see anyone.' He forced lightness into his voice. 'How'd you and Frankie go with the cake?'

Logan smiled. 'All right. It looks pretty damn good actually.'

'That's great.' It felt so wrong talking about cake after the way he'd just betrayed his brother. He'd never felt more like scum in his life. Angus faked a yawn. 'I think the exercise worked, I'm ready to hit the sack now. See you in a few hours, hey?'

Logan nodded. 'See you, bro. Thanks for coming up here with me. I owe you one. Sweet dreams.'

'You too,' Angus managed before retreating into his room and letting out a deep breath as he closed the door behind him. Maybe he should have come clean. Confessed his sins and let Logan punch him in the face or whatever he felt like doing. There was no doubt he deserved whatever his brother would dish out, but he couldn't bear to hurt him.

Logan and Olivia were all he had in the world, and he never wanted to do anything again to jeopardise that. They were all he needed and all he wanted—anyone else would come with a risk he wasn't prepared to take.

Chapter Sixteen

'Rise and shine, sleepy head.'

Simone groaned at the sound of Frankie banging on her bedroom door. She sounded way too chirpy for someone who'd been up most of the night making cake.

'I need coffee,' Simone called back.

'On it. Now get your butt into the shower.'

With another groan, she rolled over in bed, resisting the urge to pull the covers up over her head and bury herself there for the day. She should be excited about watching Stella and Adam tie the knot, but the thought of facing Angus and Logan had her stomach twisting in knots.

The only way she was going to get through the day was to pretend last night hadn't happened. Which would be simple, if muscles she'd forgotten existed weren't currently crying out from overuse.

'Oh *Lord*.' She shook her head at her stupidity as she dragged herself out of bed and escaped into the adjoining bathroom. Moments later she was standing under the hot water, wishing it would ease her aching body, wake her up and somehow miraculously wash away the memories of Angus's touch.

But no matter how much her brain wanted to forget, her body had other ideas. As she swept the soap over her skin, she shivered, recalling how wonderful Angus's tongue and hands had felt exploring every nook and cranny. He'd well and truly broken her sexual drought and she was turning herself on just thinking about it. Annoyed, she wrenched off the hot water and shrieked as ice-cold shards rained down on her.

'You okay?' Frankie called through the door.

'Yep—just dropped the soap on my foot,' she replied as she turned off the water.

'Did you have a visitor here last night?'

Simone froze, stark naked, as she reached for the fluffy white towel on the rack. How the hell had Frankie known?

'There's a wine glass and a beer bottle on the coffee table.'

She let out a sigh of relief, but kicked herself at the same time for not thinking about this evidence when she'd retrieved her jumper. 'Angus came back to watch a little bit of TV,' she said, trying to sound nonchalant. 'Everyone else left and they wanted to close the restaurant so we brought our last drinks here.'

Praying that Frankie would accept this excuse, Simone started vigorously drying herself. Although she desperately wanted to confide in someone, she could never tell her sister what had happened as Frankie had a black-and-white view of cheating. Understandable, considering how she'd unwittingly been the other woman in an illicit affair, but this felt so different to that situation. It wasn't like she and Logan were married—hell, they'd barely even kissed.

'Right. Hurry up then. We're supposed to be at Stella's already for hair and make-up.'

'Coming!' Simone turned to check herself in the mirror for any evidence of Angus. They'd completely lost their heads last night and given no thought to anything except their raw need for each other. Explaining the beer bottle had been one thing, but a love bite on her neck would be an entirely different matter.

A couple of minutes later, she stepped out into the living area to see a steaming mug of coffee on the table in place of the empty bottle and glass. Frankie was sitting on the couch, looking like she could fall asleep at any moment, despite her insistence that they needed to hurry.

'How'd the cake turn out?' Simone asked as she picked up the mug and took a long, much-needed sip. With only a few hours' sleep, she'd need gallons of caffeine to make it through the day.

'Good,' Frankie replied, not even turning her head to look at Simone. 'Amazing, even.'

'You must be so exhausted,' Simone said, feeling guilty that while her supposed boyfriend and sister had been slaving away in the kitchen all night, she'd barely given them a thought.

'I'll be fine.' She all but leaped off the couch, almost making Simone spill her coffee. 'Come on, let's go.'

Frankie had crossed the room and flung open the door before Simone could finish her next mouthful. Figuring she could make another cuppa once they got to Stella's room, Simone put the mug down on the table and hurried after her.

At not quite eight o'clock, the air outside still had a bite to it but Simone barely noticed, still hot from her nocturnal activities. She had to walk fast to keep up with Frankie, who seemed to be a little jumpy. Simone put this down to lack of sleep and the stress of the whole cake fiasco. They arrived at Stella's villa and Simone waited behind Frankie as she rapped loudly on the front door.

It opened almost immediately, and there stood Faith, looking far too alive for a woman who was supposedly suffering morning sickness.

'Hello,' she sang and then frowned. 'You two look terrible.'

'Geez, thanks,' Simone replied. 'Love you too.'

'Sorry.' Faith slapped a hand over her mouth. 'Ever since Monty knocked me up I seem to have a habit of speaking first and thinking later.'

Simone forced a laugh.

'Which means we do look crap, you just wish you hadn't said it. Well, I don't know what her excuse is but I've been up all night,' Frankie said, before marching past them into the villa.

'What's up her nose?' Faith asked, surprised because Frankie rarely got grumpy.

'It's a long story, which I'm sure will come out later, but please be kind to her.' Simone gave Faith a quick hug, vowing to forget about the night before and focus on the day ahead. 'Is the hair and make-up lady here yet? How's the bride?'

Faith grinned. 'Crazy excited. I'm not sure who's worse, her or Heidi. It's like they've both overdosed on red jelly beans. Come on.' She linked arms with Simone and led her into the lounge area, which although bigger than the one in Frankie and Simone's apartment, was already looking crowded.

'Aunty Simmo!' Having just unwrapped herself from Frankie, Heidi rushed over to Simone and wrapped her arms around her. 'We're getting married today.'

Simone laughed at the way Heidi said 'we' and scooped the little girl into her arms. 'I know,' she said, wiping some hair out of her eyes. 'I can't wait to see you in your pretty dress. You're gonna look like a princess.'

'Princess Heidi,' squealed the little girl, squirming to get out of Simone's arms and back to the action.

'Frankie, Simone, this is Camille,' Stella said, waving at them from her position on a stool in the middle of the room.

The pink-haired woman wielding a hair dryer glanced up from her task and smiled at the sisters. 'Love your red hair,' she gushed. 'I have clients pay big bucks for that colour.'

'I'd pay big bucks to get rid of it,' Frankie replied, slumping onto the couch. 'If the upkeep wouldn't be more trouble than it's worth.'

'Thanks,' Simone said, then turned to Ruby, who was standing in the kitchen, placing croissants on a tray. 'Is the kettle on? Frankie and I are in dire need of caffeine.'

Ruby wriggled her eyebrows suggestively. 'That's right,' she said, 'how was your big night, Simmo?'

Simone blushed. 'Fine. Did you sleep well?'

'Perfectly, thank you,' Ruby replied, exchanging a look with Faith before they both sniggered. 'But we're more interested in *your* night.'

'Yes.' Faith nodded, resting her hands on her bump as she leaned back against the kitchen counter. 'What was it like? Was Logan worth the wait? What time did he get here?'

Her cheeks burning, Simone thought she might be sick. Just hearing Logan's name amplified the guilt she was already struggling with. She should just tell them that nothing had happened, but that would only invoke a plethora of further questions. Maybe she could admit that she wasn't feeling it for Logan anymore— which was true, but what if someone said something to him before she had a chance to talk to him? He'd be hurt and embarrassed. And she certainly couldn't tell them about Angus, because Frankie was supposed to be taking him to the wedding.

She nodded towards Heidi. 'I don't think this discussion is one for little ears, do you?'

'Don't mind Heidi,' piped up Stella. 'This'll all go over her head. And I'm desperate to hear the gossip as well.'

'Um … well … I …'

'Will you guys just leave Simone alone?' Frankie glared from where she'd collapsed onto the couch. 'Listen to yourselves. You sound like a bunch of teenage girls. If Simone doesn't want to talk, then back the hell down.'

Simone blinked at Frankie's outburst, although she appreciated the sentiment.

'Oh, God, I'm sorry, Stella,' Frankie rushed, running a hand through her hair, which didn't even look like she'd bothered to brush it that morning. 'I'm just tired after being up all night.'

Stella, Ruby and Faith raised their eyebrows in unison. 'Why were *you* up all night?'

'Did you and Angus—'

'No!' Frankie interrupted before Stella could finish. She looked appalled by the idea and Simone was thankful no-one was looking at her.

'Did the migraine keep you up?'

Frankie looked momentarily confused.

Simone jumped in to save her. 'That's why you had to skip dinner last night. The migraine, remember?'

Frankie must have been too tired to carry on the charade. 'I'm sorry, Stella, there was an accident with the cake yesterday,' she admitted, her shoulders slumping.

'What?' Stella's eyes widened and her hand rushed to her mouth. Until now she'd been the absolute opposite of a Bridezilla but something in her eyes told Simone she could be capable of losing it if hit with an emergency this close to the actual wedding.

'Oh no,' Ruby said.

'Cake?' Heidi asked eagerly.

Camille switched off the hair dryer and looked like she was enjoying the drama.

'Relax,' Simone said, taking a step closer to Frankie. 'It's all good now. Isn't it?' Preoccupied with her own thoughts, she hadn't really paid much attention when she'd asked about the cake earlier. She'd just assumed they'd conquered the task.

'Yes, it's beautiful.' Frankie nodded, pulling out her mobile phone. She stood up and crossed the room to shove an image under Stella's nose. 'I stayed up all night with Logan making a new one. It's not the same as the original but I hope you like it almost as much.'

Simone's heart stopped as she waited for the bride's reaction. The room was deadly silent for about ten seconds and then a smile burst across Stella's face.

'Oh, my.' She pressed a hand against her chest and sounded close to tears. 'I love it. I think I love it more than the original. And if people don't want to eat their share at the reception, it'll be so much easier to give them a cupcake to take home. Oh Frankie, I can't believe you did this for me.'

'It was the least I could do,' Frankie said, a tear snaking down her cheek.

Stella reached up and hugged her. 'You must be exhausted. Ruby, where's that coffee? Or would you like to go take a quick nap and we'll do your hair and make-up last?'

Frankie shook her head and wiped her eyes with the back of her hand. 'I think if I nap, I might not wake up. Caffeine will have to be my friend today because I don't want to miss a moment of all this excitement.'

Not long after that, Ruth arrived with Aunty Esther, Harriet and Grace in tow, so thankfully there was no more questioning about Simone's non-existent fooling around with Logan. She didn't know how people kept secrets for years; this one was already eating her up inside. She hugged her daughters, happy to see them, even if Harriet didn't return the feeling.

'Breakfast is served,' Faith announced as she and Ruby carried two trays of warm pastries over to the table, where there was already freshly squeezed orange juice and a big bowl of fruit salad.

The hair and make-up progress was halted long enough for Stella to scoff a croissant. Simone watched as everyone else ate; all the emotions churning through her stomach made eating impossible.

'I wish I had your metabolism,' Aunty Esther said as Grace polished off her second large croissant in a matter of minutes.

'We used to once upon a time, sis,' Ruth said, sitting down between her granddaughters. 'Remember? Mum used to say we all had hollow legs when we were teenagers.'

Esther nodded. 'Certainly not the case anymore.' But she picked up an apple Danish anyway. 'You're growing into quite a beautiful young lady, Gracie. You've lost all your puppy fat since I last saw you.'

Grace blushed and Harriet perked up. 'What about me?'

'You're tall and slender and gorgeous as well,' Ruth said, patting Harriet's hand. 'Just like your mother.'

As Grace slipped out of the room, Harriet made a face, showing her grandmother exactly what she thought about that comparison. Simone was too tired to laugh or cry, so she took another long gulp of coffee and retreated to the couch to sit next to Heidi, who was playing some kind of drawing game on an iPad. At least Heidi wouldn't grill her about her love life.

Stella's hair done, Faith took her turn in the hot seat and Ruby, Esther and Ruth cleared up the breakfast mess, but Simone barely registered the buzz of conversation around her. She was in her own little world till Harriet marched out of the bathroom.

'Have you got morning sickness, Faith?' she accused, her arms perched on her hips like a proper madam.

'Huh?' Faith looked up from where Camille was brushing her hair.

'The bathroom reeks of vomit.'

'Harriet, don't be so rude,' Simone yelled, tired of her daughter's insolence. She didn't want Harriet ruining Stella's day and she really wasn't in the mood to deal with her teenage dramatics right now.

'Yes, why are you always so horrible?' Grace asked, glaring at her sister.

'I think I'm finally over morning sickness actually.' Faith shrugged, offering a conciliatory smile. 'I've been fine the last couple of days.'

'Well, I definitely smelt *something*.'

'Everyone else feeling okay?' Stella asked, glancing between them.

They all nodded; Simone did feel a little queasy—she wasn't sure if it was the alcohol or everything else—but she'd have known if she'd thrown up.

'In that case,' Ruby said, holding up a bottle of champagne. 'Who's for a little pre-wedding bubbly?'

★ ★ ★

At ten o'clock, after five hours of tossing and turning in bed, Logan gave up the pretence of sleep and ventured out into the living space of their rented villa. Angus's door was still shut, so he filled the kettle and switched it on, hoping the smell of coffee would rouse him. He needed his brother's help to transport the cake from the resort manager's house to the function room where the staff would no doubt already be setting up for the reception. And he needed to do that soon, so they had time to come back and get ready for the one o'clock ceremony on the beach.

He grabbed a couple of mugs out of the overhead cupboard and then leaned against the counter and groaned. Damn, today was going to be interesting. At some stage he needed to tell Simone that he didn't think things were working out between them, but he had no idea when the right time would be. Breaking up at a wedding didn't seem the done thing, but he couldn't let things continue the way they were. He liked her—just not in the way he liked Frankie—and he didn't want to ruin her weekend, or lead her on. They'd had a lot of fun together, but he had to concede Simone was more like the big sister he'd never had than the lover he wanted.

He'd pursued things with her for longer than he should have because they'd clicked so well online and also because he'd wanted to prove something to Angus. He'd wanted to show his brother that he wasn't flighty and irresponsible and that his ideas should be taken seriously. But in his drive and determination to achieve that, he'd ignored the fact that he and Simone simply didn't have the spark necessary for a relationship.

Fuck. What a mess. The kettle started whistling and the noise brought Angus out of his room.

'Morning.' Logan nodded to his brother, who looked as bad as Logan felt. You'd have thought they'd both been on all-night benders. He didn't know what was messing with Angus's mind and he doubted he'd tell him even if he asked. Perhaps Angus was simply regretting agreeing to come to the wedding. Logan himself was having serious second thoughts. 'Want a coffee?'

'Thanks.' Angus ran a hand through his eternally scruffy hair and slumped into a seat at the small table. 'Do we have anything to eat?'

'Nope.' Logan glanced at his watch. 'The hotel restaurant stopped serving breakfast half an hour ago, but I think there's a bakery in town. Why don't we grab something from there?'

Angus grunted something that sounded like agreement and then practically snatched the mug when Logan put a coffee down in front of him. The two men drank in silence—Logan thinking he'd need a few more cups to get through the day. It'd be okay if tiredness was his only problem, but dealing with his fatigue and juggling Simone and Frankie was going to be tricky. As much as he wanted to spend more time with Frankie, he was going to have to keep his distance today and probably for a while after too. That thought made him feel antsy; patience was not his strongest virtue.

'Was last night too painful?' Logan asked, not wanting to think about his dilemma. Sometime in the early hours of the morning, he'd briefly considered asking his big brother's advice. Knowing Angus, he'd probably think the whole situation was hilarious, but it wasn't and he didn't plan on confiding in him anytime soon.

'Huh?' Angus barely glanced up from his mug.

'Dinner with Simone and everyone else?' It was kind of weird that Angus had met all the people he'd been hearing about from Simone before he had. 'What were they all like?'

'Fine,' Angus said, back to his old one-word answers. He'd been quite talkative the last couple of weeks—chirpier than usual—but all good things must come to an end eventually.

'That's it? Fine?' Logan couldn't keep the annoyance out of his voice. 'Did you stay late?'

Angus shuffled in his seat like he had ants in his pants. 'Not very. Everyone else was eager to get an early night, so Simone and I did the same.'

'Thanks for going with her,' Logan said, a little surprised that Angus hadn't just retreated to their villa. 'I know stuff like that isn't really your thing, so I appreciate you making the effort.'

'Do you want to go to this bakery then?' Angus asked, ignoring Logan's sentiment.

Logan knew when he was beaten. There was no point pushing Angus for details of the dinner if he didn't want to talk. He'd probably hated the evening—having to make small talk with strangers. 'Yep, but can you just help me move the cake first? I promised Frankie—' His voice hitched a little on her name and he hoped Angus didn't notice. 'I promised her I'd make sure the cake got to the reception safely.'

'Like she could complain if you didn't,' he grumbled. 'Her fault you had to make a new one anyway.'

Logan raised his eyebrows. Angus was acting even more like a grumpy bear than usual, which wasn't a good omen for the day ahead. The last thing he wanted was for Frankie to have to put up with his brother's crap when she was already tired and anxious. 'It was an accident. Now, are you gonna help me or not?'

In reply, Angus downed the last of his coffee, slammed the mug on the bench and pushed back his chair. 'I'll just put my boots on.'

Chapter Seventeen

Left together, right together. Left together, right, together. Frankie repeated this over and over in her head as she walked down Kalbarri Beach towards the small crowd. Thankfully Heidi was two steps in front of her, looking absolutely precious and stealing everyone's attention, which meant nobody noticed the way Frankie looked longingly at Logan or the wink he gave her as she passed him. At least she hoped not. He'd been on her mind all morning. And right now he looked unbelievably hot in a dark suit, light shirt and even a tie. She'd always thought she liked her men looking more country, more rugged, but right now all she could think about was ripping off that tie and undoing all those buttons.

Her mouth watered at the thought and her hands tightened on the bouquet as she continued to where her cousin and the four groomsmen waited at the makeshift altar. She smiled at Adam, who was even more handsome than usual in his black suit, formal in contrast to the relaxed beach setting. Behind the boys, the ocean looked like a postcard—crisp and inviting, the sky a slightly paler shade of blue right above it and the sun shining. The weather could not have been more perfect for this joyous occasion. As Heidi greeted the groom and his men with her usual flamboyant hugs, Frankie padded across the sand to her place and turned to watch Simone, Faith, Ruby and then finally Stella coming down the beach.

Although she'd seen the bride in all her glory only moments before, it was the expression on Adam's face when he first saw Stella in her lovely flowing, white A-line gown that squeezed Frankie's heart. While the rest of the guests made oohing and ahhing noises as they gazed at Stella, Frankie couldn't keep her eyes off her cousin. His smile looked as if it could light up whole countries and there were happy tears streaming down his face as he clung to his new daughter and waited for his bride. Frankie had never seen him looking so happy as he had been in the past few months and her heart felt like it could burst.

When Stella finally arrived in front of Adam, she kissed Heidi on the forehead before he passed Heidi to Ruby, who held her hand as the ceremony begun.

Adam and Stella only had eyes for each other. Stella reached up to wipe the tears from Adam's cheeks and he kissed her fingers in return.

The celebrant—a tall, wiry woman Frankie guessed to be in her mid-sixties—cleared her throat. 'I don't think I've given you permission to kiss the bride yet, Mr Burton.'

The crowd laughed, Adam blushed and even Frankie felt some of the tension that had been inside her since the early hours of the morning waning. Although she was tired, she wanted to enjoy this day—to truly participate in the celebration with her friends and family—so she angled herself more towards the bride and groom and tried not to look back at the guests.

'Friends and family of Adam, Stella and Heidi, thank you for being here on this very important day. We are gathered on this beautiful beach to celebrate the love between Adam and Stella, by joining them in matrimony.

'All of us want to love and to be loved,' continued the celebrant, 'and I invite you to leave behind the worries you might be experiencing in everyday life and focus solely on Adam and Stella as they come together today. It is also a time for those of us who are married or in committed, loving relationships to reflect on our blessings and reaffirm our commitment to our partners.'

At these words, Frankie's mind went straight to the one thing— or rather person—she was trying not to think about. She wasn't in a relationship like the celebrant described, but boy oh boy did she want to be. Logan wasn't just someone she wanted for sex, although she reckoned that would be off the Richter scale as well; she wanted so much more. She wanted a companion, a friend and a partner. She craved his eyes on her as she walked into a room, the way Adam always looked at Stella.

'Although marriage is an ancient tradition, we are not going to focus on the past, but rather what marriage means today to Adam and Stella. They love each other and this day is about that very special love.' The celebrant looked from the crowd back to the bride and groom, who were now holding hands, still gazing into each other's eyes, Heidi looking up adoringly at both of them.

'Adam and Stella, your marriage today is the public and legal joining of your hearts, souls and bodies. But entering marriage is also an emotional and spiritual decision to commit yourself to each other and each other only. To stand by each other in good times and in hard times, to work together, to play together, to laugh together and to cry together.'

Frankie found herself tearing up, but wasn't sure if it was down to the celebrant's beautiful words and her happiness for Adam and Stella, or for herself and Logan. It was surely too early to be thinking about that sort of commitment, but she couldn't help it. Her mind had superimposed her and Logan onto Adam and Stella and she couldn't help imagining the two of them standing together in front of family and friends and declaring their love for each other.

Was it the forbidden nature of the relationship—the fact that he'd been Simone's boyfriend first—that was making him so attractive? She didn't think so, because she'd felt something from that first moment he walked into her café. But maybe it was her nature to want things she couldn't have. She certainly hadn't known her ex, Michael, was married, but maybe he'd given off those vibes and she'd picked them up subconsciously. It was something she'd pondered a lot in the years following their split. Yet, Logan *did* want her; he'd made that more than clear this morning, so being with him should be easy.

Except it wasn't. Frankie sighed and realised she'd missed half the wedding ceremony while lost in her own little world.

'I promise to give all of myself and all of my love from now until the end of eternity. I love you, Stella; you are my missing half.'

A little sigh went up from the guests as Adam finished his vows and the celebrant nodded at Stella, indicating it was her turn.

'I, Stella, take you, Adam, to be my husband and the father of my daughter. Your love has anchored us, your trust has given us strength. I never thought I would find a man I wanted to live with and laugh with and work and dream with. A man who loves my daughter as much as I do.' Stella paused a moment and glanced over at Heidi, who still held Ruby's hand, beaming at the proceedings. 'I promise to fill your heart, to feed your soul, to share with you and grow with you as we live our lives together. I will always love you, all my life.'

They'd written their own vows and the way both Adam and Stella had involved Heidi in their sacred promises touched Frankie's heart. Following the vows, the rings were exchanged and Adam even had one for Heidi, which he slipped onto her finger as he kissed her cheek. Onlookers would never have guessed that she wasn't his real daughter. Somewhere there was a father who hadn't wanted her because to him she wasn't quite perfect. But he was wrong and he was the one missing out. He didn't deserve Heidi like Adam and Stella did.

Next, Adam's mum, Esther, read a poem about the meaning of true love. Again, Frankie felt her throat closing up and her eyes burning with tears.

Finally the celebrant declared what they'd all been wanting to hear since the moment Adam admitted he was more than a little smitten with Stella. 'Congratulations, Stella and Adam. You came here today to marry and exchange precious vows in front of family and friends and you are now joined as equal partners in love and with all that entails. By the power vested in me and with the blessing of all in attendance today, I pronounce you husband and wife. Adam, you may kiss your bride.'

And what a kiss it was.

Adam leaned forward, cupped Stella's face tenderly in the palms of his hands and then kissed her for almost a minute. Frankie looked away and her gaze caught on Logan. He was standing next to Angus, but she barely registered the other man as Logan's eyes met hers. He didn't smile or give any kind of acknowledgement that anyone else might notice, but she could tell he was thinking about their kiss, or rather kisses, as well. All she wanted right now was to feel his lips on hers again, to enjoy the rest of the wedding and the night ahead with him by her side.

Why did life have to be so complicated?

'Oi, enough is enough,' called best man Monty, startling Frankie back to the scene in front of her as the newlyweds wrenched apart to the sound of laughter all around them.

Frankie rubbed her lips one over the other and tried to ignore the low and deep response of her body that happened whenever she thought about Logan Knight. She'd almost been at the point where she could control it, but the last twenty-four hours had gone and ruined any progress she'd made in that department. Now that she knew he also had feelings for her, trying to resist them was going to be like putting the pieces of the broken wedding cake back together—impossible.

Chapter Eighteen

The wedding of strangers had not changed Angus's opinion of such events. He still disliked them and couldn't wait for this one to be over. This felt like one of the longest days of his life—it was torture being in such close proximity to Simone and not being able to touch her again. He leaned back in his seat, took another slug of his beer and watched as most of the guests boogied it up on the dance floor.

The bride and groom were dancing as if they were the only people here; Heidi was dancing with one of the groomsmen; Simone's daughters with their grandparents; Simone and Logan together, and everyone else was in on the act too. He, Frankie and a couple of elderly guests were the only ones sitting down.

'Are you sure you wouldn't like to dance?' Frankie asked from the other side of the table. She'd been sitting there for the last half an hour, fiddling with the little hand-painted tin—a gift with chocolate in for all the guests—while trying to make small talk, but it was clear they had little in common. The only thing he could think to talk about was Simone, but asking anything about her might make Frankie suspicious.

'No, thanks.' He barely looked at her as he spoke for his eyes were trained on her sister and Logan laughing and smiling at each other as they did the Macarena. Watching them together reminded them of the way he and Simone had danced together last night. The sight made him want to punch his hand through the table.

'Suit yourself.' Frankie dumped her serviette on the table in front of her and then strode to the edge of the dance floor where Frankie's mum and Grace grabbed her hands and welcomed her into the line. Within seconds she was Macarena-ing with the rest of them.

Angus immediately regretted being rude to her because she seemed like a nice woman, but this weekend had got way too weird. He glanced at his watch. When would Adam and Stella decide to call it a night? Didn't they want to get down to wedding night business? They'd had the speeches, they'd cut the cake— well, as much as you could cut a whole bunch of over-decorated cupcakes. He had to admit Frankie and Logan had done a good job with them; even though he considered cupcakes the fare of children's birthday parties, what they'd created looked and tasted damn good.

Then again, he wasn't a chef or a food critic, so what would he know?

You know you don't want to be here any longer.

Deciding that no-one would notice or care if he left, he downed the last of his beer and was about to make a sneaky exit when a shadow arrived beside him. He looked up in time to see Simone pull back a chair and sit down next to him. Her face was pink and shiny from exertion but she still took his breath away. He quickly schooled his expression into one of nonchalance, for although most of the wedding guests were busy dancing, he didn't want to risk anyone picking up any vibes between them. Not that there were vibes—last night had been a one-off. He'd lost his head for a few moments, okay, a few hours, but that was all.

And the way he'd kept looking at her all day … that was because she was about the only person he knew.

'Hey,' he said, trying not to stare at the way her deep blue strapless bridesmaid dress hugged her body and enhanced her already impressive cleavage.

'You could at least make a little bit of effort with my sister,' she hissed, staring at the dance floor as if she weren't actually talking to him.

'What?' She had to be kidding. 'I don't want to give Frankie any false expectations.'

She scoffed. 'There's no danger of that, Angus. You've got tickets on yourself if you think she'll fall in love with you simply because you act a little pleasant. You're not that irresistible, you know.'

Damn, she was hot when her nostrils flared. 'You didn't seem to feel that way last night.'

'Shh!' She turned her head to glare at him. 'Someone might hear you.'

He shrugged one shoulder and nodded towards the dance floor. 'Doubt that.' The closest person to them was sitting two tables away and had a hearing aid in each ear. 'I take it you haven't told Logan you're breaking up with him yet?'

'Who said I am?'

Now it was his turn to glare.

She smiled at him but it wasn't warm at all. 'You made it clear that last night was a big mistake, that you aren't interested in more, so why should I ruin a good thing with someone who does?'

'Because …' His jaw was clenched so hard it felt like it might snap at any moment. He'd told Simone he didn't want to ruin things between her and Logan, but she couldn't be serious about continuing to see him. If she'd felt anything at all for Logan, she wouldn't have done what she'd done with him last night.

'Relax,' she said. 'I'm going to end it with him. Tonight. As soon as the reception is over and then we can all escape to bed.'

Although Angus knew Simone didn't mean she would be doing so with him, his mind conjured up fantasies of another hot night between the sheets with her. 'Good,' he grunted as he pushed back his chair and stood. 'Good luck with that. I'm going to call it a night.'

'What? You're going already?' She looked and sounded disappointed, and he couldn't help wishing the situation was different. He'd have happily danced with Simone again. Last night hadn't been so bad with her by his side.

'I only met Adam and Stella yesterday,' he said, 'and I'm tired. No-one is going to miss me if you don't make a big deal of it.'

'Hey.' She held up her hands in surrender. 'I couldn't care less what you do. Sweet dreams.'

Angus hated to leave things between them like this, but really, what choice did he have? It was probably better if she hated him. Without another word, he turned and made a quiet exit.

★ ★ ★

Simone watched Angus go and then dropped her head into her hands, hoping to suppress the tears that were threatening. The fact she could barely keep her eyes open from fatigue didn't help the guilt, sadness and desire mashed up inside her. The intoxicating scent of him still lingered in the air and she inhaled deeply despite herself.

'Simone?'

She dropped her hands from her face and straightened at the sound of Logan approaching.

He looked down, concern in his eyes. 'You all right?'

'Yep. Fine.' She forced a smile. 'Just tired—' *oh so tired* '—and I think I maybe had a touch too much to drink. One day I'll learn.'

He smiled warmly, pulled out the seat beside her—the seat Angus had been warming less than a minute ago—and sat. 'Where'd my brother go?'

'Back to your villa. Something about a headache. I think he was lying. You're right, he is a grump.'

He chuckled. 'I suppose being on his best behaviour for two nights in a row was just too hard.'

Simone raised an eyebrow, wondering if Logan would think Angus well behaved if he knew what they'd gotten up to last night. Just talking about him with Logan made her feel as if her stomach might expel her dinner at any moment.

'Are you sure you're okay?' Logan placed a hand across her forehead. It was warm, but it didn't make her heart stop. 'You look a bit pale. Why don't we go outside for a bit of fresh air?'

She gulped at the thought. Outside alone he might try to kiss her. No, surely he wouldn't try anything when he thought she was ill. And maybe it would be a good chance for them to have the talk they had to have. That thought made her feel sick again— she'd never dumped anyone in her life—but she steeled herself and nodded. 'Okay.'

Logan stood and offered her his arm. Feeling like a fraud, she linked hers through his and allowed him to lead her through the tables and past the dance floor to the exit. Frankie looked up from where she was twirling Heidi around and gave her a smile, no doubt thinking that she and Logan were sneaking off to get up to mischief. She'd have to think of something to tell her later, and the girls, who were going to be disappointed their attempt at matchmaking didn't prove successful.

'It was a good wedding,' Logan said, when they emerged into the fresh evening air.

They sat down on a bench a little way along the verandah.

'Have you had a good day?' he asked.

She nodded. 'Yes, it was gorgeous. I just love weddings—the dresses, the flowers, the dancing. Oh, and weren't Adam's and Stella's vows just lovely? I honestly can't recall another couple quite as perfect for each other as those two. I'm not sure who Adam fell in love with first, Heidi or Stella, but I know he thinks of Heidi as his own. I wonder if they'll have any more children. Probably, I mean—' She stopped abruptly, realising she was babbling. Damn nerves.

'You're right,' Logan said. 'It was a perfect day. Thanks for inviting me.'

Oh, he was just so *pleasant*. Why couldn't she like him the way she liked Angus? He was by far the nicer brother. But although Logan was kind and good-looking in a football hero kind of way, he didn't push her buttons the way Angus did and she couldn't keep up this façade any longer.

'You're welcome. I hope you had a good time,' she said, dithering.

'I did. Your friends and family are really great ...'

Why did it sound like there was a 'but' coming? Was he about to say 'but now I want to be alone with you'? *Oh God.*

'But,' he continued. 'I'm not sure ... this thing between us ... are you feeling it?'

He knows. Her stomach turned inside out at the prospect that he knew, but she didn't want to give anything away in case he didn't. 'Um ... It's just ... this is all very new.' Dammit, why couldn't she just admit the truth. *No, I don't want to jump your bones the way I did your brother.* Of course, she couldn't say that because she wanted to keep Angus out of it. Even if he didn't deserve her protection, she didn't want to hurt Logan any more than necessary.

'I'm not sure that's it,' Logan said, a resigned look in his eyes. 'You're a beautiful woman, Simone, and I've had lots of fun getting to know you, but I just don't think there's any chemistry between us. I don't know why. Maybe it's because you're still in love with your husband—and I wouldn't blame you for that—but I don't think we should try to force something that's not there.'

'What are you saying?'

He took a deep breath. 'I think we should just be friends.'

He was dumping *her*? Why hadn't she seen that coming? Despite the fact she'd been about to do the same, his confession that he didn't feel any spark still hurt. *It's for the best*, she told herself; her pride hurt far more than her heart. Of course they couldn't really stay friends after this—the fact of the matter was they would never have attempted a relationship in the first place if it wasn't for her conniving daughters. And now, after Angus …

'I agree,' she said, reaching over to squeeze his hand. 'You're such a good man, Logan Knight, and I know there's a very special woman waiting somewhere out there for you.'

He didn't say anything, simply smiled and then snuck his hand out from hers. They sat in silence for a few moments longer, the music from the reception overpowering the sound of the waves lapping against the shore only a few hundred metres away.

'You feeling any better now?' Logan asked eventually. 'Do you need me to go and get you a drink of water or something?'

'No.' She waved his suggestion away with her hand. 'We should probably go back inside. I think the happy couple will be making their big exit very soon.'

Logan smiled at her. 'Good idea. We wouldn't want to miss that. Maybe you'll catch the bouquet.'

She laughed, feeling better already now that Logan had had the awkward conversation for her. 'As long as Harriet doesn't. I'm not ready to be mother-of-the-bride just yet.'

As they re-entered the function room, the last song was just wrapping up and Adam and Stella were the only ones still on the dance floor.

'Hey Mum,' said Grace, coming over to them. Harriet was a step behind, carrying a sleepy Heidi in her arms. Her eldest daughter actually smiled at her, making Simone wonder if she hadn't snuck some alcohol.

'Adam and Stella are about to leave,' Harriet said.

'Oh, good.' Simone nodded and reached out to sweep Heidi's hair out of her eyes.

'Well, folks,' announced Monty, who'd been acting as MC as well as best man, 'it's time for our blushing bride and her lucky groom to call it a night, but we've got one last thing to do before they go. Can I have all the single ladies on the dance floor, please?'

'Ooh, me, me, me.' Without asking Simone's permission, Harriet thrust Heidi towards her and flounced over to Monty.

'Anyone else?' he asked, looking around. 'Come on, Frankie.'

Looking as if she were stepping towards her executioner, Frankie walked over to join Harriet and Monty.

'Simone?' Monty looked to her expectantly. She cradled Heidi against her and shook her head, taking comfort in the little girl's warm body. It seemed so long since Harriet and Grace were this small.

Ruth came over. 'You may as well go too,' she said to Grace, ushering her granddaughter onto the dance floor. 'This wedding is seriously devoid of single women.'

'All right, Stella,' Monty said into the microphone as Grace arrived beside her sister and her aunt, looking like a kangaroo caught in the headlights, 'turn around and give us your best throw.'

It felt like the whole room held their breath as Stella grinned and then hurled her beautiful rose bouquet over her head with both hands. Grace stayed frozen, Harriet dived for it like a star footballer, but she stumbled and Frankie's hand shot out and closed around it. She looked surprised and uncertain as everyone cheered.

Although Simone wasn't superstitious, she couldn't help but let out a sigh of relief. Her sister deserved to find a good man and she was ready to settle down and start a family, whereas her daughters had plenty of time.

'Congratulations, Frankie,' Monty said. 'About time we got you married off.'

Frankie stuck her tongue out at him and then, clutching the bouquet, joined Simone.

'Congrats, little sis.' Simone smiled at her. 'Just promise me you won't make me wear a pink bridesmaid dress—you know how pink clashes with our hair.'

Before Frankie could reply, Monty spoke again. 'And now it's time for the garter toss. Come on, Adam and Stella, don't be shy.'

Monty sounded like he was enjoying this gig and in the unlikely event of Simone tying the knot again, she made a mental note to ask him to be her master of ceremonies as well. Under Monty's instruction, Drew carried a chair onto the dance floor for Stella to sit on and as Joe Cocker's 'You Can Leave Your Hat On' started playing, Adam knelt down in front of his bride. Everyone laughed at the song choice but the love between the bride and groom was obvious.

Adam's smile looked fit to burst as he snuck his hands under Stella's dress. She blushed and giggled terribly and Simone suspected he was taking his time on purpose, but finally he made a whoop of victory and a few moments later, he'd slid the pretty lace garter down her leg and over her sparkly heels.

The crowd applauded as Monty gathered the single men— Logan and a couple of Adam's football mates. The footballers were so drunk they could barely stand up, so it was no surprise when Logan reached up and caught the garter as if it were something he did everyday.

'Well, well, well,' Monty said, half-laughing. 'Frankie get back here so you can get a photo with Logan.'

With an awkward glance at Simone, Frankie headed back to the dance floor and the two of them stood there looking as if they'd rather be anywhere else as the wedding photographer snapped a shot.

'I won't predict you'll be marrying each other,' Monty continued, looking towards Simone, 'because Simmo might murder me, but maybe there'll be wedding bells for our favourite sisters very soon.'

Both Frankie and Logan turned a bright shade of red, glancing at each other and then quickly looking away again. Simone suddenly saw how perfect they would be together—they were both neat freaks, they both loved cooking and reading, they were closer in age, and neither of them had kids yet but they'd both make awesome parents. Not to mention the fact that standing next to each other right now, they looked really cute together. But how weird would that be? Quite aside from the fact she'd dated Logan herself, how would she deal with being related to Angus if Logan and Frankie got married? *Awkward.* Definitely *not* something she wanted to suggest.

'Now, the time has come to farewell Mr and Mrs Burton,' Monty announced.

Adam took Stella's hand and held it up to the crowd. 'Thanks everyone for joining us for our big day. It's been amazing and we're so glad we had each and every one of you here to help make it so special. Now if you don't mind, it's time to take my bride to bed.'

Simone didn't think those two would be getting much sleep that night.

With this announcement, he swept Stella up into his arms and she squealed like a little girl. They paused briefly to kiss Heidi goodnight, and then Stella waved goodbye to everyone as Adam carried her off into the night. Simone couldn't help thinking about her own wedding night—being heavily pregnant hadn't stopped her and Jason making the most of their first night as husband and wife. She smiled at the memory. Although she still missed him, it was getting easier each day, and however much of a debacle sleeping with Angus was, it made her feel confident that when the right man came along, she would be able to enjoy another relationship.

'What are you smiling about, Mum?' Harriet asked.

Simone looked down at her daughter. 'Just remembering my wedding night with your father.'

Harriet made a face. 'Eugh, yuck. TMI!'

Despite the fact that she hadn't actually given Harriet any information, Simone laughed. 'I was young once too, you know.'

Harriet put her hands over her ears as Aunty Esther and Uncle Dave came up to join them. She held out her arms to Simone.

'Can I steal our darling girl?' she asked. 'It's been a long day for her and I want to get her into bed ASAP.'

'Of course.' Simone reluctantly handed Heidi over to her new grandmother and kissed her on the forehead. 'Sweet dreams, sweet girl.'

'Night, everyone,' said Esther and Dave in unison. 'See you in the morning.'

The hordes departed pretty fast—the snoozing elderly relatives needed to be awoken and the drunken footballers assisted out the door.

'What a beautiful wedding,' said Ruth, with a yawn. Simone caught it immediately, the lack of sleep finally catching up with her. 'Come on, young ladies, time to get you to bed.'

'Night, Mum.' Grace hugged Simone and she squeezed back tightly, not wanting to let her go. After the events of the last twenty-four hours, she needed the comfort of her girls.

'Good night, my sweet.' She looked to Harriet. 'Do you have a hug for your old mum, too?'

Harriet rolled her eyes but she obliged, giving Simone the quickest of hugs before pulling back. 'Whatever you and Logan get up to tonight, I do not want to hear about it.' She pointed her finger as if she were a teacher telling off a student. 'Understood?'

'Goodnight, Harriet,' Simone said, wishing for an earthquake that might split the floor and swallow her. She didn't know what was worse—letting them think she and Logan were off for a dirty night together or telling them they'd broken up. Luckily her mum and stepfather whisked her girls away before she had to confess anything.

'Well, I guess I'll see you guys later.' Frankie wiggled her fingers at Simone and Logan. 'Have a good night.'

'Actually,' Simone said, 'I'm coming with you. Goodnight, Logan.'

'Goodnight, Simone,' Logan said at the same moment as Frankie said, 'Oh?'

'I'll see you both tomorrow before we go?'

Simone nodded at Logan. 'Of course and thanks again for coming.' She couldn't bring herself to tell him to thank Angus.

The three of them left the function room together and then Logan walked towards his villa and she and Frankie went in the opposite direction. Simone expected the Spanish Inquisition from Frankie but maybe she was tired, because all she said was, 'You okay?'

'Uh huh.' Simone nodded, feeling anything but. 'Logan and I have decided to call it quits.'

'I'm sorry.' Frankie wrapped her arm around Simone's shoulder, comforting her as they walked.

'It's all right.' Simone leaned her head against her sister. 'It's not like I need a man in my life. Remember after Ryan came out of the closet? I said I had a beautiful marriage once and maybe that should be enough. Well, I think the universe is trying to remind me of that.'

'Just because Logan isn't The One doesn't mean he isn't out there,' Frankie said.

Simone shrugged. 'Whatever. Right now all I want to do is go to bed.'

But she couldn't help thinking of Angus and how, briefly, she'd thought she might have found him.

Chapter Nineteen

A week after the wedding, Angus was still beating himself up with guilt. Logan had been working from home, researching and writing articles at night and helping on the farm during the day, but he wasn't his usual sunny-natured self. On the journey home from Kalbarri, he'd admitted that he and Simone had called it a day and while he'd made out like this had been a mutual decision, Angus had insider knowledge he couldn't reveal to his brother— the fact that it had been Simone who'd instigated the break-up. Logan's mood indicated he was pretty bummed about it.

He couldn't blame him—he'd also found himself distracted by thoughts of Simone whenever he should have been concentrating on something else. He'd tried to change the oil in his ute and ended up with the wrong container. Luckily he realised his mistake before it was too late; his ute wouldn't have thanked him if he'd filled the sump with hydraulic oil. Then he'd tried to measure up some steel to cut and kept forgetting the numbers. Three times he'd had to walk back to the seeder bar to re-measure it.

If he could turn back time and change that night, he would, but as that wasn't possible, he felt the need to do something else to make it up to Logan.

He was in the shower, scrubbing off the dirt from a day's work servicing the harvesting machinery for the upcoming season, when the answer came to him. The wind-farming bizzo. His motives for resisting Logan's ideas about renewable energy on the farm had been unreasonable he knew, and who was he to hold Logan back? If leasing some of their land for wind-farming meant Logan didn't have to be as tied to the place, then they should do it. He preferred working with his brother over farm contractors, but he didn't want Logan to feel obliged and come to hate working on the farm, to eventually come to resent him.

Feeling lighter already and happy to have thought about something in the shower other than Simone—that was progress indeed—he turned off the water, grabbed a towel and wrapped it around himself. As he opened the door to walk down the hallway to his bedroom, he caught a whiff of something alluring coming from the kitchen. One of the many good things about having Logan home was that they ate well. He was as good as any wife, whipping up cakes, slices and the like for smoko, and he always cooked a full-on meal for dinner. Angus told him he didn't have to but Logan reckoned he enjoyed it and Angus wasn't going to argue with that.

He went into his bedroom, dressed quickly and then grabbed the literature from the renewable energy company that Logan had given him to read months ago. Shamefully, he hadn't even opened the brochure, but Logan had told him enough and it was time to trust his brother. Logan might not be as active on the farm as Angus, but they owned equal shares, along with Olivia, who was studying to be a teacher and happy to be a completely silent partner.

'We'll do it,' Angus said as he entered the kitchen a few moments later.

Logan turned around from where he was tossing something in the wok. 'Do what?' he asked, frowning.

Angus held up the wind-farming booklet and Logan raised his eyebrows.

'What's brought this on?'

Angus swallowed, hoping guilt wasn't scrawled across his face. He wasn't about to admit the truth—that sleeping with Logan's girlfriend had filled him with such a heavy weight he had to do something to try to ease it. 'I've just been thinking,' he said, heading for the fridge and grabbing two bottles of Carlton Dry. He handed one to Logan, cracked the lid off his, sat down at the table and took a swig.

Logan simply stared at him, waiting for some kind of explanation.

'Well,' Angus began, taking a deep breath, 'the truth is I've realised my reasons for objecting are neither sensible or logical.'

'What exactly are your reasons? Until now, you've shut me down every time I've tried to talk about this. What's changed?'

'This is going to sound stupid, but wind-farming just sounds like something Sarah would be excited about. You know what she was like, how environmentally aware she was. However unreasonable it is, when she walked out, I developed an aversion to stuff like that.'

Logan frowned. 'Seriously? That's why you didn't want to consider my suggestion?'

'See? Stupid.' Angus took another slug of his beer.

'You really need to get over her, brother. She's been gone, what? Ten years?'

'I *am* over her,' Angus said, perhaps a bit more forcefully than necessary. It was the truth. Any love he'd had for her was long gone. It wasn't Sarah who had stopped him pursuing another relationship. It was the fact he'd lost too many people in his life and each loss had taken a chunk out of him. He couldn't risk losing someone else.

'When was the last time you were with a woman?' Logan asked, as he took the wok off the heat and retrieved two bowls from the overhead cupboard.

Angus was thankful his brother didn't see his reaction to that question. 'Not that it's any of your business,' he replied, trying to sound casual, 'but you don't need to worry about my sex life. I find satisfaction when I need it.'

'Being acquainted with your right hand doesn't mean you have a sex life, and besides, I'm not just talking about sex. I'm talking about companionship.'

An image of Simone landed in Angus's head. He'd had such a good time with her the night before the wedding, and not only when they were roughing up the sheets. They'd talked, they'd laughed, and having dinner with her friends and family had reminded him what it was like to be in a couple. As much as he hated to admit it, he'd liked it and he kept thinking about what it would be like to see her again.

'How did me agreeing to your wind-farming proposal turn into a conversation about sex?' Angus asked.

Logan grinned and set two bowls down on the table. 'We're blokes. Isn't everything about sex?'

Angus rolled his eyes but at least Logan was smiling again. 'Maybe. Speaking of which, are you going to try your luck again on that Rural Matchmakers site?'

'Nah.' Logan shook his head as he sat down and picked up his fork. 'You were right. You can't properly gauge whether you have a connection with someone online. Guess Miss Right will come along when she comes along.' He held up his beer. 'You sure about pursuing a deal with the renewable energy guys?'

'Yep. It's not fair of me to be keeping you back from advancing your career. As you say, if we have some extra income, then I'll be able to pay people to do some of the stuff you currently have to come home to help with.' He'd miss Logan if he wasn't around so much, but that wasn't a reason not to do this.

'That's not what this is about,' Logan said. 'The extra income will give us a bit of a buffer for the not-so-good farming seasons and insure against a market downturn. I've probably already said this, but one farmer I interviewed referred to the land he leased to wind farmers as his vertical crop. That sounds good to me. If we're lucky, we might even save a bit. You could take some time off, go on a holiday.'

Angus snorted. 'Where the hell would I go? Relaxing by the beach isn't really my thing.'

'Whatever. I just meant you wouldn't have to feel so tied to the farm. You could go visit Liv a bit more.'

'Maybe.' Angus shrugged.

'If we do set up a partnership with the renewable energy company—and there's no guarantee they'll even choose us for their purposes—but if they do, it doesn't mean I'll be taking a back seat here. You're not going to get rid of me that easily. I might not live and breathe the farm like you do, but that doesn't mean I don't love it here. Farming's in my blood too, remember? And I don't want to give it up any more than I want to give up journalism. I think this will be a smart move, going forward. More wind turbines are going to be installed in this region regardless, so we may as well get some benefit from them. Yes?'

'I already agreed. No need to go on about it.'

Logan laughed. 'In that case, let's drink to it instead.' And he lifted his bottle and took another slug.

* * *

As the beer slid down Logan's throat, he realised this was his perfect opportunity to tell Angus why he was so keen on inviting renewable energy developers onto their property. It wasn't that he didn't want to work on the farm anymore; the truth was he just wasn't sure how many years he had left where that would be possible. He was thinking ahead, forward planning before his medical situation became dire, but he wasn't ready yet to say why. Once Angus knew, he'd have to tell Olivia and they'd both pity him in a way he couldn't bear.

'What's the next step then?' Angus asked, jolting Logan from his thoughts.

'I'll register our interest with my contact and we'll attend the information session in Geraldton. We'll be able to ask questions and hear more about the whole process. You up for that?'

Angus nodded and Logan still couldn't quite believe he'd agreed. He appeared to be becoming more easygoing in his old age. First agreeing to come to the wedding and now this— he wasn't quite sure what had come over his brother, but he wasn't about to complain.

The wedding sent his thoughts right back to Frankie, which was exactly where they'd been before Angus had walked into the kitchen and delivered his surprising news. In fact, Frankie had taken up permanent residence in Logan's head, so much so that everything he did was taking twice as long as usual, due to his daydreaming. He still couldn't believe how fast his feelings had developed—they'd only met twice before the weekend in Kalbarri.

It had been a week since he'd seen her and it felt like years. The yearning to talk to her was driving him crazy and if he didn't do something about it soon, he thought he'd explode. The problem was he didn't have any contact details for her and he was worried that if he rang the café, Simone might pick up and question why he was calling.

'Earth to Logan. Are you in there?'

'Huh?' He shook his head and looked at Angus. 'Did you say something?'

'I asked you when this meeting was,' Angus said. 'I'm thinking of taking a trip to see Liv before harvest and just wanted to make sure I wasn't away then.'

'Next Wednesday night, in Gero.'

'Okay.' Angus nodded. 'Where were you?'

'What do you mean?'

'It was like you were in another zone just then. If I didn't know better, I'd say you had a woman on your mind. You still upset about Simone?'

Logan forced a chuckle. 'Nah, just thinking about an article I have to work on tonight,' he lied. Although he did have work to get on with, he doubted he'd be able to concentrate with thoughts of Frankie filling his head.

'I'll clean up here then,' Angus offered, as he dumped his fork in his empty bowl.

'You sure?'

'Yep, least I can do after you fed me. Go work. And try not to stay up too late. You're no use to me if you're burning the candle at both ends.'

'Thanks.' Logan finished his last mouthful, pushed back his seat, dumped his bowl in the sink and escaped into his bedroom. As he shut the door behind him, he saw the book that had arrived in yesterday's post. It was Ruth Park's *The Harp in the South*, which he'd ordered to replace the copy he'd left in his hotel room in Broome. One of his favourite books of all time, he could not be without it. And as he picked it up now and flicked through the pages an idea came to him.

He wondered … had Frankie read it?

Chapter Twenty

Ten days since Frankie had last seen Logan. That's if she was counting. Which of course she was. Although you could barely call their goodbye on the Sunday after the wedding talking to each other. It had been awkward between Simone and Logan, and Frankie and Angus had just kind of hung on the sidelines looking uncomfortable. Lifting her hand to wave farewell had physically pained her, because she'd wanted to do so much more.

Ten days! If she didn't see or hear from him soon, she wouldn't be safe to work in the café. Her stomach was a constant knot of anticipation, wondering if this would be the day he'd make contact. She only half-heartedly listened to customers when they gave her their orders, for she always had one ear cocked to the phone on the wall. It was the only phone listed under her name in the White Pages. She didn't have a home phone and she'd never seen the point of listing her mobile number—anyone she wanted to call her had her number. Until now.

She'd even searched for him on Rural Matchmakers, but he must have taken down his profile when he'd started seeing Simone. And he didn't appear to have a Facebook account. In this day

223

and age! It was infuriating. If she ever did see or talk to him again she would give him what for about that.

Two more days. If he hadn't called or emailed or *anything* by the weekend, she would sneak his number off her sister's phone. Which could be tricky considering they hadn't seen much of each other either this last week and a bit. Frankie felt guilty every time she looked at Simone, so she'd been making excuses about being busy. She missed her though, and her nieces, so she'd have to work out some way forward with Logan and her family.

That's if he hadn't changed his mind.

Her hands froze over the carrot cake she'd been icing on auto-pilot. Could that be why he hadn't made contact? *Argh.* That thought shouldn't have left her so bereft when she'd barely known him a month and kissed him only twice, but it did. It made her whole body feel achy and flu-ish. Panic set her heart racing.

She put down the spatula and leaned back against the counter, hoping neither of her staff had noticed her little turn. But they were both busy—Stacey at the counter with a customer and Monique waiting on a table.

'I'm just going out the back for some fresh air,' she called through to Stacey, who waved her hand in acknowledgement and kept chatting to the customer.

Frankie pushed open the rear door of the kitchen and escaped into their little courtyard, inhaling the fresh mid-morning air in gulps. She felt like crying at the injustice of her situation but if she started, she might not be able to stop and the girls would need her when the lunch rush hit.

The door opened behind her and she straightened quickly, not wanting to be caught in such a state.

'What are you doing out here?' said Simone, stepping out to join her. The girls must have directed her through.

'I felt a little queasy,' Frankie lied, putting a hand against her stomach to enhance the excuse. 'Thought some fresh air might help.'

Simone made a face and rubbed her tummy at the same time. 'Must be something going around. I feel a little off this morning too.'

Frankie frowned. 'What are *you* doing here?'

'And it's nice to see you too.' Simone held out a bunch of envelopes, most of which looked like bills, and one slightly bigger package. 'I stopped in at the post office and thought I'd bring you your post. Feels like we've hardly spoken this last week.'

'I've been busy.' Frankie took the post, hoping her sister wouldn't ask her exactly what had been keeping her occupied.

'So you've said. I need you to come over and play mediator between Harriet and me.' Simone sighed and Frankie noticed her eyes looked bloodshot, as if she'd been crying or not sleeping well. 'All we seem to do is scream at each other lately.'

'How about I bring dinner round tomorrow night. That's if you're not already busy?'

Simone put her index finger against her chin as if in deep thought. 'Let me see … because I have such an active social life … Nope. Nothing comes to mind. Dinner would be lovely.'

Frankie smiled. 'It's a date.' And then she glanced down at the envelopes in her hand. Yep, mostly bills as predicted, but she had no idea what the package was. It felt like a book but she hadn't ordered anything recently.

'What's that?' Simone nodded towards the package.

'Not sure.' Frankie slid her finger under the flap to open it. She pulled out a book—*The Harp in the South* by Ruth Park. There was no note.

'You and your books,' Simone said, shaking her head as Frankie flicked open the first page.

Her heart slammed up into her throat and she snapped the book shut, hoping Simone hadn't seen.

'What is it?' Simone asked.

'Just something I ordered a while back.' She hugged the book to her chest, warmth rushing through her at the knowledge Logan had sent it. There'd been no time to read the inscription, but she'd caught his name at the bottom. 'Been meaning to read it for ages.'

'I don't know how you find the time to read,' Simone said. 'Anyway, I'm on Meals on Wheels delivery today, so gotta fly. See you tomorrow night.' She leaned forward and kissed her sister on the cheek.

'Yep,' Frankie managed, barely able to contain her excitement as she watched Simone head back into the kitchen. She waited a good five seconds after the door had shut behind her and then peeled back the cover of the book again.

Frankie—hope you haven't got it yet. Can't wait to talk about it with you. Logan x

And then a phone number and an email address. Oh hallelujah, God! She did a little jig around the courtyard, in a much better mood than when she'd come out. Only problem was that now she had hours ahead of her before she could call him as she couldn't risk doing so at the café where anyone might hear.

But she could send a text message. Grinning, she slipped her phone out of her apron pocket, opened the book and copied his details into her phone, saving them as *LK* rather than *Logan Knight*. Then, she sent a message: *Got the book. Thank you. Will call you tonight. Frankie x*

With a little sigh, she slid the novel back into its packaging and then went inside and tucked it into the bottom of her bag. She floated on air for the rest of the day with the knowledge that it was there.

★ ★ ★

Logan's phone started ringing in his pocket as he placed the lasagne on the table. 'Help yourself,' he said to Angus, who had just sat down. 'This is an important phone call. Gotta take it.'

And then he hurried down the hallway to his bedroom and shut the door behind him before swiping his finger across the screen to answer the phone. 'Frankie!'

'Hey there.'

He took two strides to his bed and fell down on top of it, so damn pleased to hear her voice. 'How are you?'

'I'm good now,' she said, 'but I've been going insane since the wedding.'

He grinned. 'Me too. Can't stop thinking about you. I think Angus is getting suspicious that something is up.'

'I've barely been able to look at Simone. I feel so guilty for even thinking about you but ...'

'I know,' he said when her voice trailed off. 'We'll work it out. But let's not worry about it now. I just want to talk to you.'

'Me too,' she whispered as if someone might be in earshot.

'Where are you?' he asked.

'At home.'

'Then why are you whispering?' he whispered.

'I don't know.' She laughed and it sounded so beautiful that he racked his brain for jokes to tell her so he could hear it again. 'There's no-one here to eavesdrop except my cats.'

'How are Fred and George?' She'd told him about her kittens the night they made the cakes. They sounded like little rascals.

'George is climbing up the curtains in my living room and—youch!' she yelped. 'Get down! Fred was climbing up my leg. They think their dinner is more important than talking to you.'

'You'd better feed them. I don't want them to eat you.' If anyone was going to feast on her he wanted it to be him, but he swallowed that thought. He didn't think they were quite at the phone-sex stage of their relationship just yet.

'I will.' Although he hadn't seen her house, he imagined her walking down a small corridor into a warm kitchen swimming with cookbooks and cooking paraphernalia. 'Thanks for the book.'

'Have you read it?' he asked as he heard a clatter in the background, followed by what he guessed to be the shaking of cat biscuits into bowls.

'Nope. I told you, I'm way behind on my Aussie fiction.'

'Well, Ruth Park isn't everyone's cup of tea but if you like that one, I've got plenty more you can borrow.' Logan repositioned himself on the bed, back against the headboard, legs stretched out in front of him.

'That'd be great. How was your day?'

'Ah you know … same old, same old. Angus and I are checking all the machinery over before harvest and I had to make some phone calls this arvo to line up some interviews for next week.'

'You sound busy.'

'No more than you, I suppose. How's the café? Had any interesting characters come in lately?' Another thing they'd talked about that night. He'd said she should write a book with the stories she'd told him.

'Actually, yes. One lady was travelling through town in her caravan and she brought her dog inside the café.'

'Oh yeah?'

She chuckled. 'It was a Great Dane and when I told her she'd have to leave him tied up outside and I could bring him out a bowl of water, she accused me of discrimination—saying that I let people bring their toddlers in and that the dog was her fur baby.'

'What? That's insane. People are crazy.'

'I know. You must meet a fair few loonies in your job too.'

'Nah, mostly people want to suck up to me,' he admitted. 'They're scared of what I'll write about them if they don't.'

'What would you write about me?' she asked.

'Now that's easy.' He cleared his throat and then spoke in a deep voice. 'Headline: Sexy red-headed café owner makes rural journalist hot under the collar, and not just because she's a red-hot cook.'

'Isn't that a bit too long for a headline?' she said, her tone amused.

'Stuff the headline. Nothing I'd write about you would do you justice anyway.'

'You're making me blush.'

'That I'd like to see,' he said, muscles all over his body tightening at this confession. 'You busy on Sunday?'

She was quiet a moment, then, 'I think this is where I'm supposed to play hard to get, but I hate games, so no, I'm not busy.'

He laughed. 'Good. I've got to go up to Carnarvon next week for a story. I was thinking if I head up on Sunday we could meet in Geraldton for lunch.'

'That sounds … great. Where are we going?'

He racked his brain but couldn't think of any café or restaurant half as good as hers and he wanted their first date to be special. 'It's a surprise. I'll text you details of where to meet me.'

'Sounds mysterious. But I can't wait.'

'Me neither.'

They talked for the next few hours without any pause. Frankie ate some quiche she'd brought home from the café while they chatted, but Logan didn't bother sneaking out for lasagne; just listening to Frankie satisfied him enough. In fact, he could have talked all night long, but just before eleven, he said, 'I suppose I'd better let you go and get some rest. Don't want you falling asleep in the soup tomorrow.'

She sighed. 'Yes, I suppose you're right.'

But neither of them seemed inclined to hang up.

'Sunday,' he said after the first moment's silence in over three hours.

'Yes, Sunday.' It sounded like she was smiling and that made him smile.

'But I'll talk to you tomorrow.' It was a promise, not a question.

'I'll look forward to it,' she replied and then they finally disconnected.

Logan put his phone down on his bedside table and stretched out on the bed. He could not remember the last time he'd talked to a woman on the phone for that long. Hell, he couldn't remember the last time he'd talked to a woman *in person* for that long—well, aside from Frankie, the night before the wedding.

And he couldn't wait to talk to her again.

Chapter Twenty-one

'Mum? Are you awake?'

At the light pressure on her arm and Grace's voice above her, Simone opened her eyes and then blinked at her daughter. Her head felt muzzy as she tried to sit up from the couch, where she'd been lying since just after lunch. 'What time is it?'

'Just after four,' Grace said, sitting down next to Simone. 'Are you okay? You don't look very well.' Grace raised her hand and placed it on her mother's head as Simone had done to her so many times when she was sick.

'I'm fine,' she told her, putting her own hand over Grace's and then bringing it down to rest on her knee. 'Just tired. I didn't mean to nap for so long though.'

Damn Angus. If thoughts of him weren't keeping her awake at night, she wouldn't have needed a nanna nap. Every time she closed her eyes, he appeared in her head—tall, rugged and naked as he had been the night before the wedding. Her mouth went dry, her insides twisted and her body temperature soared at the thought. Sometimes she even found herself half-wishing she was still going out with Logan so she could grill him about what

231

Angus had been like since the wedding. Was he thinking about her—about their night together—as much as she was?

The not knowing was making her loopy. Or loopier.

'Did you have a good day at school?' she asked, mentally telling Angus to take a hike.

'Yep.' Grace nodded. 'Mrs Beaton gave me the highest mark in our class for our English essays.'

'That's awesome. I'm so proud of you.'

'Thanks, Mum. Can I have a snack? I'm starving.'

'Sure, honey. There's some of Frankie's chocolate cake in the fridge.'

'Yum,' Grace said, leaping up with the kind of energy no adult ever had.

Simone heaved herself up off the couch and followed her into the kitchen. 'Where's Harriet?'

Grace frowned as she retrieved the container from the fridge. 'She went to Alyssa's from the bus. I thought you knew.'

'Nope.' Simone shook her head, irritated by Harriet's lack of communication and continuing disrespect, especially after last year's high jinks. She had a good mind to drive over to Alyssa's house and make a big scene about hauling Harriet home, but … she didn't have the energy. Maybe she *was* sick, because right now all she wanted to do was head back to the couch.

'Do you want a piece, Mum?' Grace asked.

Simone smiled. 'No, thanks, honey.' Frankie's chocolate cake was something she usually couldn't say no to but today the thought of eating made her want to throw up. 'Do you need any help with your homework?'

'No, we don't have much, 'cos tomorrow is the sports carnival. Are you still coming?'

'I wouldn't miss it for the world,' Simone said, hoping that by then she wouldn't be feeling like death warmed up. 'I'm just going to have a shower and text your sister. Thank God one of you is good to your mother.' Simone leaned forward and kissed Grace on the forehead.

Grace smiled and then sank her teeth into the cake as Simone headed for the bathroom. En route she messaged her older daughter, aware Harriet likely wouldn't bother with a reply.

I heard you're at Alyssa's. Next time it would be nice if you asked my permission before you go somewhere else after school. You might not think about anyone but yourself, but I happen to worry if I don't know where you are. Be home for dinner. Frankie's cooking. Love Mum.

The knowledge her beloved Aunty Eff was making dinner would ensure Harriet came home in time to eat. Simone intended to tell her that if she didn't start toeing the line, she could kiss goodbye to her boyfriend, because she'd be grounded for the rest of the year. She had never grounded either of her daughters—she'd always thought it sounded like such an American thing to do—but how else were you supposed to punish a sixteen-year-old who insisted on acting like she was twenty-one? Simone couldn't help but wonder if Harriet would have been so much of a handful if Jason was still alive. Single-parenting was not for the fainthearted, that's for sure.

With a sigh, Simone stepped into the bathroom and stripped. She was usually conservative with showers and encouraged her girls to be the same, but today she couldn't bring herself to hurry. She needed the comforting warmth to refresh her. Finally, after about ten minutes, she turned off the water and wrapped a towel around herself.

'I thought you were never going to finish,' Grace said, sneaking into the bathroom the moment Simone opened the door. 'I need to pee.'

Simone raised an eyebrow. 'Since when do you two worry about things like privacy?' For as long as she could remember her girls had been barging in on her in the shower and even Harriet still had the occasional conversation while one of them was on the toilet.

'Mum!' Grace looked horrified. Simone wondered if maybe she'd been too quick to think she wouldn't go through the same awkward stage as her older sister. Then the door was shut in her face.

She blinked and headed off to her bedroom to get dressed. When she emerged, Grace was in the living room watching TV. It was some show about teenage rock stars that held absolutely no appeal to Simone, so she decided to head out into her studio and try to make up some of the time she'd lost that afternoon.

'I'm going to do some work,' she called to Grace. 'Can you come get me when Harriet comes home or Frankie arrives?'

Grace didn't look up from the TV but she raised her hand in acknowledgement. 'Sure, Mum.'

Simone lost herself in her latest textile project for the next hour and a half and was startled when the knock came on her shed door. The door opened and Gracie appeared.

'Aunty Eff *and* Harriet are here.'

'Oh good.' Simone put down her scissors and stood.

'I'm not sure you're going to think that when you see Harriet.'

Simone's stomach clenched. 'Why? What's she done?'

'I think you should come see for yourself.'

Her heart hammering, she charged past Grace, up the garden path, not even caring about shutting the shed door, and stormed into the kitchen. Her eyes landed first on Frankie laying plates out on the bench and then she turned to see Harriet half in the fridge, drinking straight from the juice bottle.

'What the hell have you done to your hair?' she yelled, unable to believe the sight before her.

Harriet put the lid back on the juice, returned it to the shelf, shut the fridge door, slowly turned to face her mother and then shrugged. 'I dyed it blue.'

Feeling her blood pressure rising, Simone put her hands on her hips. 'Don't be smart with me, young lady. I'm not colourblind. I'll rephrase my question. Why the hell did you think it was a good idea to dye your hair blue?'

Harriet narrowed her eyes, thrust her shoulders back and stuck out her chin as she flicked her fingers through the ends of her long *blue* hair. 'Jaxon loves it.'

'Oh, well that's okay then,' Simone snapped. 'Never mind what your mother thinks. As long as *Jaxon* approves.'

'Mum, don't be so boring. I swear you act twice as old as you actually are.'

'Harriet—a word of aunterly advice,' piped up Frankie from where she was dishing out her pumpkin, spinach and ricotta cannelloni. 'Now might be a good time to be quiet.'

'I thought you were at Alyssa's,' Simone said, forcing herself to calm her breathing. If Harriet gave her one more word of cheek, she wasn't sure she'd be able to resist picking up something hard and hurling it at her.

'I was, but Jaxon and Brad were there too,' Harriet said like it was nothing at all and Simone decided there and then that it was time to show her daughter who was in charge around here.

'You know very well you are not supposed to see Jaxon outside of school without my permission. I would have thought you'd know that dyeing your hair without talking to me about it first was also a no-no.' She sighed. 'Honestly, Harriet, you leave me no choice. I'm grounding you for a month. You'll go to school and come home and don't even bother asking me if you can go to anyone's house or have a friend over here because the answer will be no.'

'*What?* You can't do that!' Harriet's hands flew to her hips, echoing Simone's stance.

'I think I just did,' Simone replied with a smug smile.

'But it's Alyssa's birthday party on Saturday night. *Everyone* is going to be there.'

'Everyone except you.'

'That's not fair. I *hate* you.' Harriet turned and ran from the kitchen. A few seconds later they heard her bedroom door slam.

Simone inhaled deeply, resisting the urge to scream after her that the feeling was mutual. She loved her daughter but she didn't *like* her very much at the moment.

'I promise I'll never dye my hair blue,' Grace said as she pulled out a chair and sat down at the table. 'And if she doesn't come back, can I have her serving of cannelloni?'

'No,' Simone sighed, her fury easing. 'She needs to eat. We'll leave it for when she's calmed down.'

'It's all right, Grace,' Frankie said as she brought the first two plates to the table. 'I made plenty. If you're still hungry after this, you can have seconds.'

Grace smiled up at Frankie and stretched across the table to grab the bowl of salad. 'Thanks, Aunty Eff.'

Simone looked down at the plate in front of her and just knew she wasn't going to be able to stomach much of it.

'Shall I get you a glass of wine?' Frankie asked, turning to the fridge. 'I could do with one myself. It's been a long week.'

'Thanks.' Simone nodded and within a few moments Frankie had poured the glass, given it to Simone and sat down again with her own drink. Simone found that even her favourite chardonnay didn't taste good. She wished she could just crawl into bed and forget about today. No, scrap that, she wished she could crawl into bed and forget about the last two weeks, but peace wouldn't come with slumber, only Angus, so maybe she should persevere with the wine.

As Frankie's and Grace's cutlery scraped across the plates, Simone picked up her glass again. 'So, how's you, Frank? Anything interesting happening I should know about?'

'Um … Not exactly.'

Simone raised an eyebrow; Frankie had deliberated too long. 'What's going on?'

'Nothing. Absolutely nothing. I wonder how Adam and Stella are going on their honeymoon?'

'I ran into Aunty Esther yesterday morning when she was dropping Heidi at school. She looked exhausted but said they'd heard from the newlyweds and they were having a wonderful time but missing Heidi.'

'I can imagine,' Frankie said. 'But Stella really deserves a holiday.'

'They both do. Esther wants to clean the house and make sure everything is nice for them before they come home on Monday, so I told her I'd take the girls over on Sunday and help. Want to come?'

'Um …' That look of discomfort flashed across Frankie's face and this time Simone was certain she hadn't imagined it. 'I can't this Sunday.'

'What's going on?'

'Um …'

'Would you quit saying "um" and fill me in.'

'Well …' Frankie inhaled and then let out her breath slowly. 'I'm going on a date on Sunday.'

'What?' Simone didn't know what she'd been expecting but it wasn't that.

'Go, Aunty Eff!' Grace cheered, lifting her arm to offer Frankie a high five. 'What's his name?'

Frankie laughed nervously and high fived her back.

'Do we know him?' Simone asked.

Again Frankie took her time answering. 'I met him on Rural Matchmakers.'

Harriet chose that moment to return to the kitchen. 'Met who on Rural Matchmakers?' she asked, sitting down at the table and making a show of not looking at her mother. Which was just fine, as Simone didn't want to look at her blue hair right now either.

'Aunty Eff's got a boyfriend.'

'He's not a boyfriend,' Frankie said, 'just someone I'm … pursuing.'

'Let's hope you have better luck than *she* had with *Logan*.'

Simone chose not to let Harriet rile her any further. She simply said, 'Yes, let's hope she does. I'm happy for you, Frank. So what's his name?'

'Uh … Clive,' Frankie said and Simone couldn't help but smirk along with her daughters.

'I hope he's better looking than he sounds,' Harriet said, her nose screwed up in disgust. Although Simone shared her sentiment, she bit her tongue.

'When do we get to meet him?' she asked instead.

'Not sure. It's early days. I just want to see how things go first.'

'I understand,' Simone said. She'd felt the same about Logan but ended up bringing him to the wedding to meet practically everyone she was close to. Look how much of a debacle that had been. Not that it was Logan's fault she and Angus had such amazing chemistry. An unwanted shiver shot down her spine at the thought.

'Thanks.' Frankie smiled and stood up. 'Now, does anyone want seconds?'

'Yes, please,' said Grace.

Chapter Twenty-two

Frankie parked her hatchback in the car park at Tarcoola Beach, grabbed her sunhat off the passenger seat and popped it onto her head. She'd tied her long red hair in a knot and now pushed it under the hat, then looked into the rear-vision mirror. Hopefully with the hat, dark sunglasses and her hair tucked up, she wouldn't be recognised if someone saw her and Logan together. And she was wearing a dress, something she rarely did.

Guilt churned the butterflies in her stomach as she locked the car and headed to the spot where Logan had told her to meet him. Mostly she couldn't wait to see him, but there was a tiny part of her that worried things wouldn't be so easy between them now they'd officially agreed to start seeing each other. Wind blew against her face as she walked, and she pressed a hand to her lips, wondering if her lipstick was overkill. Her make-up ritual usually consisted of a layer of tinted moisturiser and a little lip gloss, but today she'd made a big effort. She hoped she didn't look like an overdressed clown.

When she'd voiced her concern that someone she knew might see them in a café or restaurant, Logan had suggested a picnic on the beach and told her he would handle everything. No guy had ever made a picnic or even cooked for her before—they all expected that because she was a chef she was happy to do the honours. But it was nice not to have to worry about the food on top of her nerves and her guilt and everything else.

There were a few kids and a young family playing on the sand on the main part of the beach but Logan had told her to meet him further along, where they could have privacy. She lifted a hand to shade her face from the sun as she peered in the direction he'd indicated and only just made out the silhouette of a man a few hundred metres away. The figure turned towards her and as he lifted a hand to wave, all her anxiety, all her doubts about her clothes, her make-up, everything, evaporated. Every cell in her body tingled with awareness. She couldn't cross the sand to him fast enough.

Logan smiled as she approached and she almost stumbled at the sight of him in black cargo shorts and a greenish-blue T-shirt, a picnic rug at his feet, and an honest-to-God wicker basket sitting on top of it. *Swoon.*

'You came,' he said as he reached his hand out.

'As if there was ever any doubt,' she replied, slipping her hand inside his, heat flooding her at the connection.

He pulled her against him, dipped his head beneath the brim of her sun hat and kissed her. It was as simple as that. And she kissed him back, because it felt more right than anything had ever felt before, as if her sole reason for being born was to kiss this man.

'Why are you hiding all your gorgeous hair?' he asked, reaching under the hat to touch it when they finally broke apart.

'It's a disguise,' she whispered with mock-seriousness, and his beautiful lips broke into a grin.

'Ah, I see.' Then, 'It's so good to see you.'

'Ditto.' Her brain was still a bit scrambled from that kiss so a more eloquent description of how she felt was out of the question.

'Are you hungry?' he asked, gesturing to the picnic rug and basket.

She nodded. Truthfully, she was only hungry for one thing but she didn't want to appear like a hussy.

'In that case, take a seat.' With the hand that wasn't holding hers, he gestured to the picnic rug—a quaint tartan number that Frankie guessed had been in his family a while. Her family had never been the camping or picnicking type—like Simone, their mum Ruth had been single for almost as long as Frankie could remember and she'd never bothered much with outdoorsy pursuits. Visits to Aunty Esther and Uncle Dave's farm had been as close to nature as they'd got.

Getting comfy on the rug, she made a vow to herself that when she had a family, she'd take them on hundreds of picnics and they'd camp out under the stars and roast marshmallows on bonfires.

'What are you grinning at?' Logan asked as he knelt down beside her.

'Oh … just the beautiful day,' she said, nodding at the ocean. Probably too early to be telling him the truth—that she'd been picturing him with a little red-headed girl on his shoulders and a little boy that was the spitting image of him running ahead along the beach holding her hand. Didn't want to scare him off.

He followed her gaze, then looked back and smiled. 'Nice, but I hadn't noticed because I was too busy looking at something even more beautiful. You.'

Although it was a cheesy line, it sounded anything but cheesy rolling from his lips. Her tummy flipped and her breathing quickened. Of course she blushed. 'I bet you say that to all the girls.'

He shook his head and looked seriously into her eyes. 'I'm not going to pretend I've been a monk since I broke up with my ex-wife, but I can honestly tell you that no other woman has gotten under my skin like you have.'

Her heart squeezed and she thought her eyes might leak.

'Too full-on?' he asked with a sheepish grin.

'No.' She leaned into him, stretched up slightly and pressed her lips against his. He kissed her back, lifting her hat off her head and sneaking his fingers up into her hair, pulling her closer. His caress on the back of her neck sparked shivers right down her spine and she moaned when he slipped his tongue into her mouth.

The sounds of the waves splashing against the sand disappeared as she cupped his cheek, loving the roughness of his jaw against her palm. His two-day stubble had to be the sexiest thing she'd ever seen or felt.

'Anyone ever told you how hot you are?' Logan whispered, pulling back a moment to look at her before dragging her lips back to his.

Emboldened by his words and the heat in his eyes, she moved her hands lower, over the curve of his broad shoulders, coming to rest on his lovely biceps. She squeezed. They felt so hard and strong—much more like the arms of a man who worked outdoors than a journalist, but she loved that he did both. He was such a well-rounded individual.

And *such* a talented kisser.

Logan's lips trekked lower and her head fell back as he kissed her neck. She dropped her hands, palming them against the ground so as not to collapse under the sensations. Before she knew it they were both lying back against the picnic rug, snogging like a couple of horny teenagers, hands going everywhere, limbs entwined. Her heart was racing so fast she thought it might leap out of her chest at any moment—she had never felt such a burning desire to touch or be touched.

Logan, his body on top of hers, pushed himself up so his hands were on the rug either side of her head and he was staring down at her. 'I should feed you.'

Frankie frowned, not giving a damn about eating, but then out of the corner of her eye, she saw two shadows walk by and thought maybe she should give a damn about the fact they were in a public place and this close to ripping off their clothes. With a sigh, she nodded, trying not to mourn the loss of Logan's body heat against hers as he rolled over and sat up. He took a deep breath and ran a hand through his hair, his arm muscles flexing as he did so. Her pelvic floor tightened in appreciation. Telling herself she should sit up too, rather than lie there ogling him as though *he* were lunch, she forced herself into a sitting position and dusted off the sand that had somehow gotten on her clothes.

As Logan lifted the lid of the picnic basket, she did a quick scan of the beach, breathing a sigh of relief that she didn't recognise the passers-by. In the rush of hormones, she'd forgotten the need to lie low. She picked up her hat and jammed it back onto her head as he conjured a paper package, which announced itself as fare from the local fish and chips shop. Then he pulled out a bottle of pink bubbly—her favourite—and two glass champagne flutes.

'Impressive.' She smiled, her mouth watering. So he hadn't cooked, but what could be more perfect than fish and chips on the beach?

'I aim to please,' he said, as he laid the parcel between them and peeled back the layers of paper. He picked up a chip and held it out to her. She opened her mouth and took a bite, loving the intimacy of him feeding her. He popped the rest of the chip into his mouth and grimaced. 'They're cold.'

She shrugged, laughing. 'Not their fault.'

'I suppose not.' He hit her with a smile that sent shivers spiralling through her body. Chris Hemsworth, move over; Logan Knight truly was the sexiest man alive.

She plucked another chip, eating it as he uncorked their drink and poured it into the two glasses. He smiled as he offered her one and their fingers brushed against each other as she took it. All she could think about was what it would feel like to have his fingers on other, more private, parts of her body.

Hopefully oblivious to her torrid thoughts, Logan lifted his glass and clinked it against hers. 'To us,' he said.

She echoed his sentiment and then took a sip, loving the way the bubbles melted on her tongue.

'Well, tuck in.' He gestured to the food. 'I'm sorry I didn't bring any plates or anything.'

'I think it's sacrilegious to eat fish and chips from an actual plate. They taste much better right out of the paper.' And to prove her point, she ripped off a bit of fish and popped it into her mouth. So, the chips had gone cold and the fish was no longer crunchy but nothing could ruin this moment.

'Good?' he asked.

She nodded and then ripped off another piece and offered it to him. He ate it right from her fingers and she knew she'd never be able to eat fish and chips again without remembering this day.

They ate and drank, feeding each other and talking between mouthfuls. Frankie felt as if she'd known him so much longer than she had. Being with Logan just felt right, aside from one annoying thing. *Simone.* She sighed, wishing she could banish her sister from her mind, just for a few hours. There'd be plenty of time to feel guilty later, but right now, she just wanted to enjoy Logan while she had him.

As if a mind reader, he asked, 'How's Simmo going?'

Frankie shrugged. 'Hard to tell. I haven't seen much of her lately but she does seem a bit down. I guess it could be Harriet—she's being a right little shit at the moment—but I think she's more cut up about you guys breaking up than she's letting on.'

'I'm sorry to put you in this position,' he said, reaching out and brushing his thumb against her cheek.

She caught his hand in hers and smiled back. 'There's two of us playing this game.' And the guilt wasn't going to stop her. 'I told her I was going on a date today.'

His eyes widened. 'You did?'

'Yep. She asked me to go visit Aunty Esther with her and I had to tell her I was busy.'

'What exactly did you say?'

'That I'd met someone on Rural Matchmakers and was meeting them for lunch. At least this way I'm partly being honest.'

'What did she say?'

'Oh, she and the girls were happy for me. They wanted details. I told them your name was Clive.'

'What?' He coughed as though the last mouthful of his drink had gone down the wrong way. 'Where did *Clive* come from?'

'I dunno.' She gave him a sheepish smile. 'It just popped into my head.'

'Couldn't you have come up with something more macho?'

She laughed. 'Like what?'

He thought a moment. 'Like Jake, or Mitch, or Hunter. Hell, Bruce would be better than Clive. I don't look like a Clive, do I?'

'No, I promise you don't. You're way better looking than a Clive.'

'Why thank you.' He puffed up his chest, making her laugh again. Then he took her hand, his expression turning serious. 'Try not to beat yourself up. We're not doing anything wrong here. Neither of us is seeing anyone else—and you just don't want to hurt your sister so are biding your time waiting for the right moment to tell her. You're a good person, Frankie. And a very sexy one as well.'

She rolled her eyes but couldn't help the glow she felt at his words. It was weird, feeling so happy and so reprehensible at the same time. 'I just feel so guilty. I've never outright lied to Simmo

before. If the girls hadn't been there, I might actually have confessed the truth but she and Harriet had just had this big barney
over Harriet's hair and I couldn't bring myself to hurt her more.'

'Harriet's hair?'

'She dyed it blue.'

'Holy shit.' Logan's expression said it all.

'That was pretty much Simone's reaction too, multiplied by a
hundred, with a few choice words thrown in for good measure,'
Frankie said. 'I've actually never seen her that mad before. She's
grounded Harriet for a month.'

He chuckled. 'I'll bet that went down well.'

'Let's just say I don't think Harriet will be talking to her for a
while.'

'Poor Simone, she's got her hands full with that one, hasn't she?'

Frankie nodded and bit her lip. 'But ... let's not talk about Simone. I don't want to waste our time together.'

'What do you want to do then?'

★ ★ ★

Frankie blushed and Logan couldn't help but imagine her thoughts.
His had been along the same lines since he'd caught sight of her
walking along the beach towards him in that cute floral sundress.
He'd silently praised God for the beautiful September weather, making a picnic on the beach the perfect option. It was so much more
intimate than sitting in a café with other people only a few feet
away. But as much as he'd have liked to whisk her away and have his
wicked way, she deserved better than a quick tumble in the dunes.

'We could go for a walk on the beach,' she said eventually.

'Sounds like a plan.' He pushed himself off the rug and then
held out his hand to help her up. As she downed the last of her
sparkling wine, he packed up their rubbish in the basket and
folded the rug. 'Let's just dump these in the ute first,' he suggested.

They walked hand in hand back to the car park and it felt so natural, as if they'd been together for a long time. His head was telling him to slow the hell down but his heart and body were ready to throw themselves off the deep end. If this were his brother or a friend telling him how they felt—not that blokes had touchy-feely conversations like that—he'd ask them what the rush was, predict that they were thinking with the wrong brain, but it wasn't like that.

'Nice wheels,' Frankie said as they stopped in front of his 1970s Holden Kingswood ute.

'Thanks.' He dumped the basket on the back tray and then ran his hand along the top of the cab. 'It was my dad's.'

She reached out and took his hand again. 'It's really nice that you have something so special of his. Was he a big car enthusiast?'

'He was a Holden man—no-one in our family was ever allowed to buy a Ford or he'd disinherit them.' He smiled at the recollection. 'His shed out the back was filled with Holden memorabilia. Mum wouldn't let him have any of it on show in the house. It's all still there. None of us have been able to bring ourselves to get rid of it.'

'I can't imagine losing someone so close to me, never mind a parent.'

He nodded as they headed back towards the beach 'It's tough. I'd just married Loretta and Angus was busy with Sarah. Olivia was still only little. We were all looking to the future and we didn't notice how depressed Dad had got.' He swallowed the lump that had formed in his throat, wondering if that guilt would ever ease.

'You must have gotten married pretty young?'

He nodded. 'Loretta and I met when we were in high school. We tied the knot when we were totally young and stupid. I don't think she could handle all the sadness in our household so she found entertainment with the guy next door. Would you believe she's still with him?'

'Her loss,' Frankie said, squeezing his hand.

They took off their shoes and strolled along the shore, the waves licking at their feet.

When they reached the rocks, they sat down and looked out over the ocean. 'Tell me about your biggest joy,' Logan said. He wanted to know everything about her. Not the little stuff like favourite food and favourite colour—that would come as they hung out together more and more—but the deep stuff, the stuff that shaped her and made her tick.

Her face lit up. 'Opening the café.'

'That is an amazing achievement,' he agreed. 'It's a great little place. Funky, cool, with to-die for food.'

'Why thank you.' She showed her appreciation with a kiss.

'How'd you get started?'

'Well …' She sighed, and spilled the story of her relationship with the married man in Perth and how she'd fled home to be near Simone. 'I worked with Liam at the pub for a bit and then the woman who'd had the café forever offered it to me for a reasonable price. I was lucky that the shire wanted someone to keep it going. They gave me a good lease and Mum and Graham helped me with the initial set-up costs. I threw my heart and soul into making the café special and slowly I recovered from the betrayal.'

'Bastard,' Logan uttered, not letting on that he'd already heard some of this story from her sister. 'So I guess that would be your biggest disappointment then?'

'What? Getting screwed over by a married man?' She shrugged. 'Possibly. But I think watching Simone lose Jason and helping her through that tough time was the hardest thing I've ever had to do. What about you?'

'Biggest joy? That's easy. Becoming an uncle.'

Her eyes widened and her mouth dropped open. 'I didn't know you were an uncle. Who has a child? Angus or Olivia?'

He hesitated, feeling a little guilty about revealing this but wanting her to know, because Angus's pain had also had a major effect on him. 'Angus,' he said. 'He and his fiancée had a baby not long after Dad passed. He was such a joy, a light after so much darkness.'

'Oh my God. Did Sarah take him when she left?'

Logan picked up a pebble from his feet. He held it in his hand for a moment, then threw it into the water in front of them. 'He died at seven months.'

She gasped. 'That's horrible. How ...?'

Logan sighed. 'Cot death. Sarah fed him at ten o'clock and Angus went to check on him in the morning and he was gone.'

Frankie put a hand to her mouth.

'Angus and Sarah were never the same again. She stayed for a while, but Angus threw himself into caring for Olivia, and Sarah just couldn't handle it. I guess it was his way of coping, but she didn't want to help raise Liv when her own child was dead.'

Tears poured down Frankie's cheeks and he hugged her close.

'Poor Angus. He's had so much sadness in his life. Kinda makes his grumpiness understandable.'

'I know. Life sucks sometimes.' But he was no longer thinking about his brother. He was thinking about this gorgeous woman in his arms and how he needed to be completely honest with her.

She sniffed and then looked up at him. 'No need to ask what your biggest disappointment has been in life. There's been so many.'

'I might be going blind,' he blurted and then closed his eyes the moment the words were out.

'What?'

He opened his eyes again. Frankie's shock was palpable. Her face had gone pale and her hand was pressed against her chest as though she were suffering cardiac problems. Goosebumps prick-led on his arms. Perhaps he shouldn't have said anything. Maybe it was too soon, their relationship too new. Then again, if this was going to be a roadblock, might as well bring it out in the open before they'd gone too far down the path they were heading.

'About a year ago I start noticing some issues with my sight,' he admitted, taking a quick breath. 'I would occasionally trip or bump into things, but mostly I found driving at night difficult. Eventually I went to the doctor, who sent me to a specialist. After a round of tests, it was confirmed I have retinitis pigmentosa.'

'What exactly is that?'

'Basically it means the retinas in my eyes are no longer doing their job and my vision is deteriorating.'

'That's awful. I'm so sorry.' She leaned into him and pressed her head against his shoulder.

'It's not your fault.'

She pulled back and looked him in the eye. 'I—I didn't mean that. I'm just upset for you. I can't imagine being faced with something like that.'

'Sorry.' He sighed, unpractised at this conversation. 'I'm … just …'

'It's okay.' She pressed her lips against his cheek and then asked quietly, 'What's the prognosis?'

'Hard to tell. There's no cure or anything at this stage. Worst-case scenario, I'll completely lose my sight. Best case, it'll go downhill further but I'll keep some vision.'

'Shit.'

He chuckled. 'That wasn't the word I used when I first found out, but I've had time to come to terms with it.'

'What can they do about it?'

'At this stage, there is no cure, but there are a number of treatments and therapies being explored. I'm hopeful that medical advances will change my prognosis before it's too late but there are worse things I could have. This isn't a death sentence, just an invitation to redirect a few things in my life. Right now I'm just trying to work out how to live with it. I'm looking into learning Braille and investigating other ways that will make life easier.' He paused a moment. 'This blindness thing is why I've been so keen to lease part of our farm to a renewable energy producer. I'm scared I won't be able to help Angus forever and I don't want to leave him in the lurch. I figure if we have an alternative source of income, he'll be able to employ help when needed.'

'It makes sense. God, I imagine it was a shock for Angus as well. Is this thing you've got hereditary?'

Logan cracked his knuckles, something he always did when he was anxious. 'I haven't told Angus,' he said. 'You're the first person I've told.'

'Wow.'

He wasn't sure if the wow was for not telling Angus or for confiding in her. He let out a deep breath and turned again to face her.

'Thank you,' she whispered. 'But don't you think you should tell your family? I know if Simone had something like this, I'd want to be there for her. You said Angus isn't a hundred per cent behind your wind-farming idea, but if he knew your real reasons, I think he'd be more supportive.'

'I dunno.' He shook his head. 'I don't want anyone's pity. I don't want it to change how people see me. Has it changed how you see me?'

'Yes,' she breathed, and his heart jolted.

It shouldn't have come as a surprise. Who wanted to spend their life with a blind man? He didn't have a choice about coming to terms with it because he would never hurt his family the way his father had, but Frankie did.

'It makes me like you even more,' she continued. 'I admired and respected you before, but now I see a man who doesn't just sit by and let life tell him how it's going to be. The fact that you're thinking about Angus and Olivia, rather than wallowing in self-pity, only makes me want to be with you more.'

'Really?'

'Of course.' She squeezed his hand again. 'What did you think—I'm some princess who is going to run at the first sign of trouble? I'm made of tougher stuff than that. Like you said, there are worse things in life. And, even if you do eventually go blind, at least I'll still be able to look at you.'

She blushed a little as if she realised what she'd just said, that they'd still be together when his eyes got really bad and dammit, he hoped they would be.

'What did I do to deserve you?' he asked, grabbing her head in his hands and kissing her hard on the lips again.

She laughed when they came apart. 'Just walked into my café and kissed the wrong girl.'

He groaned. 'Am I ever gonna live that down?'

'Um …' She pretended to think about it a moment. 'I doubt it. I think it's the perfect story to drag out every Christmas. Once we tell Simone we're together, that is. Looks like we're both keeping secrets from our siblings. The question is who will tell first?'

He shrugged, then pulled her close and kissed her on the forehead. 'But no secrets from each other.'

She was quiet a moment. 'Actually, I do still have *one* secret.'

'Oh yeah?' He raised his eyebrows. 'Are you gonna tell me?'

'I'm not sure if I should. Promise you won't get mad?'

Now he was curious. 'Promise.'

'You know how you and Simone were talking on Rural Matchmakers for a couple of weeks before you met?'

He nodded.

'What would you say if I told you that you weren't actually talking to Simone?'

'I'd say please explain.'

She smiled and then bit her lip to cover it up. 'Harriet and Grace signed Simone up to the site—they thought it was time she got herself a man—but she had no idea about it until you turned up that day.'

'What?' He dropped his head in his hands and then looked up. 'Are you telling me I spent two weeks chatting up a couple of teenage girls?'

She started to laugh. 'It's kind of funny if you think about it.'

'It's kind of *mortifying*,' he choked, thinking this would likely be another story that he'd never live down—that's if he didn't kill Frankie's two nieces first.

She nudged him in the side with her elbow. 'You know … you're kinda cute when you're embarrassed.'

He shook his head and then started laughing as well.

Chapter Twenty-three

'Just ignore them,' Logan said to Angus as they approached the Geraldton Senior College gymnasium where the renewable energy company was holding the meeting for landholders interested in hosting wind turbines.

Angus raised an eyebrow, guessing he was talking about the protesters jumping up and down in front of the building with signs on pickets. He read a few for amusement's sake.

SAY NO TO 400FT MONSTERS
YOU DON'T GET USED TO THEM, YOU GET SICK
THE SHIT IS GONNA HIT THE FAN

He chuckled a little at that one.

PLANT TREES NOT TURBINES
DUMB, DUMBER AND WINDPOWER SUPPORTER

That's right, insult the meeting attendees—that's really gonna win me round to your way of thinking. He shook his head, wondering how many of these people had truly done their research and how many were just blindly following like sheep because they liked the drama. Either way, he'd promised to give this serious thought and he owed Logan more than he owed any of these people.

The protesters screamed slogans at them and tried to thrust flyers into their hands as they entered the hall. He and Logan politely declined and were rewarded with scathing looks. One woman even swore. There were two cops standing at the door—he guessed to ensure the protest didn't come inside.

Despite the ruckus going on outside, the hall was pretty full and they found seats a few rows from the back. As Logan checked something on his phone, Angus looked around to see if he recognised anyone. It was unlikely they were the only people from Mingenew considering the option. Although there were many locals who were opposed to the idea of wind turbines, there were just as many who, like Logan, thought it a viable option for additional income.

While Angus didn't see anyone from home, his heart jolted as his eyes came to rest on the back of a head a few metres in front. She had hair the exact shade of Simone's and it was cut in the same sensual style—bouncy and wavy. He remembered running his fingers through that hair and the recollection made his body wake up and take notice. He shifted in his seat, trying not to be obvious while he ascertained if it were really her. Though Simone wasn't a landowner, so he didn't know what business she'd have at the meeting.

He didn't know how he felt about seeing her and was worried that if she, he and Logan had to make small talk, he'd give away his discomfort. Hopefully Logan would be too invested in the wind-farming information to notice.

'Testing, testing.'

A hush fell over the crowd as a smartly dressed woman spoke into the microphone at the front of the hall. As the crowd noise dropped, the irate pleas of those locked outside filtered into the hall.

'Okay, I think we're ready.' The woman's smile looked too big to be real as she began her introduction. 'My name is Sandra Winters and I'm from Future Power. It's my pleasure to welcome you here tonight and I want to thank you all for taking the time to come and hear how Future Power can work with the community to both our benefits. There will be an opportunity for questions after the presentation, but first I'm going to hand over to Charlie Myers, Future Power's director of new development. Thank you, Charlie.'

Charlie stepped up to the microphone, dressed in the kind of black suit that rarely saw the light of day in these parts. He was all smarmy smiles as well and Angus thought he looked like someone out of a James Bond movie. One of the villains.

'Good evening, ladies and gentleman.' Charlie beamed at the crowd like a clichéd used-car salesman. Angus turned to Logan and they exchanged a look.

'Give him a chance,' Logan mouthed and then turned back to watch the flashy PowerPoint presentation.

Angus folded his arms across his chest and tried to be open-minded as he listened to the spiel. The presentation included lots of pretty photos and graphics, rave reviews from landholders already contracted with the company, a few measurements about the size of turbines, but very little actual information about how the part-nership progressed. Needless to say, when Charlie finally finished extolling the wonders of wind-farming, a number of hands shot up in the audience to ask questions.

'How much land is needed for the turbines?' asked a bloke right near the front. Logan couldn't see him but he sounded fairly elderly. Perhaps this was a way for farmers nearing retirement to still live and work the land but have a slower pace of life?

'Very little actually,' Charlie said, clapping his hands together as if this excited him. 'You'd be surprised. We estimate less than one per cent of most landholders' properties. Of course, easements are sometimes needed for access tracks, but we do our best to use existing farm roads where possible. Although we reserve the right to upgrade the road to cope with large loads during construction, so—' he shrugged and grinned '—this is often a win for the landowner.'

The next question came from the woman sitting next to the possible Simone. Angus couldn't help staring in case she turned to look at her neighbour.

'I've done a lot of reading on this,' the woman said, 'and I'm not a hundred per cent convinced. What do you say about the group outside who are adamantly opposed to the whole wind-energy business due to the effects it has on people's health and a farmer's livestock?'

Charlie cleared his throat, his smug smile appearing again as he leaned into the microphone. 'I'd say they should get their facts straight before they try to scare others.'

'Facts?' asked the woman.

'Research has shown absolutely no detriment to livestock from the actual turbines,' Charlie stated. 'Most of the bad press can be traced back to a case about thirty years ago in the United States where turbines on one wind farm were poorly located in the flight path of migratory birds. Things have progressed a lot since then and here in Australia, planning conditions for new wind turbine developments require extensive research on local bird life at all stages of the process. As a result, bird deaths or other animal deaths in rural regions rarely have anything to do with wind farms. The only effect of having turbines on your property is that livestock need to be kept away from the site during construction. Obviously for their own safely.'

'What about crops?' shouted a man down the back.

Angus didn't hear Charlie's response properly because the red-haired woman turned towards the speaker and his stomach clenched. It wasn't Simone. He shouldn't have felt so damn disappointed by this fact, but deep inside he'd wanted it to be her. She was still on his mind ninety-five per cent of the time, but Logan seemed to have moved on. His mood had improved dramatically since the weekend—although he'd been working away the last couple of days, they'd talked on the phone. And when Angus had seen him again today, Logan had been decidedly chipper. Angus wondered if maybe he'd found someone for a one-night stand in Carnarvon. Either way, maybe he wasn't as cut up over his split with Simone as Angus had initially predicted. Should he really make such a drastic decision about the future of their farm because of his guilt over one mistake?

'Next question?' Charlie asked and then pointed to a guy a few seats along from Angus and Logan.

'You mentioned minimal effect on cropping and livestock, but what about the farm as a whole? Any limitations we'll be locked into?'

'Very few and all such things would be negotiable when you enter a lease.' Charlie took the next question.

'Speaking of leases,' asked the lady who had kicked off the Q&A, 'can you tell us anything about them? I've read about an "option to lease". What exactly is that?'

'We start with an agreement known as an "option to lease", which means our team can access your property to assess wind-farm feasibility with the option to move into a lease agreement at a later stage,' Charlie explained, subtly glancing at his watch before continuing. 'This lease agreement usually comes into being when developers commence construction on the turbine site.'

'So can the farmer back out at this stage?'

Angus liked this woman. She was asking all the right questions, but he didn't think Charlie shared his opinion.

'No; option to lease is usually binding to the landholder,' he stated, his tone becoming condescending, 'whereas the developer can withdraw at any stage before construction commences.'

'Doesn't sound fair to me,' exclaimed the lady. 'I think this is a waste of my time. I'm going home to watch *The Big Bang Theory*.' And with that, she got up and walked towards the back of the hall, a ripple of laughter from the audience following behind her.

Angus sighed. He liked *The Big Bang Theory*.

Charlie seemed to think everyone had been laughing at the woman, rather than him, and he continued undeterred.

'I think what we all want to know,' asked a tall woman, also near the front, 'is how much money will we make?'

The crowd laughed again and a couple of people clapped. 'Amen,' shouted someone down the back.

Charlie shook his head. 'I'm sorry, but that's like asking how long is a piece of string. Remuneration varies significantly and of course depends on many factors, such as the performance of the turbines, location of the site, distance from major transmission lines. Payments are of course based on a percentage of gross revenue, but I'll be happy to discuss this further with you following the meeting if you are interested. Next question?'

'How long are the leases?'

'Lease agreements are generally for the life of the wind farm, which is usually about twenty-five years, with the option for renewal.' Charlie took a white handkerchief out of his pocket and wiped the sweat from his shiny brow.

'Will it decrease the value of my land?' Again, the crowd muttered their approval.

'Actually, we believe the opposite to be the case. A senate inquiry found that the value of properties that are host to wind turbines should increase, as long as the contract states that the rights to rentals for the turbines transfer with any property sale.'

As Charlie looked to the crowd for another question, Angus sighed. Before he made a decision he'd like to hear the other side of the argument as well, but from sensible people with factual evidence rather than the group of dissenters outside.

'What about noise pollution?' asked someone else. 'Do houses have to be a specific distance away from the turbines?'

Charlie shook his head. 'Generally we assess the location of all houses on a potential turbine site before going ahead with a development. Although there are no legal restrictions on how close a house can be to a turbine, mostly we prefer to be away from residential dwellings due to the noise emissions.'

'So you're admitting noise is a problem?' shouted the tall woman.

'That's not what I said,' Charlie said, looking past her and pointing to the audience. 'Last question, I think. You at the back there?'

'What about spraying? Will I still be able to spray any crop grown under the turbines?'

'All that information is our booklet.' Charlie held up a thick brochure—the one Logan had been trying to make Angus read for months. 'Now I'm sorry, but we're going to have to finish question time,' Charlie said, not sounding apologetic at all. 'Sandra and I will be available to speak with individuals who are interested in considering Future Power's proposal. While I don't want you to rush into an agreement, I will be honest and say that we have had a lot of interest from landowners in this region, so don't dither for too long. Thank you for your time.'

Logan turned to Angus. 'Well, shall we go talk to them?'

Angus frowned, not yet convinced that this was the right move. 'I'd rather sleep on it. Do a little further research of my own.'

'I've done loads of research,' Logan said, his tone frustrated. 'You heard the bloke, we don't want to miss out.'

Angus wasn't so sure. 'Look, if our property is suitable, then taking an extra twenty-four hours to think things through is not going to stop them. You heard them, they have to assess potential sites and I'll bet they'll be looking at quite a few properties before they make a decision.'

'But what about …?' Logan paused. 'Ah, fuck it. Whatever.' He shook his head, stood and stormed out of the hall.

★ ★ ★

Logan waited by Angus's ute, cursing his damn terrible night vision, which meant he'd driven all the way home earlier today so he could come to the meeting with his brother rather than come here straight from Carnarvon. Dammit, he should have known Angus's change of heart was too good to be true.

'I didn't say no,' Angus growled as he approached the ute and beeped it open. 'I just said I want to think about it a bit more.'

Logan climbed inside, shoved his seatbelt into its lock and then folded his arms in exactly the manner Angus had the whole way through the meeting. Before Charlie Myers had even opened his mouth Angus had been scowling, not at all open to this exciting opportunity. Logan was too pissed off to reply. He'd been trying to get Angus to think about this for months.

Angus started the ute and drove them out of the car park. Neither of them said a word until they reached the turn-off onto the Geraldton-Walkaway Road and Angus finally broke the angry silence.

'How much research have you done into this Future Power company? That guy seemed like a tool.'

'Of course I've done my research,' Logan scoffed, tired of not being taken seriously. 'Being a journalist is mostly research and I'm good at it. They're a financially sound business with a good track record. This wouldn't be their first project; we wouldn't be guinea pigs. Don't just rule it out because you don't like the face of the company.'

'That's got nothing to do with it,' Angus sighed. 'I don't want to be responsible for anyone getting sick. I've got enough lives on my conscience already.'

Fuck. Logan's fists clenched tightly. He understood the guilt Angus carried around but this reasoning was ridiculous. 'All that stuff about adverse health effects is hearsay. There's been nothing proven that living close to wind farms has any kind of ill effect on humans *or* livestock.'

Angus shrugged. 'Maybe so but that doesn't mean people don't listen to the hype. I don't need the grief from our neighbours.'

Logan couldn't believe what he was hearing. 'Do you really give a damn about how Loretta and Brad feel about this? Are their opinions more important than mine? Hell, for all we know, they're considering this too. We could miss out, have the turbines on the property next door and not reap any of the benefits.'

'I meant everyone in our area, not specifically Loretta and Brad. You know I don't give a toss about those two.'

Logan closed his eyes and rubbed his fingers against his forehead where a headache was taking hold. He thought about Frankie's belief that telling Angus about his eye condition might help convince him they needed to give leasing a shot. He didn't want to manipulate anyone, but Angus didn't have all the facts. If he was still against the idea once he knew why Logan was so keen on it, then at least they could consider alternatives.

He took a deep breath and opened his eyes. 'I know you think I want to do this to get away from the farm, to further my journalism career, but that's not true.'

'So you keep saying.'

Logan's jaw tightened. 'You don't know everything, okay? It's got nothing to do with my career. The reason I want to pursue this,' he said firmly and slowly, as if he were speaking to a naughty toddler, 'is because I'm going blind.'

Angus turned to look at him and the wheel turned with him. The ute swerved but Logan's hand shot out to bring them back to the middle of their lane.

'What the hell?' Angus said, slowing right down. 'What do you mean you're going blind?'

'Why do you think I drove all the way home today, so you could drive us tonight? Wouldn't it have made sense for us to meet in Carnarvon and me drive home after that?'

'I just thought you wanted to make sure I attended the meeting,' Angus said, his voice catching a little.

'Well, that too,' Logan admitted. 'But the main reason is my night vision is all but gone.' He swallowed. In some ways admitting this to Angus was even harder than admitting it to Frankie. 'I can't safely drive at night anymore and this is only the beginning.'

'Hang on. Can you go back a little? What's causing this blindness?'

And in the dark, as they travelled the lonely road home, he told his brother all about retinosis pigmentosa—the symptoms, the prognosis and the fact it runs in families.

'Bloody hell!' Angus said when he'd finished. 'How long have you known?'

Logan considered lying but decided against it. What would be the point? 'I've been noticing my night vision getting worse for a while now—particularly when driving—but it was only diagnosed a couple of months ago.'

'What?' Angus exclaimed. 'And you've kept it to yourself till now? Does Liv know?'

'No. I didn't want to burden either of you. I've probably got a few more years where life won't really be hindered by this thing anyway.' He also didn't want pity. It would just make everything so much more real.

'But if it's genetic, don't we have a right to know?'

Logan raised his eyebrows. 'I didn't think either you or Liv were in the baby market anytime soon, so I didn't feel there was a huge rush. I needed to come to terms with this myself before I told anyone.'

'Babies?' Angus screwed his face up at the thought. 'This isn't about babies. Didn't you think we might need to know because we also might be affected by it?'

He stared ahead and then blinked. Was the road blurry?

'I'm telling you now, aren't I?' Logan said. 'I'm sorry ... but I needed time.'

Angus heaved out a breath, pushing aside his own fears for the moment as his brother's reality finally dawned. 'No, I'm sorry. Fuck. I don't know what else to say.'

'You don't have to say anything. You can sleep on it, but after that we need to start thinking about the future. There's every chance I'll only be able to help you on the farm for a few more years.'

'Do you have a ... like a date or something?'

Logan laughed. 'Yep. Twenty-first of November 2019.'

'I guess that's a no,' Angus said, not laughing.

'I don't know exactly. I might not ever completely lose my sight or it might be gone in a couple of years. Either way, I don't want to wait until it's too late to make plans. I think the wind-farming option is a good one. Of course, once I can't work on the farm anymore, I won't take any income—' Not that he took much now. He mostly lived on his writing income. 'So you'll be able to put that into hired help—or you could find a wife who happened to love the land just as much as you.'

Angus snorted. 'Yeah, like that's likely.'

'There are plenty of women farmers as hands-on as their husbands. I've even seen some on the Rural Matchmakers site.'

'Fuck.' Angus glared at him. 'That's why you signed up for the internet dating thing, wasn't it?'

Logan grinned. 'Guilty as charged. I honestly did have to write an article about it, but then I thought if it worked for me, maybe you'd consider trying it as well.'

Angus shook his head. 'No way. You know my stance on relationships.' He paused, then added, 'You're an optimistic tosspot, you know that?'

Logan chuckled. Being a glass-half-full type had helped him when the specialist gave him the bad news. As had the bottle of Bundy he'd drunk in his hotel room afterwards.

'You're a good man, little brother, worrying so much about me. But I don't deserve it.'

'We'll have to agree to disagree on that one,' Logan said. And that was about as mushy as they got.

'What about you?' Angus asked. 'What will you do?'

'I'm considering applying for a radio gig. I've got some experience and there's a position going at ABC Geraldton. If I get it, I'll have been there a few years before things get really bad and if I move to Gero I won't have to drive much. Plenty of blind people hold down normal jobs.'

'Good for you,' Angus said. 'You're handling this so much better than I would.'

Logan wasn't so sure but he didn't want to dwell on it anymore tonight. They were nearing home and he couldn't wait to head to bed and call Frankie. 'You still going to Perth this weekend to see Liv?'

'Yep. I'll leave Friday lunchtime 'cos I've got an appointment in Geraldton in the afternoon. Do you want to come?'

'Would love to,' Logan lied, 'but I've got a few articles that are pressing and I want to knuckle under this weekend and get them done.'

'Okay. Do you want me to tell her … about your eyes, or would you rather do it yourself?'

Logan thought a moment. 'I think I should. If she has questions, I'll be best able to answer them. But I'll call her tomorrow, so you don't have to keep the secret for me.'

'Righto,' Angus said as he turned down their gravel drive.

Logan smiled. He'd been anxious for months about telling his siblings about his condition, but he actually felt lighter now that he'd begun.

Chapter Twenty-four

After the week she'd had with Harriet, the last thing Simone felt like doing was meeting her friends for afternoon tea for the official viewing of Adam and Stella's wedding photos, but neither did she want to be a sourpuss. She pushed open the door to Frankie's café and saw she was the first to arrive.

'Hey, sis.' Frankie stuck her head through the hatch from the kitchen and waved. 'Not like you to be early.'

Simone glanced at her watch as she plonked herself down on one of the couches in the corner. Truth was she'd been pottering around the studio for the last couple of hours, unable to concentrate on anything, so although she wasn't particularly enthused about looking at the wedding album, she'd been happy for the excuse to stop pretending to work. She shrugged at Frankie. 'Maybe I'm turning over a new leaf?'

Frankie snorted and went back to whatever she was doing. Stacey appeared a few moments later.

'Hi Simmo, can I get you anything?'

Simone frowned, unsure whether she wanted a drink, something to eat, both or nothing at all. In the end, she went for the safe bet. 'Just a skinny flat white, thanks.'

As Stacey smiled and headed back to the counter, Simone leaned forward and picked the latest edition of the *Bunyip News* off the table. She flicked straight to Drew's column, the only thing worth reading in her opinion. The last sergeant—pudgy O'Leary—had written dreary columns that read much like a church sermon, but Drew always made her laugh with his anecdotes about what was happening in town. He had a way with people, especially the young ones, and a way with words. Ruby was one lucky girl.

The bell on the café door tingled and Simone looked up to see Ruby enter. Speak of the devil, she thought, as she smiled up at her friend and patted the couch beside her. 'Hey there.' She held up the paper. 'I've just been reading Drew's column. He's a busy guy.'

'I know. I barely see him.' Despite this acknowledgement, Ruby smiled in the way lovers do when someone mentions their partner and then raised her eyebrows. 'I didn't expect to see you here first,' she said as she gave Simone a quick hug.

Simone smiled tightly. 'Was in dire need of caffeine.'

Ruby nodded in understanding as Stacey returned and deposited a steaming mug in front of Simone.

'Hi Ruby,' Stacey said.

'Hello,' Ruby replied. 'Could I have a white hot chocolate please and a black coffee for Drew?'

'Sure.' Stacey retreated again.

'Where is Drew?' Simone asked.

'He's working but he's going to pop in for a few minutes soon.' She sighed and leaned back against the couch. 'How are you anyway?'

'Good,' Simone lied, pasting a smile on her face. Hopefully Ruby wouldn't see how much of an effort it was because if she asked what was wrong, Simone wasn't sure she could answer. She just didn't feel herself at the moment but couldn't pinpoint whether it was the animosity with Harriet, the fact her mind kept drifting to Angus Knight and their illicit night together, or something else entirely. Maybe she needed a change. Maybe they all did. Although she could just imagine Harriet's response if she told them they were leaving Bunyip Bay.

But dammit, she was the mum—the one who worked her arse off to pay the bills and buy them the latest fashion items, who cleaned their clothes and, more often than not, their rooms. If she wanted to move them all to Timbuktu, then Harriet could just suck it up.

'How's things with you?' she asked Ruby.

'Oh great.' Ruby beamed. 'I'm crazy busy with lessons after school and on the weekends, and I'm thinking of getting another pony. I don't like having to turn down any kids who are eager to learn.'

'I'm so pleased for you,' Simone said, which was the truth. When Ruby had first returned to Bunyip Bay last year, she'd just come out of an abusive relationship and then there'd been so much drama and bad feeling when her parents' ag store burned down. It was more than time that life cut her a break.

Before either of them could say anything else, the door opened again and in walked the Burtons. They were all holding hands—a grinning Heidi in the middle—so they had to turn and come in sideways. Simone and Ruby laughed at the sight.

'What?' Stella asked, as Heidi broke free and rushed to hug them. First she wrapped her arms around Ruby as if she hadn't seen her in weeks and then she gave Simone the same treatment before settling on the couch between them. Ruby and Adam took the couch opposite.

'You three looked just like a family of elephants travelling in a line when you came in,' Ruby said. 'Anyway, sit down and tell us all about your honeymoon. How was it?'

Stella smiled in a way that gave her daughter's massive grin a run for its money and Adam looked adoringly at her as if she were the only woman in the café.

'Fantastic,' Stella breathed. 'We were so indulgent, some days we slept till noon and then spent the next few hours on the beach or lazing by the pool before—' she broke off abruptly, looked to Adam and then blushed, '—before going out to dinner.'

Simone exchanged a knowing glance with Ruby. She reckoned they'd indulged in another activity to work up their appetites before those dinners, but she didn't really want to dwell on the thought of her cousin having sex. 'Sounds fabulous. I could so do with a holiday.'

'Me too.'

'Hey, everyone.' Frankie arrived, laid a plate of red velvet cupcakes on the table and then pulled up a chair, only to be ambushed a moment later by Heidi. She laughed as the little girl climbed up into her lap. 'Want a cupcake, gorgeous girl?'

Heidi nodded and helped herself. Within a few seconds she had icing smeared all over her face.

'What'd I miss?' Frankie asked.

'Not much,' Stella said. 'We only just arrived. Is Drew coming?'

Ruby opened her mouth to reply as the door opened again and there stood Sergeant Noble, a tall, impressive figure in his smart uniform. He strode in like a man confident in his skin, then leaned over and kissed Ruby on the lips. Simone had to admit, there was something about a guy in uniform. Although Angus was just as sexy in his well-worn farmer's attire.

No! She banished that thought from her head and waved her hand against her cheeks, trying to cool her temperature. Luckily the others—all greeting Drew and asking if he'd had any interesting call outs that day—didn't notice.

'Nothing too out of the ordinary,' Drew replied, 'although I did have to rescue Dolce's cat from up a tree because none of the firies were available. I've got scratches all up my arms.'

'Aw, baby, let me have a look at them,' Ruby said as she slid along the couch to make room for him. It felt very squishy with the three of them there.

'What's up with you, Frankie?' Drew asked, looking over at her as Ruby examined his arms.

Frankie blinked. 'Me? Nothing. Why?'

He raised an eyebrow. 'You look different. You're glowing or something?'

'Am I?' Frankie asked, fiddling with her collar.

Although Frankie had her hair tied back in her trademark plaits and was wearing her usual uniform of black chef pants and the café polo shirt, Simone could see what Drew meant. There was something different about her today. 'That'll be down to her new man,' she said, without thinking.

'What?' exclaimed the others.

Frankie gave them a shrug and a sheepish smile.

'Spill,' Adam said, leaning forward.

'There's not much to say … yet.' Frankie's cheeks flushed. 'We've only … just started seeing each other.'

'What's his name?' Stella asked.

'Is he cute? What does he do for a living?' This from Ruby.

'Um …' Frankie looked at the counter as though hoping for a reason to escape this interrogation, but Stacey had everything under control.

'Leave her alone. She'll tell you when she's ready.' Simone remembered how awkward and pressured she'd felt when her friends were teasing her about Logan. They all meant well, but they were so blissfully happy in coupledom that they'd forgotten how hard dating and trying to find The One could be. She shouldn't have put her foot in it and told everyone about Frankie's new man.

'Sorry,' Stella said, glancing down at her hands, looking chastised.

Ruby nodded. 'You don't have to tell us if you don't want to.'

Frankie smiled. 'It's fine. There's really nothing to tell yet and besides, we're here to look at Adam and Stella's wedding photos. I, for one, can't wait.'

'And I can't stay too long,' Drew said.

Simone raised an eyebrow, biting down on the impulse to remind him that he was the one who raised the distraction.

'You'll love them.' Stella leaned down to grab her iPad out of her bag. 'But first I want to thank you for your parts in our wedding—you all made the day extra special.'

'Yes,' Adam agreed and patted his stomach. 'Thank God Heidi finished off the leftover cupcakes while we were away or I'd need new jeans.'

Everyone laughed. Adam didn't have an ounce of fat on his hard, lean body.

'And Simone, thanks for helping Esther clean our house for us. It was lovely to arrive back and have nothing to do but relax some more.'

'It was my pleasure,' Simone said. 'But if you don't show us the photos soon—'

'Okay, okay.' Stella put the iPad on the table, flipping back the purple cover to make a stand, then angled it so everyone could see. 'These are only the proofs. The album won't be ready for a while but we need to choose the best ones. You guys can help.'

They all leaned in to get a closer look, Ruby swiping from photo to photo because she was the closest. They spent the next fifteen minutes oohing and ahhing over the beautiful photos—first of the ceremony on the beach, then the shots of the bridal party, most of which had been taken in Kalbarri National Park, and then photos of the fun and frivolities at the reception.

Stella kept a running commentary until Adam patted her knee and reminded her that everyone here had also been at the wedding so they probably didn't need quite such a detailed description.

'Sorry.' Stella bit her lip. 'I'm just so happy.'

'And who can blame you?' Ruby said, smiling over at her. 'These photos are amazing. You look gorgeous.'

Simone and Frankie murmured their agreement.

'Heidi!' The little girl shrieked and pointed at the screen, clearly excited to see a picture of herself in her white princess dress.

Looking at these photos, Simone couldn't help thinking of the night *before* the wedding. Snapshots from that surprising evening kept landing in her head and giving her hot flushes.

'Stacey?' she called. 'Can we get some water over here, please?'

'Sure. Coming right up.'

'Sorry,' Frankie said, looking up. 'Does anyone want anything else?'

Too engrossed in the photos, nobody replied. Frankie shrugged and went back to them as well.

Stacey arrived with a glass bottle of water and six icy-cold glasses. 'Here you are.'

'Thanks,' Simone said, taking one and filling it quickly.

'You're welcome.' Stacey lingered and peered over Frankie's shoulder at the iPad.

Simone lifted the glass to her lips just as she caught a glimpse of Angus in the background of one of the photos. Even looking like he'd rather be anywhere than at the reception, he was way hotter than any man had a right to be. *Oh Lord*. This was just what she needed. She'd spent the last ten years comparing every guy she met to Jason, all of them coming up short. And now her one night with Angus had probably ruined her again. Even if it weren't for the complication with Logan, it was clear that Angus was emotionally scarred and not a good prospect for a committed, ongoing relationship. But knowing this didn't stop her wishing things were different.

She downed the whole glass of water in two seconds flat.

'I'm sorry, but I need to get back to work.' Drew stood. 'Your photographer did a top job with these shots.'

'And gave us a great price too,' Stella said, looking up at Drew. 'Maybe you guys should use him for your wedding.'

'Have you set a date yet?' Frankie asked.

Simone tried to look interested, but the prospect of another wedding so soon didn't fill her with warmth and joy. Weddings were fine for couples, but if you were single they were hell. Just like Valentine's Day. Maybe Frankie's new man could set her up with a mate? She chuckled inwardly at the thought and then wrote it off. Nope, she was done with men.

Ruby and Drew exchanged a look and then Ruby said, 'We haven't quite settled on a date yet but we have settled on a location.' She paused.

'Well?' Stella asked after a few moments. 'Don't leave us hanging.'

'Bali!' Ruby clapped her hands together. 'Of course you're all invited.'

The others all shrieked their excitement but despite the fact Simone had just said she needed a holiday, this was not what she'd had in mind. Not that she had anything against Bali, but having to keep an eye on two teenage girls—one of whom wasn't currently talking to her—wasn't her idea of a rest. And no way would she be able to relax if she left Harriet behind. Who knew what the girl would get up to home alone?

No-one appeared to notice Simone's lack of enthusiasm, so she cuddled into Heidi and chatted to her about why she wasn't at school today.

'Having a holiday with Mum and Dad.'

Simone smiled at the way Heidi referred to Adam and before she knew it, the others were also saying goodbye.

'Come on, Heids,' Stella said, reaching out her hand. 'We're going for a walk on the beach.'

Simone said her farewells but couldn't find the energy to raise herself from the couch. She had fifteen minutes before she needed to be home for the girls.

'You okay?' Frankie sat down beside her as the door clanked shut behind the others.

'Not really,' she said, contemplating whether to confess everything to her sister. Surely Frankie would understand. One little slip up didn't put her among the likes of serial cheaters and marriage wreckers. And the Knight brothers were ancient history now anyway.

Frankie picked up a cupcake and held it out. 'Here, this'll help.'

Simone shook her head. 'I'm not hungry.'

'Are you sick? That's not the first time you've turned down my cake recently.' Frankie raised her eyebrows as she laid her hand on Simone's forehead. 'You're actually really hot.'

'Am I?' Probably due to the torrid thoughts she'd just been having about Angus, but maybe she actually was sickening for something. She'd been so drained the last week.

'Yeah.' Frankie nodded. 'I think you should go see the doctor. Get some drugs and rest up. Are you sure you're going to be up to looking after the café for me this weekend?'

'Where are you going again?' Simone asked, trying to remember if Frankie had actually told her. 'Seeing your new boy?'

'Yes. We're meeting in Geraldton again.'

'For the *whole* weekend?'

'Don't look at me like that!' Frankie exclaimed. 'You're not my mother. Besides, we have to make the most of the time we get together.'

'Just be careful, little sis,' Simone said, forgetting about her own woes for a minute. 'You only met this guy last week.'

Frankie was quiet a few seconds, then, 'I will be. Don't worry about me.'

'Okay.' Simone sighed. 'And I'm sure I'll be fine to watch the café. I think all this business with Harriet is just getting to me. But I'll drag her and Grace along to help in here. The compulsory time together will probably be good for us.'

Frankie laughed, but, like Simone, she didn't sound like she completely believed that.

★ ★ ★

'Simone McArthur,' called Dr McDonald from just outside the door of her consulting room.

Simone put down the ancient magazine she'd been flicking through and stood. She felt the other locals in the waiting room following her with their eyes as she headed to the doctor's open door; no doubt the moment she was inside they'd be speculating about what her issues were. That was the problem with small country towns—everyone seemed to know your every move.

She smiled as Dr McDonald closed the door behind her.

'Hello, Simone. Take a seat.'

'Thanks,' she said, doing as she was told.

Dr McDonald sat too and swivelled her chair to face Simone. 'What seems to be the problem?'

'I'm not exactly sure. I had a bit of a fever yesterday afternoon and I've been feeling tired and a little off lately.'

The doctor frowned. 'Can you describe what you mean by "off"? Flu-like symptoms? Nausea?'

She nodded. 'Kinda queasy. Don't feel like eating.'

'Okay.' Dr McDonald grabbed a sample pot off the back of her desk and handed it to Simone. 'Do you think you can do a sample for me?' At Simone's confused expression, she continued, 'You'll be amazed what urine can tell us. I just want to rule out a few things before we investigate further.'

'All right.' Simone rose and went into the little bathroom that was off the consulting room. As she dropped her pants and sat down on the toilet, it suddenly hit her.

She thinks I'm pregnant!

Her first reaction was a giggle, but then a cold feeling consumed her, freezing her heart and clenching her stomach. The fatigue she'd felt this last week was akin only to two other times in her life. She'd been so tired in the early months of pregnancy with Harriet and Grace that occasionally she'd laid down on the floor wherever she was and napped. And, now she thought about it, her period was a few days late. *Oh fuck!* How had she been so stupid? Maybe she'd gotten her dates wrong that weekend with Angus, so crazed with lust after a ten-year man drought that she'd convinced herself she was safe. The least she could have done was gone and got the morning-after pill!

Hoping she was wrong, she screwed the lid back on the pot, pulled up her pants and went out to face her fears.

'I'm pregnant, aren't I?' she said as she thrust the little pot at the doctor.

'Is it a possibility?' Dr McDonald asked, keeping her face carefully neutral.

'Perhaps.' She placed a hand on her stomach, which felt like it was home to a pack of angry moths—or whatever the collective term for a group of moths was—and sank into the chair. As Dr

McDonald unscrewed the lid and dipped in the little cardboard stick, Simone held her breath. How the hell would she cope with a baby? It wasn't like she was doing a stellar job with the two she already had.

The doctor drew out the stick and looked at it. 'I'm not sure whether to congratulate or commiserate, but yes, you're pregnant.'

No! Simone sat there in shock for a moment. Just her luck that the first time she had sex in ten years she got pregnant. This had to be her body's idea of a sick joke.

'Do you know the date of your last period?'

'Huh?' She couldn't think straight, so she dropped her head into her hands and cried.

After much comforting and assurances that she would be there whatever decision Simone made about the baby, Dr McDonald saw her out of the office. Like a zombie, she paid her bill and then made her way out onto the street. As she arrived at the Pajero, her mobile beeped with a message.

Without thinking, she tugged the phone out of her handbag and glanced at the screen.

Hope you're feeling better. If not, Stacey said she can hold the fort over the weekend. I'm setting off early. See ya Monday! Frank x

Her hand shook around the phone as she stared down at the message.

She no longer had any choice about telling Frankie about Angus, but at least she had the weekend to get her head around it.

And oh, *dear God,* how the hell was she going to break the news to Angus?

Chapter Twenty-five

As Logan grated chocolate to go on the top of his tiramisu, he surveyed the kitchen—once again clean after his mad cooking afternoon. His duck ragu simmered on the stove and his handmade pici pasta was draped over a dowel, ready to be cooked when needed. Everything smelt amazing and he only hoped Frankie thought so too. Earlier in the week, during one of their long phone conversations, he'd grilled her on her tastes. Most chefs had an open mind where food was concerned and were willing to try just about anything once, but he wanted to make sure he didn't serve up something she didn't like.

He wanted everything about their weekend together to be perfect, starting with dinner.

With that thought, he glanced at the time on the microwave again. Although he'd been busy in the kitchen since just after Angus had left for his appointment, time had dragged all day, but now it wasn't long until Frankie would here.

Time to get a move on. Just the chocolate to sprinkle on top, then a quick shower and change and he'd be ready. Emptying the grated chocolate into a bowl, he looked out the window and felt the blood pump through him at the sight of her little white hatch-back churning up the gravel drive. Judging by the speed it was going, she was as eager to get to him as he was to see her.

With no time to change now, he abandoned the chocolate, wiped his hands on a tea towel then ran them quickly through his hair before hurrying outside to greet her. Angus's dogs got there first, though, leaping up and trying to lick her as she tried to climb out the car.

'Well, hello there, cute stuff,' she said and he almost felt a prick of jealousy that she was referring to the mutt, not him.

'Oi, you two, leave her alone. She's mine.'

Frankie laughed, trying to fend off the dogs as she met his gaze. Her gorgeous smile lit up her whole face and hit him like a blow to the solar plexus, before heading lower. Ignoring the ache in his groin, he lunged forward and pulled the dogs away.

'Go on,' he yelled at them. 'Back to your beds.' Their heads drooped at being chastised and they slowly turned and trundled back in the direction of the front verandah.

'Damn dogs,' he said, standing in front of Frankie and hoping she wouldn't glance down. He didn't want her to think him some kind of sex maniac, but it had been a long time since he'd felt such attraction to someone and his body didn't care for waiting. 'Sorry about that.'

'It's fine.' She dusted herself off and his gaze flicked down her body, taking in her cute black T-shirt, short denim skirt and knee-high boots. Good God, how was a man supposed to control himself when his girl turned up in an outfit like that?

He swallowed. 'Did you find your way easy enough?'

She nodded, then rubbed her lips together and Logan decided that was enough small talk. He'd waited almost a week to kiss her again and he didn't want to wait another moment longer.

'Good,' he said, and then he stepped right up close and pulled her against him, their lips colliding in a frenzy of lust, need and desperation. She tasted delicious, felt so damn good—her soft breasts pressed up against his chest—and he couldn't get enough of her. He slipped his hands up into her hair, which was down for the first time he'd ever seen it, and her arms wrapped around him, gliding down to cup his butt.

He groaned into her mouth. Impossible to hide the package in his pants now, but somehow, the way her tongue was sliding over his, he guessed she didn't mind it at all. His hands started an exploration of their own, first caressing her neck, then moving lower and slipping around the front, one thumb grazing the bare skin at her throat before dropping down to cup her breast. It fit perfectly in his hand and his patience for the material between them started to wear thin. Realising if he didn't slow things down, they'd be consummating their relationship on the bonnet of her car, he reluctantly ripped his mouth from hers and jammed his hands in his jeans pockets.

She smiled at him, her lips raw and red. 'Hmm … you taste like chocolate.'

He grinned. That'd be the chocolate he'd broken off and popped into his mouth before grating the rest of the block. 'And you taste better than anything I've ever tasted before. Have you got a bag or something?'

She nodded. 'My stuff's in the back seat.'

He opened the door, grabbed her backpack and hitched it over his shoulder. 'I'm so glad you're here.'

'Me too,' she said, slipping her hand back into his as they started towards the house. 'Lucky Angus decided to go away for the weekend. Would have been risky you coming to Bunyip Bay.'

'Yeah, we've got much more privacy here.'

The dogs roused their heads from their beds again as he and Frankie stepped up onto the verandah, but one look from him and they stayed put.

'Do you want me to take my boots off?' Frankie asked as she glanced down at his bare feet.

He had visions of taking them off himself later, but he simply shook his head and said, 'Nope, Angus doesn't mind about stuff like that.'

He opened the door and held it as she stepped inside. She breathed in deeply and looked back at him. 'Something smells good. And what cute décor you have. I wouldn't really have picked it as your style, or Angus's.'

He chuckled. 'What? You don't take us for vintage kind of guys?'

Her look said it all.

'It's Mum's doing. Sarah, Angus's ex, hated it—her style is more hippie chic.'

'That's a thing?'

He shrugged. 'Who knows? But Dad didn't want anything changed and then she got busy with the baby and it was always one of those things they were going to get around to doing. You know the rest.'

'Where did you and your ex live when you guys were married?' Frankie asked.

'We were in Perth—both at uni, but we spent a lot of time up here. Anyway, let's go put your bag down and I'd just better check on dinner.'

He led her into the kitchen, dumped her bag by the door and crossed to the stove to check that his ragu hadn't burned while he'd been busy outside. That *would* be embarrassing.

'That smells amazing. Duck ragu?' she guessed.

'You are a pro,' he said, turning off the stove. 'I'm almost ready. Just need to have a quick shower and change, then I'll cook the pasta.' He gestured to his jeans, which were covered in flour and other ingredients.

She raised an eyebrow. 'Bit of a messy cooker, are ya?' Before he could reply, she stepped close to him and placed her hand against his chest as she looked into his eyes. 'Would you like some company?'

It took him a second to realise what she meant. And then he almost choked, not because he didn't like the idea but because he liked it very much. 'You sure?'

She walked her fingers up his chest and then touched one to his lips. 'Never been surer of anything. And I am feeling a little … dirty.'

That was all the assurance he needed. He picked her up, threw her over his shoulder and relished the sound of her squeals as he carried her down the hallway and into the bathroom, where he gently deposited her on the vanity bench. It was not the way he'd envisaged the weekend; he'd planned a very civilised romantic dinner in the dining room and was hoping things would lead to the bedroom later, but he hadn't presumed. He'd told Frankie there was a guest room if she wanted it. Still, he couldn't be happier with the way things were progressing.

Frankie reached down to her boots, but he stilled her hands and shook his head.

'You're my guest, so let me assist you.'

She licked her lips and nodded as he lifted one of her incredibly sexy pins and slid the zipper down on the first boot. He sucked in a breath as he tugged it off and ran his hand down her silky smooth calf.

'It's hot in here,' she said, her tone breathy as he started on the other boot.

'Damn right it is.' When she was bootless, he stood between her legs, her little skirt ruching up along her thighs. He put his hands on them and she whimpered as he stroked his thumbs against her skin.

'Oh Logan,' she whispered, leaning back against the wall. He knew exactly what she meant because he felt it too.

'Come on,' he said, lifting her off the bench. 'Let's get the rest of our gear off.'

She smiled and reached out to touch the hem of his T-shirt. 'I may be the guest, but I like to do my bit.'

And with those words, she yanked his shirt up and over his head, tossing it on the floor. He dropped his arms and took care of her skirt. Then she made short work of the buckle on his jeans. As he shucked them and his jocks down his legs and discarded them along with his shirt, Frankie ripped off her top, leaving her standing before him in nothing but a black cotton bra and panties. They may not have been Victoria's Secret but on Frankie they were the sexiest things he'd ever seen.

It seemed a shame not to spend a little time admiring them, but he didn't know how much longer he could hold out.

'Are you gonna turn on the water?' she asked.

'Are you gonna take off your underwear?' he retorted.

She cocked her head to one side. 'I thought … since I was the guest … that was your job.'

Logan didn't needed to be asked twice.

★ ★ ★

'Mum! Mum!'

Simone blinked herself awake and looked up to see Grace peering down at her. It took her a few seconds to orientate herself and then she realised she was lying on the couch. Again. 'What time is it?'

'Five-thirty. And I'm starving. What's for dinner? How come you're so sleepy all of a sudden? This is the third time in the last few weeks you've napped and you never nap. I thought you hated naps.'

Grace's babbling was making Simone's skull pound. She sat up, but Grace didn't stop, frowning at her like she was an alien.

'Are you sick or something? Please tell me you're not dying of cancer.'

Oh God. Telling Frankie and Angus was going to be hard, but what about the girls? Harriet especially would think her a hypocrite. She'd told her daughter to practise safe sex—preferably abstinence—and then gone and done the exact opposite. With life-altering consequences.

'I'm fine,' she said very matter-of-factly, reaching out to squeeze Grace's shoulder as she stood. 'Now, I brought some left-overs home from the café. Can I interest you in some quiche or maybe some lasagne?'

'Or both?' Grace asked hopefully.

Simone raised an eyebrow and shook her head, gazing at her daughter who seemed to have the appetite of a horse lately. 'You must have hollow legs. Now, go get your sister and tell her we're having dinner now and her presence is required whether she likes it or not.'

She turned towards the kitchen, thinking that Grace might have more luck luring Harriet out of her room than she would. She'd come home from school in a right strop, looking as if she'd been crying. Thankfully her blue hair was already fading. When Simone had asked her what was wrong, she screamed: 'Leave me alone! As if you give a damn about my feelings.'

So many responses had jumped into Simone's head at this accusation, but Harriet was in no mood to be reasoned with and quite frankly, Simone wasn't in the mood to bang her head against a brick wall. Instead, she'd thrown her hands up in the air as she listened to Harriet's bedroom door slam shut, and then gone to lie on the couch. Right now, she had enough problems of her own to deal with.

In the kitchen she opened the fridge and was retrieving the plastic containers she'd brought home from the café when Grace rushed in waving a small piece of paper in front of her.

'She's gone, Mum. She's gone!'

'What?' Simone's hands froze around the containers as she stared at Grace. 'Is this a joke? What do you mean she's gone?'

'It's all here. In her letter.'

Dumping the food on the bench, Simone crossed the kitchen and snatched the paper out of Grace's hand. She stared down at it, the words jumbling in front of her eyes.

Hate it here. Life sucks. Going away for a while. Not that you'll care.

When Harriet had shouted these words earlier it had been like water off a duck's back, but now they felt like a knife twisting in Simone's heart. She clutched the note to her chest, her heart thumping. 'What do you think this means?'

Grace shrugged, looking like she was about to burst into tears.

'You don't think …' Simone didn't finish her sentence, not wanting to alarm Grace. She bit her thumbnail and thought hard.

'Should we call her friends? And check if she's with any of them?'

'Yes. Good idea. Thanks, sweetheart. Can you go grab the phone?'

As Grace rushed off to get it, Simone took a deep breath and did something she very rarely did. 'Please, God,' she whispered, 'don't let anything happen to my baby. Don't let her do something stupid.'

'Here, Mum.' Grace returned, thrust the phone at her and Simone immediately dialled Harriet's mobile. It was a long shot and she wasn't surprised when it rang out.

She grabbed the local Bunyip Bay directory out of the top kitchen drawer. 'I'll start with Alyssa,' she told Grace. 'Can you write a list of any other girls you can think of?'

'Yep. And shouldn't you ring Jaxon's house too?'

Simone nodded as she punched in the number of Alyssa's house. Thank God one of them was thinking straight.

Alyssa's home phone rang out as well and Simone started down the list. As there was no high school in Bunyip Bay and most of the teenagers went to Geraldton or away to boarding school in Perth, Harriet didn't have loads of local friends.

'Hello?' answered Jaxon's mum after a few rings.

'Oh, hi, Julie,' Simone said, trying to keep the panic out of her voice. 'It's Simone here. I'm just wondering if Harriet is over there.'

'She better not be,' Julie replied. 'Jaxon is in his room and I've told him he's not allowed to take her in there, but I'll go check for you. Just one minute.'

It felt like Julie was gone for ages.

'I'm sorry,' she said when she finally returned. 'Jaxon says he and Harriet broke up last weekend.'

Simone frowned, her heart turning to ice. Harriet had been home all weekend, except when they'd gone to visit Esther. The rest of the time Simone had kept a beady eye on her so she hadn't been able to sneak out. It didn't make sense. 'All right, never mind, thanks, Julie,' she said and then disconnected, her palms now sweaty and her heart still beating so loudly she could hardly think.

She took a quick breath. 'Grace, do you know anything about Harriet and Jaxon splitting up?'

Grace shrugged one shoulder. 'She hasn't said anything to me but I saw Jaxon kissing this other girl on the oval yesterday at lunchtime.'

Oh, fuck! Poor Harriet. Poor darling girl. Simone's heart felt as if it were breaking for her daughter. Young love could be bitterly cruel and when it went wrong you honestly felt like the world was ending. She should have been there for Harriet, holding her close, wiping her tears away and spoon-feeding her ice-cream but she'd been too consumed with her thoughts of Angus to notice that behind Harriet's anger was a whole load of sadness.

What a poor excuse for a mother. She pressed her hand against her stomach, thinking of the tiny life growing there. Another life for her to stuff up.

'Do you think we should call the police?' Grace asked, interrupting Simone's self-deprecation.

'Yes.' She could barely say the world. Involving the police made it all too real, all too scary. 'And can you use my mobile and ring Aunty Eff? I think it's next to the couch.'

Grace nodded and went to get it from the lounge room. Simone's hands shook as she called Drew.

'Hey Simmo. How are you on this fine Friday evening?'

Ignoring his chipper tone, she rushed to explain. 'Harriet's gone. I don't know where to look or how long she's been gone. Well, can't be more than an hour because she came home from the bus. Oh God, Drew, I'm scared she's going to harm herself.'

'Simone! Calm down. Take a breath. What do you mean she's gone?'

Tears started down her cheeks but she swiped them away as she tried to speak clearly. 'She left a note. It says she's had enough of everything and is going away for a while.' She paused a moment. 'Hang on, "a while" means she's planning on coming back, right? So she's not going to kill herself?'

'I doubt that,' Drew said. 'She's probably just letting off steam. Mike and I will have a drive around town and see if we can see her. Any ideas where she might go?'

'No. And I've called all her friends. Except I couldn't get through to Alyssa's house.'

'I'll check there first. Don't panic. And you stay at home in case she comes back. We'll keep in touch.' With this promise, he hung up.

Don't panic?! Drew didn't have kids so he didn't know he was asking the impossible of her. If anything happened to Harriet she would *never* forgive herself.

'She's not answering, Mum,' Grace said as she returned to the kitchen. 'Shall we send her a text message?'

Simone blinked. 'Who?'

'Aunty Eff.'

'Oh. No.' She shook her head, feeling marginally better now that Drew was on the case. 'We'll call her later.' *Hopefully Harriet will be home again by then*, she added silently as she started pacing the kitchen.

★ ★ ★

'You hungry?'

Frankie smiled up at Logan from where she was lying naked in his arms, in his bed, after what was without a doubt the best sex of her life. Right now, she couldn't have cared less if she never ate again, but she'd seen and smelt all the trouble he'd gone to and for him she'd make the effort. 'A little,' she said, 'and we really should keep our strength up.'

His fingers playing with her hair, he kissed her forehead. 'I like your thinking.' And then he untangled himself from her and climbed out of bed.

She bit her lip to stop from moaning at the sight of him buck-naked, standing before her unashamed as he grabbed some clean clothes from his drawer. God, he was gorgeous. Tall and tanned and muscular in all the right places. Her fingers tingled from the memory of their acquaintance and itched to trail themselves all over him again. She couldn't help but notice that he pulled on jeans but didn't bother with underwear. This made her smile and he turned around and caught her perving.

'What are you looking at?' he asked, his lips turning up at the edges.

She gave him her best innocent expression. 'Not my fault if you have the cutest butt I've ever had the pleasure of looking at.'

He snorted. 'Yours isn't so bad either.'

With a contented sigh, she rolled over, surprisingly unselfconscious at the thought of having to dress in front of him, until she realised her old clothes were in the bathroom and her clean ones in her backpack in the kitchen. 'Um … do you mind going and getting my bag from the kitchen?' she asked. Dressing in front of the man who'd now seen every intimate part of her body was one thing, but walking through the house naked was another. She wasn't *that* confident in her skin.

Logan folded his perfectly masculine arms over his perfectly masculine chest and slowly shook his head. 'Actually I do.'

She frowned. 'You *do* mind? You *won't* go and get my clothes?'

'Nope. I've decided I like seeing you in my bed too much.' He smiled and a hot flush rushed through her, both from his words and his irresistible grin. How could she argue with that?

'Then what about dinner?'

'I'm going to bring it to you in bed. You stay right there and relax.' With that he turned and swaggered out of the room like a man who'd just gotten laid and planned on a re-enactment very, very soon.

No arguments here.

Frankie relaxed into the pillows, quite happy to stay here all weekend if that was what he so desired. The bed smelt like him—a manly aroma that turned her on something chronic. She brought the doona up to her nose and inhaled deeply at the exact moment he returned to the bedroom.

'That was quick,' she said, sitting up and dropping the doona like it was on fire.

He held up her mobile, which she must have left in his kitchen when they'd retreated to the bathroom, and her backpack. 'Since I'm not sure I'm going to let you out of my bed all weekend, thought you might need these.'

She laughed as he dumped them on the bed. 'Thanks.'

He leaned over and kissed her on the lips. And, *man*, each time was better than the last. 'Back soon.'

Not wanting to be caught sniffing his blankets again, Frankie grabbed her phone—she could check Facebook or something while she waited for the return of her new sex slave. Or was she the slave, because she was forbidden to leave the bed? Not that he'd tied her to the bedposts or anything—though that thought turned her on more than she wanted to admit. Either way, she had no plans for escape.

She swiped her finger across the screen to wake the phone and saw she had a missed call from Simone. Her insides twisted but this time it felt different from the way they did whenever Logan touched or even looked at her. This time it was the undeniable, horrid feeling of guilt. Her finger hovered over the return call option but she couldn't bring herself to press it. Simone was probably ringing to sound off about another fight with Harriet, but what if it was something else? What if something had gone wrong at the café this arvo?

Her head ached—a war going on inside it about whether or not to call back. And then she had a brilliant idea. She could text Stacey to check on the café. After shooting off the quick message, she put her phone on Logan's bedside table and tried to distract her thoughts by taking a proper look around the room. She'd taken little in when they'd stumbled into it, still wet from the shower. It was neat and tidy but manly. The bed itself was solid wood and the doona cover blue stripes. There was a desk in one corner with a funky black lamp and a laptop set up on it and a whole row of bookshelves, spilling over with books. Other items in the room included a tennis racket, a stereo, some prints of old Holdens hanging on the walls—it seemed Logan inherited the passion from his dad—and a couple of photo frames on an old chest of drawers.

Her curiosity piqued, she snuck out of bed, wrapped herself in the stripy doona and tiptoed across the room for a stickybeak. There were pictures of a couple she guessed were his parents, looking very happy with each other. She sighed with the knowledge of the tragedy that had befallen them and moved on to look at the next photo. Two lanky teenage boys—one blond haired, one brown—with a cute little toddler standing between them. It had to be Olivia and she was blonde like Logan. The graduation class photo next to it made her frown.

'Geraldton Senior?' she said out loud. But that's where she and Simone had gone. She didn't remember him—although it was a big school and he would have been a few years ahead of her—but she'd sworn he'd mentioned going to boarding school in Perth like Angus and Olivia had.

'Got bored waiting for me, did you?'

Logan startled her as he came back into the room and she almost dropped the doona. She tightened her grip and turned her head to him, noticing he was holding a glass of wine. 'Sorry, couldn't resist a look.' She pointed at the graduation photo. 'Bet you had all the girls chasing after you at school.'

He shrugged. 'Maybe a few.'

She smiled and said nonchalantly, 'I thought you went to boarding school in Perth?'

'Ah …' He looked sheepish. 'I did … until I was expelled.'

'What?' She almost dropped the doona again.

He stepped closer and offered her the wine. 'Thought you might like this while you wait. Won't be much longer.'

'Oh no, you don't,' she said, taking the wine. 'I need this story. Now.'

'The pasta might overcook.'

'Then you'd better be quick.' She leaned back against the chest of drawers and took a sip of white wine.

He ran a hand through his hair. 'Okay. Promise you won't laugh?'

She cocked her head to the side. 'I make no guarantees, but if you don't tell me, I'll get dressed.'

'You're an evil woman, Frankie Madden.' But she'd won. 'Okay, I had this business going in the boarding house. It was quite profitable actually. Started in year ten and by halfway through year eleven, I'd made a couple of grand.'

'What were you doing?' she asked, all sorts of possibilities running through her head.

'Selling vodka oranges to the other boarders.'

'*Vodka oranges?*'

'Yep—I conned Sarah into buying the vodka and gave her a percentage of the profits. It was our secret; Angus would never have helped me.'

'How did you inject them?'

'With syringes I borrowed from Dad on the farm.'

She raised her eyebrows. 'Borrowed.'

'Okay, stole, but that's just semantics. He didn't miss them.'

She smiled. 'And no-one ever told on you?'

He pointed a finger at her. 'I told you not to laugh. Sometimes the boarding masters asked me why I was always getting fruit from the kitchen but I think they just assumed I liked oranges. I got away with it for over a year because everyone knew that if they said anything, the supply would stop, but eventually, some nerd dobbed me in. That's when I got expelled.'

She couldn't help it. She cracked up at the image of Logan hiding away in his dorm room injecting vodka into fruit.

'You promised.' He shook his head but he was chuckling as he left the room.

Frankie was still smiling at the story when he returned a few minutes later with a tray that carried the bottle of wine, another glass, and two steaming bowls of the most delicious smelling duck ragu. Maybe she was hungry after all.

He put the tray on the bed, which she'd climbed back into. 'Madam, your dinner is served.' He handed her a bowl and a fork and then went to get in with her.

'You better not be thinking of coming back in here with clothes on. If I have to eat in the nude, I don't see why it should be any different for the chef.' She felt so confident around him, far more so than she ever had around any other guy.

'Fair point,' he said. And then he undid his buckle and pushed his jeans down his legs before stepping out of them. Her eyes were drawn to one thing and it wasn't his handsome face.

He snuck into bed beside her, and she felt the heat from his thigh only centimetres from hers. She downed the last few sips of her wine. How she was going to manage to eat with all that beautiful nakedness so close, she had no clue, but at least they wouldn't have to waste time taking off their clothes when they were done.

Logan topped up her wine and poured a glass for himself. They began to eat.

'Oh, this is amazing.' She was thinking that if they ever got married he could be the household's chief cook because although she loved it, she put all her enthusiasm into the café and couldn't usually be bothered to cook when she got home. Of course, she kept this little fantasy to herself. Even though it felt like she'd known him forever, it was still early days and she didn't want to jinx it. Or scare him off.

'I can't imagine going to boarding school. What was it like—were they really strict on you or was it like one long sleepover with your mates?'

Logan laughed and, from the twinkle in his eyes, she could tell he was recalling more mischief. 'Some of the boarding masters were stricter than others but we got to know who'd let us get away with stuff and who wouldn't. One night I organised a midnight cricket match down the corridors between the rooms and we'd played for a good half an hour before anyone discovered us.'

'You were a ratbag,' she said, thoroughly enjoying hearing about his youth. He was entertaining her with more boarding school stories when her phone buzzed with a text message.

'That'll be Stacey, one my of my employees,' she told him as she picked it up. She smiled with relief at Stacey's message that everything was A-OK.

'Good news?'

'Oh, kind of.' She sighed as she put her phone back down. 'I had a missed call from Simone and I wondered if something had gone wrong at the café, but I really didn't want to call her back. I feel sick just thinking about lying to her like I am.'

'Aw, come here.' Logan put down his empty bowl and wrapped his arm around her, pulling her against him. 'I know it's going to be hard, but we're going to have to tell her sooner or later. Sooner might be better because then she won't feel like we've kept her in the dark a long time.'

'Yes, you're right.' But her heart beat too fast at the prospect.

'Do you want me to come with you when you tell her?' he asked.

While she appreciated his offer, she shook her head. 'I think this is something I need to do by myself. And I'm going to do it as soon as I get home. I don't want my guilt and deception to overshadow our time together anymore. She might be angry at first but we've never held a grudge for more than a few hours.'

'Good plan,' Logan said, removing her empty bowl and placing it on the tray on the floor with his. 'Now, are you ready for dessert or would you like to wait a while?'

Frankie felt his large warm hand on her bare thigh and quivered right down to her core. 'If you're referring to your tiramisu, then I think I'd like to work up my appetite again first.'

He grinned as she hooked one leg over the top of him and leaned in for a kiss.

Chapter Twenty-six

Cruising down the Brand Highway, Dire Straits on the radio, Angus tapped his fingers on the steering wheel, excited about seeing Olivia. Now that she'd started uni in Perth, her trips home were less frequent than when she'd been at boarding school, and he missed her. Logan saw her more often because of all the travelling he did for work, but if it weren't for Liv, Angus would have little desire to visit the big smoke.

As he passed the turn-off to Bunyip Bay, he made a conscious effort to think about the weekend ahead, rather than about Simone. A crazy part of him contemplated turning into the little town and paying her a visit but he didn't know exactly where she lived and the café would be closed by now. Besides, if he went into the café and Simone wasn't there, what excuse would he give to Frankie about seeing her? And what exactly was he planning on saying to Simone anyway?

Hey good-looking, I can't get that hot night we had together out of my head and was wondering if you wanted a repeat sometime soon?

The fact that Simone had registered for Rural Matchmakers proved she was looking for something more than he was, so the best thing to do would be to exorcise her from his head. Problem was, that was proving harder to do than he thought.

He was contemplating ways to achieve this when he saw a hitchhiker up ahead, her thumb held out to the road. She slowed her pace, turning his way as he approached and the first thing he noticed was her blue hair. He grimaced, unable to understand why anyone would want to draw such attention to themselves.

The second thing he noticed was her age—mid-teens—and then he slammed his foot on the brake and pulled over because he recognised that she wasn't just any old teenager, but Harriet, Simone's daughter. What the hell was she doing hitchhiking? Hadn't her mother ever told her how dangerous it was?

He cursed, thumped the heel of his hand against the steering wheel and then pressed the button to open the passenger window.

Harriet smiled—she obviously hadn't recognised him yet—as she walked the short distance to the vehicle. 'Hey there,' she said, leaning into the window like some kind of streetwalker. Thank God he'd been the one to stop for her.

'Hi Harriet,' he said and her eyes widened in shock as recognition dawned. It looked like she'd been crying.

'You're Logan's brother.'

Nice, after the effort he'd made to chat with her when she'd visited the farm, she could have at least remembered his name. 'I have a name. It's Angus.'

She shrugged. 'You going to Perth?'

He nodded. 'Sure am. What about you?'

She hitched her hot pink backpack higher up onto her shoulder. 'Yep. Wanna give me a lift?'

He thought about it a moment—no way was he taking a sixteen-year-old girl all the way to Perth without her mother's permission, but nor was he about to leave her on the side of the road for the first sick fuck to come along and take advantage.

He thought of what he'd want if this was Liv. What choice did he have?

'Get in,' he said, grumpy because this diversion was the last thing he needed. Seeing Simone again was going to ruin all the good work he'd done so far towards forgetting her. Not that he'd been so successful in that mission.

Harriet's expression brightened as she yanked open the door and climbed inside. 'Thanks. I was beginning to think I was going to have to walk the whole bloody way.'

'You've walked a fair way already.'

She dumped her backpack at her feet, clicked on her seatbelt and thrust a finger at the stereo. 'Can we change radio stations? This stuff is ancient.'

He raised an eyebrow but nodded his head. It didn't appear she knew the first thing about hitchhiking. 'Why's your mum not driving you?' he asked, as he pulled back onto the highway and the ute's doors locked automatically.

'Because I'm done with her,' Harried said, perching her feet on the dashboard. 'I'm done with this whole dump of a town.'

'You got a plan for when you hit Perth?'

'Yeah. I'm gonna live with my grandma. She's so much cooler than Mum.' Something young and boppy—he guessed Taylor Swift—filled the cabin as she succeeded in changing stations.

'And your mum is okay with this?'

She didn't answer and he glanced sideways to see guilt scrawled all over her face. Just as he'd suspected.

'She doesn't know, does she?'

'So what? She won't care. I only cause her stress. I'll call her when I get to Grandma's. Where exactly are you going in Perth? Gran lives in Inglewood. Do you know where that is?'

It wasn't at all far from where Liv rented in Bayswater but he didn't tell Harriet this. Instead, he checked the rear-view mirror, then indicated right and did a U-turn so they were facing back towards Bunyip Bay.

'What the hell are you doing?' Harriet screamed, looking back in the direction of the city. 'I said I want to go to Perth.'

He nodded. 'I heard you. And once we've checked with your mum, if she's agreeable, I'm happy to give you a lift all the way to Inglewood, but you're not choosing the music the whole way.'

Harriet didn't seem to care about the music anymore. She grabbed the passenger door handle and rattled hard, trying unsuccessfully to open it.

'I wouldn't suggest leaping from a car travelling a hundred-and-ten kilometres an hour,' he said, keeping his eyes on the road ahead.

'You can't keep me in here against my will,' she spat, folding her arms across her chest and glaring at him. Thankfully looks couldn't kill because if so he'd have been a dead man.

'Fine. Give your mum a call and let me talk to her. As I said, if she gives her permission, we'll turn around.' He was calling her bluff but his heart rate jumped at the prospect of speaking to Simone again.

Harriet didn't say anything; she turned away from him, sighed and leaned against the window. He contemplated changing the station back to his preferred one but didn't want to rile her unnecessarily. After a few minutes he heard her sniff and although she was still staring out the window, he could tell she was crying.

His grip tightened on the steering wheel. He wasn't good with women and tears. 'You okay?'

She wiped her eyes with the back of her hands and glared at him again. 'Do I *look* okay? I'm trying to run away from home here and you've spoilt everything.'

'You want to … talk about it?' He wasn't a big talker but he figured they only had a few minutes and they'd be back in Bunyip Bay.

'You wouldn't understand.'

'Possibly not, but you won't know unless you try me.'

She peered at him as if trying to make a decision. 'You ever been in love before?'

He thought of his son, Liv and Logan, and then nodded.

'Love sucks. My boyfriend dumped me and I know Mum is going to be all smug and pleased when she finds out. She hated him anyway.'

'I'm sure that's not true,' he said, although as Liv's guardian he understood that a parent never thought anyone good enough for their child.

She screwed up her face. 'And what would you know? You barely know my mother.'

You have no idea, he thought, but didn't say this for obvious reasons. 'Maybe not, but I raised my little sister from when she was six years old and I know I'd have died if anything ever happened to her. Your mum will probably be worried sick right now. Do you really hate her that much that you want to cause her so much grief?'

'How old's your sister?' she asked, not answering his question.

He decided not to press the issue. 'She's nineteen. It's her I'm going to visit in Perth. Now, are you going to give me directions to your place or am I going to have to drive around guessing?'

She sighed. 'I'm never going to forgive you for this.'

He stifled a smile. 'Fair enough. But I'd rather that than some crazed axe murderer pick you up on the side of the road.'

'You obviously watch too many horror movies,' she said and then rattled off her address. 'You turn at the next right and we're the fifth house along.'

'Thanks, Harriet.'

Neither of them said another word until they turned into the driveway of the house she said belonged to her mother. 'This it?'

'Yep.' She scooped up her backpack and put her hand on the door. 'Thanks for the ride. I'll take it from here.'

He switched off the ignition, unclicked his seatbelt and shook his head. 'I don't think so.' Despite having sweaty palms at the thought of seeing Simone, there was no way he'd backtracked and delayed himself only to have Harriet run off again. 'I'm taking you inside, and don't think about running or I'll chase you.'

'Whatever.' He couldn't see her expression as she climbed out of the ute, but he'd bet his life savings she'd rolled her eyes.

She stormed ahead of him up a path cluttered on either side with overgrown plants and an assortment of garden ornaments. Along the verandah hung mismatched baskets, overflowing with bright flowers. The house was an old fibro, also painted odd colours, and suited Simone down to a tee.

He forgot his nerves and smiled just as the front door opened.

'Oh, thank God,' Simone shrieked, dashing out of the house and throwing herself at Harriet. She flung her arms around her daughter and held her in what looked like a very tight grip. As Simone sobbed and made a number of unintelligible utterings, Harriet stood like a wooden soldier and Angus waited awkwardly a few feet away.

Finally, Simone pulled back and, still clutching Harriet by the arms, gave her a thorough once over. 'Where the hell have you been?' she asked, her voice still choked. 'I was so worried.' She blinked as if fighting further tears. 'Oh, my sweet baby.' She pulled the silent girl against her again and then looked up and met his gaze. She blinked as if she hadn't noticed him until now, but he'd sure as hell noticed her.

She was wearing a Frankie's Café polo shirt and denim cut-offs, which showcased her tanned, taut legs perfectly. Despite the uniform, her hair was messy, as though she'd just woken up, which of course took him right back to the memory of them being in bed together. He tried to focus on the situation to cool his rising desire—to remind himself that the object of his sexual fantasies had two teenage daughters, one of whom was more than a bit of a handful. Even if there could be something more between them, the last thing he wanted was to raise someone else's kids. He'd been doing that for the last thirteen years and although he adored Olivia, it was good to only have himself to worry about now.

'You brought her home.'

The way Simone spoke, he couldn't tell if it was a question or a statement, but he nodded, cleared his throat and said, 'Yep. Don't think I'm her favourite person anymore, but I doubted you'd approve of her hitchhiking.'

Simone gasped. 'Hitchhiking! What were you thinking?'

Harriet, taking the opportunity to extract herself from her mum's embrace, shrugged and looked at the ground, not saying a word.

Simone, still clutching her daughter's hand like she would never let go, looked at him with tears in her eyes and offered a heartfelt, 'Thank you. I've never been so scared in my life.'

Something shifted inside his chest and he fought the urge to hold her close, to tell her everything would be okay. But it wasn't his role to comfort her.

'I'm going inside,' Harriet said, yanking her hand from Simone's.

Simone looked torn—as if she wasn't sure whether to chase after her daughter or stay and talk to him. 'Don't you think about running off again,' she called, 'Drew and Mike are out looking for you.'

Harriet turned back, hands on her hips. 'You called the police?'

At that moment Grace appeared at the front door and flung herself at Harriet. 'You're back. I missed you so much.'

'Get off me, squirt,' Harriet replied, but she sounded kind of chuffed. 'I'm starving. Let's go inside and eat something.'

As the girls disappeared into the house, Simone hugged her arms around herself and smiled at him. 'What did she think I'd do? Throw a party?'

Her smile did weird things to his insides and he couldn't help smiling back, secretly pleased he'd had the opportunity to see her again.

'Thank you,' she said again, her voice shaky. 'I can't thank you enough.'

'I'm glad I could help. And I hope she opens up to you. She's hurting pretty bad at the moment.'

Simone closed her eyes briefly and cursed so softly he barely heard it. 'She talked to you?'

'A little,' he confessed, not wanting to upset her but also wanting to prolong their time together. 'I asked her why she was running away and she told me she broke up with her boyfriend. The one you hated. She was planning to go live with her grandma.'

'Oh God.' Simone ran a hand through her hair, but her fingers got caught in the tangles. She yanked them out. 'I must look like a mess. I *am* a fucking mess. And I'm a terrible mother.'

'You're not.' He couldn't help stepping closer to her and placing his hand against her arm in an attempt at comfort. A jolt of heat shot through him at the connection and he told himself to get a grip. Now was not the time to make a move—Simone was upset and vulnerable and hadn't he already decided that making a move would be a very bad idea? 'Just talk to her. If she's really hurting, then deep down I'm sure she wants her mum.'

Lord knew, even as a grown man, there'd been many times he just wanted his mum to wrap her arms around him and offer him the kind of comfort only a mother could.

She nodded. 'Good advice.'

He dropped his hand and smiled back. 'Good luck.'

'Would you like to come in for a coffee? Or even dinner?' she asked. 'Not that it'll be anything flash, but I'm good at heating up stuff in the microwave.'

He chuckled. 'Thanks. That sounds almost too good to refuse, but I told my sister I'd have a late dinner with her when I get to Perth. And I think Harriet needs to talk to you more than I need a coffee right now.'

She nodded again. 'Yes, you're right. Guess I'm a little bit nervous at that prospect. I don't want to fail her again.'

He loved that she was so honest with him. They barely knew each other but it didn't feel like that. He felt strangely invested in Simone and even in her daughters. 'You won't,' he promised and then he turned to go before he could change his mind.

'Can I have your number?' she called after him when he was almost at his ute.

He stopped, closed his eyes a moment and then finally turned around. 'Why?'

She blinked. 'I just thought maybe we could … catch up sometime? I could thank you properly for bringing Harriet home.'

Images of exactly how she might choose to thank him ambushed him, every red blood cell in his body overheating. But remembering the weekend of the wedding and how hurt Logan would be if he ever found out, Angus took a deep breath. 'Seeing you guys reunited is thanks enough. Goodnight, Simone.'

And then he got into his ute and drove away.

★ ★ ★

Simone closed the door behind her and then banged her head against it, welcoming the pain as a momentary distraction from all her other crap.

Seriously … could this day get any worse?

Her cheeks burned from the mortification of Angus's brush-off. She'd thought she'd felt something between them when he was standing there, but it must have all been her imagination.

He'd looked at her with pity at her request and then hadn't been able to get away fast enough. She was glad he'd been the one to stop for Harriet and not some crazed psycho serial killer, but she could have done without the awkward reminder that what they'd shared was nothing but sex for him.

When he asked why she wanted his number, she should have told him outright. *Because, Angus too-hot-to-be-true Knight, I'm pregnant with your child and I thought maybe we should discuss what we wanted to do about that. You know, before it turns twenty-one!*

She sighed and rested her hand on her flat stomach. 'I'm sorry, baby,' she whispered. 'Mummy is a coward and Daddy is a dick.' But she hadn't been expecting to see him again so soon, so hadn't had time to prepare what to say to him. Hell, she'd barely had time to comprehend the news herself.

'But he's a good-looking dick,' she added, rubbing her hand back and forth. She hated that her damn hormones, which should have been taking a back seat now that she had bigger issues to focus on, had stood up and panted like puppies at the sight of him. It had been so difficult to focus when she was struggling not to gape and drool over the impressive specimen of masculinity standing before her. If anything, his appeal had increased since the last time they'd met.

And maybe, Simone had to concede, he wasn't really such a dick after all. If so, he would have left her daughter stranded on the side of the road.

The powers that be must have a sick sense of humour because surely there were better candidates for third-time motherhood out there. Women who didn't have one-night stands with near strangers. Women who could cook and knew the right things to say when their teenage daughter was obviously falling apart.

Thinking of Harriet reminded Simone that she was the number-one priority right now. There'd be plenty of time tomorrow and the day after that to worry about Angus and the baby. She had quite some time before anyone would notice the pregnancy, so there was no need to make any decisions just yet. It was time to heave herself up off the floor and have a long-overdue chat with her daughter. But first she'd better call Drew and tell him the good news.

'That's great,' Drew said, sounding genuinely relieved. 'I was just about to come around and make this official.'

'Sorry about the trouble. I hope you and Ruby have a good weekend.'

'No worries, Simmo. I'm sure we'll have our own kid problems one of these days and then you can give us advice because you'll already have all the answers.'

She half-laughed. 'I doubt that. But thanks again.'

After hanging up on Drew, Simone found Harriet and Grace sitting on the couch in the lounge room, stuffing their faces with café leftovers and watching *Neighbours* as if this was a perfectly normal Friday evening.

'Harriet, can we talk?' she said, speaking loudly over the noise of the TV.

'Do we have to?' she whined. 'I'm busy here and I'd rather just pretend today never happened.'

'Yes, I think we do,' Simone replied. 'You can bring your dinner into my bedroom.'

Harriet let out an exaggerated sigh, dumped her near-empty plate on the coffee table and stood. 'Don't even think about finishing that,' she said to Grace before walking out of the room.

'Go on into my bedroom,' Simone said. 'I've just got to get something.'

Without a word, Harriet did as she was told. *Progress*, thought Simone, as she headed into the kitchen, grabbed two spoons and a tub of cookies and cream ice-cream from the freezer. Thank God she'd been too tired and queasy that afternoon to drown her own sorrows with it.

When she entered her bedroom, she found Harriet leaning against her dresser, as if hoping this talk would be over ASAP.

'Take a seat on the bed.' Simone nodded towards it, wanting to sound firm but not pushy. She needed to find the fine line between being a friend and a mother.

With the speed of a sloth, Harriet made her way to the bed and perched herself on the very edge. Simone took it as a step in the right direction and sat down beside her. She opened the ice-cream and handed Harriet a spoon. 'Dig in.'

Harriet glared at the spoon. 'What is this? Your attempt at some kind of mother–daughter bonding? Are you trying to lull me into a false sense of security before you unleash your fury?'

'I want you to feel secure here,' Simone said. 'I feel terrible that you felt the need to run away. I love you and it breaks my heart that you don't feel like you can open up to me anymore.'

'And whose fault is that?'

'Mine.' Although she thought Harriet had at least a small share of the blame, Simone choose not to mention this. 'And I want to fix it. Will you at least give me a chance?'

In reply, Harriet gouged the ice-cream with her spoon and then shoved it into her mouth. Simone followed suit, thinking it might be best not to say too much and to give Harriet the opportunity to open up. They ate in silence a few moments and although Harriet kept her eyes trained on the tub of ice-cream, Simone took the time to really look at her daughter.

The blue hair didn't look *that* bad now that she thought about it. Perhaps she'd overreacted. As a teenager she'd gotten henna tattoos, frequently changed her hair colour—although not quite as dramatically—and had her nose pierced without asking her mum's permission. She reached out her hand and brushed it over Harriet's hair. 'You know, I think blue kinda suits you.'

Harriet flicked away Simone's hand like it was a pesky mosquito and then dumped her spoon in the tub and folded her arms. 'You've changed your tune.'

Simone swallowed her pride. 'I haven't really. You just got me on a bad day. And I would have preferred it if you'd asked my permission.'

'You'd probably have said "no".'

'I'd probably have asked if you could wait till the school holidays but I'm not a complete ogre. I do remember what it was like to be young.'

Harriet rolled her eyes. She really was very good at it. 'Because of you, Jaxon dumped me.'

Simone frowned. 'What do you mean?'

'You grounded me, so I couldn't go to Alyssa's party, and he hooked up with someone else.'

'Oh, honey.' Simone wrapped her arms around her and surprisingly Harriet didn't pull back. 'If he could do that to you, he doesn't deserve you. You deserve a boy who treats you like a princess.'

Harriet came undone, her tears spilling down her cheeks as she clung to her mother. Simone held her close and stroked her hair, making soothing noises, exactly like she'd done when Harriet was little and upset because she'd scraped her knee or couldn't find her favourite Barbie.

They sat this way for at while before Harriet sniffed and said, 'I think it might also be because I refused to sleep with him.'

Although she was hurting for her little girl, pride surged through Simone at this confession. She couldn't help smiling, but thankfully Harriet was still buried against her chest and couldn't see. 'Good for you,' she whispered. 'That's one thing you don't ever want to feel pressured into doing before you're ready.'

Harriet pulled back slightly and looked her mum in the eyes. 'I know. And I don't want to get pregnant or anything, but it still hurts.'

Simone almost choked on her own tongue at Harriet's words. Turned out her daughter had more smarts than her and had thankfully been doing as she said rather than as she did. 'You're a good girl, Harriet. I'm sorry I've been—'

Harriet interrupted. 'It's okay, Mum. I've been a little bitch, I know. I'm sorry.'

'I love you,' Simone said, tears sprouting in her eyes too.

'I love you, too.' This time Harriet initiated the hug and emotion clogged Simone's throat. She made a silent vow to be a better mother, from this day forward. To be there for her daughters, no matter what ridiculous scrapes she'd gotten herself into.

'I really want to be here for you,' she said. 'You know you can talk to me about anything. I'll never judge you. And please don't ever run away like that again. That hour you were missing was the worst time of my life.'

'I'm sorry, Mum, I promise I won't do it again.'

That was music to Simone's ears. 'And I promise I'll try not to fly off the handle again,' she said.

'Deal.' Harriet looked down at the ice-cream. 'It's melting.'

Simone laughed. 'Guess we'd better go put it back in the freezer then.'

'Can I go watch TV again?'

'What do you say I make some popcorn and we all watch a movie together?'

'Do I get to pick?'

Simone pretended to consider this a moment, then, 'Yes.'

The two of them left the bedroom and while Simone put the ice-cream back in the freezer, Harriet went to select a DVD.

Simone didn't care what she chose, she was simply happy to have her daughter back.

Later, as she sat on the couch, squished between her two girls watching *The Fault in Our Stars*, she thought about the news Dr McDonald had delivered that afternoon. Being a single parent again terrified her, but there was no way she was getting rid of this baby or giving it away. She'd been mothering alone for ten years and it might not always be a bed of roses but it was the most rewarding thing she'd ever done.

Even if Angus didn't want anything to do with this little one, she would love it with all her heart.

Chapter Twenty-seven

Angus stabbed his fork into his seafood linguine, twisted it round and then lifted it to his mouth. Opposite him at their favourite Italian restaurant sat Olivia, her blonde hair tied back in a neat, high ponytail and her blue eyes radiant as she spoke, gesturing enthusiastically with her hands.

'They've just given us our placings for teaching practice and all my friends have got these fancy private schools and you'll never guess where I'm going?'

Liv and Logan were alike in looks and also in their sunny personalities, but right now, he couldn't help seeing a likeness to Simone's daughters as well. Dammit, why did every single thought he have come back to her?

Olivia sighed and he realised she'd asked him a question.

'What's going on?' she said, her head cocked to one side, scrutinising him. He was pretty sure that wasn't her original question.

Although he'd had the four-hour drive to Perth to contemplate his feelings about seeing Simone again, he still couldn't get his head around them and was finding it hard to concentrate on Liv's conversation. 'I'm sorry. What were you saying about uni?'

She waved a hand in dismissal. 'Nothing worth repeating.' Then she narrowed her eyes at him. 'What's going on with you?'

'Nothing,' he was quick to answer, although his gut clenched with the denial. Since the wedding, it felt as if someone else had been walking around inside his body and he'd hoped a weekend with Olivia would help him get back to his old self.

She raised a sceptical eyebrow at him and picked up her wine glass. 'You might be able to fool Logan,' she said, 'but not me. You've been acting weird since you arrived. Is there a problem on the farm or is this about Logan?'

As Liv took a sip of her wine, the knot in Angus's stomach twisted even more. She couldn't possibly know about him betraying Logan with Simone or she wouldn't have greeted him that evening with such an enthusiastic hug. 'What about Logan?' he managed.

She blinked. 'His eyesight,' she said, as if he were dense.

'Right.' He nodded, guilty when relief swept over him. 'Yeah,' he lied. 'I can't believe it. I guess he called you?'

She nodded and sniffed. He knew her well enough to know she was fighting tears and he reached across the table and wrapped her small hand in his.

'I know. I thought things like this only happened to old people. Is he really handling it as well as he makes out?'

Angus shrugged. 'No idea, he only just told me as well, but knowing him, he's probably trying to put on a brave face for us. You know there's a possibility we might have it too, or at least carry the gene?'

'Yes. I'm going to get tested. Are you?'

'I haven't even thought about it.' He'd had other things on his mind and he picked up his glass to try to distract himself.

'Well, I guess you only need to consider it if you meet someone and decide to have kids,' said Olivia.

Angus almost choked on the swig of beer he'd just taken. 'You know I'm not interested in anything … anything like … that.'

Liv was quiet a moment, staring at him as if he were a book she was trying to read. And then, 'What aren't you telling me, big brother?'

'Nothing,' he said, but his whole body heated with the lie.

'Oh my God,' Olivia shrieked. 'You've met someone!'

'Shh,' Angus hissed, glancing around the restaurant to see people looking at them.

Liv simply laughed. 'What's her name? Where'd you meet her? Does Logan know? I demand you tell me every intimate detail.'

So much for her helping to take his mind off the dramas with Harriet and Simone. Olivia wouldn't back down until he'd convinced her there was nothing to get excited about. And how did she do that anyway—simply look at him and *know* things? If he protested too much, she'd guess something was up, so he tried another tack. 'Don't wet your pants or anything, because nothing will come of it.'

Liv's smile faded. 'Why not?'

As the whole truth was out of the question, he improvised, sticking as close to it as possible. 'I may have met someone I like a little but it's complicated.'

'How so?'

'She has kids. Teenage daughters in fact—and I've only just gotten rid of you.'

She poked her tongue at him. 'Does this woman have a name? And what's wrong with kids? You were great with me and …' Her voice drifted off but he could guess what she'd been about to say.

'Of course she has a name but not one you need to know. And if you don't mind I'd prefer you didn't say anything to Logan. He knows her and I just … Well, I don't need him ribbing me about it.' Worry made him sound harsher than he meant to.

'I promise I won't say a word but if she's making you tense, I really think you should do something about it.'

He shook his head. 'Not going to happen.'

'Because of the kids?'

He nodded, not meeting Liv's eye. 'Too much hassle. Her daughter was the reason I was late today.'

'I thought you were late because you had a meeting.'

'That was earlier. I met with the wind-farming developers that Logan is so gung-ho about to try to get some more information—that's a secret by the way. The meeting ran late but then Harriet way-laid me even more.' He realised his mistake the moment he said this.

Liv's eyes sparkled at this nugget of information. 'And Harriet is this mystery woman's child?'

'Yes, one of them.' Angus racked his brain for a way to redirect the conversation. 'So, what do you think about wind-farming?'

But Liv was not going to be deterred. 'How did this Harriet make you late?'

With a sigh, he told her about finding the girl—blue hair and all—on the side of the highway as she tried to hitch her way to Perth.

'She sounds like quite a character,' Liv said, smiling, when he'd finished the story. 'And it sounds like you were really good with her. Maybe a solid male role figure is just what she needs in her life and maybe her mother is—'

'Stop.' Angus held up his hand for her to be quiet before she could finish her sentence. He'd come here to try to forget about Simone and so far she'd dominated not only his thoughts but much of the evening's conversation.

'Okay, okay, I'm sorry.' Olivia smirked, not sounding sorry at all. 'Tell me about the wind-farming thing instead. Are you coming round to Logan's way of thinking?'

Angus still wasn't sure what he thought, but this topic was much safer than the alternative, so he took another sip of his beer, sat back in his chair and endeavoured to answer the question.

Chapter Twenty-eight

Although the café was closed on Mondays, Frankie still had cooking and preparation to do for the week ahead, but she wanted to speak to Simone first. She couldn't go another day, another hour, without telling her sister the truth about herself and Logan—that they'd fallen in love.

She'd barely slept last night, despite her energetic weekend, and had been unable to stomach breakfast that morning, but she needed to wait until Harriet and Grace had left for school before making her confession. This was not a conversation she wanted to have within earshot of her impressionable nieces.

'Do you think I'm doing the right thing?' she asked Fred, who leaped onto the table where she'd been sitting for the last half an hour staring at the microwave clock.

In response, he nuzzled his furry head and wet nose against her chin and rubbed, purring loudly.

'What choice do I have?' she asked as George jumped up beside his brother. These two were inseparable—they ate together, played together, slept together and she reckoned if cats talked, they'd tell each other everything. Exactly like she and Simone had always been. And she wanted to get back to that. Having Logan to play with and confide in was magic, but she didn't want to lose her other best friend in the process.

'You're right.' She pushed back the chair, stood and stared down at her two adorable cats. 'Just do it. It works for Nike, right?'

They looked up at her blankly but she guessed felines didn't have much call for sportswear. After ensuring they had full bowls of water and clean litter trays, she collected her phone and keys, took a big breath and then walked the short distance to Simone's house.

Her heart was racing by the time she arrived, and it wasn't from exertion. Shivering despite the pleasant September morning sun, she walked—one foot, then the next—up to the door and knocked. This was something she never did because she had a key and usually it was unlocked anyway; she always showed herself in.

She waited, her foot tapping against the doormat, for what seemed like an eternity, but was probably only about fifteen seconds, before the door swung back and Simone appeared, still wearing her pyjamas.

'Frank, I'm glad you're here,' she exclaimed, making no comment about the fact that she'd knocked. 'There's something we need to talk about.'

Wasn't that supposed to be my line?

Simone dragged her into the house and all but slammed the door behind them. 'Would you like a drink? Coffee? Tea? Diet Coke?'

Is it too early for wine? Oh, this is ridiculous. She just needed to get it off her chest. Whatever she imagined Simone might say was likely far worse than the reality. Knowing her sister, she'd just laugh and ask if he was good in bed. Want to know what she'd missed out on.

'No, I'm fine,' she said. 'And thanks for the message about Harriet.' Late Friday night, Simone had texted telling her that Harriet had tried to run away but that all was good now, so not to worry and just enjoy the weekend. 'I can't believe she did that. Are you sure it's all good now?'

Simone smiled, but she seemed a little agitated. 'Yes, we had a good chat,' she said as she headed for the kitchen.

Frankie followed, wondering how the heck to open this conversation.

'I haven't got any milk, sorry,' Simone said as she grabbed two mugs and flicked on the kettle. 'You don't mind black coffee?'

Something weird was definitely going on. Sure Simone was scatty at times, but it was like she hadn't even registered Frankie's answer. 'I already said I don't want a drink.'

'Oh, right.' Simone turned away from the counter and gestured to the table in the middle of the kitchen. 'Sit then.'

She pulled back a chair and sat but Simone leaned against the bench, remaining standing. Now that they were at different eye levels, Frankie felt like she'd been called to the principal's office for punishment and that wasn't how she wanted this conversation to go.

'I had a good weekend,' she found herself saying—not exactly the way she'd planned on starting the discussion, but anyway.

Simone held up a hand. 'Look, Frankie, I really do want to hear all about your weekend, but—' she paused a moment and for some reason it looked like she was fighting tears '—I won't be able to concentrate until I tell you this. I need to get it off my chest.'

A horrible thought landed in Frankie's head. Had Simone already found out about her seeing Logan somehow? 'Tell me what?'

Simone inhaled deeply and then let out a long breath. 'I'm pregnant.'

Frankie's heart turned to ice and the cold spread through her body like nits through a kindergarten. She pressed a hand against her stomach, feeling as if she were about to be sick. 'But you told me you didn't sleep with Logan.' And he'd promised her things had never gotten to that stage either.

'It's not Logan's.'

'What? Then who?' She was torn between utter relief and even more shock. And here she'd been thinking *she* was the one with secrets.

'It's Angus's,' Simone confessed.

Frankie couldn't believe it. Speechless, that's what she was.

'Don't think badly of me,' Simone pleaded, finally pulling out a chair and sitting down opposite. 'It just happened.'

'When?'

Simone tried to tuck her crazy, untrainable hair behind her ears. 'The night before Adam's wedding. You and Logan were off cooking and we were both bored and we just ... well ...'

'You just fucked!' Frankie's tone was cold, but she couldn't help it. There was a stranger sitting in front of her. All this time, she and Logan had been feeling guilty about being together when Simone and Angus obviously hadn't shown any regard for Logan's feelings. 'But you were going out with Logan. And *I* was supposed to be Angus's date for the wedding. Geez, no wonder he wasn't interested in me that day.'

Simone looked taken aback. 'Don't be angry. I know you hate cheaters but this is hardly the same as you and that loser in Perth. I need you, Frank.' She sniffed and reached for a tissue. 'I'm not going to get through this without you.'

Frankie shook her head. 'Does Angus know about this? And what about Logan? How do you think this is going to make him feel?'

Simone frowned. 'Logan and I were barely together five minutes. He'll get over it. Anyway, what do you care about him? Shouldn't you be more concerned about me?'

'I care because—because I'm in love with him,' she declared. And it felt good to say it.

'What?' Simone reeled backwards; her turn to look shocked. Then she narrowed her eyes. 'Since when?'

Frankie lifted her chin high, her nerves about confessing the truth to Simone gone now that she and Logan weren't the ones who'd done the dirty first. 'Possibly since the day I met him.'

'You mean, before *I* met him? Why didn't you just say something?' When Frankie didn't reply, Simone continued, 'Oh my God. He's your mystery guy, isn't he? No wonder you were so secret squirrel about it all. Did you fuck up the stupid wedding cake on purpose?'

'Have you lost the plot? You know how much time and effort went it that cake!' Frankie exploded.

'Yes, but if you hadn't stuffed it up, I would have been with Logan that night. Angus and I would never have happened.'

'Oh, so this is *my* fault?' Frankie pointed a finger at her chest, unable to believe her ears. 'I'm not the one in the wrong here.'

'Only 'cos I'm the one who ended up pregnant,' Simone spat. 'But I don't see you apologising for messing with *my* boyfriend.'

'As you just said, you were barely together at all. And I didn't sleep with Logan until you guys had broken up.'

'Oh, so that makes it all right then. Perfect Frankie. As usual, you can do no wrong.' Simone shook her head and looked at her like someone who kicked kittens.

'What the hell's that supposed to mean?' Frankie asked, leaning forward, her hands curling into fists on the table.

'Well—' Simone shrugged '—nothing is ever your fault, is it? It started when we were little—I was always the one who got into trouble even if you started it. I worked my butt off at school and you still got better grades than me. Mum never considered my art to be a real job but hey, cooking for a living is perfectly fine. Oh and it wasn't your fault you hooked up with a married man. No, you didn't notice any of the signs; you'd *never* be a marriage wrecker.'

Frankie blinked, unable to believe what was coming out of Simone's mouth. It sounded like she had plenty more where this came from.

'Perfect Frankie goes away to college and learns a trade, comes home and opens a café, whereas silly Simone gets herself knocked up accidentally.'

Simone opened her mouth as if to add more, but Frankie got in first. 'And it looks like you've done that again, haven't you? Most people learn from their mistakes, but not you.'

They stared across the table at each other like worst enemies, not the best friends Frankie had always thought they'd been. If she wasn't so angry this thought would probably have made her cry, but she was still upset from all the hurtful things Simone had said. Still reeling from her news.

Simone broke the silent standoff first. 'Look, if you're not here to be supportive, you might as well get the hell out.' She pointed at the door. 'I've got enough on my plate right now without you coming into my home and making me feel worse.'

Oh, and what about Simone making her feel like crap? Frankie wasn't going to be made into the bad person here. 'Fine,' she said, shoving back her chair and standing. 'I don't want to be in this pigsty anyway.'

Without another word, she snatched up her phone and keys, charged down the hallway to the front door and slammed it shut behind her. If her heart had been racing when she'd arrived, it was ready to leap out of her chest now. She stormed down the street in the direction of the café, imagining herself as a cartoon character with steam pouring from her ears and nostrils.

Had she ever felt this angry in her life? Finding out she was Michael's other woman paled in comparison to finding out what

Simone really thought of her. All these years, she'd been there for her sister through good and bad. She'd changed the girls' nappies, babysat, made meals, cleaned on occasions and even paced the hallway with their mother late at night when Grace was suffering terrible colic so that Simone could get some sleep. And what had Simone ever done for her?

'Hello, Frankie love,' called Dolce as she passed by. Normally she'd stop to talk to the old gossip, maybe help her pull a few weeds from her garden, but today she just kept walking.

She wanted to call Logan but she needed to wait until she was in the safe confines of the café—thank God it was Monday—so no-one would overhear. Not that she cared what they thought of Simone right now, but she didn't air her dirty laundry in public. Keeping her head down, she practically jogged down the main street, hoping that everyone could see she wasn't in the mood for chitchat. She breathed a sigh of relief as she opened the café and then locked herself inside.

Once in the kitchen, she flicked on the lights, filled a glass of water and then downed it in almost one gulp. Then she wiped the sweat off her brow and took a few deep breaths to try to regulate her breathing. Being in the kitchen was already settling her. Who needed therapy when there was baking? When she was angry, she made cake. When she was sad, she made cake. When she wanted to celebrate, she made cake. Right now she was experiencing a maelstrom of emotions and the need to bake was stronger than ever.

But first, she needed to speak to Logan. She heaved herself onto the counter and dialled his number. He took so long to answer that for a moment she worried it was going to ring out but then he picked up and she heard his beautiful voice.

'What's up, buttercup?'

His voice brought tears to her eyes. She wished so badly he was here right now to hold her. 'Are you busy?'

'I'm just about to head out and interview a local farmer, but I can always make time for you.'

She contemplated asking him to call her after his interview because she didn't want to mess up his work but in the end, she couldn't wait. *This* couldn't wait. 'I went to see Simone.'

'I see. And ... did you tell her?'

'Yes, but she had something to tell me first.' Her gut squeezed at the memory. Suddenly she wasn't certain she wanted to be the one to tell him this, but maybe it was better coming from her than Angus—and who else was she supposed to confide in?

'And are you going to tell me what that was?' Logan sounded amused but that probably wouldn't last.

'She's pregnant.'

'Really? Did you know she was seeing anyone?'

'No.' Frankie snorted bitterly, but Logan didn't appear to notice. He chuckled. 'I guess she wasn't too worried about us then?'

'I wouldn't say that. She accused me of all sorts of things and then basically told me to fuck off.'

'What? Why?'

'I think she was hoping we'd never find out.'

'So who's the father?' Logan asked.

'Are you sitting down?'

'No, why? What's going on?' Logan's tone had changed from amused to anxious.

'I'm sorry to have to tell you this—' she paused briefly '—but it's Angus.'

There was another silence, then, *'Angus?* Hang on ... are you telling me they've been seeing each other behind our backs?'

'Well, Simone said it only happened one time—the night before the wedding when we were doing the cupcakes—but I don't know if I believe anything she says anymore.'

'Bastard,' Logan hissed. *'Fucking* bastard.'

'I'm sorry,' she said, wishing again that they'd been together for this conversation.

'Does he know?' Logan asked after another long silence.

'I don't know,' she whispered. 'I asked her, but now I think about it, she never answered. I got the feeling she'd only just found out.'

'I can't believe he'd do that to me. And there we were trying to do the right thing, waiting until I'd broken up with her.'

'I know. More fool us. Although Simone doesn't see it that way.'

'Makes sense now,' he said. 'Why she didn't seem all that shocked or upset when I broke up with her. I'd thought she must have agreed that we weren't suited, but actually it was because she preferred my older brother.'

'She's a stupid woman.'

He laughed a little at that but it didn't sound genuine. 'I'm sorry, Frankie. I'd better go, but I'll talk to you later, okay?'

She wanted more than talking and she hoped this thing between Angus and Simone wouldn't ruin the wonderful thing she and Logan had going. 'Do you think you could come here after your interview? I really want to see you.'

'I'd like that,' he replied and then they said their goodbyes.

Although she was worried about Logan, Frankie did feel better after talking to him. Her fury and hurt had calmed a fraction, but she still needed to cook. So, she put on her apron, turned on the oven and set to work.

★ ★ ★

Spurred on by anger, Logan hastily packed a suitcase with clothes, his favourite books, his toiletries and the photo of his parents, and then shoved his laptop in its bag. He stood at the door and surveyed the room, staring at the bed and remembering the weekend just past, when he and Frankie had barely left it. The best weekend he'd had in a long time, sullied only by the thought that maybe Simone would be hurt by what they were doing.

What a joke! He shook his head, not wanting to believe it. Not because he was upset by Simone's unfaithfulness but because the big brother he'd always looked up to, always stood by when things got tough, had thought nothing about betraying him. *That* hurt.

Being cheated on by his wife hadn't been a pleasurable experience, but in the end he'd accepted that they'd been too young and not at all right for each other in the first place. He'd forgiven Loretta long ago but this was an entirely different kettle of fish. Did blood and family mean nothing to Angus? The evidence spoke for itself. He'd lied about that night—so much for going for a late-night run—and he'd been lying about it ever since. Logan doubted Simone meant anything to him either—he'd just been bored and unable to keep it in his pants. Perhaps it was even his way of punishing Logan for dragging him to the wedding in the first place.

Feeling like such a bloody fool, he slammed his hand against the wall but it did nothing to relieve the storm raging inside him. His breathing ragged, he grabbed the suitcase and laptop and thundered out of the bedroom. Normally a peacekeeper, he'd planned on leaving without confrontation—let Angus wonder why he didn't come home—but as he was heading down the hallway he heard his brother taking off his boots at the front door and talking to the dogs.

When Angus entered the house, Logan dumped his luggage and charged at him. He put his hands against his chest and shoved hard.

Angus stumbled back, his butt smashing into the hallway table as he let out a cry of shock. As he straightened, he looked at Logan like he'd gone insane. 'What the hell? What did you do that for?'

Logan pushed his shirtsleeves up to his elbows, angling for a fight. 'The name Simone ring any bells?'

Before Angus could reply, Logan slammed his fist into his brother's face. Pain shot through his knuckles but he didn't care. It was worth it.

The confusion left Angus's eyes, replaced by a sheepish expression. 'Mate, I'm sorry. I never meant for it to happen.' He wiped the blood off his upper lip. 'How did you find out?'

'Simone told Frankie,' Logan said. 'And don't call me mate.'

'And you ran into Frankie because …?'

Logan swallowed, wondering if he should punch him again. If he admitted he was seeing Frankie, Angus wouldn't see why he was so angry. But it wasn't about the girl. 'Frankie and I … We … we're together now.'

'Really?' Angus grinned as if it was the funniest thing he'd ever heard. 'So I wasn't the only naughty one?'

'Shut your face or I'll punch it again,' Logan warned. 'I may have had feelings for Frankie but I didn't act on them till I was a free man. I know how to keep my dick in my pants, which is more than I can say for you.'

'Look. I'm sorry,' Angus began, offering his hand to Logan, 'I admit it wasn't my finest hour and I promise it was never about hurting you. That's the last thing I ever wanted to do. There's just something about Simone that—that made me lose control. I—'

'Save it.' Logan held up his hand, not wanting to hear his brother's excuses. If he didn't know better, he'd almost think Angus was in love with Simone. He bent down to pick up his suitcase when it suddenly hit him.

'Oh my God, that's why you changed your mind about wind-farming.' The timing certainly made sense.

Angus looked like he was about to deny this, but at the last moment he hung his head. 'Yes, which shows you how bloody bad I felt about what happened. Speaking of which—'

'It shows no such thing,' Logan interrupted. 'All it shows is that I've been a fool all these years worrying about you, when you don't give a damn about anyone but yourself. You can have your fucking farm and do whatever the hell you want with it.'

'What do you mean?'

'I mean I'm done here,' Logan said, slowly this time so his idiotic brother could understand. He picked up his stuff and charged past Angus, but he stopped at the front door and turned back. 'And by the way. That night you "lost control"? Your sperm hit the jackpot. You and Simone are going to be parents.'

Chapter Twenty-nine

'Parents?' Angus breathed the word to an empty hallway as he heard Logan's ute door slam in the distance. He steadied himself on the side table, the blood on his face and the wrath of his brother no longer his biggest concerns.

Logan's parting words kept repeating in his head until he felt like it was going to explode.

No. It can't be true.

Simone had said she was safe. He hadn't given her words much thought while they were in the throes of passion, but he'd assumed she'd meant she was on the pill. And wasn't the pill 99.9 per cent effective? Besides, the wedding was what ... three weeks ago? Surely she wouldn't be able to tell so soon.

He glanced at his watch. It was only mid-morning but he needed a beer. Forgetting his busted lip, he headed into the kitchen and opened the fridge, hoping to find a cold one. Neither he nor Logan were big drinkers but they had the occasional quiet beer of a night when Logan was home. When he was away, Angus stayed off the grog; drinking alone was never a good idea. But this was a one-off and he needed something to calm the rising panic inside him.

'Thank God,' he muttered as he spotted a bottle right at the back. He snatched it up, cracked it open and then sank into a chair at the kitchen table. He raised the bottle to his lips and took a long slug but after a mouthful, he realised he'd need a whole carton to stop the noise inside his head.

Simone. Beautiful, lovely, funny Simone. Pregnant. With *his* child.

He put the bottle down and pushed it across the table, his other hand tapping a tattoo on the surface in time to the heavy beat of his heart. When staring into space didn't help either, he dropped his head into his hands and closed his eyes but that only made everything worse, because when his eyes were shut, all he could see was the tiny lifeless body of his baby son. Cold. An unnatural tinge of blue under his soft skin. His special spark gone. That was a sight he never wanted to see again and the only way to ensure that was to never have another child. No commitments apart from Liv and Logan.

The plan had been going just fine until his brother had brought Simone home.

If anyone should be angry here, it was him. Angry at Logan for meddling in his life—for trying to get him to socialise, for conning him into going to that damn wedding. If he'd just let him be the way he was content to be then none of this would be happening.

A tiny part of his brain wondered whether perhaps Logan had been messing with him. Maybe there was no baby—he'd seen Simone on Friday night after all, and she hadn't said anything then. Maybe Logan was so angry at the betrayal that he'd said the one thing he knew would really throw Angus into alarm.

He could sit around here all day drinking beer and thinking bitter thoughts or he could confront Simone and find out the truth. Decision made, he pushed back his chair and stood, thankful that because of Harriet he knew where to go.

The dogs leaped up in excitement when he went outside, thinking they were off for a ride in the ute to some part of the farm, but at the shake of his head and one word from him, they sank back down into their beds, disheartened.

'You're living the dream, boys,' he told them as he yanked on his boots and tried to make light of this shitty situation. 'No bills, no worries except where you're going to bury your next bone, and best of all, no women.'

Although it was only a fifty-minute drive between his farm and Bunyip Bay, it seemed to take forever. The grey nomads with their caravan clubs were out in abundance, doddering along the road as if they had eternity to get to wherever they were going. And then he had to stop for ten minutes for bloody road works. What the so-called workers were actually doing to the road he couldn't figure out—from where he sat, impatient in his ute, it looked like the only people doing anything were the two men turning the stop/go signs.

All this time to think wasn't what he needed. He wanted the facts—straight from Simone's mouth—before he started analysing everything and working out what the hell to do about it.

Finally, a fat, balding man wearing an orange hi-vis vest spoke into his walkie-talkie and then turned his sign. Angus pressed his foot against the accelerator and ignored the go-slow signs as he zoomed ahead. He only slowed again when he passed the 'Welcome To Bunyip Bay' billboard and realised he'd be with Simone very soon.

His hormones woke and battled with his anxieties as he turned into her driveway and parked the ute. Hearing she might be pregnant should have been cold shower enough, but despite the difficult conversation they were about to have, he still worked up a temperature at the thought of her.

He closed his eyes, took a deep breath, told his eager libido to take a hike and then climbed out of the ute. In a few strides he was on her porch, lifting the little metal knocker on the door and pounding hard. He shoved his hands into his pockets as he waited.

And waited.

After about two minutes, he tried again and after another long wait, he finally accepted that she might not be at home.

Bunyip Bay wasn't a big place so it wouldn't take him long to track her down but he didn't want to risk running into Frankie. Dammit, he thumped his boot against the ground. Why didn't he give Simone his number when she'd asked for it on Friday night? They could have exchanged numbers like normal people and he'd have been able to call her. Admitting defeat, he was turning back to his ute when Simone's Pajero pulled up alongside it—half in the garden because the driveway was so skinny. He'd been so distracted when he arrived that he hadn't even noticed the four-wheel drive wasn't there. *Pathetic.* If there was a baby, it had drawn the short straw when it got him for a dad.

He swallowed, thoughts of the baby sidelined as Simone climbed out of the vehicle. She looked different from the other times he'd seen her—today she was wearing black tracksuit pants and an old, oversized T-shirt—but somehow was just as gorgeous as when she'd been all dressed up at the wedding. Maybe even more so. Barely acknowledging him, although he knew she'd seen him, she opened the back door and leaned in, emerging a few moments later with a handful of plastic shopping bags. He rushed forward to help her as she bumped her butt against the door to close it.

'Hi, and thanks,' she said, as he took the bags. 'I needed to stock up on a few supplies.'

He glanced down at the bags in his hands and glimpsed ice-cream, biscuits, packets of chips and chocolate. Comfort food, Olivia would call it.

'Don't judge me.' She sniffed. 'I had a fight with Frankie.'

'No judgement here.' He tried to offer a sympathetic smile but it didn't quite work out that way.

'Oh my God,' she gasped, slamming a hand over her mouth and gaping at him.

'What?'

'What happened to your face?'

'Oh, that.' He'd almost forgotten all about it. 'I had a fight with Logan.'

She sighed. 'I guess that means you're not just here for a chat or to check up on how Harriet is after the Friday debacle?'

He shook his head.

Her shoulders slumped. 'You'd better come inside then.'

An awkward silence followed as Simone unlocked the front door and pushed it open for him to go inside. The situation had gone well past small talk.

'Head straight down the hallway and you'll find the kitchen,' she told him as she closed the door behind them. Inside the house was much the same as outside—a mix of colours and styles, as if the decorator had kept changing their mind on what kind of look they wanted.

As predicted, he found the kitchen easily and dumped the bags on the 1970s orange Formica bench top.

'Thanks,' she said again, her voice a little shaky as she came in behind him. 'Let me just put away the cold stuff and we'll talk.' She began, then paused a moment and looked over to him. 'Unless you'd like some ice-cream?'

'No, thanks.' He shook his head. He'd never understood women's inclination to eat sweet stuff when they were down in the dumps. Alcohol seemed like a much better idea but it was still early-ish in the day and, of course, she was pregnant.

'Take a seat then,' she said, gesturing to the small table in the middle of the small kitchen. 'Or would you rather have this discussion in the lounge room?'

Truth be told he'd rather not have this discussion at all. 'Are you pregnant?' he blurted, still standing exactly where he'd been when he dumped the bags.

The tub of cookies and cream she was holding slipped from her hands. She cursed, stooped to pick it up again and instead of putting it in the freezer as had been the plan, grabbed a spoon and sat down at the table. She peeled back the lid and dug in. 'So what if I am?' she asked, before shoving a very large spoonful into her mouth.

Was that a yes or a no?

As if she could read his mind, she sighed. 'Yes. I am. I suppose Logan told you the good news? And yes, it's yours.'

At her confirmation that his worst nightmare was coming true, his heart rate shot up again and he dealt with the terror the only way he knew how. He folded his arms across his chest. 'Isn't a bit early to be mine?'

For all he knew she could have been sleeping with every Tom, Dick and Harry for weeks before she did the deed with him. She'd cheated on Logan at least once, who knew how many other times she'd done so?

She narrowed her eyes and pointed the spoon at him. 'Are you accusing me of making this up?'

He shrugged. 'The wedding was three weeks ago. I thought you couldn't tell till at least four weeks?'

'Oh, so you're a pregnancy expert, are you?' She obviously didn't expect him to reply as she continued, 'As it happens, I went to the doctor because I wasn't feeling well and she picked it up. I said the same as you and apparently I must be one of those women who ovulate earlier in the month. *Lucky me*. But don't worry, it's still very early days. No guarantees it'll stick. The poor child's living in a body stressed out to the max at the moment. Not exactly ideal thriving conditions.'

'Is that what you want? To lose it or ... get rid of it?' Angus asked, unsure how he felt about that.

'No!' she roared, waving the spoon around as if she might hit him with it if he came any closer. 'And don't use that tone of voice with me in my house.'

'Right,' he said, nodding as he tried to get his head around this news. Maybe he did need some ice-cream. 'So when were you planning on telling me?'

She shrugged and gobbled some more ice-cream. The way she was eating, the tub wouldn't last the hour. 'You made it pretty clear you didn't want anything more to do with me,' she mumbled through her mouthful. 'I assumed the same went for little people.'

'How dare you assume anything about me. What do you think? I'd shirk my responsibilities? What kind of bloke do you think I am?'

She glared right back. 'How the hell do I know? We had one night together.'

That was true, but it had been a night he'd thought about ever since.

The problem wasn't only a baby that had the potential to steal his heart. It was that he thought Simone might already be halfway there. And dammit, he didn't want that.

'You told me you were safe,' he accused, regretting the words the moment they were out of his mouth.

The spoon froze midway between the tub and her mouth. She raised her eyebrow and gave him a look no man ever wants from a woman. 'You don't want to start down that road, buster. As you so aptly taught me, it takes two to tango. You were very much present and accountable the night this little bundle was conceived.'

This time she dumped the spoon back in the tub and placed her hands on her stomach in the way pregnant women often do. There was no evidence of pregnancy there but his chest tightened at the vision of what she might look like seven or eight months from today.

A baby. Oh God, he was never going to sleep again.

'Look. I don't need your crap today. I've already had Frankie's.' Simone's chair scraped against the tiles as she stood and set her hands on her hips. 'I've done this twice before on my own and I'm quite happy to do it again, so go.'

'Simone,' he pleaded as she thrust her finger in the direction of the front door.

'You know the way out!' she yelled, her cheeks red with fury. 'What are you waiting for? I'm giving you permission to leave and not come back. Pretend you never met me and retreat to your solitary existence. Go!'

Go? Before he fell any harder for Simone and before the baby became real to him. Angus considered her offer for all of two seconds, then turned for the door and hurried back out the way he'd come in. He jumped in the ute and reversed out the drive, narrowly missing the Pajero in his haste to get away.

★ ★ ★

Simone waited until she heard Angus's ute start up, then retrieved the spoon from the ice-cream and started to eat again. That was two people she'd argued with and tossed out of her house in one day. God help the next person who came knocking!

Her bravado lasted about as long as the ice-cream. *What a fucking coward*, she thought, as she swallowed the last mouthful. She recalled the expression on his face when she'd confirmed she was pregnant and then again when she'd told him he was off the hook. She hadn't been so naïve as to imagine that news of a baby would have him dropping to his knee and proposing marriage. Hell, until that morning, they'd only met each other three times, but each of those times she'd felt an intense connection she hadn't felt with anyone since Jason. And yes, she'd thought that once they got past the fact she'd dated Logan first, maybe down the track they could have a future.

But his reaction just now was about as bad as it could get and had dashed all such fantasies. He'd all but accused her of getting pregnant on purpose.

As if she *wanted* to raise another child all by herself. Because, oh yeah, doing so was a walk in the park, a piece of cake, easy as pie and a whole load of other stupid clichés. *Not.* And he, who'd practically raised his kid sister, should understand that.

And then, when she'd given him the chance to walk away, he'd run. Her fists clenched tightly at the memory. Surely she couldn't *love* a man like that? Surely walking away from a woman pregnant with your unborn baby trumped all the wonderful things he'd done, like make her laugh, rescue her teenage daughter from possible death, and give her toe-curling orgasms. Yes, there were so many things that ranked higher than those.

So why did his departure hurt so bloody much? She stared into the empty tub of ice-cream and, despite her best intentions not to cry over a man who didn't deserve the time or effort, she began to sob; big, heavy tears that shook her whole body and wreaked havoc with her breathing. In the absence of an actual box of tissues, she stumbled into the bathroom, slid to the floor and tugged on the toilet roll, using it like a continuous hanky to wipe her eyes.

Could she have done something differently? Broken the news to him more gently? Not been on the defensive from the start? Maybe, but after her horrible argument with Frankie, in which she'd said so many things she didn't mean, she'd been all off-kilter. Not at all in the right headspace to have a civilised conversation with the father of her unexpected baby. Perhaps she shouldn't have given him such an easy out. Maybe she should have demanded that he step up to the plate and at least pay maintenance, but she didn't want that for herself or her child. She didn't want her baby to feel like it was a burden to anyone and she certainly didn't want a man who was with her simply because he felt obliged.

Why did everything have to be such a mess? Why couldn't Angus want her, and the baby, as much as she wanted him?

Although Logan had told her his brother was practically a hermit, happy to live in his own little world, she'd spent the last couple of weeks fantasising that she would be the one to draw him out of his shell. She was probably the most stupid woman on the planet.

Yanking off another length of toilet paper, she sniffed again and blew her nose hard. She craved the company of her sister, who would wrap her arms around her and say all the right things. But Frankie probably didn't want to talk to her any more than Angus did right now. And calling her mum wasn't an option, because once she'd explained, Ruth would likely side with Frankie.

Simone had never felt more lonely in her life—even in those dark, dark times after Jason died, Frankie had always been there with some sort of sixth sense about what she needed. The sad thing was, Simone didn't really care about Frankie getting together with Logan. Hadn't she realised at the wedding that those two were perfect for each other? She didn't begrudge her sister's happiness, it was simply that she'd expected sympathy, understanding and support and when she hadn't got any of those things, she'd snapped. She'd lashed out in a way she'd never have done if she wasn't already an emotional wreck.

In a matter of hours she'd offended her sister, perhaps irrevocably, and given her baby's father permission to walk out of their lives. What the hell would she tell the child when it started asking questions?

'Oh God, what have I done?' she sobbed, thinking what a pathetic sight she must be, sitting on cold, hard tiles, leaning against the toilet bowl, snivelling into double-ply toilet tissue. Thank goodness the girls were still at school.

Chapter Thirty

Late Monday afternoon, Frankie had just arrived home from the café when a knock sounded on her front door. She glanced down at Fred and George, who were winding around her legs, demanding dinner and attention.

'That better not be Simmo,' she told them. Tired of her phone ringing every fifteen minutes for the last couple of hours, she'd eventually turned it off, hoping her sister would get the message. Annoyed, she headed back to the front door, fully prepared for confrontation, but was pleasantly surprised when she opened it to find Logan standing on her porch—his laptop bag slung over his shoulder, a fully stuffed suitcase at his feet and a disheartened expression on his face. In all her anger, she'd forgotten he'd promised to drop by after work.

'I'm not moving in.' He gestured to his stuff. 'But I just need a place to stay for a couple of nights while I make other arrangements.'

In reply, she reached out, grabbed him by his collar and yanked him against her, kissing him hard on the lips and then sliding her tongue in to taste him. She'd never been happier to see anyone in all her twenty-eight years and she didn't care how many local gossips saw them on her porch, making hay.

'You can stay as long as you like,' she said, when they finally broke apart to breathe. With him around, Simone was less likely to barge her way in and demand Frankie's attention. Of course, there were also a zillion other reasons why she wanted him here. 'I'm so happy to see you.'

'Me too.' His dejected expression transformed into a smile as he took the hand she offered, picked up his suitcase with the other one and followed her inside.

'How was your interview?' she asked as she closed the door behind them.

'Not bad. Was a bit hard to concentrate.' He took off his laptop bag, dumped it on the floor next to his suitcase and looked around. 'This is a great place. Love that wallpaper. It's warm but also really modern.'

'Thanks.' It was weird to think he'd never been here before, when in so many ways it felt like they'd been together forever. 'Renovating has been my project for the last little while, but I still have to save up to get the bathroom and kitchen done.'

'And they must be Fred and George?' Logan stooped and peered under the side table in the hallway, where two little furry heads were only just visible, peeking out. He held out his hand and tried to lure them out with soft noises and Frankie looked on, amused. She didn't get many visitors—apart from Simone and the girls—so the cats were wary of strangers. They had a number of favourite hiding spots they retreated to whenever someone came to the door.

Yet, to her great surprise, both Fred and George emerged within a few seconds and rubbed themselves against Logan's hand. 'I've always been a dog person,' he confessed as the cats allowed him to scoop them up. He held one in each arm and smiled down at them. 'But I've gotta admit, these guys are pretty damn cute.'

'I think so,' Frankie said, stealing Fred off him and cuddling the cat close. 'They're also hungry. Come through to the kitchen and I'll feed them or we'll never get any peace.'

'What do you feel like for dinner?' she asked, when the cats were finally munching their smelly wet food and Logan was sitting at the table sipping a beer.

'You,' he said, wriggling his eyebrows suggestively as he grabbed her hand and pulled her onto his lap. He kissed her neck, then travelled lower to her cleavage, and all thoughts of cooking flew out the window as warmth filled her from head to toe.

She laughed, feeling sexy and desirable at his words and his touch.

'You smell really good,' he whispered right into her ear.

His warm breath sent shivers down her spine. 'That's because I've been baking cakes all day.'

'Good enough to eat, even,' he said, sliding his hands under her T-shirt as he nibbled on her ear. She let out a little gasp of pleasure. Only yesterday she'd been in his bed, but after all that had happened today, it felt like so long ago and she wanted to plaster over today's horribleness with Logan's magic touch.

'Go ahead.' She lifted her shirt off her head, tossed it away and then reached around to unclip her bra and did the same with that.

'Don't mind if I do.' He gazed at her a moment as if she were a work of art, before dipping his head and taking one nipple into his mouth as his hand closed around the other.

She closed her eyes and arched her back, pressing herself closer, loving the feeling as his tongue swirled around her nipple, shooting pleasure right to her core. As his mouth attended to her breasts, he slipped his hand lower, inside her shorts, violating her underwear as he pushed one finger and then another deep inside. She held onto the back of the chair to steady herself as her body began to tense around his fingers.

Oh, he was so … *very* … good at this.

Her breathing quickened and just when she was about to fly over the edge of ecstasy, he withdrew his hand. She blinked her eyes open, confused at his smug expression.

'I said you were good enough to eat,' he said as he eased her off him. She stood before him, a topless, shivering bundle of frustration, before he nudged her back against the table.

She gazed up at him, her eyes wide, her pulse quickening again as he slipped off her shoes and then tugged her shorts and knickers down her legs. Then he put his hands on her thighs to push them wide before dropping to his knees and hooking her legs over his shoulders. As his mouth touched her most intimate place, she looked sideways to make sure she'd closed the kitchen curtains. That was her last thought before he robbed her of her ability to think any more.

Much later, after Frankie had whipped up a creamy chicken carbonara fettuccine and they were eating it on the couch, with a glass of wine and a cooking show on the TV in the background, she told Logan all the horrible things Simone had said about her. Sadness overcame her and she tried to hold onto her anger rather than burst into tears.

'I'm sure she didn't really mean all that,' he said, reaching up to stroke an errant hair out of her face. 'We all say stupid things in the heat of the moment.'

'She's been calling me all afternoon and if I thought she was really sorry, maybe I'd pick up, but I know she'll only be grovelling because she needs me. The girls will need dinner or she'll want sympathy over morning sickness or something. Well, too bad. I'm done with being used.'

'Good for you.' Logan smiled and nodded approvingly. 'And me, too. I told Angus I quit the farm.'

'What?' She'd been lifting her glass to take a sip of wine, but halted in midair. 'But you love it there.'

He shrugged. 'Yes, I do. But I'm tired of feeling like my opinion doesn't matter. Angus refuses to listen to my ideas or budge on most of his and I've realised he's never going to change. Besides, I love my other work too and now I love you, so I've got plenty of things to keep me busy.'

Her heart stopped still. Had she heard him right? 'Did you just say you love me?'

'Maybe.' His cheeks flushed and he didn't quite meet her gaze.

She put her index finger on his stubbly chin and forced him to look at her. He was the most beautiful thing in the world. 'Maybe you love me? Or maybe you said it?'

'Neither.' He grinned and cupped her cheek with his hand. 'I definitely love you. And I definitely said it.'

She opened her mouth but the emotion whooshing through her made it impossible for her to speak.

'You don't have to say it back if you don't want to,' he said, gazing down at her. 'But I couldn't hold it in any longer. I know it's happened fast, but I know my heart and I wanted you to know it too.'

'I *do* love you,' she managed, before her tears broke loose. Right now all the crap with Simone felt worth it, just to hear those words. 'More than I've ever loved anyone.'

He kissed the tears on her cheeks and then kissed her properly, taking the wine and putting it on the table in front of them as he wrapped his arms around her and held her close. If they didn't have to work, she reckoned she'd be content to stay there on the couch, in his arms, forever.

'So how'd Angus take it when you told him you're leaving?' she asked, after Fred and George had jumped up to join in the snuggles.

Logan gave the little brown bundle a chin tickle as he spoke. 'You know, I'm not sure, because I hit him with the baby news before he really had the chance to say anything. When I left, he was standing there liked a stunned mullet who'd just swallowed a whole lemon.'

Frankie couldn't help but snigger at the image. 'I wonder if he's made contact with Simone? How do you think he'll feel about being a father again?'

'Fuck knows.' Logan shrugged. 'But he'll probably come round eventually. He can be a right wanker, but he was a doting dad to his son and he was always good with Olivia. Whether he and Simone get together or not, he'll be there for the kid, I'm sure.'

'That's good.' A tiny part of Frankie wanted to go see her sister or at least call to check she was okay, but then she remembered Simone's hurtful words and she settled back into Logan's lovely strong arms. She was still angry and didn't want that feeling to ruin the novelty of having her boyfriend—her boyfriend who *loved* her—to stay the night.

'What is Olivia going to say about your big bust-up with Angus?' she asked, stroking her fingers across his red knuckles, which he'd admitted were sore from punching Angus in the face.

He sighed. 'That's one conversation I'm in no hurry to have. Let's forget our sibling woes tonight and focus on enjoying the time together.'

'Now that,' Frankie said, 'is one of the best ideas you've ever had.'

Chapter Thirty-one

As Angus stopped the ute and looked ahead to his empty house, an unfamiliar feeling sat heavy in his chest. Was he lonely? He couldn't remember ever feeling this way before. Even when Liv was in Perth and Logan off on one of his work trips, he never felt like the recluse they teased him about being. Most of the time he loved the solitude—he could watch whatever he wanted on TV, eat a packet of biscuits for dinner if that's what he so desired, not have to make conversation at the end of a long, laborious day, and no-one nagged him about tidying up his mess. If he wanted to talk, he had his dogs and acres and acres of open air. He loved his work and couldn't imagine ever doing anything else.

But over the last two days, since returning from his brief visit to Bunyip Bay, loneliness had seeped right into the marrow of his bones. The silence around him was eerie. He felt as though he were the last person on the planet, and the satisfaction that usually came from getting up and achieving stuff on the farm was missing. When he came in from working outdoors, there were no tantalising aromas wafting from the kitchen indicating that Logan was in there doing one of the things he did best.

Angus kept expecting to hear his brother's ute tearing up the gravel or music wafting from his room while he tapped away at the keyboard, but so far Logan had stayed true to his threat to stay away.

The desire for conversation had Angus looking for an excuse to go around and talk to Loretta and Brad, which showed how insane this was making him. If he was like this after two days, what would happen if Logan never came back? Suddenly the prospect of living the rest of his life in this manner—like a robot with little purpose, no friends and no family—didn't appeal. Hell, another day like this and he was going to become an official mental case. He'd even trawled Facebook, of which he was a member but rarely checked, to feel some kind of human interaction. He missed Logan and wanted to apologise for his actions, but Logan refused to answer his phone. Calling Liv was his only option, but if he told her the whole sorry story, she'd be furious with him for hurting Logan and deserting his baby.

Hell, *he* was furious with himself. If some guy had knocked Olivia up and walked away from her the way he'd done with Simone, he and Logan would have taken the loser to a deserted paddock and shown him exactly what they thought of cowards. Because that's what he was—terrified. Every time he thought about Simone—and that was pretty much every second of the day and night—his chest tightened, his breathing grew ragged and he felt like he was being buried alive.

It wasn't that he couldn't imagine Simone and her daughters setting up residence in his life, in his heart, in his home. Quite the opposite, in fact. Whenever he went inside, he visualised what the house would be like with a family living there. It wasn't hard to picture himself and Simone in the kitchen, both as bad as each other at cooking, yet trying to concoct something edible. He imagined Olivia's and Logan's bedrooms taken over by Harriet and Grace; the house no longer quiet but filled with the sounds of boy bands and … a baby gurgling happily.

He'd been working towards that years ago with Sarah and then one dark morning, all hopes and dreams of a house filled with happiness and children's laughter were snatched away. Death was hard to accept at any age, but when a baby died, everything changed. He'd lost so much in his life and he didn't think he could go through such devastating loss again.

Although he'd come home from the sheep yards to grab an early lunch, the prospect of going inside to that empty, cold house didn't appeal. Everywhere he looked there were reminders of his past and fantasies of a future he wasn't sure he was man enough to reach out for. With a heavy sigh, he flopped down onto his mum's old swing chair that still sat on the front verandah and occasionally swung back and forth even when there was no wind. He looked out over the horizon but the usual rush he got from surveying his land didn't come.

Do you really want to live alone out here forever, my darling boy?

He startled at the sound of the voice, so soft yet so clear, so real, and then turned his head to see his mother sitting beside him, her legs tucked up on the seat the way they'd always been. His heart grew still and he blinked, expecting her to disappear, but when he opened his eyes again, she was smiling at him.

Well? Do you really want to? The look in her eyes told him exactly what she thought about all of this. Even when she was alive, she hadn't always agreed with or approved of the things he wanted to do but she'd always offered a listening ear, wisdom and her love, whatever stupid decision he ended up making.

'What do you think?' he asked.

She gave him a reproachful look. *I think the fact you're scared shows how much you want this woman. Baby or no baby. I think fate has given you a second chance and you'd be stupid not to take it. Look around. I want more for you than this. And don't I deserve another grandchild?*

He half-laughed and reached out to take her hand but his fingers landed only on the firm material of the seat cushion. 'Mum?' He swallowed, wishing she'd reappear again, wishing he could have just a few more moments talking to her.

But she was gone. She'd been gone for more than fifteen years and he still missed her every moment of every single day.

Simone, however, was very much alive. He thought of her vivacious smile, her contagious laugh and the messy red curls that drove him crazy. She'd done what he'd thought impossible—she'd made him *feel* again. Awoken inside him emotions and desires he'd thought were buried alongside his mum, dad and baby boy. He may not have known her long, but she'd gotten under his skin in a way no other woman had since Sarah.

The way he saw it, he had two options. He could stay out here alone, going through the motions from day to day but never actually living; in essence, become his father. Or he could choose to risk his heart and take a chance on what life was offering.

It might take a while and a heck of a lot of grovelling to win Simone around but he planned on stepping up to the plate and accepting his responsibilities to her and their baby. He *wanted* to. And he owed it to himself, to Simone and to their unborn child to go and talk to her, to give her an explanation for his gutless behaviour and to promise he'd never act in such a manner again.

Decision made, Angus forwent lunch, jumped back in his ute and hightailed it to Bunyip Bay. He'd been there more in the last week than ever in his life and drove on autopilot, already feeling better now he'd made the decision. He puffed out a breath of relief when he saw her Pajero in the driveway and parked right behind it. Demons spoke in his head, reminding him of all the possible hurt and pain he was opening himself up to by coming here, but he pushed them aside, climbed out of his ute and charged up the path to the front door. He rapped hard and waited.

'If you're here to yell at me or to throw more accusations, then you can turn back around,' she spat the moment she opened the door. 'I don't need that right now.'

He opened his mouth to speak but the words caught in his throat as he drank her in. She looked awful. Beautiful but awful. As if she'd been crying for the last two days and hadn't had a good meal in that time either. He had a crazy urge to cook something for her and he never had an urge to cook for anyone. The thought that he'd walked away from her made him sick.

'Well, are you just going to stand there like a codfish or are you going to tell me why you're here?'

That she was angry wasn't unexpected but the absolute emotion in his heart was. Until he'd seen her again, he hadn't realised just how much he wanted her. Needed her. The thought that she might not forgive him, might not want to give *them* a chance, left him cold. 'I'm sorry,' he blurted, wishing he had Logan's way with words. He'd never been good at knowing what to say to women and he shouldn't have just barged over here before thinking up some kind of speech.

Simone perched her hands on her hips and raised her eyebrows at him. 'What exactly are you sorry for? Sorry you slept with me? Sorry I'm pregnant? Sorry you're a coward? Sorry you're a total dick? Sorry you're taking up space on my porch and wasting my time when I could be watching daytime TV and devouring the entire contents of my pantry?'

He held up a hand and, to his surprise, she went quiet. 'How about … I'm sorry for all of the above? And a lot of other things too.'

She cocked her head to one side as if contemplating his response. 'And what exactly does this apology mean? Because "sorry" is a lovely word but—'

Again he interrupted. 'Can I come inside? We need to talk.'

'Now there's a turn-up for the books, a man who *wants* to talk.' She moved back a little and gestured down the hallway, although her tone was still cold. 'Well, sure, come on in.'

He stepped inside and she closed the door behind them and then indicated he should follow her into the lounge room.

'Take a seat,' she said, pointing to an armchair in the corner.

He did as he was told and Simone sat down on the couch opposite. She folded her arms and glared at him expectantly. He felt like some naughty kid in the principal's office and wished she'd offer him a coffee so he'd have something to do with his hands. But she obviously wasn't in a hospitable mood.

'I was an idiot the other day, when I found out about—' he swallowed '—our baby.'

'No kidding.' She rolled her eyes and he saw where Harriet got it from.

'And while there's no excuse for leaving you like I did,' he continued, 'I was in shock and needed time to think things through.'

'Look,' Simone said, leaning forward, 'I understand the shock. When the doctor told me, I couldn't believe it. I'm thirty-five years old, I have two teenage daughters and I was pretty sure I was done with shopping in the nappy aisle. The question is, how do you feel now you've had time to digest the news that you're going to be a dad?'

'Did Logan ever tell you that I am a dad?'

Shock flashed across her face. 'To Olivia you mean?'

He shook his head and hoped he could get it all out. Although this was something he thought about constantly, he'd never told anyone who didn't already know. 'Sarah and I had a little boy,' he confessed. Simone frowned and he continued. 'We were quite young and he wasn't planned but we loved him from the second we found out. We called him Tim and he was born not long after

Dad committed suicide. He brought so much hope and joy into all our lives.'

He paused. Even after all these years, it was hard to speak of that day. Hard not to wonder if they'd missed something, if there was something they could have done to help him. 'He died at seven months.'

'Oh my God,' she gasped, her hand flying up to cover her mouth, her eyes wide.

Although she didn't ask, he wanted her to know the whole story. He didn't want any secrets between them. 'It was cot death—or at least that's what they called it. Basically no-one knows why. Sarah fed him at ten o'clock, then we put him to bed healthy and happy, and when I went in to him the next morning, he was gone. Sarah was never the same again. I was still responsible for Liv, but she didn't want to help raise my sister when her own child was dead. And I couldn't blame her.'

★ ★ ★

Simone swiped at her eyes, wishing she'd bothered to buy tissues. Her heart ached at Angus's story. It ached for him. She couldn't even begin to imagine how she would feel if one of her daughters died. Harriet going missing for an hour had taken a decade off her life. And in less than a week, she'd already become attached to the life inside her.

'How did you handle so much tragedy?' she asked, feeling terrible about how snarky she'd been when he arrived. If only she'd known this before. It must have been so hard for him to come, to open up like this.

Angus shrugged. 'I guess the truth is I haven't handled it. Logan and Olivia are right—I locked myself away from the world, figuring that if I didn't make connections with people, I could protect myself against further hurt. But life doesn't work that way.'

'Life sucks sometimes,' she said, fighting the urge to go over and hug him. That might be weird. He might think she was making a move when what they needed to do was discuss the future of their child.

'I didn't tell you this to make you feel sorry for me,' he said, raking a hand through his thick mop of hair. 'I just hoped maybe you could understand my terrible reaction when I first found out you were pregnant. I'll understand if you can't, but I'd really like you to forgive me for running away. And I'd like to try that conversation again.'

'The baby conversation?' she asked, her heart swelling with love for him. She'd suspected her feelings for him were stronger than lust but now he'd opened his heart to her, she just wanted to jump inside it and take up residence. Hope sparked within her.

He nodded. 'I'd like to talk about us as well.'

'Us?'

He pushed off the armchair and crossed the room, sitting down beside her on the couch. They were close—Angus's thigh and shoulder pressing against hers, his breath warm against her face as he took her hand. She almost squeaked at the electricity that zapped between them. Even if she had wanted to stay angry, her body had other ideas.

'Simone,' he said, his tone deep and serious.

'Yes?' She was helpless, able only to look into his dark brown eyes.

'I'm not good with saying how I feel,' he began, 'but I want you to know that until I met you, I was content to live in my own sad world. Sure, I had the odd liaison, but no woman ever made me lose control the way you did. What we did—sleeping together when you were with Logan—was wrong, but also more right than anything I've ever done. I'm man enough to admit that my feelings for you scare me shitless, and adding a baby into all that just makes my fear a hundred times worse. The thought of losing you, of losing another child, is too awful to contemplate, but I don't want fear to control my life anymore.'

'What are you saying?' she whispered, wanting to be sure before she made a total fool of herself by confessing she was head over heels for him.

He rubbed his jawline with his free hand. 'I guess I'm asking if you'll let me into your life.'

'You guess?' She couldn't help but smile at the uncertainty in his voice. He was adorable when he didn't know what to say.

'Yes. I mean, no. I *am* asking if you'll let me into your life. I want to give us a shot and I want to be there every moment of this pregnancy and our little one's life.'

The tears that had only just subsided welled again in the back of her throat. Happiness like she hadn't felt in years flooded her, so that she needed a moment before she could reply.

Angus reached into his pocket and pulled out a clean plaid hanky. 'Here,' he said, wiping away a tear that had snuck down her cheek.

'You carry a hanky?' she asked, unable to keep the amusement out of her voice.

He shrugged, his cheeks flushing. 'It's something Mum always made us do. Hard habit to break.'

She smiled and took the hanky from him, wiping her nose and inhaling his unique scent. She was never going to give it back. 'It's cute. Your mum sounds like a very special woman.'

He nodded. 'She was. I wish she could have met you and our baby.' Angus reached out and pressed his hand against her still flat stomach; butterflies fluttered in her belly at his touch.

'Me too,' she whispered back, placing her hand on top of his, loving the warmth seeping from his skin.

'Does that mean ...' He cleared his throat. 'Does that mean you're willing to give us a try?'

In reply, she leaned towards him, cupped her hand around the back of his head and drew his lips to hers. Although this time there was no illicit aspect to their kiss, Simone's body still shivered with the heat of it. And the knowledge that it was the first of many to come only heightened the experience. To have made peace with Angus was wonderful and she felt confident that in time, they would do the same with Logan and Frankie. The thought of Frankie not being an aunty to their baby ... well, it was inconceivable and Simone silently vowed to do everything within her power to make amends.

But later. Right now, she had other priorities.

'I guess that's a yes?' Angus said, looking at her as though he'd like to devour her when they finally pulled apart.

She licked her lips and nodded, then leaned forward and whispered into his ear. 'Shall we seal the deal in the bedroom?'

His eyes widened. 'You feeling up to that?'

She laughed. 'I'm pregnant, not ill. I still have needs and from now on, it's your duty to take care of them.'

'In that case, I'd better get to work.' And with those magical words, Angus swooped Simone up into his arms and carried her into the hallway.

'Which bedroom?' he asked with a gruff caveman voice that turned her insides liquid with desire.

'Second on the right,' she replied, every nerve in her body on fire.

Who knew something so wrong could turn out to be this right?

Chapter Thirty-two

Frankie looked up at the sound of the café door opening, hoping it might be Simone come to offer an olive branch. It was the next best thing—Logan. Smiling, she wiped her hands on her apron and went around the counter to greet him.

'Hey there,' she said, leaning in for a quick kiss. 'Can I get you something for lunch?'

He grinned sheepishly. 'That may be why I decided to take a break from writing.'

She shook her head. 'And here I was thinking you'd come to see *me*.'

'That too. You guys busy today?'

'Steady. But I'm ready for a break. How about I get us both a slice of pie and I'll come sit with you.'

'Sounds just about perfect.' With a playful pat on her bum, Logan went to find a table and Frankie treated herself to a quick perve. He really did have the best arse in the history of arses and no-one wore jeans like he did. Granted they'd only been together a few weeks, but she still had to pinch herself every time she thought about the fact he was hers. The only thing that put a dampener on this was the fight with Simone.

The two days since they'd last spoken had been the longest two days of her life. Maybe she was being stubborn, but after all the horrid things Simone had said, Frankie felt it should be up to her to make the first move. She could tell Logan was more cut up about his altercation with Angus than he was letting on as well, but she didn't know what to do about it. With a sigh, she turned and headed into the kitchen to get their pie.

'Geez, that looks and smells amazing,' Logan said, when she brought two plates to his table a few minutes later. He patted his washboard abs. 'You're gonna make me fat.'

She laughed and sat down opposite him. 'I think you've got a little way to go yet.'

They both picked up their forks and dug in, Logan moaning with pleasure as he slipped the first mouthful into his mouth. She loved that it was her cooking that made him sound like that.

'What's your secret?' he asked. 'I can never get mine this flaky.'

She wriggled her eyebrows at him. 'I could tell you but then I'd have to kill you.'

He leaned towards her and whispered in his most seductive voice, 'I'll get it out of you later.'

She didn't reply but took a mouthful of pie because the truth was he probably could seduce it out of her. His hands and tongue had amazing talents and if he used them against her, resistance would be futile.

'Guess who I just saw parked outside Simone's place when I drove past?' Logan asked, giving up on the pastry secret for now.

Frankie's stomach turned hard. 'Stella or Ruby?' So far, she'd seen neither of their close friends since the fight and didn't like the idea that Simone might be poisoning them against her. *She wouldn't, would she?*

'Angus,' Logan said. 'Well, his ute.'

'Really?' Relief swamped Frankie as she raised her eyebrows. 'I wonder if they're an item now.'

A look of disbelief crossed Logan's face. 'I don't think Angus knows how to be "an item" with anyone anymore, but I guess they might try to make a go of it because of the baby.'

'Are you still angry at him?'

He shrugged one shoulder. 'I was fucking furious to start with, but now I'm hurt more than angry.'

'Me too,' she admitted. 'But I hate all this bitterness between us. I love my sister and I love my nieces and I'll love a new niece or nephew too. I don't want this to be one of those families where nobody talks to anybody else.'

'Me neither,' Logan agreed. 'I've lost too many people I love to give up on the ones I have left.'

'So what do we do then?'

'Personally, I was hoping Angus would come grovelling, but then I guess I haven't answered any of his phone calls.'

Frankie half-laughed. 'And I haven't answered any of Simone's. I was waiting for her to turn up in person. I wanted to *see* her grovel.'

'We could be the bigger people I guess,' Logan suggested.

'What? Go to *them* and apologise? But we didn't do anything wrong!'

He laughed at her indignation. 'Well, maybe we don't apologise exactly. Maybe we try a different tack instead and take them a congratulatory gift. Give them our blessing, so to speak.'

'What exactly did you have in mind?'

Before Logan could reply, Monique called to Frankie from the counter. 'Phone call for you,' she said, holding the café's cordless phone against her chest. 'Someone from Geraldton High.'

Frankie frowned as she slowly got up. Her heart clenched as an overwhelming feeling of dread washed over her. 'I'm emergency contact for Harriet and Grace if Simone can't be contacted,' she explained to Logan. Not that the school had ever had cause to call her before. 'Something must be wrong.'

She jogged the few steps to take the phone from Monique. 'Hello?'

'Is that Francesca Madden?' asked a woman's voice.

'Yes,' Frankie said, not used to hearing her full name. 'Has something happened?'

'We have you down as emergency contact for Grace McArthur, is that right?'

'Yes!' Why wouldn't she just tell her what was going on?

'This is Mrs Beaton, Grace's English teacher,' explained the woman, who sounded as if she not only taught English but had once resided in that country. 'I've been trying to contact Grace's mother, but she's not answering her phone. Grace had some sort of seizure in class and she's been taken to Geraldton Hospital.'

'Oh God,' Frankie said, her hand rushing to cover her mouth. 'Is she okay?'

'She's in the hands of the paramedics. We let her sister go with her and the assistant principal is heading to the hospital as we speak. I don't know if you have any other way to reach Simone, but I'm sure Grace would like to see her mother as soon as she can get there. And if not, maybe you could come?'

'Of course. Thank you for the call.' Feeling as if she'd been knocked in the head by a plank of wood, she held the phone close. Logan was already at her side and Monique too looked worried. 'It's Grace,' she explained. 'She's had some kind of seizure at school and they can't contact Simone.'

Frankie squeezed her eyelids together, trying to fight her tears. She'd die if anything happened to Grace. And Simone had already suffered so much loss—she didn't deserve any more.

'I'll call Angus,' Logan said, his phone already at his ear. 'You try Simone again.'

Ten seconds later, he shook his head. 'He's not answering.'

'Neither is she.' Frankie couldn't keep the anguish out of her voice.

'Let's go to her house—see if she's there.' He turned to Monique. 'Are you and Stacey okay to man the café?'

Monique nodded and made shooing movements with her hands. 'Go. And I hope Grace is okay. Don't worry about anything here.'

Frankie, unable to think straight, was grateful as Logan ushered her outside and over to his ute.

The short journey to Simone's house seemed to take forever. 'What if …?' She couldn't bring herself to finish her sentence.

'Relax.' Logan reached across the gearbox and squeezed her thigh. 'There could be a number of reasons why Grace had a seizure and there's no point getting all worked up until we know the facts. Right now, we need to find Simone and then get to Geraldton as soon as we can.'

Frankie nodded.

Despite knowing that Angus had been visiting Simone, it was still weird to see his dirty ute parked outside her house. It crossed Frankie's mind, as she and Logan rushed out of the car and up the front steps, that they might not be answering their phones for a reason.

'What if they're … you know … busy,' she said as she unlocked Simone's front door and pushed it open.

Logan's brows shot up his forehead. 'I think Simone will still want to know about Grace.'

Frankie nodded and charged down the short hallway towards Simone's bedroom, preparing herself for the worst. The door was open and there were *noises* coming from inside. She felt the few mouthfuls of pie she'd eaten churning in her stomach. She paused before she could see inside, cleared her throat and called out, 'Simmo?'

The noises ceased. She heard the squeaking of a mattress and hurried whispers, then, 'Is that you, Frank?'

'Yep—cover yourselves because I'm coming in.'

She counted to five and then barged into the bedroom. Although she'd suspected, it still shocked her to see Angus shirtless (probably trouserless as well) in her sister's bed. She didn't know where to look.

'What the hell?' Simone shouted, her cheeks a deep red colour.

'Hi,' Angus said, with a sheepish wave as Logan came up behind Frankie.

'It's Grace,' Frankie said, not wanting to waste time. 'The school just called me. She's had some kind of seizure and been rushed to hospital.'

'Oh my God. The phone. It was ringing and we …' Simone clutched the sheet tightly against her chest. 'Did they say anything else?' Before Frankie could reply, she continued. 'I need to go to her. Now. I need to get dressed.' She leaped out of bed, completely naked, and started opening and closing drawers looking for clothes. Her actions were manic and she didn't seem to care that Logan bore witness to her nakedness.

'I'll wait in the lounge room,' he whispered to Frankie and then retreated in a hurry.

'I'll drive you,' Angus announced, also climbing out of bed and reaching for a pair of jeans lying on the floor next to the bed.

Frankie averted her gaze and went over to Simone. She'd felt like a basket case until she'd delivered the news to Simone, but now she realised she needed to keep a level head. It was Simone's right to fall apart and Frankie's job to take control. Her sister's hands were shaking and as she struggled into a pair of shorts,

Frankie found a T-shirt in her drawer and then helped her pull it over her head. Angus joined them, still buttoning up his navy chambray shirt, his boots already on his feet.

'Will Grace need a change of clothes, do you think?' he asked and Frankie was impressed by his forethought.

Simone looked as if she couldn't even comprehend the question.

'Good idea.' Frankie smiled at Angus. 'You take Simone to Gero. I'll get a bag together for Grace and we'll follow as soon as we can.'

Angus nodded, then wrapped an arm around Simone and drew her into his side. He placed a kiss on the top of her head and spoke softly to her. 'Come on, let's go see Grace.'

As he guided her out of the bedroom, Frankie couldn't help noticing how tender he was with her sister. The way Angus looked at Simone was the look Frankie saw in Logan's eyes when he looked at her, and it made her heart sing.

It didn't matter that they'd started out with the wrong people; what mattered was that now they were all with the right ones.

Chapter Thirty-three

Angus had to jog to keep up to Simone as she flew from his ute and charged into Geraldton Hospital. He hadn't been here in years and it looked like they'd flashed it up a bit since he had, not that it mattered what the place looked like. All he cared about was that they had top-notch professionals who would know exactly how to treat Grace. He couldn't bear the thought of Simone having to go through the loss of a child like he had.

'I'm here to see my daughter, Grace McArthur. She's just been brought here in an ambulance,' Simone declared to the woman behind the reception desk. She sounded like she'd run a marathon.

'Let me see ...' The woman tapped her fingers against her computer keyboard, taking her own sweet time to tell them anything.

Angus gave Simone's hand an encouraging squeeze. She looked like she was about to explode if she had to wait another ten seconds.

'Ah, yes.' The receptionist smiled victoriously. 'She's still in emergency being assessed, but family can see her.' She turned to him. 'Are you her father?'

Angus opened his mouth, unsure of what to say. He wasn't, but wanted to be there for Simone.

But she got in first, turning to him and placing a hand on his chest. 'The girls don't know about us yet, so it might be best if you stay in the waiting room. Do you mind?'

He shook his head. 'Not at all. But I'll be right here if you need me. Love you.' His breathing hitched. He hadn't known he was going to say those two words, hadn't known how true they were until they were out.

Simone smiled. 'I love you, too. Thank you.' Then she turned to the bemused-looking receptionist. 'Which way to emergency?'

Angus took a seat on the cold plastic chair in the waiting room and contemplated how dramatically his life had changed in the course of a few weeks. In hooking up with Simone, it wasn't only her and their baby he was taking into his life, but also two teenage girls who hadn't had a father figure for years. He wasn't naive enough to think that it would be plain sailing, but he found himself looking forward to getting to know Harriet and Grace more than he'd ever have expected.

Not long after Simone rushed off in the direction the receptionist had pointed, Frankie and Logan burst through the entrance doors. He stood as they headed over.

'Where's Simone? Do you have any news on Grace?' Frankie asked, bypassing traditional greetings and seemingly unperturbed by the fact that she'd seen him naked less than an hour ago. *This is what family is all about*, he thought, as he nodded an acknowledgement to his brother.

'Simone's gone through to emergency—they're still assessing Grace,' he told Frankie. 'As you're family, they might let you in too.'

That was all the encouragement she needed. Without a word to either of the men, she turned and hurried down the corridor in the same direction Simone had gone, leaving Angus and Logan alone. Angus shoved his hands in his pockets and they both stood there awkwardly, a metre apart. This wasn't the place he'd imagined having the talk he needed to have with Logan, but he guessed there probably wasn't any ideal place for this kind of conversation.

'I'm sorry for punching you,' Logan said eventually, the scowl on his face saying this apology didn't come easily.

Angus chuckled. 'I'd say you had a pretty good reason for doing so.' He sighed and ran a hand through his hair. 'I'm sorry, bro. What I did was indefensible and I know I don't deserve your forgiveness, but I'm really hoping that in time, you'll come to offer it.'

'So, you and Simone?' Logan nodded in the direction of emergency. 'Are you going to make a go of this parenthood thing together?'

Angus hoped the truth wouldn't upset Logan further, but he was through with lies. 'Yes,' he said firmly. 'She's the best thing that's happened to me in a long while and I hope you'll be able to give us your blessing. We want you and Frankie to be a big part of our baby's life.'

'Wow.' Logan puffed out a breath of air. 'A baby, hey? You ready for that again?'

'Truthfully?' he said. 'I'm terrified, but I don't think anyone's ever ready for a baby.'

Silence reigned for a few more moments before Logan said, 'Of course I forgive you. We can't all be perfect like me.' He smirked and Angus smiled too. 'Frankie and I are happy for you. We were only talking an hour or so ago about what to get you guys as a gift.'

'Really?' Angus felt the last bit of tension that had been clenching his muscles since fighting with Logan and discovering he was going to be a dad slipping away.

'Really.' Logan nodded, smiled and offered his hand. 'Congratulations, brother.'

'Thanks, mate.' Angus accepted the handshake. 'And you and Frankie? Things good there?'

'Better than I could ever have imagined,' Logan told him, his grin stretching across his face. 'She's the best.'

★ ★ ★

When Simone stepped into the emergency room and saw her baby lying on the bed, her heart leaped into her throat. Grace looked so young, so vulnerable, and all Simone wanted to do was sweep her into her arms and hold her close. But there were medical people hovering over her, so she held back.

'Mum?'

She turned to see Harriet in the corner of the curtained cubicle and rushed to her instead. Her oldest daughter sniffed into her chest.

'I was so scared when I heard about Grace,' she said, 'but they say she's going to be okay.'

'Of course she will be,' Simone said, with a conviction she didn't feel. People didn't just have seizures for no reason, did they? She needed answers.

Thankfully, one of the people stepped away from Grace and approached them. 'Are you Grace's mother?' the woman asked.

She nodded.

'Hi, I'm Dr Lacey.' The woman smiled briskly and offered her hand. 'Can you step outside a moment? We need to talk.'

Simone didn't want to leave Grace but Harriet stepped out of her mother's embrace and went over to her sister, so Simone followed the doctor to just outside the cubicle. There she recognised the assistant school principal, Tracey Palmer, waiting in a chair.

'Oh, hello,' she said. 'I'm sorry I didn't see you before. Thank you for coming.'

Tracey smiled as she stood up. 'Grace is a special girl.'

'As you know, Grace convulsed at school,' Dr Lacey said, talking to the both of them. 'We have assessed her and I believe the seizure was caused by dehydration or ketoacidosis.'

Simone had no idea what the latter was but she didn't like the sound of it. 'Is it serious? Will it happen again? What can we do?'

'Mrs Palmer has informed me that one of the girls at school confessed to their teacher after Grace's episode that she has been throwing up food in the bathroom after breaks for quite some time. Both dehydration and ketoacidosis can be related to eating disorders. Did you have any suspicions your daughter was bulimic?'

'What? No! Grace loves her food.' This was too much for Simone to take in. What more could life possibly throw at her?

Dr Lacey's expression softened. 'Don't be too hard on yourself. Girls with eating disorders are very good at hiding it from those closest to them, and bulimia is even harder to notice than anorexia. I'll bet Grace has been eating all her meals. Her lunch box coming home empty?'

Simone nodded, thinking about how Grace was the first to ask for seconds, but how she retreated to the bathroom immediately following almost every meal. How could she have missed something this big? She felt like the worst mother on the planet. 'I had no idea.'

'The good thing is we'll be able to talk to her now, work out how long this has been going on and why she feels the need to go to such drastic measures. Our first step is to get her rehydrated and to treat her physically, so we're going to transfer her to a ward in a moment, but I'll also be referring Grace to a psychologist who specialises in dealing with teenagers who have eating disorders. She's very good at her job and I know Grace will be in good hands. Do you have any questions?'

Simone guessed she should have many but she couldn't think of them right now. All she wanted to do was see her little girl. 'Can I see her?'

Dr Lacey smiled. 'Of course. We'll talk more later.'

'Thank you. And thanks to you too,' Simone said, looking to the assistant principal.

'You're welcome,' Tracey said. 'I'll head back to school now you're here, but do let us know if there's anything else we can do to help.'

'I will.' Simone turned away from the other women and slipped back into the cubicle. There was only one nurse left in the room now and Harriet was perched up on the bed, snuggling with Grace. The sight had Simone's heart turning in her chest—she couldn't remember the last time her girls had been so close.

'Room for one more?' she asked, crossing over to the bed and squeezing up on the other side of Grace, mindful of the tube attached to her hand.

Grace turned to look at her and promptly burst into tears. 'I'm so sorry, Mum.'

Simone could only just make out the words through the sobs.

'There, there, it'll be okay.' She held Grace close and stroked her hair until her crying subsided.

'I didn't know I could have a seizure,' Grace said, her lower lip quivering. 'Now everyone at school has seen me. How embarrassing.'

'Don't worry about the kids at school; if anyone gives you any trouble, they'll have me to deal with,' Harriet assured her.

Simone gave Harriet a thankful smile. 'Why did you feel you needed to—to do this?'

'Oh Mum, I just wanted to be beautiful like you and Aunty Eff and Harriet. I just wanted to be thin.'

'You are thin. And beautiful!' Harriet sounded outraged.

'You're always telling me I'll get fat if I'm not careful,' Grace said.

Harriet's face fell. 'I'm so sorry.' She sounded as if she too were close to tears. 'I didn't mean it. This is all my fault.'

If it's anyone's fault, it's mine, thought Simone, but she kept this to herself. 'It's no-one's fault,' she said, 'and we're going to get through this together, okay?'

Both her daughters nodded and she drew them close again. This was the way Frankie found them when she appeared around the corner.

'Aunty Eff!' Harriet and Grace said. Her daughters' delight at seeing her sister confirmed that Simone needed to mend the rift that had formed between them. They all loved and needed Frankie. She smiled, hoping that Frankie could read in her eyes how sorry she was for everything she'd said in the heat of the moment on Monday.

'What's this I hear about you getting to ride in an ambulance?' Frankie asked as she approached the bed. Simone slipped off so that Frankie could give Grace a hug. 'Did they put the siren and the flashing lights on?'

Grace giggled.

'All right,' said the nurse who'd been keeping out of the way in the corner of the room, 'we've got a room ready for you. If I can ask everyone to give us a few moments while we transfer Grace.' She mentioned a ward and room number. 'Grace will be ready for visitors in about fifteen minutes, but not for too long. She needs her rest.'

Simone, Harriet and Frankie bid Grace farewell and told her they'd see her soon and then they left the emergency department.

Frankie pulled her purse out of her handbag and handed a twenty-dollar note to Harriet. 'Go get us some refreshments, kiddo.'

The fact Harriet took the money and walked away without protest showed just how shaken up she was by Grace's hospitalisation. They'd all had some major life lessons over the last few weeks.

When Harriet was out of earshot, the two sisters turned to face each other. 'I'm sorry,' they blurted at the same moment. And then before either of them said any more, they rushed into each other's arms. Simone had thought she was all cried out after the last few days, but happy tears trickled down her cheeks.

'I'm so sorry I said all those horrible things,' she gushed. 'I really didn't mean any of them.'

Frankie pulled back and raised one eyebrow at her. 'Yes, you did, but that's okay. We're sisters—we're allowed to fling the odd cutting word, but if anyone else ever dares say a bad word about you, I'll—'

Exactly what Frankie would do was lost in Simone's laughter. 'I missed you so much.'

'Me too. Let's never go that long without talking to each other ever again.'

'Deal.'

'We can talk more later about everything else,' Frankie said, 'but right now I want to know what's the matter with Grace. Do they think it's serious?'

'Serious enough.' Simone sighed. 'She has an eating disorder. Bulimia.'

'Shit.' Frankie screwed up her face. 'But she loves my cake.'

Simone nodded. 'So much that she eats more of it than anyone else and still doesn't gain weight. I can't believe I didn't notice. What kind of crap mother am I?' She'd managed to maintain a sense of calm in front of the girls, but with Frankie she couldn't keep up the act. 'My oldest daughter tries to run away from home and I don't even notice my youngest daughter is fading away? What hope does this little one inside me have?'

Frankie put her hand on Simone's stomach. 'You are not a bad mother. You're the best mother I know and your girls are lucky to have you. It's not your fault you didn't know what Grace was doing. I'm around her almost as much as you and I had no idea either. But the important thing is that we know now and together, we'll help her through it. You're not alone, sis. I've been by your side every moment of those girls' lives and I'll be there for you and for number three as well.'

'And you've got me now too,' said a deep voice behind them.

They spun around to see Angus and Logan only a few metres away. The women had been so engrossed in conversation that they hadn't even noticed the brothers approaching.

'And,' Angus added, smiling in the way that always melted her heart, 'I'm not going anywhere. You're stuck with me.'

'And me,' Logan added. 'I'm ready and willing to step up to my uncle duties, and that goes for Harriet and Grace as well as for the little munchkin. We're family.'

Frankie squeezed Simone's hand. 'I couldn't think of two better blokes to be stuck with. What do ya reckon?'

Simone smiled through the tears that had started up again. *Damn hormones.* 'I reckon you're right.'

Angus moved towards her and she could already feel the comfort of his arms wrapped around her. How had she gone so long without him in her life?

'What are you guys doing here?'

At the sound of Harriet's voice, Angus dropped his hands to his side like a schoolboy caught with a girl behind the sports shed.

Her arms laden with soft drink cans and bars of chocolate, Harriet raised an eyebrow and looked from Logan to Angus and back again. 'I thought you and Mum broke up,' she asked, her tone almost accusatory.

Simone smiled. 'We did,' she told her, 'but then … things got a little complicated. It's a long story, but one I'll happily tell you and Grace together, very soon.'

Eight months later

'Any news yet?'

At the sound of Grace's voice, Logan roused from an uncomfortable, restless sleep, in which he'd sat upright on his future mother-in-law's couch, with Frankie's head in his lap. He yawned and looked down at his watch, blinking at the sun coming in through the still-open curtains. They'd been in vigil here since yesterday morning, waiting for news of a new niece, cousin and granddaughter. Certain there'd be news during the night, he and Frankie had decided not to go to bed, promising Grace, Harriet, Ruth and Graham they'd wake them the moment Angus called.

'No, not yet.' He shook his head as he tried to work out how to stand to go to the bathroom without waking Frankie.

Grace sighed and slumped down in the armchair across the room. 'Mum's been in labour for hours. Is that normal? What if something's wrong with her? Or the baby?'

She sounded close to tears and her panicked voice woke Frankie.

'Has he called?' Frankie asked as she shot upright into a sitting position, flinging off the heavy blanket that had been keeping them warm. She ran a hand through her hair and Logan smiled, still amazed that she looked so gorgeous first thing in the morning.

'No.' He squeezed her hand and looked to Grace with a smile. 'I wouldn't pretend to be an expert on giving birth but I'm sure if there was a problem, Angus would call us. The way I've heard it, long labours are not unusual.'

'Except this is Simone's third baby,' Frankie said, sounding uncertain, 'and her other labours were relatively easy and quick.'

Logan turned to see her forehead furrowed in concern. Great, now he had two panicked women on his hands.

'See?' Grace glared at him and then looked to Frankie. 'Oh, Aunty Eff. I'm scared.'

'Look, ladies,' Logan said, trying to sound confident, 'stressing is not going to help anything. Let's get dressed, eat something and then we'll go and wait at the hospital.'

The commotion had awoken the rest of the household. Harriet, Ruth and Graham all appeared, wearing dressing gowns and slippers. Logan couldn't help thinking how much easier it would have been if it was the middle of summer, rather than a particularly cool autumn.

'What's going on?' Harriet asked, rubbing her eyes. 'Has Mum had the baby yet?'

'No!' Grace shrieked and rushed at her grandmother. 'Do you think something bad has happened, Granny?'

'Now, now,' Ruth said, smoothing her hand over Grace's hair. 'Don't work yourself into a state. I'll make us all some breakfast and maybe they'll have called by the time we've eaten it.'

Breakfast was a subdued occasion. Everyone's mobile phones were on the table and nobody spoke for staring at them, willing them to make a sound. Logan had tried to call Angus but it had gone straight to voicemail and even he was starting to get a little sick in the gut. Nobody ate much and eventually they all decided to go with his plan and head to the hospital.

The weather was terrible—thunder roaring above them, lightning flashing across the sky and rain so heavy that even a person without his vision issues would find it hard to see the road ahead.

'I'll drive,' Frankie announced, smiling knowingly at him.

'You sure?' he asked. He knew she was stressed but he wouldn't be confident driving in these conditions.

'Of course.'

They all piled into her hatchback, the girls deciding to go with him and Frankie because she drove faster than Graham. After trying to make small talk with them to no avail, Logan tried to relax into the seat for the rest of the journey. He thought about how much had changed in the past whirlwind of a year. He was well on the way to learning Braille and adapting his life in preparation for future hurdles. He'd taken the job in Geraldton and Frankie was talking about moving there with him and opening a second café. It didn't seem five minutes since he'd found out about his deteriorating vision, but at the same time it felt like he'd been part of this crazy family for much longer than he had.

Frankie had given him hope of a good future, no matter how bad his eyesight got, and Simone had breathed life back into Angus. Olivia, who he'd texted to meet them at the hospital, already loved Frankie, Simone, Harriet and Grace like sisters and was so excited about the prospect of having a niece that she'd taken up knitting. Her first project was a pair of pink booties that Logan swore were far too small to fit an actual human.

'Are we there yet?' Grace asked, bouncing in the back seat.

'Almost,' he and Frankie said in unison. He smiled—they often said the same thing at the same time. Sometimes he honestly wondered if she could read his mind, but he didn't care if she could.

Just as they were turning into the car park at St John of God Hospital, all four mobile phones in the car beeped, signalling a message. After waiting for news forever, everyone jumped.

'Is it them?' Frankie asked and Logan could see her grip tighten on the steering wheel. 'What does it say?'

Harriet—her phone permanently in her hand anyway—was the first to open the message. 'She's here,' she squealed, sounding more like an excited child than he'd ever heard her before. 'Apparently labour didn't progress as it should but they got her out and she's perfect. Mum's good too,' she added. 'There's a spot over there, Aunty Eff. Hurry.'

Grace's earlier anxiety was forgotten. 'I'm a big sister! I'm a big sister! I'm a big sister!'

Logan laughed, glancing over at Frankie as she parked the car.

She sighed as she pulled the key out of the ignition and looked over to him. 'Congratulations, Uncle Logan,' she said, her grin stretching from ear to ear.

'Congratulations yourself, Aunty Eff,' he replied, leaning over and putting his hand behind her head to draw her lips to his. Who cared about the weather? This had to be pretty much the most perfect day ever.

'Will you two lovebirds quit that?' Harriet was already out the car and rapping on the windscreen with her black talons. 'We have a little sister to meet!'

★ ★ ★

'She's magic.' Angus leaned over and kissed his new wife on the forehead as he stroked his newborn daughter's silky, soft head. Wrapped in pink muslin, her skin the same pale shade as her mother's, she looked like a porcelain doll. 'You did well, darling.'

Even though Simone was still lying on the operating table, all sweaty, red and exhausted from a twenty-hour labour followed by an emergency caesarean, she beamed in the way only a woman who had just brought a new life into the world could. And he, dressed head to toe in navy blue theatre scrubs, felt like the luckiest guy alive. They stayed like that, simply gazing at their little miracle, for about two minutes, before Simone said, 'I don't think she looks like a Charlotte, do you?'

He frowned and he looked from her to their daughter. They'd spent the last four months—ever since they'd found out they were having a girl—arguing about names and had finally settled on Charlotte Rose. 'I'm not sure you look like anything when you're only five minutes old,' he told her.

She laughed and then winced, indicating that the epidural was already wearing off.

'Sorry. Are you all right?' he asked, hating to see her in any further pain. 'Do you want me to take her?'

'Yes, please. My arms are a little shaky.' She nodded, smiling at their girl as he lifted the baby off her and cradled her in his arms. She was so tiny and perfect. He'd forgotten how little newborns were.

'So did you have something else in mind?'

'I was thinking Celeste Ruth,' Simone said.

A lump formed in his throat. 'Celeste was my mother's name.'

'I know. And Ruth is mine. Do you like it?'

'Celeste Ruth.' He tried the name on for size as he rocked their little bundle. The baby opened up her eyes at the sound of his voice and his heart melted. He couldn't remember the last time he'd shed tears but he sure as hell shed them now.

'You big baby,' Simone said, her tone warm and amused. 'I guess this means you either hate it or love it.'

He blinked back the tears and laughed, loving the fact that after being awake for almost thirty-six hours, Simone could still see the humour in things. 'I love it. Celeste Ruth Knight,' he said again, putting his little finger in the palm of his daughter's minuscule hand. 'Almost as much as I love the two of you.'

'Oh, stop.' Simone shook her head. 'You'll turn me into a big blubbering mess as well. Do you think they're going to move me to a room soon? Or should I try to feed Celeste in here?'

The middle-aged, motherly midwife who'd been hovering nearby approached them. 'Your obstetrician has given you the all clear and the pediatrician said your baby is perfect, so I'm just waiting on an orderly to take you to your room. Shouldn't be more than five minutes but I'm happy to help you feed her here if you'd like?'

'Nah, it's okay. I'll have a five-minute rest,' Simone replied.

The midwife chuckled and Angus grinned, not at all upset about having to hold his girl for little longer. 'I reckon you deserve it,' he said.

True to her word, the midwife introduced them to an orderly just under five minutes later, then together they pushed Simone, holding Celeste in her arms, to her room with Angus walking alongside them.

'I'll stay with you and help you with your first feed,' said the midwife once she'd settled Simone into her bed. 'This your first baby?'

Simone shook her head. 'Number three.'

The midwife smiled. 'One for you, one for him and one for the country, eh? Good work. Are your other two boys or girls?'

'Two girls,' Simone said, 'but—'

Before she could explain further the midwife chuckled and turned to look at Angus. 'Ooh, three princesses! Completely outnumbered, aren't you, love? And I bet they all have you wrapped around their little fingers.'

Simone looked at him, discomfort flashing across her face, but he grinned and nodded at the midwife. 'They sure do. As does their mother. I'm a lucky man.'

And this was one hundred per cent the truth. Over the past eight and a half months, he'd grown to love sweet little Grace and feisty Harriet in a way he could never have anticipated. Grace had been having counselling for her eating disorder and was ecstatic to be living on the farm. She'd already made him promise to teach her all the tricks of the trade. Harriet couldn't wait to be a big sister again. He thought of them both as his own and truly loved them as much as he did Simone and little Celeste.

He'd lay down his life for all of them and Lord forbid any boy break any of their hearts, because he had a gun and he wasn't afraid to use it.

'Ah, you're a natural at this,' the midwife told Simone, jolting Angus back to the present.

He stared down at his woman and child and had to agree. Simone's chest was bare and Celeste nuzzled against her, her tiny hand resting on her mother's breast as she made quiet suckling noises. The picture before him was more perfect than any postcard sunrise and even if he didn't have a camera to take a photo—which he did—he knew it was a moment he'd remember forever.

Marriage, babies, new directions ... none of this might have been in any of their plans, but sometimes the best things in life were unexpected. And from now on, Angus Knight was just gonna go with the flow.

Acknowledgements

As usual I am in debt to a number of people who helped or supported me during the writing and publication of *Outback Sisters*.

My first thanks must go to my publisher, Sue Brockhoff, and the awesome team at Harlequin who work behind the scenes on my books. There are so many of you who do so much that I'm now too scared to list you all in case I miss someone. But know I appreciate you all and everything you do.

Thanks to my brilliant editor, Lachlan Jobbins, who always makes my least favourite part of writing a book not so bad after all and also Kylie Mason who helped edit this time around.

To my agent Helen Breitwieser, who is always so enthusiastic about my books and works damn hard to make sure others all over the world will one day be able to read them as well.

Thank you to my die-hard readers and all the reviewers who have taken time to read my books—with a special shout-out to those who send me lovely emails, chat on Facebook or write glowing reviews.

I think most writers suffer doubt at some stage or another during the writing of every book. Because the plot of *Outback Sisters* was a little bit complicated, this doubt came to me in spades about halfway through when I was certain the story was ridiculous. Without my faithful writing support crew (aka the buddies who understand the voices in my head) I may never have finished—so thank you to all who hold my hand and chivvy me on, you know who you are.

And a special mention to lovely readers Julie Hutchins—you know why—and Bec Climie for the vodka oranges (you naughty girl, you).

talk about it

Let's talk about books.

Join the conversation:

 on facebook.com/harlequinaustralia

 on Twitter @harlequinaus

www.harlequinbooks.com.au

If you love reading and want to know about our authors and titles, then let's talk about it.